Early praise for James Braziel's

SNAKESKIN ROAD

"*Snakeskin Road* bores into the brutal heart of human nature. Yet James Braziel still finds hope in man's need for redemption, his capacity for forgiveness, and his ability to offer the most unstinting, selfless love. This is a fantastic, thought-provoking read."
— ALAN DREW, author of *Gardens of Water*

"With imaginative grace and poetic intensity, James Braziel has written an apocalyptic masterpiece that will keep any reader on edge. Though filled with the grim realities and sometimes hallucinatory violence of a devastated United States, *Snakeskin Road* also reinforces our hope that love and compassion can survive."
— DONALD RAY POLLOCK, author of *Knockemstiff*

Praise for James Braziel's

BIRMINGHAM, 35 MILES

"Poetic, grim and hallucinatory, this harrowing work is not for the faint of heart, though it will appeal strongly to anyone who loved Cormac McCarthy's *The Road*."
— *Publishers Weekly*

"Braziel's ambitious tale is vividly imagined."
— *Entertainment Weekly*

"*Birmingham, 35 Miles* is just the novel we need in these scary times. Devastating, full of hard truths, but also beautifully written, deeply felt, and full of hope. I couldn't put it down."
— BROCK CLARKE, author of *An Arsonist's Guide to Writers' Homes in New England*

"*Birmingham, 35 Miles* is part tender and gritty blue-collar family drama, part environmental dystopia novel. Braziel provides an allusive catalog of the last century of Southern literature, invoking everything from Faulkner's *As I Lay Dying* to Walker Percy in his postapocalyptic mode to—most powerfully—a terrifying literalization of the old Agrarian ideals of home and soil. Braziel's characters are so attached to the land and each other that they're willing to stay even as prisoners, miners who literally scrape a living out of the clay by night and hide from the brutal sun by day. Smart and subtle— this is a chilling, promising debut."

—MICHAEL GRIFFITH, author of *Spikes: A Novel*
and *Bibliophilia: A Novella and Stories*

"I welcome James Braziel's debut novel as an extraordinarily lyrical and innovative work. It is both a speculative novel about the brutal consequences of global warming, and a traditional work that memorializes the landscapes and relationships of the rural South. Most of all, it is a rumination on love and survival that is visionary and inspiring."

—ANTHONY GROOMS, author of *Trouble No More: Stories* and
Bombingham

SNAKESKIN ROAD

SNAKESKIN ROAD

JAMES BRAZIEL

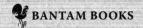 BANTAM BOOKS

A Bantam Books Trade Paperback Original

Published in the United States by Bantam Books, an imprint of The Random House Publishing Group, a division of Random House, Inc., New York.

BANTAM BOOKS and the rooster colophon are registered trademarks of Random House, Inc.

"Swimmer, Blessed Sea" and "Sparrow Bones" from *Red Suitcase* by Naomi Shihab Nye, copyright © 1994 by Naomi Shihab Nye. Reprinted by permission of the author and BOA Editions Ltd., www.boaeditions.org.

LIBRARY OF CONGRESS CATALOGING-IN-PUBLICATION DATA

Braziel, James.
Snakeskin road / James Braziel.
p. cm.
ISBN 978-0-553-38503-8
1. Women refugees—Fiction. 2. Environmental refugees—
Fiction. 3. Climatic changes—Fiction.
4. Desertification—Fiction. 5. Regression (Civilization)—
Fiction.   I. Title.
PS3602.R398S63 2009   813'.6—dc22   2009018753

Printed in the United States of America

www.bantamdell.com

2 4 6 8 9 7 5 3 1

Book design by Carol Malcolm Russo

For Jana

SNAKESKIN
ROAD

Chicago 2044

Delia took her hands and swept the edge of the bed, wip-ing away what few wrinkles were there, then sat down, and stared at the wall. There was no sound from the kitchen, no water coming up from the furnace, nothing from the apartments below, the ones boxed on either side, the one above, no sound except her cat, Pearl, footing into the room, wandering behind her on the white bedspread, paws catching in fabric. She looked from the edge of the bed to the south wall and listened to the absence pool around her until she could do it no more.

Her sister, Bobbie, was working. She worked all day as a city-state interpreter for Chicago, and stayed out evenings as much as she could, anything not to be lonely "like you," she admonished Delia with her long jaw set open, breathing in, waiting for a challenge. But Delia would just firm her lips, lock them shut. They had a lifetime of sisterhood behind them and had shared an apartment for nine years, yet seldom found ways to comfort each other. Bobbie's resentments of her older sister no longer made sense — with Delia at fifty-six and Bobbie at fifty-two, they were going the other direction, age now a liability rather than a privilege. Surely, her younger sister needed comfort, though she never said so and never offered. Delia did.

Sometimes in this silence, she heard her first husband, Everett, calling for her as if he were in the living room waiting, and simply wanted her company. But Everett had died in the clay mines at Bogalusa years ago when a thunderstorm brushed over him and drowned him. He was eighty feet down, buried in Mississippi mud.

Sometimes Terry, her second husband, called for her. He had always greeted Delia after his night-digging by gathering her up in his skinny arms, his hands too thin to hold anything right, lifting and lifting—what a skinny man should never have the balance and strength to do.

"Put me down. We're not kids," she had demanded. It was the kind of lift that hurt. But the moment he let go, Delia inhaled as deep as she could, trying to breathe him back closer. He could be standing right there, calling, "Baby. You so sweet, my baby," in that sing-sweep voice of his, scratchy, sweeping like a broom across the floor, and still be too far.

He died in Alabama, coughing up blood and clay, those skinny arms shaking. "I can't hold down my breath," he said to them, the other workers at the mine. "Help me breathe." But they couldn't, they told Delia, and they were sorry for his passing, *So sorry, Mrs. Philips*, as if apologies could erase his death, his voice, his touching her. She still held them responsible, and God.

Jennifer was the only one left in the Southeastern Desert—her daughter and Everett's daughter by blood, and every bit of Terry's child, too. After Terry passed, Delia migrated to Chicago, the Saved World, and moved in with Bobbie. Jennifer stayed behind to marry Mathew Harrison, a clay rock miner like both Delia's husbands. He worked the Alabama River.

"Why don't you come north?" she had pleaded. "The desert will never give you a fair life, Jen. It can't." That was nine years ago, 2035, and she hadn't seen her daughter since.

There was no communication allowed between families halved by the Saved World and Southeastern Desert except by letters. It had been that way since 2014 when the government created the border and patrolled it after a tear in the ozone and the dust-bowl winds refused to change pattern, to heal. The government censored what her daughter mailed to Chicago, and, she knew, what she sent down, but still Delia was able to make out her daughter's handwriting and enough of the sentences to know her girl was alive.

Most of the time, most every day, Jennifer's absence, the full length and shape of it, stretched north to south along the wall thinly, unbearably, weighted in counted seconds— *one-fifty, three hundred, six hundred.* Where was Jennifer exactly on the Alabama and Coosa rivers? *Nine hundred, one thousand*—What town? What home had she found to live in? Was she okay?—until Delia got tired of counting.

Jennifer had sent a letter in April, saying that Mathew's father had passed, and she would be coming to Chicago, that she would talk Mathew into it. *There's nothing here for him now, Mama.*

So Delia cleaned the spare room and bought her daughter a dress, a pattern of yellow and blue flowers, a spring dress, and laid it across the mattress, with yellow shoes on the floor, matching. Then she waited. It was too much to hope—that they would finally come. But every day for months she walked in and looked at that dress and shoes, saw Jennifer pick the corners up, lift it over her shoulders and down, shake out her long black hair, and smile. In the garden of that dress, all their distance gone—they could make amends.

Jennifer's last letter had arrived in June—she was taking the bus to Birmingham and from there, flying to Chicago.

She had saved enough money and had her visa, but she wasn't sure if Mathew would come.

It was early November now, getting colder. She hadn't heard from Jennifer, hadn't opened the spare room since August, the dress flat and empty as the sheets. Bobbie said the room held too much loneliness and never went in.

Each day the new cold seeped into the apartment, into her room, and bedspread. By January the cold would fray her skin and splinter into her bones. Another winter Delia wanted no part of. She no longer even bothered to change out of her nightgown and robe.

Each day, after her breakfast and coffee, she walked back to the bed, pressed out its wrinkles, sat down, and stared into the wall, the flat taupe color, hoping for a letter, wondering where her daughter was. Delia had written and written, but Jennifer hadn't replied.

Someone knocked at the front door. It wasn't Bobbie—she had a key. Besides, it was too early for her. Maybe a package, or the landlord, or a neighbor. She hated it when the neighbors wanted to borrow something—sugar or shoes or a solar bulb. Just because she was home all day on a government pension, that didn't mean she was a hotel clerk.

Delia tied her robe and rubbed Pearl, who was bumping her head into Delia's hand for a scratch. The more she obliged, the harder the cat pushed until, "Okay, okay," Delia said to the knocking, and left the room, checking to see who was in the hallway—a woman—and opened the front door. It was a young woman, but no one's daughter in the apartment building she recognized, wearing a torn gray dress, her hair cut short like a man's peach fuzz. So thin, the cheekbones in her face had swollen against her sunken cheeks. The girl was shivering. Filthy.

At first Delia thought she must be one of the homeless. They snuck into the bottom apartments from time to time, especially when the richer neighborhoods had a street purge. One tenant had shot a homeless man asking for money in the entranceway. But this was the twenty-first floor. None of the homeless had gotten past the first floor and wandered up here. Then Delia saw it, the girl's arms wrapped tight around a black stationery box. It was the box she had given Jennifer before her daughter's wedding. *I'll write every week*, Jennifer had promised, and until June she had done just that.

"Who are you?" Delia asked the girl. This wasn't how the government told you about your dead, someone in tattered clothes carrying the deceased's belongings.

"I'm Mazy," the girl answered, reaching into her pocket. She brought out a crumpled sheet of paper and handed it over, then slipped back into the hall, a long stride back. Delia stepped toward her. She wasn't going to allow the girl to just leave.

"I can see the resemblance in you two," Mazy said. "All that hair." She smiled. "And that grace through your eyes and cheeks, how it comes out in the light. She comes from you."

"Is she here?" Delia asked, and stepped out further. She realized she was breathing faster and she stared down the hallway, its tunnel of light-shade-light, but there was no one.

"No, ma'am." The girl shook her head.

"Where is she?"

"I wish I could answer that, ma'am. I wish she was here now. She made me promise I'd come find you."

The drop in the girl's voice sunk into Delia's stomach, the hum of the words vanishing back into disappointment too familiar and numbing.

Mama, the crumpled paper read—

> *I'm not going to make it to Chicago today. But this is Mazy Elis. Take care of her—promise me that. She is only fifteen and has been in my care for months now. I hope I'll still get to you, but if I don't, here is my box, your wedding*

gift to me, I'm giving to Mazy until she finds you and gives
you my letters. I have tried to send them and been unable.
They are my last details, Mama, my last trace if I
shouldn't get to Chicago. And Mazy, she holds traces of
me. I have to get Mazy out now. Take care of her. Promise.
*   I love you,*
*   Jennifer*

"What happened?" Delia said. "She was supposed to take the bus."

"The bus never made it to Birmingham," the girl explained.

"You knew her, then?"

"I knew her in Alabama and later in Cairo, Illinois. But I don't know where Jen is any longer. We got separated." The girl shook her head, kept looking off to the side, shivering, that dress ripped and frayed. There was dried blood and dirt on her legs and arms. "I'm sorry. I wish I could tell you. Wish I knew."

Maybe this last thing, her daughter not able to make it here, maybe this would be the thing to break Delia. How much longer could she keep staring at that wall each day, soundless, empty?

"I just want her to be here," Delia said.

"I understand. I want that."

She told the girl to come inside and took her where the bathroom was, and said for her to get a shower, did she want one? A bath, the girl said. Delia got her towels and snatched up the flower dress on the bed without thinking on it and handed it to Mazy and left her to bathe. She checked the kitchen pantry and refrigerator for food, something to fix her daughter's friend a good supper—maybe even chicken—they had a frozen bag of bread crumbs and chicken—something she hadn't cooked in a long time.

Then the fury of energy left her. She plopped down on the couch, the box sitting heavy in her hands like a black heart. Its surface was scratched, the lacquer completely gone at the feet and edges. She rubbed across the lid but couldn't smooth it any and pulled the latch.

On top were envelopes sealed and torn, mostly addressed to Delia Philips, 355 Turner Avenue, Apt. 2118, Chicago, each with a date—June 22, 23, July, September—they were all wrinkled like the contents had gotten soaked, but all of it was in order. She almost began to cry.

Jennifer always organized her things. It was something they shared—but crying wouldn't do any good.

Some of the envelopes were addressed to Mathew and underneath she found letters that she had sent Jennifer, old letters, none of the new ones, and a notebook of drawings, and a book of poems: *The Red Suitcase*. She would ask the girl later to tell her what she knew and where Jennifer was. Maybe she was close. That made Delia even more anxious. The government wouldn't help, not even her sister could help. All she had of Jennifer was this girl, these letters.

June 22, 2044, the envelope on top read. Delia recognized the faded green color of the paper. Stationery she had mailed to Jennifer for her birthday. She twisted the edge back and forth until it opened.

Talladega National Forest

Dear Mama,

The bus is on its side, and we're trapped within it, trapped within a dust storm. One man has already died because he fell against the window—we all fell against the windows or into the gray ceiling—but it was the way he struck the glass, somehow, some place on his skull vulnerable, rattling. It's not that there was blood, Mama, not from him anyway. He just didn't move again. I grabbed my stomach, but there was no cramp, nothing there, nothing that made me feel the baby had been hurt, thank goodness. Yes, Mama, I'm pregnant. I wanted to surprise you with the news when I got to Chicago. And I'm okay but alone. Mathew didn't come with me. I was dizzy. That's all. I kept grabbing at the seat, the side of it like I was drowning, trying to lift—I felt that way—waiting for the sky to turn upright.

Then this man crawled around me, his name's Darl, he went over to the other man and said, Are you okay, buddy? Come on, buddy.

Darl shook the man's shoulder, but he didn't move. His face was pressed up against the glass, and just outside, the desert floor that wouldn't give, holding us up, the man's neck bent at the wrong angle.

I think he broke his neck, Darl said.

Everyone wanted it to be a broken neck—not something that happened to his mind, because we had all hit the windows or fallen over the seats like tossed clothing, like clowns, bumped into something, and we were okay and wanted to continue to be okay. Yes, there was one person with a cut ear, glass still in her hair, the skin stretched over the bones of her face, but nothing deep, nothing that couldn't be fixed. A woman named Lavina had a pair of tweezers and she picked at the glass, the pieces that had gotten down into the cuts, while her daughter held the flashlight and a small jar.

Be still, honey, Lavina said to the woman whenever she flinched, then dropped a sliver into the jar. You be still, too, she told her daughter. The girl's hands kept shaking.

Two people with concussions were carried to the

rear and set down on the windows, heads stretched on the bubble of the ceiling so they could breathe, revive. We all thought if they were turned a certain way, if they were left alone long enough, then maybe, maybe something in them would reconnect and be fixed. They mumbled and shook. It was dark. We all moved to the front so we didn't have to see them except for Darl—he moved back and forth from the hurt ones to us.

Next morning, Darl and the driver took the dead man to the front and the other men helped. They pulled open the doors facing the sky, creaked them open, and hauled him up into the wind, the blowing dust falling, this crazy wind that had, the night before on our way to Birmingham, curled the sand to the sky, hit the windshield with the tiniest of rocks, flashes like shooting stars, thousands coming on. The driver tried to swerve out of the storm's way, and the bus flipped—there was so much dust, anger—the air dry, always dry, and diesel, everyone coughing.

We reached up, crawled toward the new ceiling, those other windows, and opened them slightly, too much—the sand fell down. So we took handkerchiefs and tore pieces of our clothing, stuffed the windows, leaving only cracks for the wind. The wind had upturned us; maybe now it would keep us alive.

Twelve—that's how many I counted—twelve people coughing, trying to find a steadiness. But the inside lights didn't work, and no one had any except for matches someone had brought, and Mazy, Lavina's girl, she held a flashlight on the woman with the glass cut into the bones of her face like jewels, her ear, and it was so dark because of that wall of sand that had curled over us and wouldn't leave. Then Darl found the one man dead. He was convinced the man had broken his neck, but I didn't believe it. He had smashed his head against the window. That's what killed him.

Beyond the glass was the ditch we had fallen into, the desert floor. Don't worry, Mama, I used my hands on my face—used them—I don't know how, but they were there, so I had a cushion when I fell the man didn't have. He hit the glass, and nowhere to go beyond it—just a ditch of hard sand.

When the sun came out, barely like it does on these days, the blowing dust adding a second and third tier of clouds, Darl and the driver and the other men took the dead man's body and lifted him through the doors, a shadow, clothes wrapped over blood and flesh and bone that was none of these things, a shadow of a body. They pushed him, scraping against the stairs—headless, shoulderless, his belt buckle hung for a moment, then up, and from there, he rolled and fell to the ground. But the bus was on its side, and all the windows faced into the ground or up at God. We could not see him fall. We could not hear him fall because the wind didn't want us to—a shadow, Mama—because the wind and the sand were busy sweeping and covering everything.

June 22, 2044—Night

Dear Mama,

It's night, and the wind has finally died some. We get lulls, stretches, like the easiest breathing I thought I'd never have again. The dust kept the sun black all day, kept the heat off. It's gone now, the sun has left us for a while, and the wind, too, looking for other places to smother.

The two people in back—Lavina and Darl have them quarantined—they moan and sleep, whisper in tongues—at least that's what happens to their voices when I dream. Lavina's afraid they'll never come to and Darl won't say much about it, except that they're trying to stay alive, fighting, then he goes to them. He whispers, Help is coming. Okay now.

They cry through his words, whatever he says or touches or moves.

Lavina's daughter, Mazy, is always close to her mama. She's fifteen. Just turned fifteen last week. Lavina smiled when she said this, her mouth full of teeth just like her daughter's, which is a silly thing to notice, Mama. Beautiful smiles, both of them, though Mazy doesn't say much. She loaned me her flashlight so I could write you, and I brushed a knot out of her hair. She has thick hair like us, though hers is a chestnut-brown. I rubbed her neck a little and she seemed to relax. Wish you were here. Or I were in Chicago, or Mathew were here.

There are only a few gallons of water to ration between us. The driver keeps them next to his foot. He's wide as the seat backs, has a bruise on his face where the radio fell and hit him. Then the radio smashed against the ceiling. He took the pieces, crammed them, shoved the wires and pushed, but it flung apart, cut his hands.

No damn good, he said, and kicked the receiver. Nothing—that's the only other word he's offered. He turns away from us constantly to look at his driver's chair stuck above the ground and the panel of numbers as if he still can't believe what happened, as if it were his fault. It wasn't—what could any of us have done differently?

It's a little funny, too, the driver's chair flipped on its side, the gearshift on its side, round panels with white numbers frozen still, and the bus driver standing on a window, fidgeting, scuffing up glass pieces in the heels of his boots, just staring at his seat parallel with the horizon, the windshield slung with dirt, alone, empty.

June 23, 2044

Couldn't sleep last night, Mama. None of us could. At times the two in back started moaning—one of them is a man but he cries so hard and high-pitched—I heard Lavina shush him. It was a soothing hush-hush like you used to do for me. Maybe, I thought, I could go to sleep, but then came the crash. All around us, Mama, a crashing like waves against rock, getting closer to the bus.

What the hell? the man next to me said—we had aligned ourselves across the unbroken windows, leaning against the roof, legs stretched out between the seats. Or some had curled against the hard green backs, using them as pillows, shirts as pillows, and one woman had gone the other way, stretched her feet to the dome light that flickered when she touched it. None of it comfortable, and all around us this crashing.

The driver said the crashing was the trees. He had gotten tired of looking at his driver's chair and taken off his blue Greyhound cap and was using it on his knee as a place to cross his arms and bear down. Occasionally he'd dip his hand at the broken window next to him as if he wasn't sure what to do with the fragments—the driver wanted to grab them or press them—he couldn't sit on top of the window. Then he wiped the sweat from the bruise on his face that was dark purple now. He has a squat face, Mama, a nose that sticks out further than you'd think. His hair was curled on the edges, greasy with sweat; all of our hair was the same way.

Another man chuckled, said that all the trees were gone in the desert, especially the big ones.

Not here, the driver insisted and told us we were in the Talladega Forest. He drove to Birmingham all the time, saw trees crashing or heard them coming.

He said sweetbays broke first in a black roller. He said, Used to, they had a smell like magnolias, but no longer. There were a lot of oaks in Talladega and huge tulip poplars, some of the biggest in the South. If one of those snapped and fell across the road, you might as well turn around.

You're not getting through it, he said. That's for sure. But he promised that all the poplars had been cleared.

What if the wind carries too strong? someone asked and the driver told him there was no wind tonight.

Besides, the black roller's gone and nothing's touched us. I've driven this. I know. We're okay.

Then he patted the hat on his knee.

Another voice started up with thanks to God but she had to clear her throat. Someone else continued with Oh Lord, thank you for keeping the trees away. Amen. Amen.

I wanted to believe in God, Mama. Not the first time I wanted to.

None of us could sleep easily after that, and when I did, I slipped into dreams, half dreams where the crashing woke me, and suddenly a large burnt poplar flared across, fell down, fell through the windows into me, until my eyes closed hard enough to make the illusion disappear for good. Over and over I had to make it disappear for good. The windows, the ones facing the sky, were black, vacant, no matter what I saw and felt.

I'm not that far from Mathew, a few hours, and all night I wanted him to drive north from Miller's Ferry, but how could he? He doesn't know about the bus. Our radio's broken. We're trapped. After they rolled the dead man out of the cab, no one asked, What're we going to do? We had to wait out the storm, so we did. Mathew's probably doing the same. That dead man—I know what the storm did to his body. Roughed it, buried it. At least he's deaf to the crashing.

Every time I woke, my stomach clenched, and it made me worry about the baby. All my nervousness couldn't be good for her. I'm so hungry. But all this thinking—I had to stop, Mama. I had to sleep. Eventually I managed to, until now because the sun's coming over, and it'll be over us fully, coming through the glass, burning. We'll die if we stay here, but we can't stay in the desert either.

What're we going to do? someone finally asked. A blue glow filled the whole shell of the bus, our skin no longer the color of skin.

What're we going to do?

In back, Mama, those people whispering.

June 23—Night

Dear Mama,

Finally it's dark and we've returned to the bus, the eleven who made it through the day undamaged.

It grew too hot once the sun began to lift this morning. You know how it is—the heat, the fine, fine sand, the haze of it all. The driver had warned that staying inside the bus meant we'd cook to death. He kept stepping over the broken glass, that one square, bearing his heels down. Already, we had raised the windows, but it didn't cool us any—how could all that wind just vanish? We found the shadows between the windows, kept ourselves out of the light.

It's no better out there, one of the older women an-

swered—a contractor. She had on one of those brown sandsuits, the ones with the zipper that goes from the ankle past the hip, around the arm to the neck. Long-sleeved wicking. Why would anyone wear something long-sleeved in the desert? You always said that was crazy. Foolish.

The driver wouldn't let up, said we had to take our chances outside, and Darl agreed with him. Darl said all we needed was a canvas to give us shade from the sun. Something to put over, so the wind could blow through. We'd be okay if we kept ourselves sheltered.

But the wind had left us, and we had nothing really—no canvas—just shirts, luggage. Fortunately, everything we brought was stowed in the side of the bus facing the sky.

The contractor said again that the sun would end us quicker.

I'm going out, the driver nodded one stroke at her. And we're not taking the sick ones.

He didn't move at all when he said this. Just looked straight at Darl, the bruise on his face, a long-knotted coal.

And Darl's so thin, Mama, like Terry was. I'd never noticed before.

We've got to take them, he argued.

We've already emptied out one dead man, the driver said. That was hard enough. That's it. Those two are going to die.

He pointed to the back where it was shaded still, cool-looking, even with the light coming in. And Darl leaned toward the driver's arm until he took it down, and they stood at each other, not moving, a pause in the air, sinking our voices, our hands. We could've helped Darl some, but the driver was the strongest. Without him, there was no way to get the bodies through the doorway.

Then the driver turned away from the crowd and pulled the metal handle. The doors swung open and a sweep of sun, the heat of it, rushed in, a cloud of sand was just left there floating, sifting down for us to slowly breathe. He grabbed hold of the door, the metal bars, lifted himself, and grunted. No way he'd make it. So two men and some of the women, they went over to help push.

I looked for Darl. He was already in the back talking to those people, the hurt ones who mumbled as if they were talking to God, as if God was talking through them. As if God was still in this place.

But I knew better. The others, I could tell they knew it, too, sucking in dust and glints of light, closing our eyes to one another, then opening them toward the entrance, shifting that way, shifting to get out into the sky. The bus driver reached his hand down, gestured for the jugs of water. He helped the contractor in the brown suit. Then Lavina and her daughter, Mazy. One by one we left that place except for Darl.

●   ●   ●

The bus itself was like a sundial and only at twelve and one, with the sun perfectly overhead, did the shadows dry up from the ground with the humidity. I thought about running to the trees—you could make out a sketch of them—black trunks shooting through the white haze— the branches were all broken, gone, buried under sand, and like the driver had promised, they stood far from the road. It was hard to tell the real distance.

As the wind picked up, the bare, thin tops knocked against one another. Then, a separate rhythm, the crashing, yet the landscape didn't shift—just huge whalebacks of sand, black trunks through a gauzy white, the sun above us and no way to pinpoint where. No real shade either. But the contractor and a woman, her name was Iona, had pulled clothes from their luggage. We were holding the clothes over our heads and pieces to our mouth to breathe through. The driver stretched a gunnysack from his wide head to his knees—he had dumped out the mail inside—then sat down and made his awning. I watched those letters flitter to the earth, slip into the white with the tree rows. I wondered if any were the ones I had sent you before I left.

I packed all the letters you had written me. That's right, Mama, an entire suitcase full. A few I keep in the stationery box, so I can look at them whenever I want— like my birthday, the flicker-photograph of you clapping as the candle lights go out. I read them over and over, until the presence of your voice is impossible to lose.

I'm sorry I've written so many pages—the government will mark through them for sure, mark these passages clear until what I've put down, most of my words, their realness is erased. I don't know what to do about that, how to tell you this truth. I don't even know if I can send this letter. I know if you read these pages, you'll worry, and the ones from yesterday, you'll worry more. But I don't know how else to tell you that despite it all, I'm okay. So I will send them. I will keep the letters until I'm in the Saved World, then I'll send them. I still have hope that I'll arrive in Birmingham, and even smile when I get in the city. From there, I'll come to you in Chicago because I can't believe the other—that we will die here.

Darl came out about two and went off from the rest of us. He didn't even ask the driver for water because we all had to ask that now. There's no food to share. I tried not to think about my hunger. Darl, he just stood alone.

It was weighing on us, the ozone, the heat, all of it drifting down. I worried about the baby. What was the sun going to do to me and the baby? Would she dry up into a shell? She's hungry. Still hungry. A girl, Mama—I feel her wanting to grow. I should've packed food, but it was only a six hour drive. That's what they told me to expect when I left Fatama.

At two, after Darl had joined us, I think it was around two when Iona tripped out from under the coat she was holding, sprung forward, and collapsed on the ground. We had a little shade, an angle from the bus fenders and tires, but the shade did her no good.

Everyone circled Iona except for Darl. Lavina called to him, and someone mentioned water, so the driver stood up and brought it as Lavina and Mazy dragged her into the shade. Another woman fanned her with a broken fan she had in her purse, so we all got close enough to cool her with whatever we were holding. I remember thinking, Is this it? Is this all we have to keep ourselves alive? All we can offer one another? Fanning?

The driver told us, If she's dead I don't want to give her anything. Make sure she's not dead. He wrapped a fist around the top of the jug, which was wrong—you should give everything, right? But he was being selfish for the rest of us. We needed someone to do that. I couldn't have done that.

Lavina yelled for Darl because he knew CPR and Iona wasn't breathing. She lay there with her cheeks as pink as ours, red and swirling, her gray hair specked with sand. And Iona didn't move and that was the scariest thing— her not moving even as we fanned her neck, her palms, up her arms and down, faster and faster. Someone called her Child, Come back to us, Child. Honey—several people said Honey. Letting her die was the beginning of our own death. We couldn't let that happen. Occasionally Iona's lips quivered as if she wanted to respond, or her head jerked, those swirling red cheeks getting darker.

Darl just flung one hand back at us, claiming he was tired. He said those on the bus were already dead.

Lavina told him, Get over here. They're dead, but she's not.

He asked, What's the difference? And crossed his arms.

Darl—Lavina said it like she was calling Mazy to attention. And so he did. She made him. So he did.

Darl kneeled down, touched Iona's face, then asked the driver for the water. There was another pause between them.

If it was you lying here, what would you want? Darl asked.

The driver wanted to know if she was dead already.

What would you want? Darl said it a second time, louder. Then he grabbed hold of the jug.

He put some on her lips, cooled her face—dripped the water, rubbed it into her cheeks, and the wind picked up and cooled her. My tongue swelled dry; I couldn't swallow. Darl touched her neck, held his fingers to her wrist, then set his palm against her breastbone. He breathed into her mouth, counted, pushed against her, counted, breathed. Over and over this ritual until something cracked underneath his hands, the far-off snap of a sweetbay. And he pushed again, harder, and breathed and counted, stopped. She said nothing and didn't jerk anymore. The water he had rubbed onto her face, what made her glisten for a moment, evaporated, leaving her red swirling cheeks full and blue.

*Darl stood up, dusting his shirt, crying, just that mo-
ment, then no more. And me, I wanted to rub my fingers
under his eyes, steal those tears—I could see where they
were—touch them to my lips and take the grit and dust
from my tongue—so selfish. Hungry. Thirsty. I couldn't
stop my wanting.*

*Like Darl, we all moved away from Iona, afraid that
the death surrounding her might enter our shoes, our sore
skin. Quietly, we did this and didn't talk for the rest of the
day; conversation was no substitute for coolness, for
water and food. We saved our energy for the next one
who fell.*

*At night, it started to get cold, so we climbed into the
bus. Even with the windows still open, there was the
smell of supper dishes left out too long and rotting—
those bodies in the back. The driver helped Darl throw
them out with the other dead. We helped, too. It took all
of us now to do it—all of us, so weak.*

*Someone thought it'd be a good idea to walk to Bir-
mingham. But the driver said that was crazy. Birmingham
was sixty miles.*

It's cool enough to go in the dark, the man said.

*You'll be lucky to track fifteen before morning, the
driver assured him. And the sun'll be waiting, the driver
assured him. That coolness won't last.*

*The man wanted to know if any mining camps were
close, but the driver said there were none.*

We're going to die, then, someone called out; there

was a new whisper of Oh Lord, Jesus, do not forsake us, do not; I know we're going to die.

Shut up, the driver said and grabbed a seat back, lowered himself down. The curls in his hair were sweaty from the work of lifting dead bodies, from the day in the sun, from the storm, the accident. The bruise was so sunburned, his left eye had been swallowed up in the knotted skin. He opened the cap on the last jug and gulped, then handed it over to me.

One drink, okay? The rest for tomorrow. He nodded and I nodded. I pulled the hair from my face, the loose strands that had dried in the corners of my lips. I closed my eyes and washed the salt, the sand from my tongue. Afterward, my tongue and throat were just as dry as if I had had no water at all, no memory of it, nothing. I couldn't hold on to that moment.

June 24—Friday early

Mama,

I can't leave much of a note here, because the patrollers have found us. Patrollers out of Birmingham, and they'll be taking us there. I was staring at the black sky, the trees not far away, splintered and pointing. I was listening to them snap off—the forest vanishing, becoming a burial of trunks and limbs and sand—when a light flashed over like a downed sun. Someone was here, but who? People were shuffling outside, talking, then laughing—they were looking at the dead bodies. One of the patrollers climbed up and beat on the door until the driver pulled it open. He shone a light in.

Found the lucky ones, he called down to his partner and yawned and grumbled for us to get out. So I'm getting out, Mama.

Birmingham

Dear Mama,

I couldn't write you for two days and now I'm worried that I'm going to die, that my baby, your grandbaby, Mathew's baby will never be born. We've made it to Birmingham, but it's not the Saved World, Mama. Those checkpoints that kept us out for years—they solved nothing. The desert has come north. Are you all right? It won't get to Chicago, I promise that. You've escaped the desert for good. I just don't know how to get to you any longer. And there's no returning to Fatama.

When the patrollers showed up, they led us to the back of a trailer, the word Horses washed out on the metal overhang. Someone asked about the suitcases, *could we bring them? An officer shook his head, warned everyone, You or your bag—choose. We don't have a lot of space.*

But all your letters to me were packed up, still in the cargo hull. I couldn't get to them.

Another woman, she already had her bags—large and red, one in each hand—she marched past the officer.

Without turning, he called for her to put the bags down, said he'd leave her in the desert. Then he squared his hat and told her again, Put it down.

She took a few more steps before flinging her red luggage on the dirt like a child would, and she ducked under the overhang, went inside the trailer. The ones who had already fished out their suitcases from the cargo hull clicked open the latches and started shoving toothbrushes and combs, small pieces of clothing, money—US bills and even mining scrip—into their pockets.

There was a brooch that kept slipping out of the contractor's hand, shiny and black like an oversized eye. It fell in the dirt, and she dug it up, blew the dirt off. The brooch slipped out once more, so she grabbed at it, and this time the pin stuck her and she jerked and the black eye stuck in the ground.

Lavina said the brooch wasn't worth that much trouble.

But Gail said it was her great-grandmother's. It was worth everything.

Carefully, she took it, closed the pin, and dropped it

into her pocket, the officers saying to get up now, come on, get inside, rounding their arms, pointing us to the open gates.

We walked forward, our clothes torn, and dark except for the flashlights, where the light fell on us, the officers shining them, spinning them, catching a hip, an elbow, down the barrel of the arm to the wrist, hands touching on something, a calf and hair. We were like horses going in.

At least, Mama, I have the black box, the stationery you gave me, and some of your letters. I wrapped both arms tight around it, smothered it so they couldn't see and couldn't take.

Come on, the patrollers said, whistling, and the whistles took off, shot through the black desert, where they warped and grew louder, refusing to come back to us. I got in, the last one.

We were told they didn't have any water, and when I tried to give my visa, the closest officer said it was no good, pushed it out of his way. Someone wanted to know about the dead bodies, but they shut the gates and pulled off. The few standing up began to fall, and the rest of us shifted so they could have a seat on the metal floor.

Sometimes metal at night can be cool, but it wasn't. Just dull and a little warm as if another group of people had been sitting here talking, whispering moments ago. It was easy to imagine that—their hands pressed on the same metal and loose straw, their knees bent into anchors.

Thank goodness we've been saved—they had said like we were saying now—*You heard him. Birmingham. That's where we're going.*

And the patrollers, Mama, they said nothing about the dead bodies, just left them.

Above our heads was a row of small windows, the sky too black and gray to change into blue, dry into blue we had read about and been promised. The sky Mathew talked of in his sleep.

It's blue, he would say over and over. *Sky,* he would say, twisting up the covers.

I'd lie there and rub his head 'cause once I get woken up, it takes me hours to calm back down. *You know, Mama, 'cause you're the same way.*

All right, baby, all right now, I'd whisper to him just like Darl had whispered to the injured ones on the bus. Then I'd shush him like you did me, like Lavina did.

He'd keep asking, *Do you see it? Blue?*

Yes, I'd finally say, *yes, it's right there.*

Sometimes I'd point as if his eyes were open, as if the gesture might convince him.

But he wouldn't let up. *Do you see it?*

I remember the ceilings of those houses we lived in—mostly dark and plaster or tin or wood, and the wind gusts blowing across, always blowing until *No,* I said, *No, I don't see the blue.*

He was right not to trust me, Mama, and I'd turn away from him for leaving me hopeless, Mathew never realizing what he'd done. Asleep. So I was unfair, and no one to talk with about it, that hopelessness digging at me worse and worse.

All night the patrollers drove toward Birmingham, the trailer bucking at the torn highway and bucking us off the metal floor, and I waited for the black to change to blue, for it to change into something good like Mathew had dreamed of. If not that, I hoped to at least find stars.

Instead I found small yellow lights as we approached the city gates, stretching across a high, black wall. Birmingham is a fortressed city—but maybe you know this already from when you came here on your way to Chicago and wrote about it in a letter that the government marked out, so I couldn't read, couldn't know what you tried to tell.

We got closer to the city gates, and in front sat the curling shadow of barbed wire. The wire and the wall extended like two rivers out of my reach, and the patrollers stopped just inside, told us to get out.

One of the officers said a food drop was in Linn Park, and pointed down the highway—State 11. He told us to follow it. He was the larger of the two and had a black band on the arm of his shirt. In the light I could see him—a rash across his neck, a birthmark, red, spreading from his left ear down, like someone had scalded him.

The patroller said the government had set up three other shelters, but the one at Linn Park was the closest and safest. Just take 11 to First Avenue. They had water and food.

The whole time he talked and pointed, I looked back at the wall where two spotlights flashed overhead. Two more officers stood on the wall with rifles pointing out. At first I assumed those rifles were meant for us. Then I realized they were aiming into the blackness just beyond, into the city, to where the darkness, the full and undertow of it began to pull. There. And beyond there, lights, too small and disparate to hold, too distant to reach, like stars that would burn your hand if you snatched them close to your neck or shirt. But I knew the sun would be up soon along with the white haze—I could feel its thick net waiting to take over, the heat of it already building. What happened to Birmingham? That's what I wanted to know. What happened to the city, the gateway from the Southeastern Desert to the Saved World?

The others kept saying, What's going on? Birmingham's not part of the desert.

And Gail said that they couldn't send her into that mess, not like this. She worked for the government.

What kind of hell is waiting for us, anyway? she wanted to know. She drew her energy from the ground through her boxy shoulders, her face wet with dirt like all our faces, and Gail told the officers, You ought to be fair about it. Her feet and shoulders perfectly still.

The officer with the black band said that a consulate had been set up in Linn Park—any problems could be taken up there. His job was to pick up everyone outside the city caught in the storm and bring them in. That's all.

Bring them in for what? the bus driver asked. I'm going out that gate.

He nodded one stroke at the officer and almost fell. The swollen bruise on his face was leaking from the eye. Since getting out of the trailer, he'd been wobbly, and he said, You're not leaving me here.

The first step he took, the officer glanced at the wall-guards. One of them drew his rifle. Then the officer stepped in front, crossed his arms, but the driver was too large and kept moving. So the officer shuffled back, and when he did, he tripped into his partner.

For a second it was a comedy, two officers falling on themselves, our driver trudging ahead until they reached for their holsters, a spotlight was on us, and their hands went down, flashlights hitting the dirt, and the wall-guards took aim. It was, of course, what we had already played out in our minds—this is how we would die, this is exactly what would happen—shot and no one to help. A comedy, a mistake. What we knew happened to desert people who crossed the wrong border. How else could it go?

But the patrollers untangled themselves and tried to stand up. For a moment, nothing.

So I did what you had done, Mama, that night years ago on the Pearl River when Terry yelled at that group of marshals fishing—he had such a temper. They had come down from Memphis with six deserters, stopped halfway to the Shreveport coke mill, halfway to "piss at some fish," they said, and laughed. We heard them, the three of us sitting inside Terry's truck, where he had taken us after work and school, pulled up on the bank. But then he got out and kept saying there weren't no damn fish here, and didn't they know that? They'd better leave, wasn't their damn river, that was crazy, like anyone owned a river—and Mama, I remember you just grabbed him and pulled him away—that crazy thing he was saying and doing—you just pulled him away before they could take him. I saw you step forward and hold Terry and remember what you said?

Love me. You stop this now and love me.

You held him so tight that he couldn't get outside of you. When you said, Love me, he turned away from the marshals, looked at you until he lost his anger, its purpose, lost himself. I had said nothing. I was just eleven. Too afraid, still in the passenger seat with the window down, watching.

So I thought of your hands, how strong they had to be, and put mine on the driver's shoulders and stood beside him. It's not that I had the strength to keep him in place or even that I could reach deep across his wide frame and hold him, but I startled him. So he stopped.

How far to the shelter? I asked the patrollers.

Less than ten miles, the other one spoke, gawky and long-chinned, first time he spoke since he pushed away my visa. He looked relieved that I had said something he could answer easy.

The driver didn't move.

Ten miles isn't so bad, I said. We can manage it.

Behind us were those lights, those tiny stars, that maybe we could web into a map and cut a path. Highway 11—isn't that what the patroller had said? I already felt the walk in my legs getting ready.

The driver shook off my hands and insisted the patrollers take us in before the sun got up, or at least give something for us to drive in with. He asked for water— Everyone's thirsty, he said, but the edge in his voice was gone.

We got nothing for you, the officer with the black band answered. I'm sorry. Water's at the shelter.

I wanted to know if we were still in the desert.

The other patroller nodded. Until there's a shift, he said, Birmingham's part of the Southern Alabama Zone.

The driver asked, What if there's no shift? Then he said, Not going to be. You know that, right? You know that already? The desert's here and going to stay here.

He was having a hard time catching his breath and he leaned against me. I thought of Iona, how she had tripped out into the sun and died and Darl couldn't bring her back. The driver kept raising his sleeve to his eye where the liquid pooled. He could barely touch his bruised face.

The patrollers grabbed their flashlights and looped around us—a big loop so none of us could get too close—and drove away, kicking sand up in their wheels the way they came in.

The gates closed behind the horse trailer, and that's when I realized we were all alone, truly alone. No one was coming for us, walking out from that darkness. The city was vacant, desolate, just those small white lights in Birmingham to lead us down.

The men on the wall didn't leave. And that's when— I hadn't seen it—that's when I noticed the posts set in front of the wall—short posts with signs—they showed up every so far. They all read: Any Person Found Beyond This Point Will Be Shot.

The driver walked over and pointed to the closest sign and all of us followed and stared. We hadn't read it wrong. The words wouldn't change. So we turned, started down Highway 11.

The spotlights clicked out, and one of the officers lowered his gun. The light glowed around him until the blue buzz of it and his body like a core of tungsten completely disappeared. The only lights were the yellow ones along the wall encased in thick glass shells, that river of them going on and on, and the even smaller glimmers awaiting us in front, just a few of them with no pattern. White stars.

I can't write any more about it today, Mama. I don't want you to worry, but I need to tell you, need to talk to someone. I can't write anything now.

Jennifer folded the stationery—*pine sky* the label read— "hardly green" is what she called it—there wasn't a hint of pine at all, just glue and paper and now heat, difficult to feel because her fingers kept shaking numb, had been doing that all morning. She dropped the letter and quickly snatched it up before the wind had a chance to take it into the exhausted crowd of Linn Park. They churned around her, heading to the refugee tents, slowly exiting back into the square, then back to the tents, where huge fans had been set up for cooling. Jennifer pushed the letter into its envelope yet couldn't feel the edges; the paper slipped, cutting, just the smallest lines of blood and cracked skin. Despite this, despite her dry tongue, she managed to seal it, and leaned against the flat bark of the oak—*This Oak Tree Planted in Memory of George Washington* is what the plaque said. She gazed as she had all day at the leaves.

It was the first time Jennifer had seen oak leaves beyond a photograph or a movie; the first time she had listened to the dulled edges cut against one another in stirs of wind dying, coming back. Each time, the leaves restarted like the wheel of some engine ever-turning. On the underbellies were green and white splotches, but mostly the leaves had shriveled brown through the veins, frozen from when the storm hit.

The trunks needed to be uprooted, she had already decided, the dirt shaken out of their wrinkled skin, like shaking out a rug, what her mama told her to do when they lived in Mississippi—shake out the rugs to rejuvenate the color. They had carried five rugs from home to abandoned home, occasionally replacing a worn-out rug or an unraveling one with a new one. Used to, she'd lay them across the chair backs and close them around her into a hiding place, a cloak. And when she stared out from between the legs, it was like being in a rocket or a smaller house—"my apartment," she called it. If she touched the walls of her fortress, dust separated from the bright weaves, floating down and at the same time up to the ceiling, fine particles wrapped and strung through light. In the same way, the people here moved about her, as if the rugs couldn't be still now, the sky sifting its dust.

As a child, the taste of dust had calmed her, and she would roll its familiar chalkiness back and forth on her tongue, refusing to spit like her stepfather, Terry. "It's mud sucking," he explained often, spitting into the sink or the toilet or sometimes into his hands, wiping the brown liquid onto his coveralls. In Louisiana and Mississippi, the dust was always brown.

"That's gross," she'd tell him, and examine the folds in her dress, the one ribbon, the sleeves, to make sure the fabric remained untarnished. Her thick hair had always trapped dust, and every night her mother grabbed up long pulls and shook them before tying them into braids. Jennifer touched the ends to make sure they weren't dipped in his brown goo.

One night when they lived in Picayune, he laughed and said, "Better on my coveralls than in my *lungs*. Why you keep all that dirt inside?" She closed her mouth, just stared at his hands.

"Don't worry," he said, "I won't touch you with these." He spread the palms forward, lumbered into the room, then followed with another clumsy stride and another until Jennifer ran out to get something, anything to hit him with. She hated it when he tried to frighten her.

Steel flat cars worked best for throwing—Barbies had a tendency to veer at the hinged legs and shoulders. But by the time she made it back to the kitchen, the laughing had switched to coughing and there he stood over the sink, gripping the metal rim, unable to spit. That coughing, it sounded like he'd never stop, like he had no more air in his lungs to help.

Terry was tall, bowed through the center like a warped strip of metal, his spine never fixing right—sometimes, she thought, like the sun skimming the edges of the moon into slivers and quarters. If he collapsed, what to do with him?

How would she possibly stretch him and raise him back up? He possessed too many ungainly bones, too much coughing that made her feel tiny, just a girl, and not older like she imagined to be. So she yelled for her mama, heavier and stronger, but in the bedroom with the door shut and locked, all the lights out.

Terry doubled over the sink, and Jennifer yelled, again.

"Don't bother Delia," he managed to say, the words coming out breathy with no force to them at all. "I'm all right. She needs to readjust. You know that, Jenny. I'm okay." The coughing wasn't as hard, that's true, but it might be a trick. He stood clamped onto the sink and swaying.

"What if you die?" His face was soaked in red as if all the blood in him was trying to get out and couldn't. Any moment he'd get even worse. But there was one good thing—he couldn't get to her. He couldn't scare her with his gross hands.

"Lord, girl, I'm not going to pass." He chuckled. "All it is is a cough." And the coughing eased up some. He breathed good and full.

Jennifer lifted the torpedo, an Indy 500 race car shaped like a skinny arrowhead, and flung it. Usually, she aimed for the stomach because it didn't hurt awful to be hit there, yet enough of a hit that he felt it, that he knew what she'd done. But this time, she flung it right for his head and hit him under the ear. He had coughed for five minutes.

"Damn it, girl. That one hurt." He rubbed the place. There was even a speck of blood.

"You can't cough that long."

"I can't help my coughing."

"Not that long," she told him.

He reached down, grabbed the torpedo, and flung it back. The car cracked into the wall.

"You put a dent in it," she said. "You're going to wake her."

"Delia needs to be."

"I thought she needed to readjust."

"Not now. She needs to see what kind of mess her daughter's up to." The red in his face had changed, was pinker and cool, like he was controlling the blood, how it flowed, how it moved through the skin and under his short, short brown hair. "She won't be happy."

Jennifer spotted the car. She looked at Terry, then back at the torpedo.

"Don't—"

But she did and flung it and Terry ducked and this time the car sailed through the thin glass of the kitchen window.

"Shit," he said. "Now we're both in trouble, Jenny. Why—" But he stopped himself a second time. A shuffling noise was coming from her mama's bedroom. "You woke her." He raised a finger.

"You did it coughing. And yelling."

"Just get me something to fix this," he said.

"Like what?"

"A shirt, cardboard, something. I got to cover this hole unless she finds it." He leaned in on the broken frame, then swiveled around. "Come on, come on."

So she went to her room and rattled open the drawer, scooped up her shirts, and carried the whole bundle to the kitchen.

"I just need one." Terry wrapped it around his hand and punched out the remaining glass; the wind swirled, blowing in debris and light.

"Why don't you use your own shirt?" she suggested.

He grabbed up another one of hers, a pink one that she wore a lot, and another, stuffing them in the window like bricks until they fit tight in the square and the wind couldn't whistle through. It looked as if the window had grown a colorful fungus, her clothes bulging and ugly.

"You think Delia will notice?"

"That's stupid. Of course she'll notice." There was a flushing noise—her mother still behind a door. "When do I get my shirts back?" She only had three clean ones left and needed them.

"As soon as I get this fixed. You're all right today." He glanced down. "We've got to measure it," and he quickly traced his finger along the frame. "I'll talk with Neil about cutting glass, or maybe plywood. But that's it. One square, you think?"

They looked at the fungus blob, and Jennifer nodded. "One square," she said.

Then, "I can't help the coughing, Jenny. Don't be so hard on me."

"I don't like it."

"I don't either." He sighed. "Don't be so hard on me, okay?"

She wasn't about to utter *okay* or even give him a nod. Then he started to rub her head, and she jerked back.

"I washed my hands," he promised, and put his hand back on her head and she let him. But she didn't feel calm, couldn't bring herself down from all his noise, such a thin body, he wouldn't hold up. He'd pass like Everett, and she'd lose another father. So she rolled the dust around with her tongue and kept at it, focused, so she never had to spit, never had to cough. Eventually, it wasn't his rubbing, it was the dirt her tongue clicked back and forth that made her relax and allowed her to readjust.

The calmness she felt now leaning against the oak in Linn Park was from that same place—the dust had simply moved from Louisiana to Alabama, had followed, that dust sifting now from the light to her, like the rugs in her apartment of chairs. Jennifer trapped those tiny particles, breathed them in, held them, and her lungs refused to let go.

Every tree in Linn Park was covered, too, not quite dead, still in shock. Water no longer ran in the fountain that the trees encircled, and the lower reflecting pools were also empty, overrun with people stepping in, out as if their movement were the only way to stay alive.

On the envelope, she wrote her mother's Chicago address, *355 Turner Avenue, Apt. 2118*, and started to put her own Fatama address in the left corner—Mathew was in Fatama, and maybe the letter had a chance of winding up at one of those places—but instead she wrote the date, *June 26, 2044*, and her name, *Jennifer Philips Harrison*. She didn't have any liberty stamps and no way to get any—every store she had passed on Highway 11, every building was broken and blacked out. As soon as she left Birmingham, she'd mail the letters.

She'll worry if I don't, Jennifer reminded herself.

Delia often said, "I just can't stop thinking about things. Wish I could."

"I'd like to know about it, Mama, those things."

"Oh, don't do that," she'd say. "Don't make me answer that."

Jennifer used to find her mother in the dining room, sitting with hands spread wide on the table, examining every crease, bend, and knot—when she checked her own palms, that's all she found. Then her mama would wipe something from her face, lay her hands back on the table, open, close them, open them more, and wiggle her hips firmly into the wooden seat. Her mother had long hair, thick with streaks of gray that never trapped much dust, and she sat through the early morning, repeating the same ritual until Jennifer asked, "What's wrong?" What else could her mama's hands possibly carry?

"Nothing, nothing, nothing." That meant something was definitely wrong, those three words given so quickly, leaving Jennifer breathless, anxious. Somehow Delia Philips knew it, too. She scuffed the chair over the tile and walked into the kitchen. If Jennifer followed, her mama would walk out of the kitchen to her bedroom, close and lock the door.

All of Jennifer's attempts to reverse the lock's click with bobby pins and clothes hangers failed—they merely scratched at the hole in the doorknob. Sometimes Delia said, "Stop it." Then the light inside the room would click off and all around the door blackness would seep into Jennifer's toes and up through her body to her black hair. That's when she felt the most empty and weak—as if she were being filled with cold black water, nothing to do until Terry got done at the mine.

Louisiana and Mississippi were like that, whatever house they moved into on the Pearl River, the schools barely open for weeks, always closing. Like that.

When Jennifer turned sixteen they kept the schools open for good, and she was in a classroom every night. She sat at her desk, and thought if only her mother had stayed at the table, had talked, then the loneliness they both felt could've been erased, or at least uprooted. But grief was something to endure alone—Delia insisted on it. First Everett's passing—a flash flood at the Pearl River mine in Bogalusa, and Jennifer so young she could recall him only in fragments—the way he pitted the sofa cushions, his arms slumped and resting next to her, no jawline, eye line, hair, only his laugh—so loud and rumbling, it couldn't be turned off.

In her dreams, even the ones now, his laugh curled up like smoke and wheeled through, vanishing as naturally as sky, skin, words—whatever the dreams put forth. Mama had pictures—the woman loved to take pictures and flicker-photographs—but they remained static against the memories of Everett plopping down and standing, his voice rolling inside her bones, unwilling to be quiet. Mama's pictures were no one she knew really.

Four years after Everett's death, Terry had moved in, and as soon as he left for the mine in New Hebron, Mama pulled and braided Jennifer's hair and said, "He's coming back at six." Then after a pause, "Isn't he?"

Jennifer swung around to face her mama's doubt—always that doubt, something hard in her eyes. Not toward Jennifer, she didn't mean it that way, but something hard and scattered that Jennifer connected to the desert, the sand undercutting her mother's gravity, in both of them, the possibility of any axis.

"He'll be home. He's always home at six, Mama," she said, and wanted sometimes to snatch her mama's hair, make her say ow, make her step out of the unending sadness.

Yet Jennifer had done the same worrying when she married at twenty-one, spent nights examining her palms for cuts and breaks while Mathew dug deeper holes in the clay loam. She counted figures in the wallpaper and the rough ceilings while he went thirty-seven feet, sixty feet down—a parallel counting of his life and hers. She measured him deep in the earth, his body growing smaller and smaller, the numbers filling up the space above him and between them, but never enough numbers to fill the distance completely.

When she started to talk to herself like Delia, she paid for Internet classes from Syracuse, went driving through the desert towns until her propane rations gave out. Back and forth she went, looking at the empty houses everyone fled in 2014. But what was she hoping to find in them? She stopped at places with the front doors missing as if the ghost people had finally returned, and left open the black space as invitation and warning.

Walk inside there, she knew, and vanish.

Maybe I'll open a business—she said that at least once a week for a year, but over half the encampment was at the mine. What was the point? Her friend Tonya had a hair place, The Great Look Beauty Shop, only the *e* and *t* kept ungluing and falling off, so it read *The Gr a Look* and sometimes *The Gr at Look*. Whenever Jennifer drove by, Tonya was sitting in the fat beauty shop chair watching TV, alone. It was like that at all of the businesses, everyone slumped in their seats, watching the one station, WAZD, the government transmitted to the camps, waiting for the dust to quiet, for the miners to be done so they could lift the town's grogginess with their mud and exhaustion.

You can only drive so far—Terry had said that. He took them on a weekend drive once a month, saving up his propane rations until he had extra, and if he had extra money, he bought propane from the black marketers. Jaunts, he called them—Let's go for a jaunt—along the full length of creek beds and upriver until he got weary. I've had enough now, he'd say when he was ready, Jennifer half-asleep against the passenger door, Mama against his shoulder. He slued the truck and always so fast, something in her got pulled through the window and left in the desert. But Jennifer didn't open her eyes to find it, that piece of herself, whatever it was.

And he was right. She grew weary of drifting over the state and county roads, was drawn back to the houses she and Mathew lived in: a two bedroom trailer in Fatama, a one floor ranch in Tensaw, the old Georgian in Selma on Abbott Street made of brick. Every August for nine years the mining camp stopped in Selma for a month; every August she made that place her home on Church and Abbott. But the ones in Fatama and Tensaw would more than likely be damaged next year, unlivable—sand and wind searing off a roof, or joists and rafters snapped from dry rot she'd seen happen so many times.

As she got older, and Mat talked less, she gave up on driving altogether and stayed in the kitchens and bedrooms, the crooked, empty hallways that had belonged to others, all of them dead now, ghost people. Where she slept, they had slept, and lived with the same insomnia, counted figures in the same walls, waiting for the desert to tire. Her only relief came from writing her mother letters and watching television. "At least I don't stare at my hands," she said to herself. At least there were other voices when the television was on.

Jennifer did this until Mat's father, Mr. Chris, moved in the year before his death, stacking his stolen library books on the kitchen floor. She began to read like she had in high school, was surprised to learn that Mathew had read a lot when he was younger.

"I've never seen him pick up a book. And he sees me doing it." Another piece of his history that Mathew kept from her.

Mr. Chris nodded. "He won't now. Can't get him to do anything now," he said, pulling clay from his beard.

Jennifer read to avoid sinking into a solitude like her mother's, those nights and early mornings, watching her stare at her hands. It was as if Mama had plunged herself into the center of a fig, and no way for anyone to get close—except for Terry, when he was home and held her.

After Delia left the Southeastern Desert for good to live with her sister, Bobbie, in Chicago, after Terry's death when Jennifer was twenty-one and chose to stay in Alabama and marry Mathew, she wrote her daughter every week, sometimes twice a week. "Forgive me," her mother had said, but for what? Escaping the desert? Giving Jennifer her loneliness? Jennifer never asked. She wanted her mama to bring the quiet existence between them all those years to the surface. What an explosion—an explosion that would never happen, would never be said. And what to do with this new woman Delia Philips had become, this attention to her daughter from a long distance? Before she left, they could barely stay in the same room—too much grief, and when Jennifer reached Chicago, she hoped the years and letters between them had altered that distance, had softened her mama toward her presence.

She'll worry about me, Jennifer told herself—the bus overturning, the dead in Birmingham. *Maybe I shouldn't send the letters. Or I should change what I wrote.* But for

years the government had censored the letters Delia Philips
sent. She wasn't about to censor her own. She shook her
head. *Got to let her know I'm coming. That's the important
thing.* As soon as she was outside Birmingham, she'd mail
them.

Jennifer twisted her hair, stuck it behind her ear. She
was sure it looked funny, her ear poking out on one side, but
there wasn't any other way to keep the bangs from her face,
to cool off. The wind that blew through Linn Park was all
heat and gritted-soot.

Then she took the letter and placed it in the black box,
pulled the box under her blouse and wrapped her arms
around it—so much sand on her arms. When the box
touched her sweaty stomach, a chill there, and she wondered if her baby felt it, too.

She had managed to keep the stationery, the accompa-
nying envelopes, some of her mother's letters with their
flicker-photographs, her visa, but no brush—her hair des-
perately needed one—and a picture of Mat, a high school
picture he had given her before the wedding so she wouldn't
forget him while he mined for clay rocks.

"Please. I'm not going to forget *you,*" she always teased
Mat before he left, and he smiled. In the picture, the bones
in his face had not yet spread and stretched his mouth and
skin into an older bloom—there was something hopeful
about that face, so she kept it in the box, along with seven
hundred US dollars she had saved, and a small notebook if
she ran out of stationery, and the one poetry book by Naomi
Shihab Nye. She went over the items again and again,
thumbed through them, so she wouldn't forget.

She hadn't opened the Shihab book since leaving Fatama. But Jennifer had written so much in the last few days,
at least the poems gave her a voice other than her own,
someone else talking, and in that way permitted her voice to
rest.

I want, I need immediate bloom—that was the line that had given her the strength to leave Fatama and Mathew. Immediate bloom. She needed that now.

Instead, here she was in the center of Birmingham leaning against an oak, the leaves cutting, dying, the box sealed under her shirt and arms so no one could know it, the baby sealed deeper inside. Yet somehow she and the baby were safe as if in a tornado's eye, as if inside her old rug fortress. All of these people churning, milling over the dead and one another—she was in the center of their misery. They were too trapped to see her, to know she existed as they swirled toward the refugee tents, the huge fans, and away from the sun to the trees and the buildings outlining the square.

The white haze—it infused the roofs with a flatness, as if nothing existed beyond the park, the roped-open tents, the Tutwiler Hotel, and across the square, the Jefferson County Courthouse, which had been the capitol building since they moved the state offices from Montgomery in 2014, the courthouse with its stone panels. She could see those panels barely—a woman sending a man away and another panel with the same woman allowing a man in—*With Justice* the first one read and *With Mercy* the other. The rest of the city had been swallowed up in white and flakes of soot. Still people kept moving until someone dropped to the ground like Iona had done, like the driver had done on the way in from the Birmingham gates. They had traveled maybe five miles at that point.

"Get up," Darl and Lavina had told him. Jennifer said, "Just a little more. We're close now."

She had put her hands again on his shoulders, but he shook them off, wiped at the pucker on his face, where his eye had been, the blistered bruise swollen, flowering, draining. "Just bring me some water when you get there," he had said. "It'll be enough to carry me." He was on the curb and there was no way to lift him.

Darl said, "I don't know how long."

"Doesn't matter." The driver lay flat. "Just bring me water."

"I could lance it. We could hold you; I could try to get some of the infection out. Then you could go on."

"You're not touching me." The driver tried to slow his shallow breath and catch it deeper. He set one finger to his face, moved it off. "Bring the water. I'm too dizzy. The doctors can fix the knot."

He said "will carry me" several more times and "water," a large framed man like Bossey, and no way to lift him. Bossey, the mining crew chief, was in Fatama with Mathew, and the driver was lying down and softly crying and then, "I'm going to lose my eye, I can tell. They won't let me drive a bus anymore."

Darl crouched lower. "Be quiet," he whispered as if the dead were listening. "I'll get water for you."

Once they reached the tents, Darl looked for a doctor, and Jennifer lost sight of him and the others.

Around her now, refugees buckled, dropped. Some grabbed hold of the closest arms and fingers and belt loops and lifted. Someone managed, "Help me, baby, I'm so tired." The others didn't get up. Two men talked about a car they had on L Street with a full tank. "If we go north." "No, they've closed it off, too." After he spoke, the second man turned and looked at the tree. He followed the trunk down to Jennifer and paused. She looked away. When she turned back, the two men had walked on. Church bells—she couldn't place where they came from. One man kept yelling to God, "These are the end times, the end times, the Lord shall make the rain powder and dirt." He was close by and the crowd pushed around the preacher. No one waited. When someone fell, the crowd swirled around them, like a rock fallen in a river, just like her; she had become a rock against the tree with its low-gnarled limbs, splitting the flow of bodies and wire and trash. They swirled around her, around the end-times man lifting up on his toes, "I will tread them with my anger," and swirled around the fallen until a group with red crosses on their sleeves and backs jagged through and took the dead away.

From another part of the city, a low sound rose and fell — "The early warning system," some of the refugees said, and a woman chuckled, "Remains of the Cold War." She had tied white bags over her arms' burnt skin. "We never got nuclear explosions, just this terrible weather." The woman laughed and stepped through the dust. The Red Crosses cut against her.

Another stray dog wove through the crowded legs. Earlier, a dog had been shot, its hind legs taken out, and the refugees peeled open a circle for the shooter to flip the animal, cut and pull through its stomach, still trembling, and skin it.

Jennifer had seen the national guard gun down a man who said he was hungry. And she realized afterward, it had not made her jump or turn away. "Can you help me with some food?" he said, walking up, then jerked in the rifle flash. She watched him slip, and she did nothing and felt nothing. The shot for a moment made her deaf, the same as the dog's whine had made her deaf earlier when he lost his legs. The Red Crosses took the man away, and her mouth so dry; she kept trying to swallow but there was nothing to swallow.

These bodies made the heat worse — the shuffling of feet and mumbling for food, the hard breathing — refugees with shirts over their heads, pillows, anything against the sun, and everyone carrying the yellow cans of water handed out at the shelter each morning.

Someone whispered, "Hey," from behind her. "Hey," he said louder. He was getting close, and Jennifer took a piece of glass she had found on the walk to Linn Park, moved it into the open so the man could see it. She kept the point of the glass ready, but when she turned, no one was there.

In one corner of the empty fountain, three refugees had torn limbs from the brittle oaks to build a fire. They cooked meat and coffee and kept their rifles upright like the guardsmen, and a black shirt knotted to a pole marked them against the others, their blue smoke too awful and delicious to avoid.

Again, the church bells denoted the time of day she no longer knew. Mille-copters appeared out of the flattened sky and whipped up dust and landed with rations and guards and took off. She was safe, she reminded herself, until the human tornado shook her out. She was safe under the oak branches that curled down like the long brim of a hat. Near her toes and the knuckled roots lay not acorns, but birds, wings pulled tight to their blackened bodies, the wind pushing, hoping to turn them like spun balls of thread. If she moved, she'd touch their feathers. She didn't, remained as still as the tree. Behind her, on the other side, she heard a woman selling sex for rations and water. Someone else, a black marketer, was selling bags of ice, changing his pitch when he traded ice for sex.

Everyone from the bus had disappeared. Two days ago as they walked deeper into Birmingham, some went into the buildings along Highway 11, the doorless entranceways, and some, like the driver, couldn't make it. As they walked, the dark gave over to the sun and ozone, and they realized just how many bodies they were stepping over. Bodies littered the highway, their blood dried in pools of fleck-dust and along thin grass barriers still green, and cars that had jammed into one another, the bodies inside them coated with powder and smoke. Some cars had struck the long corridor wall that followed Old 11, the driver called it. Heavier trucks had broken through the concrete before stalling and burning into soot.

There was one girl, she couldn't write to Mama about that girl, lumped on the black pavement, her face swollen and purpled as if she had been stuffed with sand. Something of her had slipped into Jennifer as if the girl had withered down into a baby. Jennifer reached under the box and touched her stomach, wished she was far enough along to feel a kick. She waited for the girl to change back and breathe.

"Don't stop walking." Lavina lifted Jennifer's elbow. "Stop looking at that girl. And if you see someone coming at you, run." She, Jennifer, Mazy, and the contractor, Gail, had walked from the gate together, a little behind the rest of the group.

"We don't have much to steal," Jennifer said.

"They don't know that. You're carrying a box. What's in your black box?"

Jennifer clutched it and didn't answer.

"Besides, can't you tell something's changed—I feel it all the way through me, a nervousness—don't you have it?"

And Lavina saying that made Jennifer worry about the death on the road, that it could be her, her baby. She saw a piece of glass, clear glass, a triangle broken clean, and stopped to pick it up.

"That's good," Lavina said. "Find something yourself, Mazy. Don't just look at the road. Look at the bodies."

Mazy nodded, "Yes, ma'am," and looped her brown hair into one hand and started to kick gingerly at the wrists of the dead. They all did the same. Mazy had a pale blue dress like a faded cornflower and the skirt of it lifted when she kicked.

"Open them up like clamshells," Lavina said, her eyes widening full and lazy into moons, and the only thing on her face bigger were the knotted bones that stuck out against her pared cheeks. Mazy had those same features. "Open them up. Kick harder. Come on, they can't feel."

One hand of the dead had tangled a necklace of black beads, and on several others, the fingers had been cut off.

"Someone's taken their wedding bands," Jennifer said, and checked hers, turned it, the metal suddenly cold; then she looked into the white. The white smog gave nothing back except the burning.

"Taken the phones, too." Gail tapped her boot under someone's ear where a peel of skin hung, where the phone had been implanted. Jennifer had seen those cuts in the bottom of the skull, faces pulled to the side, and thought it was a marking of the dead, the first cut of a scalping, and that whoever did it would be back once the bus group left.

"Collectors," Gail called them. "Filthy scrap hunters, I tell you." She shook her head and stretched the neck of her small body.

Mazy pried a half bottle from a hand, and fitted her own hand around the green neck.

"Good. That's good. Keep it until you find something better," Lavina said.

"Where you from?" Gail asked.

"The Milner plant—I'm a coal blaster, but we have relatives in Birmingham and all the way to Nashville. My cousins live in Hooper City. My aunt." Lavina pointed up Highway 11, then slightly to the left as if she had divined the location exactly. "That's where we're going. My cousins said we could stay with them if I got out of Georgia."

"My mother's in Chicago," Jennifer offered. "My husband's down at Miller's Ferry."

"Clay rock miner?"

"Yes," she said.

"Why isn't he with you?" Lavina asked.

"I don't know," Jennifer said at first, but that wasn't the real truth. "He had a visa, but I couldn't make him leave."

"A visa? He could leave and he didn't? Crazy."

Jennifer wished she hadn't said anything. Since Mathew's father died, Mathew had barely talked to her. The desert had overtaken his mind like she had seen it do to other people. He was lost. Still, she didn't like hearing Lavina say he was crazy, and she didn't want to think about the other possibility—that he didn't love her enough to come along.

"I've been all over the Georgia and Alabama Zones,"

Gail told them, and coughed into a blue rag. Her wrinkles squinched tight, so many wrinkles stacked on top of one another above the brown sandsuit—not at all like Delia's crossed face, or even Lavina's narrow one. "My company's Kile, water filtration."

Jennifer had seen those people. They kept the huge filters changed, the machines carrying the sluck from the mines working. There wasn't a Kile woman at the Miller's Ferry camp though. They lived with the rest of the government agents, separate from the miner families.

"I live just north of Birmingham, in Fultondale. Gone for a year, and I tell you, Birmingham didn't look like this. It's a mess." Gail blew her nose. "These walls weren't broken. That's for sure. They were still protected zones. Now, in the east it was different—Redmont and Crestline Heights—you didn't want to live in those places. Collectors would start digging at your skin the minute you stepped in the open."

The walls had started at the Birmingham gate and continued along 11, turning at every intersection—but how far did they go? Jennifer wasn't sure. Then an emptied restaurant would appear, the Alabama Tearoom, Dexter's Barbecue, or a store selling catfish bait, and a street sign for Avenue Y and Hullman, and then the wall in long, empty stretches. In some places, the wall consumed the sidings of factories and offices, their windows and doors bricked up or boarded up.

"I wish I could see over them," Lavina said. "It's making me claustrophobic—I hated that about coal blasting, too."

"They're no good now. Everyone's stuck and crashed, even the rich." Gail kicked hard at a shoulder. "That's why I live in Fultondale. Birmingham has too many damn sections. The city's an onion, walls wrapped inside more walls, I tell you. It all started in Tarrant after the riots in the twenties. Tarrant built this concrete fence around themselves twenty feet high." She raised her arm. "Lastis, which was next to them, did the same, only they made it twenty-two feet and barbed wire on top, and then Killough Springs and the neighborhood next to them, until the whole city became an onion of higher and higher walls. A damn onion." She opened her hands at the sky, shooed the sky and smog away. "These walls are worthless. Looks like a bull's-eye spiraling out if you get up in a mille-copter. I've seen it before. You ever been up in a mille-copter? And the poor got squeezed between the walls, the open pockets that were left.

"Two years ago, some neighborhoods were quarantined with Martz disease. I had friends in Vestavia, but I couldn't see them. The people there died off and no one goes in those places now except for collectors, and the poor who've got nowhere else to go. If you get down one of these side streets, you'll see what I'm talking about. They don't stop— the walls just keep going until you hit a gate, and the guards'll let you in if you have the right credentials. Otherwise, they'll send you packing. But Fultondale is just one walled city, the whole city, I tell you. Here, every part is segregated—Vulcan, Tarrant, Center Point. They bricked up the old downtown so people could mille-copter to work—the roads have gotten dangerous. And on the south side is the city border to keep people from crossing in from the desert, the Birmingham gate where we came in. They thought it might keep the desert back, too." She laughed, breathy, and that started her coughing into the rag, choppy like bits of gravel like Terry used to do, and Jennifer shut her mouth, clicked the dust with her tongue until Gail breathed slower and fluidly.

"But why did the patrollers bring us to the gate, send us into Birmingham, if no one wants us here?" It was only the second time Mazy had spoken since they started walking.

"It's crazy what they did. I agree with you. They might as well left us in Talladega," Gail said.

"We need to be in Birmingham. Our cousins are expecting us," Lavina said.

Mazy rolled her lower lip under her teeth and bit down.

"They don't want us," she said quietly. Lavina walked up, stood over her daughter, and "Yes, ma'am," Jennifer heard Mazy say. "No, ma'am, I don't have any more sass."

"The desert's here," the driver shouted from up front. "You heard the patroller. They're keeping us locked up *here* so we can't go north or anywhere else." He didn't look back when he said it, just flung his arms at the sky like Gail had done, then let them drop and his whole body seemed to drop again. So loud. Would the noise bring people from behind the walls? Jennifer squeezed the clear glass in her hand until the edges started to cut.

Of course, it was the desert. It had made its way to Birmingham like it had always threatened to do. No one said anything after that. Those lights she had seen in the dark, those lights that were stars and would be maps—they had vanished. Nothing to guide them except a car smoldering, or a home in the distance still in flames. Jennifer wondered, was everyone crazy now? Setting fires? Cloistered behind walls until the sky and smoke settled back? Not everyone could be dead and vanished. Any second they might appear and come after her.

Three mille-copters dove in and they had to duck. She had seen mille-copters on TV—rescue vehicles that hovered just above roads, but could also sail higher. Tiny. They held four people—two in the cab, two facing the other way in the backseat, the rumble seat, open to the air with legs dangling out. The engine was sandwiched between the box-cab and the short blades. Sometimes the copters were hooked together into trains, the lead mille-copter cutting a path for the others to dip into and follow like water channeled into a sluice. And so here they were, flying, blue lights flashing, speeding over the dead bodies and smoke and traffic jam, so close to the ground that Jennifer and the others had to duck out of the way.

They're heading to the consulate, she decided, her heart cutting out and back in as if the blades might reverse her exhaustion, its speed might lift and make her better—so close—if she reached up, she'd touch a dangling foot. It seemed possible. Everyone in the group, they looked up, too—the wind from the blades rushing, cooling, something of the dust and the sky in this. The mille-copters shot ahead, the faces of the patrollers in the rumble seats—they continued to look out, fixed and tired and dirty. The wind eddied, then a crosswind turned the other way.

The mille-copters became like the other noises in Birmingham, the gunshots and explosions, buildings collapsing—something was being destroyed in the white haze, but always at a distance. The whir fell to a hum, then vanished, and only their steps echoed through the wreck of bodies.

At one point they came upon a man, his left arm missing, sawed down at the shoulder, his right hand cradling a gun. Darl pulled it free and pulled the chamber. He squeezed the trigger. Nothing. Squeezed it again, with the same result, and grasped the stock more firmly, kept it in view.

"I used to drive this street all the time," the driver told them. "Drove up 11 last week, through all the checkpoints, all the way to the downtown, and then the airport on East Lake Boulevard." He shook his head, kept walking though it was hard for him. No one stopped walking. Jennifer's heart stayed with the girl with the purple and blue face. Someone destroyed like that—she couldn't force that girl from her mind.

June 27

Dear Mama,

This is what Birmingham is now: people walking around moaning, or just staring, falling. The sun's gotten to them, the white haze and the smoke—everyone *coughs, is turning crazy. I wish I could tell you I was flying to Chicago and would be there soon, so soon. But I've already been to the consulate. The official said all visas have been suspended. Maybe tomorrow they'll be reinstated. She said, Check back tomorrow.*

It took me an entire day just to get to the front and talk with someone and sign my name in their book, tell them why I'm here, why they should let me go. The guardsmen have set up fans to cool us, but mainly to keep the smell down from the sick and dead. I'm okay, Mama. I just wish I could find a way to send this letter.

And the storm that hit Talladega also hit Birmingham. The sky hasn't cleared. I don't think it's going to change—that's what everyone's afraid of, what the guardsmen keep saying. No one knows what the government will do with us. I don't think the government knows. They refer to us as people of concern, POCs for short. I wonder what is meant by concern—their concern for us or their concern we'll do something to them. They feed us, shut us in, and while we wait to see if the sky reverses itself, people are slowly dying. The sky won't let anyone free. I know that's what happened when I was born, what you lived through. I love you, Mama. I wish I could send this letter.

It was afternoon, and more people had fallen, marked by purple spots the size of quarters where dehydrated blood had come to the skin's surface. The Red Crosses took the ones breathing to the hospital and later culled through, tossing the dead into harvesting machines that rotated the bodies in sheets of plastic, spit them out for the Crosses and guards to turn with poles, turn the cocoons toward wheel loaders engulfing and lifting the dead into gravel trucks and driven away.

"Like mummies, these POCs. Wrapped so tight, they can't stink," a guardsman said, leaning on his pole. "Spooky." He twitched his fingers at the train of plastic bodies, then jumped back against his partner.

"Stop fooling," the other guard said, and shoved him out of the way.

"All right, all right. You don't have to hit so hard. I mean, shit." He brushed at his vest, tugged his collar down, dust swirling the air.

The other guard shook his head. "Could you help me? Because I don't know about you, but I want a break." Together, they stabbed their poles like long river oars on top of a cocoon, pinning the feet and head until the wheel loader had troughed six bodies, taking theirs last.

They walked down six more bodies. "This is spooky shit."

"Shut up."

They leaned on the poles and waited for the loader to return.

For two days, Jennifer had hidden under the oak, then at night moved to the entrance of the consulate and food drop where the guardsmen were stationed. At night they cut the whirring fans off and set up a barricade. But as soon as the noises in the park swelled with high-pitched cries and gunshots, the fans were turned back on, and people who could make it to the front, bleeding, injured, did.

One man walked to the barricade, his hand against the side of his throat, his body pressed to that side of himself like the flat bottom of an iron. The crowd had parted around him like a sea, everyone afraid his bad luck might rub off.

"She's cutting me," he said, and turned halfway, pointing into the crowd, one face, then another—but which one?

A guardsman stepped up to the thick cables and rails. "You can't come in here. This is a sanctuary until tomorrow." He had a yellow patch on his sleeve and vest and stood like the patrollers at the Birmingham gate—would not lean forward, would not give.

"If it's a sanctuary, let me in."

"Tomorrow."

"But I'm dying," the man argued, and that's when Jennifer noticed the black diarrhea seeping, wherever he turned, a glistening down his clothes. And he didn't say "I'm dying" loud. He didn't have the energy to say anything more.

The guardsman turned, went back to talking, left the man standing, one hand on his throat, one holding the thick high cable, until he wilted into sleep. Occasionally a guard looked over at the body lumped on the sidewalk or into the crowd, but it wasn't until the shift change that he was hauled away.

"I'm tired of cleaning up your messes," the officer from the new shift called after them, but the departing unit kept their heads down, their shoulders down, and walked.

"Leave him for the Red Crosses. Let them take care of it," one of the new guards said.

"I don't want to look at this dead POC my whole shift, do you?"

"No, sir," the guardsman answered quickly and whistled for help, and "On three" they leaned down, the hard shells of their hats almost touching, then separating as they lifted the body up. The harvest machines sputtered nearby and fizzled, a sound they made all night.

When the man collapsed, Jennifer had wanted to turn away, wanted not to watch, but she did and didn't help him because what if that made her noticeable. For so long she had stayed unnoticed. A few times, hands had grabbed her, but she pulled loose, kept walking.

In the morning, and then, again, the middle of the day

when the sun broke up the ozone, and at evening when it cooled just a little, enough that you could feel yourself breathe again, the old Cold War sirens launched into their slow whir as if the city were under attack, as if *attack* were an experience about to happen and they should prepare. The church bells and fewer and fewer explosions sounded, as if that part of the city had exhausted itself. The siren was a marker of when the others woke up, when they ate, how much the sun was willing to give. Afterward there were no stars. None to follow.

She had been given rations of food and water, canned beef that tasted of ash, and vegetables that tasted the same. Three people had been killed over rations. And the guardsmen went on missions into the square with the Crosses to bring the dead to the harvesting machines, the sick to the hospitals, and from the hospitals to the machines with their steel mouths open like bullfrog planters—that's what they looked like. Jennifer had planters like that once. She'd taken them from a house in Alma and kept them and loaded the stone mouths with dirt and zinnia seeds, tulip bulbs that sprouted then withered until in disgust she threw the planters away in a backyard in Montgomery. The following night, they were already covered under sand drifts, and she forgot where she had thrown them.

The guards wouldn't venture out into the square at night, and once a guardsman said over a loudspeaker, "*No firearms,*" repeated it over and over. But that group inside the fountain with the black shirts, they were still there. And yesterday in the afternoon she had seen a collector after the last Red Cross detail had receded into the crowd. He moved his hand over the new dead as if he might heal them. Something round, half-round in the belly of his palm occasionally glowed a faint red and that's when he stopped and took out his short knife. She watched him peel a phone from under someone's ear, making sure to remove the long wiretaproots undamaged, cut fingers and shake the rings into a bag, clamp down on teeth with pliers and take them, and volt-chips, optic-steel—whatever had been implanted in scars and hips and skin, all of this into his bag, wet at the bottom as if it had been slung through mud. She knew then that she couldn't fall asleep.

By now she had been in the park for three days. She moved back under the oak where a few leaves still twisted, refusing to splinter in the barrage of heavy gusts, though most of the leaves had been carried away. Under the tree, there were people fixing themselves into the branch-shade. On one side, a family, and on the other, several couples huddled together. The woman selling herself was gone. Beyond them more people in stacked tight bands, and no longer clearings between the haze and the buildings, opening, closing, swirling open.

The dead birds had all been scattered by the children. They played with the bodies, burying them and digging them up. One boy arced them high above the crowd like grenades, footballs, and when they awkwardly dropped, wobbly and spinning, he shouted, "Touchdown! Boom," then slapped his hands together until the mother said, "Quit. Leave those birds where they are. They might have disease."

He gravitated toward her slightly, his shoulders and head shifting—the only hair he had was a helmet of peach fuzz—then back, leaning the other way, a more sure foot into the crowd. Too much chaos for rules to hold, the power they had a few days ago, no matter how strong and familiar the voice. There was too much chaos not to be independent if you wanted.

So he set off and Jennifer lost the boy. His mother called after him, went after him as other children pressed in close to the tree. Jennifer held their movements in ribbons of light and dust for only a second as they stroked the dead birds, drew their feathers open like paper fans then petted the wings back. Sometimes the children held one bird, as many hands as it took until they swallowed it fully inside their grip.

"Where did birdie go? Where did he go?" some of them began to chant.

"I don't know, I don't know," the others answered back.

"In my hand. In my hand," the first ones said.

Then "Let him fly, let him fly," the others said.

Then "One, two, three," they jerked their hands away and spun.

"There he goes." They looked up. East, west, north— their bodies forming the points of a compass. "There he goes," they echoed one another until someone picked the bird out of the dirt and knee-roots.

One girl sat a bird on top of her head and nested it there, balanced, on her stringy hair, and one girl tried to feed a bluebird dirt, and another traced the cracked beak of a bird to its eyes, pinpoints of wooden glass. Then off they went just like the boy with the peach fuzz head who had arced the birds like footballs, legs knifing between refugees, a yell to get back here, that's too far. This time the voice had enough sway; the legs and feet stomped back to the tree and Jennifer's eyes drifted, shut down. Time had started to slip around her.

She could no longer depend on its continuity, that the world unfolding would do so in unbroken threads. Time had slipped outside of her fingers where it jerked and fluttered and spiraled beneath her, so deep, she could only breathe silt and loam, choking, her body shaking, her blouse ringed with salt, caked and dry under her chafed breasts and arms. She kept staring at her arms for the purple spots to appear, to bubble up under the skin, her mouth to run dry in a milkish foam. Then she would surely pass like her two fathers. She would follow them out of this world.

There were flickers of Mathew, the trailer in Fatama, the desert, Mama. Something in Jennifer said, *This isn't the right world. You're not in the right world, Sweetie. Sweetie,* like her mama called her on good nights.

She jerked awake. But it didn't last, and she fell again into time's misflow, its dark eddies swirling around the children's legs and crossing up their chants, muddled.

"Come on," Mathew called, and waved her down to where her breathing plunged. He was already at the foot of the bank, the water turning fast and making her thirsty.

"I'm so tired," she said. "And I can't go in that water, not now."

"What do you mean, you can't go? It'll be fun, Jen." He kept prodding her and knocked the side of his boots against a metal shaft, an old piece of the dam, until clay rolled off like sloughed wood. He kneeled and started to unlace his boot as she sat next to him.

"Because I'm pregnant."

"Pregnant?" He looked up. "When did this happen?"

She hit him in the shoulder. "I don't like that question. It happened with *you.*"

"I didn't mean it like that. I just—I didn't know."

"You don't want children, remember? So I didn't tell you." But why hadn't she told him before leaving? Maybe he would've come to Chicago. But she had asked him to come for months, and he never answered, and so she didn't say the other, and he didn't.

Jennifer had to get to Chicago. She started to get up, then stopped and asked, "Why didn't you come with me?"

"The water's not going to hurt the baby." He put his hand on her stomach and it was warm. That touch, relaxing. He smiled and leaned in, the thick ridge above his eyes visible like dull plows, familiar, and trapped in his skin, the iron from the clay upturned, allowing Jennifer to breathe.

"Come on. It's just water." He went back to unlacing his boot and she grabbed his hand, put it back on her stomach.

"Don't you know what you're supposed to do by now?" she said. The river kept rushing, just that sound over their

breathing and would not end, would keep going until someone poked her arm.

"You can't go to sleep here." It was Lavina, and behind
her, Mazy.

She said their names, reminding herself, placing herself,
and Lavina trailed her fingers through Jennifer's hair. Jennifer grabbed hold of her wrist.

"It's all right, girl. We found each other a second time.
That's a good omen. We need good omens." And the river
where Jennifer had held Mathew slipped through the heat
and shade, down tunnels thirty-five feet, fifty feet. The mining tunnels filled with mud faster than she could count,
until she lost that dream of him completely.

"It's all right," Lavina whispered.

"Just good to see you. Where's Gail?"

"They let her out. I suppose they need their contrac-
tors."

"And Darl?"

Lavina shook her head and pulled away, stood up.
"Haven't seen him. You're the first one we've come across.
But there are so many people here." She looked around, her
neck just a stalk, too thin to balance that head with its clut-
tered bush of hair. Dirty-blond is what Tonya who owned
the beauty shop would call it. "Even when I get finished
washing and cutting and drying—dirty-blond." She always
finished a hair statement with lips pinched shut, raising her
scissors—"$200 scissors," she pointed out, "that will cut into
anything"—to the ceiling, to God. Punctuation. There were
certain absolutes that Tonya maintained, and all of them
had to do with hair—thickness, length, cowlicked, colored,
straightened, permed, weaved, and extended. But Jennifer
doubted absolutes in her own life, they never seemed to
take hold, and so she had none to offer Tonya. She just

listened—dirty-blond. Lavina's hair was dirty-blond. Beautiful, like Mazy's chestnut-brown.

Lavina kept staring at the refugees as if trying to find passengers from the bus, like she should've kept up with their whereabouts, a duty owed Jennifer simply for inquiring. She didn't say the other, that they might be dead, swallowed up in the deluge of bodies that kept expanding. Maybe her look was just a way to avoid speaking that truth.

Jennifer had wanted to ask about the driver, but not now. For days, she had looked for him, checked the hospital tent, and even the rows of cocooned bodies, so big he'd be quick to spot, at least two people taken up in his wide skin. His absence pulled through her in flashes without warning, like the moment on the bus he paced over the broken window, crushed the glass into bits, or his face, the bruise growing, swelling, his button-eye swallowed up until gone. She had looked and looked and looked.

Mazy reached across, traced Jennifer's hair more gingerly than Lavina had done.

"Why are you so far away?" Jennifer said, and pulled the girl in, hugged her, then gasped—the girl's body was much too light, and Jennifer worried she wasn't getting enough food. There were tins saved in her pocket, but her baby was growing, needed these.

Too selfish, she thought. Still she didn't offer Mazy a thing. Jennifer let go and pressed her hand against a root between them.

Mazy brushed her arm. "Why you so far away?"

Jennifer started to tell her, *I'm right here*, started to say other things, but her arm tensed and Mazy pulled back.

"I'm not feeling too well," she answered the girl, the lie rehearsed and ready.

"Me either," Mazy said, and when Jennifer reached over to touch her, Mazy didn't move and neither did Jennifer's guilt.

"I'm sorry," Jennifer said, and Mazy nodded, but that didn't help either, so she asked, "Have you been to your cousins'?"

"No." It was Lavina who answered. She was still watching the crowds push slowly to the tents. "It's not really good once you get outside the square, especially for a journey that long." She marked a direction with her finger. "They're up north. They've set up shelters in the north, too—that's what I heard. A place close to Lincoln, but we haven't chanced it," and she rubbed the back of her neck, rubbed the sweat into her jeans. "I did find a place to sleep. It's too hot right now and too much daylight. People could follow us. But in evening we'll go over. Can you make it?"

Jennifer nodded.

"It's better us three than you by yourself. You still got that glass?"

Jennifer pulled it carefully from her pocket, then slid it back, and as she did, her arm caught on the stationery box wrapped underneath her shirt.

"No one's taken it," Mazy said, pointing at the box like Lavina had pointed north, that same response of touching at the air. "What's inside?"

And Jennifer grabbed the squared edges to hide them deeper and fuller, make the box invisible somehow, as if she could make these things invisible. But she had already turned Mazy away once.

"Letters to my mother in Chicago," she said. "Would you like to write something?" She got the box out, pulled the top off.

And Mazy bit her lip, gazed down at her hands. The skin had already shriveled along the backs of Mazy's knuckles like ditches the river channels carved into slumped beds, then left to dry, not at all like Mazy's face, still full over the knobbed bones, those same bones so pronounced on Lavina.

"No need for letters, her mama's right here," Lavina offered. "Besides, she can't write. I never put her in school."

"It was a long time before I went to school," Jennifer said. "In fact, I was older than you are. I bet you can draw." She took out the small notebook and pencil and handed them to the girl. She closed the lid and gave the box to Mazy to use as a desk.

"Ma'am?" Mazy looked up at her mother, pencil flat to the paper.

"Of course, you can draw. Go ahead. She can," Lavina said to Jennifer. "Loves to. I keep notepads just for Mazy, but they're in our suitcase on the bus. No good now."

"I'm not trying to upset you," Jennifer said.

"You're not upsetting *me*." Lavina crossed her arms and hooked her thin neck back, indignant at what Jennifer had said, or had she been caught off guard? Jennifer wasn't sure.

Mazy stopped drawing and looked at her mother again.

"Go ahead, Mazy. Show Jennifer a picture." She waved her hand at her daughter. "She's good with faces. Besides, you might be doing that all day, which is more than we'll be doing. I'm not mad," Lavina chuffed. "There's too much else to be mad at. The government, for one. And all these people—it's damn making me claustrophobic. I wish they'd just move out." She shooed a hand at the crowd, rubbed the back of her thin neck.

"Just in case someone decides to mess with us . . ." She pulled up her shirt to reveal the butt of a knife, her stomach drawn and the bottom of her ribs showing. Jennifer noticed a scar across her stomach like a long worm.

"You see that?" She turned in closer to Jennifer. "That's where they pulled Mazy out of me, and Lord," she grimaced, "I know what it's like to be sliced into. And holler? Lord did I holler. 'Won't feel a thing,' the doctor said. 'Okay, Doctor. Okay.' " She nodded. "Let me tell you, didn't know what the hell he was talking about. The anesthesia didn't last, and I just lay there, couldn't even twitch." She drew her body in. Her eyes closed down. Then opened. "Mazy, you owe me for that one. Always going to owe me."

But Mazy was busy sketching, watching the boy with the peach fuzz head. He had come back and sent another bird sailing, diving. He whistled like the dropping of a bomb, and Mazy glanced at him, sketched, didn't look up at her mother.

"Too many people," Lavina whispered; the Cold War sirens started, middle of the day. The sun was sitting over them, and it would only get hotter. Jennifer tried not to think of the heat, how it swelled her tongue, left her mouth chalky, and the taste of metal—*middle of the day, middle of the day*, she kept telling herself, a piece of time to hold on to.

Jennifer had drawn pictures when she was younger but never liked what she drew. Nothing looked like it was supposed to be. Houses looked like blobs with diagonal windows, cars looked like flat houses ready to swoon, and her faces? They were gnarled like thrown-away paper and blurry, boring. When she got bored enough, she cleaned: windows, ovens, cabinets—especially the hinges on cabinets—the sand was always trying to get in, grit everything up. Or she slept against the passenger door while Terry drove the riverbanks, the truck's engine humming in her stomach.

Her mother had taught her to write, and the lessons carried over during those few weeks a year the mining schools opened until she was sixteen. Delia taught her when she wasn't having a spell, and sometimes after her mother locked herself in her room, Jennifer wrote small notes and slipped them under: *Come out*, or *Please, come out*. She stood completely still, listening, waiting for Delia to pick them up. But those requests never worked. So she tried another strategy: yelling, which worked on two occasions, and got her spankings for it.

Since her mama kept the television in her bedroom, Jennifer had the rest of the house and its loneliness to carry. Sometimes Jennifer stood by the door listening to the voices, imagining actors, creating their lips and white teeth, tilts of head and how confidently they strode across floors and fields, and the audience, that matchbox of people dark in front of the stage. But most of the time the TV wasn't on. It was quiet, and Jennifer had the whole house. She cleaned until her arms got heavy and became a dull silence she wanted to cut off—arms, legs, all of her had become boring. And no cleaning, no drawing, no rugs wrapped around chairs could reverse it.

In their home in Picayune she had busted a window. It marked the beginning of one of her mama's longest spells. For twenty-seven nights the wind shook the frame, Terry promising to get it fixed and not doing it; twenty-seven nights her mama locked herself in the bedroom. The quietness and the shaking window built up a feverish pressure all the way to the ceiling that would eventually get to her mama, had to, and she'd come out. But Jennifer had told herself the same thing last night and the week prior, and the one before that.

Twenty-seven. Jennifer was twelve. Twelve plus twelve was twenty-four, and this spell had lasted twice her age—too long. She couldn't breathe, and walked up to the window, unplugged the shirts stuffed in the gap, let the wind blow the sand in. She stuck her hand out and felt around, all gritty and dirty hot that didn't make her feel better. But once she pulled her hand inside, she noticed the cut. A scrape on her lower left arm just above her wrist, a bleeding, just a little. *Stupid, stupid.* She wrapped her arm tight with one of the shirts, but the dirt inside it was too rough, and she unwrapped it, washed her arm in the sink, beat the dust out of another shirt, wrapped it again.

Then she went to her mother's door and started to knock.

All afternoon, Mazy sketched and Jennifer and Lavina watched the crowds. More and more people fell, and they didn't help them, not a single one, and even the Red Cross details gave up and left the bodies where they lay.

After the evening siren washed through, the collectors started in like oversized locusts, how Jennifer had always pictured locusts swooping down, covering a field, landing on blades and leaves with twitching legs and wings, eating. The collectors started in like that, had become so aggressive, and Jennifer followed Lavina and Mazy to another park: Kelly Ingram.

It wasn't long before they came across two men and a woman turning down a street.

"They might've seen us," Lavina whispered and led Jennifer and Mazy the other way, across Bestoe to Eleventh, then back up Seventeenth. The small group might be a group of roamers, a bishop gang, or a bombing gang—that's what Lavina called them, what the guardsmen called them.

Lavina had seen the bishop gangs in action—they holed up in churches and took people as soon as they walked inside to "Have a word with God." Repent. Sanctuary. The explosions were from bombing gangs shelling into wealthy neighborhoods. "They're destroying Gail's onion." Lavina had laughed when she said this because that's what Gail called the labyrinth of Birmingham walls. "It's getting sliced up now, those rich places. Everything's getting looted. And the people there still trying to leave." She had pointed to a string of mille-copters slipping up into the sky beyond the food drop; all day the mille-copter trains slipped in and out. "City's about empty, except here."

So when they saw the two men and the woman, they went the other way across Bestoe to Eleventh, and down to

Kelly Ingram. The sign in the brick said: *In Honor of Osmond Kelly Ingram, First American Killed in Action in World War I. Medal of Honor. War Cross—Italy.*

Cars had been piled into the square, and a long transit bus and the bricks from one building, the entire façade had collapsed into the park, leaving a dark cave, an open hull of pews and stained glass and beams like a rended ship. In the park was a statue of Dr. Martin Luther King, and nothing else except the last of the sun where the ozone had disappeared for the moment, giving a new depth to the world— shadows left behind from coiled metal, wires, the high tops of buildings, and car hoods. They walked between two sheets of bronze—dogs growling out from bronze walls frozen and sharp. What had happened here? Jennifer wondered. She couldn't move away from thinking the dogs might be real. If they had been, they would've cut into her and Mazy and Lavina. Mazy stroked a muzzle, felt along the sharp bottom row of teeth.

"Don't do that," Lavina told her.

At the end of the dogs sat a van, pale blue, but it was hard to tell the color in the grayness, the way dust had settled over the body, the hood crushed beneath the underbelly of a truck. Lavina jingled out a set of keys and opened the rear doors.

"Don't get in yet," she whispered and walked to the front, opened those doors, too. She did it slowly, carefully, so the hinges creaked only slightly against the lull.

"I don't think the roamers followed us," Lavina said.

"There were two dead bodies inside," Mazy said, staring at the van. "We dragged them out."

"To Ninth Street," Lavina added. "Heavy as washing machines."

"Then we took the keys," Mazy said.

"Don't talk so much," Lavina told her. "We don't want any roamers to find us."

Jennifer held on, tried to keep herself, her balance, but

there was a flutter in her mind she couldn't get hold of, ravel. She needed sleep, and the flutter spiraled down her body, down her spine and hit her legs with a numbness—she couldn't feel her feet, and she couldn't judge her distance to the open van, the buildings, the sun.

"Got to let it cool off," Lavina said. "I haven't seen any people here, and none have seen us, but we got to be quiet."

"Mama, stop talking," Mazy said.

"Don't tell me what to do."

"Mama."

Lavina crossed her arms. "Just a few more minutes till it's cool enough."

The shadows kept growing wider and wider as if they were being poured into the square like some cool, thin liquid, trying to hide them. There were lights in the distance, but not like the lights that had come before. A fire—that's what it was. Something else burning farther away and smoke.

Lavina stepped into the van, scuffed around, then poked her head out to say it was cool enough, come on, so they joined her and hid themselves inside, locked the doors. The van was black inside except for a swath of tiny rust holes near the front, and the windows had been shut up with cardboard and plastic, the air kept still with heat and dust and the thinnest traces of grease and metal. Lavina turned the crank on the flashlight and set the base down. The blue light curved through the van's belly, revealing blankets and a tire and that was it.

In one corner, Lavina lifted out a stack of provisions, added two more. "We've saved nine," she said. "That should do for a while." Mazy plopped down with a moan. She had given the notebook back to Jennifer in Linn Park, and was stretching her hand out now, her arm. And she hadn't said a word about the faces she had drawn and decided to keep, the ones she scratched over.

"People do a lot of walking at night," Lavina explained.

"I've seen them. Roaming. One group I saw shoot a collector. Took everything that he'd lifted from the dead. Then they started in on his body. We couldn't get away from where we were hiding. They would've shot us. Would've done the same with us. I've seen bodies blown up, you know. When we're blowing a shaft, before we light any chesa-sticks or fill any boreholes, we try to clear everyone, but sometimes people are there you don't notice, or they step into the wrong place. I've seen what explosions can do. But nothing like what they did to that collector. I covered Mazy's eyes. Wrapped her up in me so she wouldn't fidget. Saw all of that."

"Be quiet, Mama," Mazy said.

"Stop it now. Just go to sleep, and let me tell it." Lavina wouldn't look at Mazy or Jennifer, not straight-on. Instead she sighed, kept scanning the walls.

"Sleep."

She said it in such a way that at first Jennifer thought it was a question, as if "sleep" were apples, cold water, and did Jennifer want some? But no, Lavina was *telling* her to go to sleep, if she could do it, wind down, slow the flutter of her exhaustion.

Jennifer stretched out on one of the blankets—it was rough and the steel beneath made her back go numb and sweaty. She shifted, kept shifting on the floor. It was a huge cage they were in. Lavina flipped off the blue light. Soon all Jennifer felt was a tumbling of dreams—those seconds of Mat and her mama, stretched out now, longer and longer reels of those worlds, their skin—Mathew's clay hand on her stomach holding the baby in place, her mama's wrinkles crosshatched and closing over her pinhole eyes, drawing her face, her chin into the V center of her neck.

Last week through the early mornings, Mat had held Jennifer in Fatama, and later they slipped out to the Alabama River—two weeks ago he had held her before work, and they listened to the old record of Billie Holiday that had belonged to Mathew's father, Mathew's grandfather. It was warped now, but they still set it on the turntable, taking in the scratched rhythms.

Billie's voice swelled against the steel of the van now, echoing the final trace of blue light and the cardboard Mazy and Lavina had pushed into the windows. One window remained cracked and wouldn't close all the way, so they worried, but it was pitch, the world was pitch—and just beyond were those fires as if stars had fallen into Birmingham, and would smolder here, burn everything, sink the city into the earth before their intensity washed out.

The sleep grew darker, fell away from Billie's voice, her song—

> *I will go through fire with only you*
> *Baby, whatever you do*
> *Take me through the fire with you.*

—the stars so deep, she would never wake from it, didn't want to, afraid at times she'd never find the way back from sleep to waking because there was no staircase, no rope out of its tunnel, just a deep, deep falling until she landed on top of a door and she knocked, kept knocking.

Jennifer was twelve, again, and she beat the door until it was upright like a door should be and she was standing in the house in Picayune, a coolness gliding along the carpet and across her toes, it was February, she was twelve, her arm wrapped tight.

"Mama," she started yelling. "Mama. I'm wounded."

She looked at her arm where the shirt was wrapped—no blood—and pressed into the fabric, first her thumb, then her nail, until a drop leaked through and a small line of blood began to smear.

"Mama," she said. "Please come out." She banged on the door, pounded as if she could knock it down. "I'm hurt bad, Mama."

Finally there was movement, her mother shuffling. *She'll open the door*, Jennifer thought. For twenty-seven nights she had kept herself hidden while Terry worked, but now she'd do it.

Delia paused at the door, just the hollow wood between them, and Jennifer screamed again. "I cut myself," she yelled. "I'm bleeding," drawing out the *ees* in *bleeding* as long as she could, like Terry's hand flat on the truck horn, telling them to come on, it was time to go for a jaunt.

The door swung open, and her mama still had wrinkles on her face—why Jennifer thought they would be gone, she wasn't sure. A ravaged face—what her mama said about herself often and hung bath towels over mirrors after staring, pinching her skin, pinching the wrinkles out. "The desert has ravaged me," or "The wind has," or "I." Delia moved the blame around.

And the long crumpled dress she wore fit too loosely on her arms and flapped at her stomach with the tiniest movements, and she seemed only half-alert, a little dopey and confused from those hours locked in her room, decaying into someone else. It was *decay*, that word that snagged in Jennifer's mind, made her realize she had stopped breathing to watch, to judge. But she couldn't stay withdrawn forever, so she screamed.

"What's wrong with you?" her mama said.

Jennifer put her arm forward as evidence and truth of her suffering. "I got cut."

Delia grabbed the arm, and in doing so, pulled Jennifer.

Jennifer almost fell, then caught herself by stubbing her toes, anchoring them deep into the carpet.

"How'd you get cut?"

She hadn't thought about that, how to answer that.

"On the window," she admitted.

"Which window?" Her mama peeked out from the doorway, and Jennifer pointed down the hall with her good hand to where the kitchen was.

"Why you messing with that window? You already broke it once. The one over the sink? You break more of it?"

And Jennifer screamed louder, "I'm hurt. I'm hurt."

Her mama pulled back the bloodied shirt and a straight line of blood was still coming, slowly, but coming, and a sticky blob of blood all along the rill in her fish-white skin.

"Did *you* cut yourself?"

Jennifer wasn't sure what her mother meant and didn't answer.

"Did you hurt yourself on purpose? Did you?"

"No, ma'am," Jennifer said. "I just got cut on the window."

"Not on the wrist, not there, not like that." Her mama's palm began to shake and it shook Jennifer's wrist, a cold engine starting as if blood were draining out of her mama fast, but from where? Everything about the woman was sealed up in that long cotton gown, including her toes. Jennifer was the injured one.

"Mama?" Jennifer started to ask if she was okay, then Delia's hand turned hot, the faucet turned on inside her, and she squeezed Jennifer's wrist, drew her daughter close, punched her in the mouth. "Don't you ever do that to yourself again."

She hadn't yanked Jennifer's hair like she did sometimes when she braided it, to straighten her head. Delia announced it in this way, "I need to straighten your head." Braid-pullings came with warnings. She hadn't spanked Jennifer—Jennifer was too old for spankings. Or simply walked back in her room and shut the door. And she hadn't embraced Jennifer either, said, "I'm sorry, Baby. Let's go wash that, Baby. Take care of you," like Jennifer wanted. No. She hit her in the mouth. And Jennifer stood there, unable to smooth out the ache in her lungs for her mama had managed to push all of Jennifer's breath back inside and trap it.

Slowly, she began to feel the numbness and cool blood

drip to her chin, circle into drops heavy enough to fall. Then she curled her head under, barreled it into her mother's stomach, pushing at her like some bull spitting blood.

"I'm hurt," she said, coughing. "Damn you. I'm hurt," and somehow their bodies got switched—they fought like two girls Jennifer saw at school, one pulling chunks of hair out of the other one's head, the other girl grunting, and two boys the same week, their fists wouldn't stop clipping, swinging until one boy said, "Damn you," and head-butted the other—he capsized with his mouth open in a big surprised O—it was like everyone had to get into it before the school closed down again. But not like mother and daughter, like their fights had been in the past and should be. Their bodies got switched. And Jennifer pulled away, slammed the bedroom door, locked it.

The room was black, all black, and smelled like chocolate, cinnamon—her mama loved the stuff—hot chocolate stirred with cinnamon sticks in winter that she saved her money for and bought from the black marketers when they traveled up to Jackson. She heard a faint tapping, her mother striking at the door, so distant compared to the blood pulsing in her ear.

"Let me back in my room, Jennifer. Let me inside," the voice whirred, and drowned in the noise of Jennifer's blood. She waited for her eyes to adjust, but still things shook—a lamp, the vanity, and on top jewelry sparkled, and bedposts, and the bubbled glass of the TV. One chair had something hanging—clothes. She inched toward them, then stopped, afraid to walk too deep into the room, into the blackness growing cold, and what she couldn't see, the nothingness— this is where faces became ravaged.

Her mama knocked louder as the pulsing subsided in Jennifer's ear.

"You don't have any right. It's my room." Delia slapped

at the door now, slapped like she was throwing water. It made a thrash, thrash like a sweeping broom. "Hear me?" Then her mama began to cry.

Jennifer went to the door.

"Unlock it," Delia said. "You don't understand, girl. Please, girl. I've got to."

And Jennifer crouched down, her hands on the hollow wood, that thin, thin wood, her mother's shadow underneath the door, clogging the small chute of light. Blood dripped from Jennifer's chin and she wiped it off, rubbing at the carpet—she'd have to clean this—blood was never easy to get up if allowed to set.

"No," she said, the blood choking her a little, caught in her throat. She spit it out.

"Please."

Jennifer kept still. And for the first time, though she had felt this before and never brought it to the surface, named it, hadn't wanted to—it was the only time her mama had ever struck her—for the first time Jennifer recognized that she hated herself for hating her mother.

Everything in her body scattered, the hatred moved so she couldn't place it, couldn't find it to quarantine, and scoop out, throw into the nothingness and be done with. Her mama's crying spread under the door, into the walls. And she knew she would never be done with it.

"Girl, there's people walking around," Lavina whispered. "Sleep, okay? It's okay. You're just having an awful dream. Come on now. Be quiet. Can't let those roamers find us."

Jennifer couldn't see Lavina's face, or her hands, but felt them, the palms like river stones, their roughness trying to smooth her hair back, trying to cool the worried skin stretched over the flat bone of her forehead, that crinkled hair. Those hands smelled like mud, as if Lavina had reached down and pulled Jennifer from deep inside the tunnel, away from her mother's door.

"So much sweat on you," she said, and rubbed the moisture into Jennifer's hair. It's something Mat had done, and she had done for him. Delia had done it, too, when she wasn't in a spell. "It's all right."

Jennifer stretched her neck out, exhaled. She had made her way to the surface of her dreams and could go down, again, no matter how much falling, no matter if she didn't want to go—she wouldn't get lost there and suffocate.

June 28—Day

Dear Mathew,

I need you now and I thought tonight of us together, holding each other—just that laying out of our bodies on top of a blanket—breathing, holding. That sweat, a line curving your back into me, and your breath—I can count it, the way your body sinks in at the lowest part of your back and rises while you sleep.

If you knew what had happened, you would be here. I need you to be here, then we could leave together, but first you would hold me, hold me so close that I could push the world away, the two of us together. I don't want to die here. Our baby—I wish I could get this letter to you. I need you to come find me, Mat. Understand?

The air in Birmingham is thick with smoke, but when I put my hand through it, I feel as if I'm reaching into nothing, there is no weight to this dense air, this place;

nothing to hold me, for me to pull inside and keep. I need
you to come find me now. Will you do that if you get this
letter?

I love you,

Jen

She didn't write her mother that morning, couldn't.
Even though the fight between them had happened eighteen years ago, and they had forgiven each other, whenever
Jennifer thought of it, her mouth became numb, and her
mama's crying rattled in her ear. She wanted to leave Birmingham, but she didn't want to see her mama, not today.
But there was nowhere else to go. Jennifer turned her wrist
over—not even a scar, a trace of what had happened, only a
small bruise from holding the stationery box for so long, and
nothing on the inside of her lip. She smoothed her tongue
over her teeth to make sure.

Lavina and Mazy had almost finished their tins. Mazy
took her finger and licked out every corner—three times Jennifer saw her do this—dipping a finger carefully, avoiding the
top sharp inner edge, making sure she had removed it all.

The consulate told them no just as the consulate had
told Jennifer no before: visas were not accepted, and Lavina
walked up, pressed her legs into the table. "You have to get
us out. We can't survive in this much longer." They had
spent all day in line, and behind them, more and more people. Didn't seem worth it, all this standing, but the fans were
blowing, it was safe.

"I'm sorry. We can't do anything like that. There's water
and food," the agent said through her face mask. The
woman was tall, taller than Jennifer, and rested her hands
on the belt at her hips. When she moved, her leg caught as
if injured, and she had to stumble-step back into place.

"At least I need to get up north in the city."

"That area's closed," she said. "There was a spill."

"A spill? My aunt's there, my cousins. What kind of spill?"

"That's all I know," and she glanced at the long string of tables, the guards helping other agents with their refugees. The yelling, the crying—it was like that booth to booth. No one wanted to leave the wheeling fans for the sun, and maybe if they carried on long enough, they'd outlast the agents and their resistance, trick them into granting asylum.

"Every time I get this far, I'm told stay put. But staying here—we're going to perish. All of us. You know that."

"Ma'am, the government's providing water and a healthy, balanced diet—" She pointed to the food tent. "You'll be okay if you eat your rations."

Lavina chuckled. "No we won't."

The woman looked over her shoulder again, but this time, she leaned out too far on her bad leg and had to cross up her step to keep from falling. As soon as she readjusted, she sighed through the blue mask, rubbed her forehead— the guardsmen were still too busy.

"We need to get out of here," Lavina pressed.

But the woman didn't answer. She put a strand of hair behind her ear, the same turn Jennifer repeated throughout the day, and crooked her neck at the tablet between them, studying it or pretending to.

The top read *United States Petition for Asylum, Southern Alabama Zone.* Underneath a list of names had been scribbled next to fingerprints, pressed into the screen and eventually scrolled out of view as new names were added. The date appeared to the right, June 28, and half a line for the petition reason: *Visa*—that's what they had put down, Lavina underlining and copying over her *Visa*, over Mazy's, but all it did was make the electronic imprint blurry to read. A little lower someone declared *Cannot*, and under that, *Citizen. Permission to Transfer*, a social security number, and *Reason of Insanity. Can you help?* And *Specialty Occupation* without any details of the specialty, and *Please*. Rebecca Eders—another name Jennifer didn't recognize, but wanted to, wanted to fill in the contour of the cursive letters with a body, a face—Rebecca Eders had simply written *Please*.

"My daughter's only fifteen years old," Lavina said. "Let her out. You do that."

"Can't, ma'am."

"Lavina. My name's Lavina." She set her palms heavy on the table.

"You can sign the petition, ma'am."

"Lavina."

"Lavina," the agent conceded.

"I've already signed." She tapped the screen. "You watched me do it. Have you forgotten? Been looking at my name, studying it for the past few minutes. I have cousins in the north. Isn't there a camp at Lincoln?"

The woman shook her head and began to rock on her pegged feet. Her shoulders turned in like honed rocks, diminished.

"Isn't there a camp at Lincoln?"

"There was. They had to close it because of the spill."

"I need to get up there. My aunt could help me. She lives in Hooper City."

"It's closed off." And that was it. The woman headed to the next booth, situating herself between a staffer and guardsman. They glanced at Lavina, then shuttered back, checked Lavina again in quick takes.

"I need some help," Lavina yelled, her hair all knotted, the blond and gray strands frizzy, going left and right out of the loose knot.

Behind them the crowd remained bottlenecked in a long S train. Jennifer tried to count the first row, but too many eyes stared back, knotted her gaze, held her up before she could move on. Others looked around her as if a *real* exit was just beyond the tables and the canvased wall. All of them had dirty hands like her hands, trembling. The fans blew fine dust through the tents, which managed to stir up and sift a coating onto their shirts and heads; occasionally a fleck caught sharp in her skin. Some people looked down at their shoes, their bare feet, or held the rope that kept the line in its S shape and held their bodies up, stacked in crooked rows, emptying at the front where the answer would be *Not today; we can't do that today*. In all the mumbling and coughing and shifting and staring, an exhaustion accumulated, churning inside Jennifer until it made her sick.

She touched Mazy's shoulder. "I'm going out."

"Wait." Mazy caught Jennifer's arm. "Why you leaving?"

"I'll be outside. Not far." She pointed to the opening in the canvas. "I promise." Jennifer started to put Mazy's hand on her stomach and explain but stopped. She didn't want Mazy to know about the baby—she shouldn't reveal that to anyone. So Jennifer exited by the large fans as a guardsman and the agent trudged back to Lavina.

Outside, the fans' humming stayed with her; the sun's heat began to swell; and she bent over, vomited on the ground.

Don't pass out, she said to herself quickly and repeated quickly. *Whatever you do, don't pass out*, trying to push through the drowning heat and breathe.

Someone reached over to help. But when she saw the Red Cross patch, she jerked away. The Crosses lifted the dead and the dying, took them to the harvesting machines, and she was neither.

"You all right?"

She nodded, stepped away, slipped inside the wall of refugees. That pull from the earth had so much strength— well fed, rested, cool, and she had none of the man's reserves. She had to sit on the ground to keep from falling and watched the legs cross and open in front of her. In between those arches, before the legs closed up, she fixed on the exit where Lavina and Mazy would eventually show.

"You need a way out?" a man said to her.

"What?" she asked.

"A way out," he said. "Don't you want a passage out of Birmingham? Consulate's no help." He stood pearled and blue like the desert at times. In his shades, certain tinges of light filtered against what she remembered—the sandbanks, washing color into the river. On him now, the same dusting of sunlight, and underneath, what he really was: curly hair, bland shirt, pants, scrubbed clean and faceless. Not even the doctors were this clean.

"What're you doing?" she asked.

"You're too close to the consulate," he said, and started into the thick mess of bodies. She got up and followed. When he stopped, another man was there, identical clean shirt and skin and shades. They nodded to each other like partners, brothers, and faced Jennifer.

"Do you want out?" the man repeated. He was younger than the other man, but something in the straight of their bodies like a tree split down the center, both halves pulled open to reveal the same burls and longness in their faces, the same deep hinge attaching their necks to their jaws, something marked them as brothers in the odd filtered light.

"Yes."

"Then we can get you out," the older one said. "You have money?"

"Yes," she said, again, but shouldn't have said that, why did she reveal that? and wished to undo the word. Jennifer had left the money in her box, and left the box under the blanket with the rations in the van. Lavina had said not to bring it. "It'll be safer here." But all morning in the cramped line Jennifer felt for the lacquered edges, her hands twitching, hesitating, and at nothing, just restless twitching.

"Not a lot of money," she added.

They kept quiet, and she withdrew a step—"I don't have

the money on me—" brushing against the refugees. If needed, she could push into the swirl of bodies and escape.

"You look healthy. Do you have any diseases?"

"Diseases?" Jennifer laughed. "Not that I'm aware of. You?"

They didn't answer. Of course they didn't, and she laughed more, unable to stop. When she was younger, she did this often: laughed in the middle of conversations, in bleak moments or the silence right before a joke's punch line, always at the wrong time. It was something Terry and she did together, cutting each other off with snickering until they had forgotten the logic of their thoughts. Her mother would scowl and slap at them, her hands like blind flyswatters, missing badly. "Stop it. You're too giddy." She slapped at the air and never hit, never caught them.

"You're missing on purpose," Jennifer had accused her mama eventually, all that laughter a contagion her mama tried to avoid.

"Oh, I'd hit you if I wanted," Delia said, and they left it at that.

Mathew used to tease her about it. "What's so funny?" he'd say. "Why you laughing *now*?" And that always got her laughing in wilder spurts. She'd shrug or close her eyes and bite her tongue until it stung. That was the marker—pain— what it took to stop. And he just eyed her, chuckled, never lost himself in a fit like Terry. Once she bit the corner of her tongue so hard she started crying and couldn't stop. "What's wrong?" Mathew said, but she just balled up on the bed and sucked at the blood, shut his hands out rubbing, rubbing and trying to soothe, shut out everything except Terry and Everett, their laughing swirling through her in wave after wave.

"I only take healthy people out," the older brother said. "It's a difficult trip."

"To where? I need to get to Chicago."

"Chicago," he said, and nodded.

"I don't have any diseases." She giggled, could hear her mother—*What will they do with you, Jenny? This is serious. Stop now.* Jennifer bit down on her tongue, and the sun curled into the afternoon haze, no longer splitting a purple light along their faces. The younger brother stepped forward.

"What're you doing?" she asked.

"Checking." He threw his hands up, opened them—nothing, nothing to hide, not even specks of dust. Then he let them down and stared at her shoes, up her pants leg, his stare sealing her inside the thick fabric, rendering her motionless. Her stomach breathed in and out, the dirty T-shirt where her baby rested, then he touched Jennifer's shoulder, pushed it too hard and she pushed back.

"Don't push on me."

His hands went up in surrender again. "No trouble," he said, and turned to get a better look at her teeth. She shut her mouth, watched him, his curly hair, the smooth flatness of his face down from his eye and nose.

The refugees were behind her, but the man was so near, and the sliver of glass Jennifer had taken off Highway 11 was too deep in her pocket to reach for.

"Your wrist, it's okay?" He reached out for her wrist and she let him take it. There was a bruise in the center and one at the bend in her elbow from carrying the box. He rubbed over the center bruise, held her lightly, rubbed as if trying to figure out the dimensions, trying to find a break in the skin, decide if this bruise was somehow dangerous, the surface an indicator of something rotting inside at the core—like an apple, she thought, and wondered what soap he used and where in Birmingham was there enough water for a shower. Maybe it was the history he was looking for, what happened between Jennifer and her mother, all those years between then and now. *Pull away*, she told herself, *Get out of here*, but he was holding her gingerly.

"Healthy," he said, and smiled and walked over to his brother.

"I'll take you to Chicago for the money. How much do you have?" his brother asked.

"I don't have any," she changed her words.

"When can you get it?"

"I said I don't have any," and Jennifer found a seam, slipped into the line of bodies, slipped as easily as the man had held her arm.

"I'll take you without the money," the older brother shouted, but Jennifer kept walking. She spotted the American flag above the entrance to the consulate—the exit was to the right, and the crowd seemed to turn like a compass, its directions shifting slightly north toward south, then swooning the other way, recalibrating around her, the center needle, the tornado eye, shifting, shifting. Someone reached a hand out, pulled, but she sped up and started running toward the exit like running in water, stepping over bloated ankles and the yellow cans and shawls people left on the ground, bodies rolled in dirt, the dead trees. She looked behind her, kept checking—the two men weren't coming.

She didn't feel safe until she got to the gate where the Red Cross stood with the guardsmen, the Red Cross who had asked if she was okay. He had on his cap now and mask, the sun bright, and she stood on the red line spray-painted in the morning that you couldn't cross. Jennifer checked behind her—no one was coming. What if she'd missed Lavina and Mazy? For a moment she was overwhelmed by panic. Then they walked out, and she ran up, hugged the girl.

"What's wrong?" Lavina asked.

"Nothing," she said. "Nothing."

"You need to get across the line," one of the guardsmen told them over the hum of the consulate fans.

"It's okay," Mazy said. Her hair was so thick, and it smelled like grass, what Mathew used to say about her own hair. She pressed her hand and face thick into Mazy's hair, as thick as she could until she felt the girl trembling.

"It's okay," Jennifer said. "Sorry. I'm sorry." Mazy held on.

"Get over the line."

"We're doing it. There's no need to come here." Lavina waved the guardsmen off, and the whole time, she kept her back to Mazy and Jennifer, facing toward the crowd. It was what Jennifer saw of her in the consulate tent, just that hair going every direction, the knot gone, replaced with tangles and loose curls.

"What're you looking for?" Jennifer asked.

"Don't leave us like that. We could've lost you. Too many bodies to separate out and find you. We might never—probably wouldn't find you a third time."

"I had to leave."

"Not like that." Lavina turned to the side, her scrawny neck keeping her head straight and angry. Then she let her chin drop, those knotted cheekbones thrown into shadow, exhausted.

"We're together now," Jennifer said hopefully. Still Lavina wouldn't answer. "I won't do it again."

"Don't." Lavina lifted her shoulders and looked out into the park above the dried-up trees, the buildings to a gold statue of a woman on a tiled roof. The statue held lightning bolts and threw back all of the sun in the brightest glare.

"I guess you need someone to be angry at."

Mazy pulled at Jennifer. "Stop it," she whispered. "Please, Jen." It could've been Delia talking to her, her voice made young and smooth.

Lavina shook her head. "You don't seem to appreciate what can happen here if we lose each other. I don't think you grasp it."

"I grasp it," Jennifer said. "I'm sorry I keep upsetting you, but I'm not your daughter, Lavina. You can't tell me—"

"You don't appreciate—"

"I appreciate you, I promise. I'm grateful we're together,

that we found each other, but I'm not your daughter." Lavina refused to turn and look at her, stare through her, glare at her, but Jennifer could tell.

"I'm grateful," Jennifer said, kept repeating that lower and lower until she had calmed down enough that she no longer needed to say it.

"Tell me what happened. I know it wasn't nothing," Lavina asked Jennifer that evening. They had finished the tins of corned beef and pale orange carrots, and Mazy was asleep on the floor of the van, breathing heavy, and all evening Lavina and Jennifer had avoided talking to each other.

After supper, Jennifer had brushed Mazy's hair, braided it, and Mazy did the same for her, brushing and shaking out as much dust as she could like Delia had done. Mazy kept the notebook with her on top of the blanket. She had drawn pictures all day—drawn and drawn—engraved faces, arms, and hard-boned knees into the pages, the pencil lead blurring in the sun, then cooling in the haze and clouds that drifted overhead.

"She snores as loud as her grandmother," Lavina said, and laughed, trying to keep it low, but the laughter kept breaking through, chopping little notches into the silence.

"I haven't heard her snore," Jennifer said.

"You're just tired. Unfortunately, I'm a light sleeper. Last night you talked in your sleep."

Jennifer blushed, was thankful for the flashlight's blue glow that kept their skin tinged in a pale blue, unreal and unchanged.

"It was gibberish. Nothing to be embarrassed about," Lavina said. Somehow, she had managed to read that blush anyway.

"I didn't mean to keep you from sleeping."

Lavina waved her off. "I'm used to it. Like I told you, she snores like her grandmother. A bullhorn. If you're awake in a few hours, you'll hear. Of course, I shove her a little like I had to shove you last night—have to get her to stop. I don't want anyone finding us." Jennifer remembered how Lavina had rubbed her head sweetly, calmly, cooled the sweat back into her hair until she had fallen back asleep and felt guilty for her silence toward Lavina all day.

"You're not sleeping," she said.

"No." Lavina rubbed her eyes and yawned. "See what you're doing—making me yawn just by mentioning sleep." She glanced over at Mazy, then settled into staring with those large eyes open full to the blueness. "I do rest, until I hear something or get triggered out of a dream."

"But we're safe in the van, Lavina."

The van was quiet just like the evening before. Around them, everything hushed except for the church bells that misfired—three bells, then ten, then six, and between the tolls, the buzz of mille-copters hovering, leaving.

"It won't last," she said. "Someone will find us. I've got to get Mazy out of here."

For a while that afternoon, Jennifer had drawn pictures with Mazy. She made the noses longer than the heads and gave her figures pinwheel ears and hair that shot straight to the edge of the page like her own tangles did first thing in the morning and Mazy had said, "Electric hair."

Jennifer had said, "My hair's electric. Touch it." Then, "Go ahead, touch it," when Mazy just looked on skeptically.

The girl reached a hand up. Slowly she touched the thick black ends, then eased a tangle further and further out, untangling, until Jennifer jumped or half jumped, her best imitation of Terry's bullfrog move, sitting still, then, boom! Mazy jumped back.

"Feel it?" Jennifer asked. "Electric," she said. "Got you," she said the next time, Mazy giggling, smiling, which Jennifer wanted. She seemed younger than fifteen. If it wasn't for her height and growing breasts, Mazy might be twelve, what Jennifer remembered of that age, too closed off inside herself to grab hold of any kind of maturity. But Mazy's body said something different, that adulthood was coming, that it would happen fast.

"What happened to you today, Jen? I don't believe nothing happened." Lavina wasn't going to leave it alone.

Directly above her, one of the cardboard pieces slipped, and Jennifer pushed it more tightly into the window. She waited to see if it would fall again, breathing in the diesel and heat—it was much hotter at the top of the van—but just standing there became as awkward as not answering Lavina, so she sat down and flipped her arm over, revealing the bruise.

"There were two men—coyotes, *guias*—who said they would take me to Chicago. Kept looking at me, examining, said they would take me with whatever money I had. Then I told them I didn't have any money, and they said that didn't matter, they'd still take me to Chicago. But I didn't know what they would do."

She looked up and Lavina was staring like the men had done, that same suffocation of her body inside her clothes. Jennifer wanted out of the van.

"You're healthy," Lavina finally said.

"That's what they told me."

"The same for Mazy. All us desert people. We're used to this weather. I've been told by *guias* since we got to Linn Park that Mazy and I are healthy. All of them saying they'll take us out of Birmingham with no problems. Now, one *guia*, he just said he'd take Mazy. Trusted him," she said.

"I didn't trust those men I saw."

"His name was Teal Dennis, told me to get Mazy out, she'd have to work her debt off in Kentucky, the tobacco fields there. He knew farmers and kept them supplied. Said he might be able to sell her as a servant to some of his people in Louisville or Memphis—those who live behind the walls, rich people. She'd be taken care of. He had connections, customers he dealt with on a regular basis, a route that stretched up through the Midwestern Free Zones to St. Louis, Missouri, and that he'd take Mazy, and she'd have to work until she paid off her debt—three years' labor."

"My God, three years?" Jennifer shook her head. "You can't do that. Mazy'll be eighteen. What about you? What did he promise you?"

"He did what you're doing—shook his head at me. Told me I was too old to bring a good price, even if I was healthy. That's the one word they all like to use—*healthy*. Like we're chickens or dogs. He said he couldn't get a buyer for me because I wasn't young enough, pretty enough. Too many sun wrinkles, don't you see?" She pushed her head forward and smiled so her wrinkles fanned out in deeper ravines. *The desert has ravaged me.*

"I told him I was a coal blaster—that didn't help. That's what I get for having Mazy at forty-five." Lavina pulled up her shirt, rubbed a finger along the worm-scar. "Still itches," she said, as if the scar were new or by rubbing it she could make it new, keep her daughter's memory attached. Then she lowered her shirt. "But he can get Mazy out. That was his promise."

"I don't know why you'd trust him."

"It's a choice among bad choices here. At least what he's offering is temporary."

"If it's real," Jennifer said.

"He showed me a contract. Said all the workers are insured."

"What good is that paper? It's no good."

Lavina crossed her arms over her knees, stretched her body down and back up, slow, painful like she was trying to work the pain out of her bones and muscles and couldn't. Jennifer felt that same ache working its way through her body, making her shift a little, and still the ache.

"I've always known about *guias*, but I never thought I'd be dealing with one."

Jennifer had known about them, too. They hung out

around the desert border and drove in when the miners got close to Birmingham, what the miners called "sweeping"— "the *guias* are sweeping"—and some of the miners and their families paid to get swept up and out of the desert and none of those people came back to say what happened.

Lavina flung her hands at the air as if slinging off water. "You're right. I know you're right. I can't send Mazy out like that, so I told this man no, I wouldn't do it," and she crossed her arms again over her knees. "The other *guias* said they'd take us, no problem. That's another one you hear, *No problem*, as if trusting them should be easy. Some of them are organ dealers. Kill you as soon as they get you outside the city limits. Gut you like an animal, take your organs and sell them up north. At least the collectors wait until you're dead before they start cutting. But this man, Teal Dennis, has been sweeping the Southeastern border for years." Lavina sighed and Jennifer leaned over the blue light that separated them.

"What if we tried to leave on our own, tried to make it to the end of the city over the walls?"

"The bishop gangs will find us, or the national guard, the patrollers. Even if we got out, where will we go? It's too dangerous."

"It's better than trusting that *guia*."

"I told him I wouldn't do it. But Jen, you have to trust somebody. You have to choose," she said. "At least he had a history, the names of places, an explanation. That's something you can't find in other people."

"I don't have that much faith."

"If you were desperate enough you would. If you had a daughter—" And she lay down. "My aunt would help us, but she's up in the north. I worry she's dead, and my cousins. I don't like to think like that, but . . ."

"They're not dead," Jennifer assured her, but it wasn't the kind of thing you could give assurance of, and she shouldn't have said it, another thing she shouldn't have said.

"I don't think the government's going to let us out of here to know. Just going to keep us corralled until we all die in the sun. Like what happened to the bus driver. He's still on that sidewalk."

"You seen him dead?"

"No," Lavina answered.

"You don't know, then. Maybe Darl got back with some help. Maybe the visas will work tomorrow. We can go back to the consulate."

"Sick of that place." Lavina kicked her feet, shifting them so the bottom of the blanket curled around her toes like loose paper, and the van rocked, settled back.

"What's in the black box?"

"Letters to my mama," Jennifer said like she had said yesterday. Her mouth was dry, and there was sand she couldn't get out from behind her teeth. She kept rolling it around with her tongue to calm herself. "That's all."

"So your mother's in Chicago?"

"Yeah," Jennifer said, and Lavina didn't say another thing except, "That's good. I hope you get there."

June 28

Dear Mathew,

　　All this time, even with food and water, I'm thirsty. I never lose that thirst. And still I'm worried about you. It's been four months since your father passed and you've been carrying his death too long. Selfishly I wish you would let him go. My body doesn't want to sleep without you here.

　　I'm afraid that I'm trapped in Birmingham. I could make a run, but I don't know where to get out safely. I think sometimes, if you could find me, but I worry I will die *and our baby will die like everyone here, never being born. Somehow, even though I've seen a lot of death since Talladega, all those burnt trees surrounding us, and I've seen bodies cocooned in plastic and the bodies when they first fall under the crowds, and later the black leather skin—but somehow putting death into this letter, its possibility seems too close, too real.*

I hope you're okay. I know you'd be here, you'd drive up here for me if you knew what had happened. But you don't. And I can't tell you, can't be in Fatama waiting when you come in from the mining or call. I don't want to go back into the desert, Mat. Even if you came for me. Even if you asked. I just want to hold you so I can sleep. Sometimes my desire is all selfishness, demanding. It's becoming more that way in your absence. Today I got sick, but I'm all right, the baby is fine.

The flashlight is going out now. If I use the crank, it'll wake Mazy and Lavina. They're friends I've made. So I have to end here. I can't sleep.

I love you,

Jennifer

She sealed the letter in an envelope, addressed it, set it in her box, closed the lid down, and watched the blue light fade in clips and clips, dimming the belly of the van blue into black. *Why didn't he come with me?* Always that question circling, pushing forward in the space around her.

The blackness spread out beyond the van, beyond Kelly Ingram Park and into Thirteenth and Ninth and Eighth Streets, filling the pews of the open church on Sixteenth with long black space, and into Linn Park, overwhelming the refugees, the guards, and Red Crosses, and to the first set of concrete walls in Birmingham, and over them into the neighborhoods, each peel of Gail's onion engulfed, layer after layer, until the blackness pooled outside the city and began flooding the desert, too much space to gather up and hold.

The night she left Fatama, she and Mathew sat on the bed holding each other, the air conditioner making its low-hummed growl, circulating the cold over the blankets she stayed wrapped in, Mathew already dressed for work. His thick rubber trousers squeaked whenever he shifted on the mattress, and underneath, his boots scuffed and scuffed at the floor like dying fish. He pulled away.

Don't, she thought, and said, "Come with me to Chicago." He just looked down at the blankets and she wondered where he was in his head. Thinking of his father who died in March. Or his uncle who died looking for blue diamonds when Mathew was twelve. But it wasn't her.

"What're you thinking? Talk to me."

"I've got to leave for Miller's Ferry," was all he said, and he showed Jennifer his watch. "It's almost 11:00. I'll be back in the morning."

"I won't be here," she reminded, and he nodded, kept looking at the blanket, where it gave way to her gown and arms.

She grabbed his chin and lifted, flaked off the mica and old clay along the ridge in his forehead, sweaty, smooth, a river rock jutting, anchoring his eyes deep under his eyebrows—"So much of your father is in you."

"Don't say that." He jerked away so she couldn't reach his face.

"It's true," she said. There had always been the similarity. But Mat had become uneasy since his father's death, so quiet, a ghost that, when she touched, nothing warm or familiar returned.

"I have to go to work." He brought his arm up again, the watch flashing in the lamp, and she pushed it down.

"The bus leaves at 2:30. Why won't you come with me?" And the baby, if she mentioned the baby, said, *I'm pregnant*, this would do it, this would get him to leave with her for Chicago.

He looked at the blanket seams, where they crossed her beige gown, the wrinkles there. She pulled the blanket further up her arms. The AC flickered, the generator slowing for a second, then it surged, fell back, and stayed in a growling lull until Mat stretched up from the bed, headed through the hallway without answering.

Jennifer listened as the front door, then the truck door opened, closed, and said to herself, *Open the door back up. Come here.* When the engine cranked, she said, *Turn the key back. Open the door back up.* She closed her eyes. *Come here.*

He pulled out of the driveway and the ghost she had known since March was replaced by the wind, the AC humming, gone.

The heat in the van started to build in the morning, and it felt as if the whole cavern had swelled up like the belly of an animal, sleep giving way to flesh and ribs bowing and bending. Usually Lavina was waking them, getting them up so they could open a few rations before the heat turned unbearable, then out to Linn Park for more food and water and maybe the consulate, trying to figure out what the government would and wouldn't do.

But this morning, it was just the heat, the smell of rubber and diesel tangled in the scratchy blankets. The black river Jennifer had dreamed of, having consumed the city and desert all night, now flowed back into the van, sunlight breaking around the cardboard edges, trying to saw open the last color of the dream. Jennifer looked at the clump of blankets where Lavina and Mazy slept and thought about going back to sleep and would have, but the note was so close that when she turned her head, the paper shifted, rattled.

Jennifer grabbed it and sat up, moved the note under the pins of light.

> *Look after Mazy. I'm gone up north for my aunt. I'll return for the both of you, take you north of the city. A way out, like you said, Jen. Please look after Mazy until I'm able.*

It was signed *Thanks* and *Lavina* and a p.s. at the bottom said, *I will pay you back.*

Pay me back? Jennifer opened her black box and dug into the bottom. The money was still there. But when she lifted the envelope, it sprung too lightly in her hands. She counted the twenties, the tens—only three hundred. She recounted. Still three hundred. Lavina had taken the other four.

She dropped the money and snapped the box lid, wrapped her body around it.

You have to choose who to trust, Lavina had said, and Jennifer had trusted Lavina, but shouldn't have. Three hundred dollars wouldn't get Jennifer and her baby to Chicago. And yet Lavina was trusting her with Mazy—or was she leaving Mazy?

All her pressing didn't make the box any tighter, any more secure, didn't bring the money back. She'd been too careless, should've kept the box hidden under her shirt like she had those first days in Linn Park, should've kept it with her no matter what until the box was invisible. *Keep your secrets in,* she told herself, pressed harder, and started working at the dust on her tongue.

Her mama was probably still in her room in Chicago.

Delia had sent flicker-photographs of the room, its walnut vanity with two oval side mirrors that opened out from the long center mirror, all three flashing up briefly in the camera light; a bed had been placed on the opposite wall, with blue covers, navy, with light yellow sheets, and sometimes the sheets were a dull taupe, but the covers remained blue, and a bedside table without books, and sometimes her mama's cat, Pearl, crossing the bed for the ten-second length of the flicker, carefully unsnagging its nails. One light in the ceiling, a square room, plain walls—her mother had kept them that way—no paintings, no framed photographs, no windows.

In the picture, her mama was sitting on the blue covers, looking at the south wall as if she could see beyond it, see the expanse between her and where Jennifer was, a gaping emptiness that she felt and Jennifer felt, miles and miles of geography neither one could touch or change. Delia knew her daughter wasn't coming to Chicago, not that day, and she kept sitting there immobile, helpless.

Jennifer put the box down, slung it; that's when she realized how angry she was. She started to reread the note, but spotted a map on the van floor, a section of Birmingham pressed flat, and another paper. The handwriting was different from Lavina's. It read:

2607 Chesson Street, Whatley
Teal Dennis
Mazy—Bonded—5:00
Wednesday.

And next to that the keys to the van and Lavina's knife gashed at three points where the blade had cut against things that wouldn't give, the gashes pinched into metal burrs.

The note from Lavina had been written on Jennifer's stationery—A way out, like you said. Teal Dennis' name was on the bit of paper, and on the map there was a pen line, routing south from Linn Park on Fifth Avenue, then Borrow Street, then Chesson. *Stay off 1st*, someone had scribbled— First Avenue was Highway 11, the road they had walked in on. *Choose*, Lavina had told her last night. Jennifer's hand started shaking. She dropped the notes on top of the box and fitted one hand inside the other, squeezed as hard as she had squeezed the box.

On the other side of the van, Mazy kept snoring, but softly, not like the bullhorn Lavina had promised. The other crumpled blanket was bodiless where Jennifer had watched Lavina lie down, pretend sleep until she snuck out.

Jennifer could do it, too, could go and leave Mazy. *Not my child, not my burden*, she said to herself. Where the windows were on the back doors, they had put up cardboard so no one could see inside, yet around the edges, the sun kept working, squares of light that bloomed milkish-pink inside the van.

Lavina wouldn't be back. Jennifer had to think that way. Even if she got to her aunt's, even if that was the truth. And Jennifer couldn't leave Mazy. A man had taken a girl in Linn Park, hustled her over his shoulder and carried her screaming over his shoulder, carried her out like a bag of sand. Jennifer couldn't leave Mazy to that even if the girl wasn't her own. But how did Lavina know what Jennifer would do? Like she had done with Teal Dennis, like she had figured on him—in the last couple days, Lavina had figured Jennifer out.

The heat was getting stronger and Jennifer felt a little sick. She shoved the map and notes into her back pocket.

"Mazy," she said, went over and shook the girl. "Get up, Mazy. Your mother's gone."

Mazy curled away.

"Get up now." Jennifer pushed, insisted, and slowly the girl did; she sat up, shoulders and head thumping against the back wall. Her arms tensed.

"Where's Mama?"

"She's gone up north for your aunt. She'll be back."

"She didn't wake me up."

"She didn't wake me either. But your mama'll be back. Here," Jennifer fished out the note and set it on Mazy's thigh.

Mazy pressed the curled edges down, then smoothed over its whole surface with her palm, kept ironing the wrinkles against the skirt of her pale blue dress. Then she handed it to Jennifer.

"I can't read. You've forgotten already."

Jennifer turned away, ashamed.

"I know it's her writing, but I can't read it."

So Jennifer read the letter, and Mazy rubbed her eyes, wiping the sleep out of them, but crying, too. "My cousins live in Hooper City. Do you know how to get there?"

Jennifer wanted to say *Yes, I know it,* or at least, *I'll get you to Hooper City,* but the lie was too great. She said nothing.

"I don't know where that place is, Jen. We need to find her. I don't think Mama meant to leave me here."

"Your mama's coming for us. That's the plan," Jennifer said. "We're going to do this together."

Mazy leaned over, her chestnut hair falling down, and Jennifer pushed one side back, but Mazy shook it so it fell down again into a curtain.

"We've got to eat," Jennifer said. "We've got to get to Linn Park. It'll be cooler under the tents. Listen to me. We can't stay here." She reached over and took Mazy's hands, shook them firmly. "You listening?"

Mazy wouldn't open her eyes, wouldn't look up.

"Mazy. We have to."

The girl nodded.

"Your mama will be back," Jennifer said. The cool wet of the tears, Jennifer took them from Mazy and put them against her own face, where they dried so fast that the coolness didn't do a thing to ease the swelling heat, the metal of the van expanding and creaking as if the ground below them would give at any moment.

June 29

Dear Mama,

We had to abandon the consulate line. All morning, we've stood outside, first for rations and water, then the consulate. We couldn't get under the tent before the sun became too much, so we're under my oak tree, the one I found when I first came here, planted in memory of George Washington. That's what the plaque says.

The limbs give us a thin shade now, leafless, crossing out lines of the sun, and by us, I mean I'm here with Mazy Elis. She's the girl I wrote you about from Talladega. Usually she draws pictures through the heat, but her mother, Lavina, has gone to find a way out, and I'm taking care of Mazy now. She's fifteen and won't talk. I don't blame her for that. She's worried about her mama. A little bit of her, I think, blames me for her mother leaving. That's probably true. If her mama hadn't found me, she wouldn't have left her daughter behind.

Already noon, and we're inside the dust and smoke, something perpetually burning the city, sooty and gritty. Something here is always burning. So the earth's white haze gets confused with our own fires. I can't separate them, and my breathing is shallow, difficult like some-

thing heavy is down in my lungs—a crowbar or hammer twisting. The workers at the shelter all have respirators for when the air is heavy like this. The rest of us pull up our shirts to our face or take a rag. A wet rag is better than a dry one—that's what you always told me, and it's true. I've seen some people tearing shirts from dead people. Forget the smell, they just need something to filter the air, to use against the sun.

Across from the shelters, a memorial points at the sky, an obelisk trying to find a cloud to pierce, to open. But it can't cut through the smoke. There's one statue on a roof, a gold woman clutching arrows. I can't see her today. The park is full of stone obelisks, bronzed soldiers turning blue-green, memorials to the dead. When you first come into the city, there's a statue of Vulcan, Birmingham's symbol, but I've never seen it because of the haze. It's gone, the residents say, pointing at where it should be. But it'll show up when the weather clears. It'll be back once the weather clears.

The evening siren has started, and still the sun is trying to break through the dust and smoke; shards of light come, then quickly get covered over. At least the heat is finally letting up; at least Mazy has drawn a picture. She hasn't started talking to me yet, but she drew a picture of a woman who plopped down a few yards in front of us, her dress rising as she fell. For a while she raised her hands, lowered them, and stretched one higher and held

herself up with the other until her arms became too wobbly. She lay down and went to sleep. I thought she might
be dead, or easing into death, but someone kicked at her
and helped her up.

Elaine, keep moving, the man who kicked her said,
and she walked toward the tents with him, disappeared.
Never saw her face, only the back of her clothes char-
coaled in dirt.

Mazy drew the hands holding on to the air as if
Elaine had found an invisible clothesline, or as if the air itself, every length of it had been compressed into a single
line for hanging on to before Elaine had to let go, and then
Mazy drew the sleep, and then the legs and arms of the
crowd like a thick grove of trees. I've got to get us out of
here, Mama. There's no electricity except for the genera-
tors the national guard have set up and the ones that
sputter in pockets through Birmingham. Lavina, Mazy's
mother, was good at pointing them out and the different
explosions. She could tell by the sound what was deto-
nated and the total weight of plastics used. Mostly plastics, she said, some launchers. She was a coal blaster
from Georgia. Today, so many blasts. Then smoke. Birmingham is caving in around us, and we can't see it.

The Red Crosses are coming through for the dead—
their last pickup of the day. They don't load the dead at
night. It used to be ten or twelve on foot, but now the
Crosses travel in armed groups alongside a small truck
and a trailer for tossing up bodies. They stack them into

pyramids until the bodies start rolling off. Then the Crosses drive to harvesting machines where the dead are cocooned in plastic so they don't stink.

But Mama, the dead aren't being hauled out of the park anymore. Seven gravel trucks are lined up, full of plastic dead bodies and the cabs empty of drivers, the trucks just sitting. The roads have gotten bombed is what a guardsman told us. So, the rest of the bodies have been taken to a courtyard behind the tents. The harvest machines wrap them, and the forklifts dump them into the courtyard. On some bodies, the plastic has already started to melt to the skin—you can see it, how the plastic changes hue, less shiny, more opaque and greasy. The courtyard bodies are as high as the withered boxwoods, starting to form into a pyramid.

Mazy is sleeping now. For supper we had canned beef stew and green beans—even more tasteless than our desert food, the out-of-date MREs we used to get. But Mazy and I are safe, locked inside the van. Tomorrow morning, the walls will start to heat up and we'll unlock the doors, return to the food drop site. We'll have our breakfast, lock the van doors, head to Linn Park—the world has become static. I've been here four days but our lives are set into this routine, so exhausting, it's getting harder to call up what the world was like, what existed before this one.

Mazy and I talked about her camp in Georgia over supper. They didn't have school like we didn't for so long in Mississippi, though friends of her mother had read to her and taught her a few words. So I showed her the one book I had, read her a poem, "Sparrow Bones," then tried to get her to read the first line—He told the secrets of his life directly into your ear—I had her sound out letters.

Remember when you did that with me? It's the only time she looked happy all day. I guess I wouldn't call it happiness. That's not right. She seemed interested. Engaged. She keeps asking, Where's north? How do you get to Hooper City? That's where her mama went.

I don't know, I keep telling her. I sit on my hands, so I won't point in any direction. I'm afraid she'll try to leave. This morning, a group of refugees opened a manhole cover and people jumped in; other refugees said they led to the protected communities that hadn't been overrun, and eventually led out beyond the desert city wall. But it depended on where you surfaced. The labyrinth opened into the broken parts, too, overrun with collectors, bishop gangs.

It wasn't long before some of the people started coming back up, said they got turned around, couldn't figure which way to go. One woman said she could get to the end of the city—a short woman, bald, her scalp black as if her hair had been burned off. She had worked for the city in the sewer tunnels, but no one joined her, no one believed anymore. She'll be back, someone said. She'll just go in circles, too, make herself crazy. Or bake to death down there.

Even the inside of the earth is baking, Mama. The dust is the same as yesterday—I see it now in this blue light floating through the van—the heat, the smoke, and the sun, finally the sun has given up for the day. And when the Red Cross detail came through, they put the manhole cover back on top.

I saw Darl today. He was the one who tried to help those people on the bus in Talladega. He was leaning against the tallest memorial, the obelisk, all sides of it burned black like the woman's scalp. I saw him after the last warning siren, and Mazy and I had begun our journey from George Washington's tree to the van.

He was leaning against the stone slab, his eyes closed. He could've still been alive like that woman, Elaine, earlier. And Mazy, she saw him, too, knew who he was. But we just walked around him, watched how the last of the sun cut over his face and body, lines of sunlight shifting as the haze shifted, the smoke sinking to the earth as if it were coming from his body, as if the last of him was sinking.

Then the Red Crosses came over and took him because he was close to the tents and their painted red line you're not allowed to pass. When they lifted him, the line of his shoulders raised as if the shoulders had been pinched up, clipped to the air. I remembered how it was when he was alive, those shoulders planting him or setting him into a strong walk. But the Crosses just slung him onto the truck bed already too full. His body rolled down, and they pushed at the other bodies with sticks.

Make a little room for the POC, someone said, then they slung him again, and this time he caught on the curved bones of the others. I know I shouldn't let Mazy see these things. You'll think bad of me here—and maybe it's a mark that I won't be a good mother, but all day we watch people die, Mama. And yes he was someone we knew, and deserved more respect than that from me.

The harvest machine was close by, ready to spin and sew him in plastic, like some huge spider cottoning him in a web until his face was entirely sealed. I know that's what happened.

Mama, I can't sleep. I keep thinking of Darl, keep seeing his face all closed up and stiffening. If I don't keep my mind busy with writing, the walls of the van start to shrink down, and I can't breathe. If only I could open the door a little, see a glimpse of the lighter darkness out- side—I must get my mind off of it—I'm tempted to get up and go out just to breathe, but I'm afraid that if I do, Mazy will wake, and I might expose her, both of us. I can't let anyone find us here. Lavina said Mazy snores like a bull- horn, and she does. I have to push her. Is it mean of me, you think? But I don't want anyone to find us.

I've had some morning sickness. I keep putting my

hand on my stomach, but there's no lump there, nothing to show. Sometimes I press down, not hard, I press to see what will happen. My stomach doesn't pop up any bigger. And I breathe and watch my stomach. Mazy caught me once and asked, Is your stomach hurt?

I got a bellyache, I told her. My stomach's full of air.

I smiled, wanted to laugh, wanted to get her to laugh.

I'm hungry all the time, was all she said and went back to drawing. She did talk to me before we got back to the van. I had forgotten that, her talking to me, and so many other things I wish I could forget.

Mama, when did you start showing with me? What's it like to carry a baby for all those months, someone growing inside you? Nine months. How do you take care of something you can't hold properly? And I can't make the smoke in Birmingham disappear. And I remember the women's babies in the mining camps. I felt Charlene's baby swing a foot against her round stomach, her skin so tight at any minute it would burst. My skin has never been that tight, but it will be. Tell me when I see you, all these things. Promise, you'll tell me.

The mille-copters are coming over again. It's the food drop for tomorrow, or maybe another train of people in the protected zones leaving. The explosions have died down some—they remind me of thunderstorms at night sweeping through the desert, leaving the morning ground so hot and wet that it sticks to your hands, all over your skin. By lunch all of it dry, too hot to keep.

Jennifer signed the letter with love and folded it and addressed the envelope to her mother. Mazy started snoring and Jennifer rubbed her head, turned her a little until she stopped, but kept rubbing, as light as possible so as not to wake the girl.

She was still troubled by the dream memory of her mother's hand on her face, the blood in her mouth. She had locked herself in her mama's room and wouldn't open it, no matter how much Delia walloped on the door and begged.

But when Terry got home, the sun just starting to come up, Jennifer had rushed out, grabbed him, and Delia shouted, "Just do that. Go ahead and hold her instead of me." Her wrinkles had swollen into pinkish-red bags from the crying, sinking her small eyes even deeper into her skull, and she marched into her room, shut the door, locked it. "I'm the one who's hurt," she said.

"I'm hurt," Jennifer shouted just as loud, waiting for Terry to pull her in, but he just kept his arms up as if someone had a gun to his spine, as if he hadn't done anything wrong—*See, Delia, see. I'm not favoring Jen* was what he said without saying a word. Too bad Mama wasn't in the hall to witness his performance. Then slowly he dropped his hands around Jennifer's shoulders.

She felt them light down carefully, like skittish birds. It left her comfortless.

"What the hell happened?" he asked, and she looked up, gripping his stomach that kept trying to wiggle free.

"Your face—what happened to your face?"

She wanted to shut her mouth, but the skin just tightened and turned numb. And she kept swallowing her own spit—the bleeding had stopped, but her saliva glands had gone berserk.

"We got to a fight, in a fight." The words sputtered. She kept repeating them until she could say it all in one breath. "We got in a fight because of my arm. Mama thought I cut myself," and Jennifer wanted to show him the place on her wrist, but he pushed her back slightly, firmly, adjusting her to a distance, as if she were a letter he was trying to read. "You didn't, did you?"

"No." She shook her head. "I cut myself on the kitchen window." She nodded one stroke toward the kitchen.

He glanced there, then down at her wrist. "What happened to your face?"

"She hit me."

Terry frowned and went over to the door, started knocking. "Open up, Delia."

"I don't think she meant to hit me," Jennifer said quietly, but a part of her didn't mean those words—it felt good to have Terry stick up for her, too.

"Honey," he yelled. Delia refused to answer. "It's okay. Open up. I'm here now. Don't shut me out." He started coughing but managed to relax himself before the cough hastened into a fit.

The silence began to build and build until only the wind outside rose and fell; the television had been clicked on, but nothing from Mama.

"Delia, I need you to talk to me. Tell me you're okay. You have to tell me that. I ain't leaving this door."

"What's wrong?" Jennifer asked.

He leaned in, started beating on the door with his skinny shoulder until the wood cracked and swung loose of the frame in a whoosh of air. Delia was sitting on the edge of the bed, watching television. Terry went to her and grabbed her, saying, "It's okay, it's okay, honey." She shook and shook in his arms.

Jennifer wanted to hold her mama, too, and wanted to be held. She felt carved up with bruised jealousy and anger. Then gravity pulled all of the jealousy and anger out through her toes, leaving Jennifer light-headed; she no longer knew who to be mad with or who deserved the most pity. She walked into the room, backed up—Terry was squeezing so tight, she wouldn't be able to get between them.

So Jennifer sighed as loud as she could and clapped her hands on her hips, stomped to the bathroom and washed the blood from her arm, rinsing the sting from her mouth until the copper taste thinned into water. A yellow towel hung over the mirror. She yanked it to the tile. But the towel didn't even make a popping noise, just drifted lazily, and her face in the mirror stopped her.

Ravaged—she thought it, couldn't bring herself to say it. All the blue places around her lips and eyes were just as swollen as her mama's. Even some of her freckles, what she had been told was pretty about herself and believed until now; the freckles had stretched in this new swollen skin, her ears red with heat. She saw more of her mama in the reflection than she had before, than she wanted to see ever. Behind those eyes, anger—still churning, rising back up through her toes—that anger hadn't left after all. A *ravaged face*—she shook her head and her black bangs came undone from behind her ears. *Not my face, not my face.* But there it was.

An hour later Terry peeled away a side of her rug tent, then a chair, and raised Jennifer to the kitchen counter, so they could see each other mostly eye to eye. He squinted, had to back up. Jennifer frowned and started to tell him he needed glasses, but he'd just wave the suggestion off like he always did and say, Don't bother me about it. He still smelled like mud, and faintly like cinnamon and chocolate, his hands cold like Mama's room was cold.

"Jen," he said, "your mama can't handle you doing anything to your wrist. Acting this way." He reached into the drawer for a rag and fished it under the spigot, then started cleaning at her mouth that she had already cleaned. She kicked her feet whenever he pressed too hard.

"I didn't do anything to my wrist. I got cut on the window," and Jennifer turned, touched the square hole where the shirts had been.

"Keep still," he said, wiggling her front teeth.

She yanked her head back.

"Keep still, they're all right. Your mama didn't knock you too bad." He started wiping at her lips again. "Your lips are bleeding like a squished tick."

"What's wrong with Mama?" she managed to say.

He just kept wiping, then washed the bright-red off in the sink, but the towel wasn't as bloody as he let on. He took her arm and rubbed the wet rag over it; her skin prickled with coolness. Only a thin line existed, a hairline where she had cut herself, and the blood had stopped leaking altogether. "Even if it was an accident, Jen, it's not as bad as you made out."

He gave Jennifer a sharp look she didn't respond to, which was as good as admitting that he was right, and a protest bubbled up in her. "She punched me in the face. My lips are bleeding like a tick."

"Next time, just wait on me, okay? Wait until I get home and can take care of you."

"But why? Why can't Mama do it? She's been in her room for twenty-seven nights. You're not here and it's lonely here."

"Twenty-seven—you been counting on her again? Look, she's having a spell, but your mama will come out of it. She always does. You've been coping with these spells longer than I have. You should know how they work."

"I'm tired of it. It gets lonely in the house," Jennifer said. "And she's my mama. She owes me."

"Owes you what? Brought you into this world."

"She shouldn't have brought me, then," Jennifer said and kicked at his leg.

Terry jerked out of range before she could get him, but the sudden move started him coughing. She wanted to tell him to relax, it would be okay if he relaxed. But she said nothing because she was mad at him. Instead, she crossed her legs and tensed them together.

He grabbed the shirts off the floor and stuffed them in the window to stop the wind's howling and rattling and his coughing died down. Then he came back to her and rubbed her hair, smoothing the flyaway parts, trying to flatten the black patches.

"Your mama's trying to find reasons to stay alive in this desert," Terry said, and Jennifer knew then she wasn't one of those reasons.

"You're making me an orphan."

"What?" Terry laughed. "You ain't no orphan."

"My father's already dead, and now you're telling me my mama doesn't love me. I might as well run away."

"Now, girl, you know she loves you. It's the desert. The desert's getting to her."

"Then what's her reason for living? It's you, not me."

This time when she kicked, he buckled and Jennifer squirmed off the counter, but before she could march out like Mama had done earlier, Terry snatched her arm, the one with the scrape.

"We're both reasons for her living. Sometimes that's not enough. Don't you understand? Or you too stubborn?"

Jennifer wasn't about to give him the satisfaction of an answer, but of course she knew. The desert stretched for miles and miles and stretched you out with it, stretched your life into the thinnest, inescapable breath, no matter how many people you loved or who loved you. Those people couldn't keep you sane and alive any more than they could keep the desert from spreading. She understood because she had no choice—over and over, she confronted the desert. Its annihilating persistence was the one absolute she was made to understand.

"Your mama has hurt herself before," he said.

"No she hasn't." Jennifer didn't believe it. She had lived

with Delia the longest of anyone and knew her best. If Delia was that vulnerable, then Jennifer was vulnerable.

"She has." He pressed tighter on her arm. "And you don't want that to happen. I don't want that. Understand? Grow up and be more forgiving."

Jennifer snatched away from him. "She didn't have to hit me."

"She didn't mean to," Terry said, "she got spooked." But then he reached up to Jennifer's mouth still puffed and swollen and made sure not to touch the sore places, set his hand close and touched her skin lightly. "Delia shouldn't have hit you. I know that. I'm sorry."

"Not your place to apologize for her. You're not the one who's with her all night, walking through this house while she's locked up in her room. Do you know how lonely I am?"

"Jen—"

"You won't do nothing about it; I know that about you—nothing," and she marched off.

For weeks she waited for her mother to apologize, but Delia wouldn't do it. The one thing Jennifer had managed was this—her mother no longer stayed holed up in her room. Delia drifted through the small house, Jennifer anticipating her steps, keeping out of their way inside her tiny bedroom or the bathroom, or hours inside her tent of rug-chairs unless she had chores—she didn't want another fight.

It was as if Delia was open to an apology, had made herself available for one, but it had to come from Jennifer first. And that was the line—pride—that neither one of them dared budge across. Her mama roamed the dining room and kitchen, the hallway, and even the porch some—Terry had bought a rocking chair. She took car trips into town. Jennifer stayed mostly in her room with nothing but clothes to change in and out of, Hot Wheel cars and pieced-together

Barbie dolls she was too old for, but that's all she had. She took naps. A lot of naps. Traced the dust rising to the ceiling light and dust drifting just as steadily to the ground.

A few times, someone visited and brought a son or daughter along. Hagen Teasdale came over twice. Half his front teeth had gone missing from a baseball bat accident, giving him an odd, mush-mouthed voice. The mining camp dentist, Elliot Sumners, had to order Hagen new teeth from the Saved World.

"Tee coming," he promised her and nodded and closed his lips tight, so he didn't have to say more—he knew how garbled he sounded, and Jennifer had no desire to pry that ugly mouth open.

His whole body was wrong-shaped to the point where even standing became a difficult task. He could walk okay, but if he stood for too long, he had to suddenly grab a bed-post or the dresser to keep gravity from swinging him down. It was as if his body had rejected its own sense of balance. Hagen kept near the doorway, fidgeting, and Jennifer sat in the farthest corner, miles of blue shag carpet between them.

"You want some Hot Wheels to play with?" she asked on his first visit. They hadn't talked for an hour. "I don't have a TV."

"All right," he said, so she gave him six—the ones she threw at Terry during their brawls, and, therefore, the ones with sideways wheels and bodies roughed up the most. It was about the only thing she used the cars for now that she was twelve, mature. But Hagen Teasdale made do with them, kneeling by the door, crashing the cars into one an-other and making boom noises when they hit until it was time to go.

"Tha you," he said because his mother made him, standing with her hand clawed to his shoulder.

"Thank you," Ms. Teasdale corrected.

"I got it," Jennifer said. She felt bad for Hagen. He

would never have the courage to head-butt Ms. Teasdale in the gut.

And that was it.

"Thank God," she said to her Barbies once the Teasdales' truck drove away. When he showed up four days later, she parceled out the same six cars; they went the whole visit without a single attempt at conversation; and yet, it was nice, Jennifer decided, to have someone in the room.

The swelling in her lips went down, and when Terry came home, the two of them didn't say much. He had definitely taken Mama's side. On weekends, they took drives without speaking—Terry no longer asked if they wanted to go for a jaunt; they were going, period. The government had sent down an extra shipment of propane by mistake and he was determined to use up his doubled rations. But their jaunts had always been silent outings, so it wasn't much different except Terry drove longer than usual, epic drives that threatened to find the end of the desert if only they had more propane tanks in the truck bed, if only they had more time before the sun broke the day open. Driving it turned out was the only thing they could bear to do as a family that still seemed normal.

She was two weeks into her standoff when she realized that she had become her mama's ghost. She vowed not to talk to herself like Mama did; instead Jennifer mulled over the number of socks in her drawer, matched and unmatched, green—her favorite color—turquoise, red, and white. The whites, in truth, were more gray than white. After two weeks of repeating the same details, the same counting, she was going crazy. She didn't have that many socks to begin with, or pants, or skirts, or blouses, her mama called them—T-shirts was what Terry called them—or cars or dolls, or bedsheets, or holes in the ceiling tiles. The constant silent procession of bodies—whether it was Hagen by the door, her mother walking the halls, or Terry fixed permanently in the driver's seat of his trucks—bodies without voices didn't help her keep her sanity.

She went to the mirror, took down her mama's towel, and looked at herself—her hair had gotten all frayed, her skin dulled; her face was shrinking, and soon, maybe, her bones, her whole cranium would shrink into a pea and crush into grains for the wind to blow out of existence.

"You," she said, pointing at herself in the mirror, "are going crazy." She nodded just in case some part of her didn't get it. But she still refused to talk to her mama. Better to die crazy than give in—that was the motto on night fourteen. Then she felt sorry for her mama, all those nights of hers, like this. But Jennifer still wouldn't leave her room. *Pride cometh before the fall* was one of the few Bible verses she knew, because Terry liked to say it like this: *Baby, now, pride cometh before the fall.*

Then on night sixteen, her mother came to her room and sat on the edge of the bed. She took Jennifer's hair and started to shake out the dust like she always had, their routine, like they hadn't missed a night of shaking and braiding. Delia pulled as hard as ever, and Jennifer bit her lip to keep from saying *ouch.* Neither one of them spoke as Delia patiently combed through the tangles, pulled strips of hair aside, then braided. When she finished, she clasped her hands onto Jennifer's shoulders.

"There now," she said. "All done." She lowered her head between Jennifer's shoulder blades. Jennifer stiffened her back to hold the weight and bowling ball shape of her mama's head, her mama's tears warm, turning cool and stinging. Jennifer did not turn around; she did not dare turn around.

"I'm sorry," Jennifer said. "I'm so sorry, Mama."

"I love you. I didn't mean to."

"I know why you did it," Jennifer said, her shoulders easing, opening the cradled space in the center of her back. She nodded. "I know why."

Despite the crying, her mother's voice had a strength to it, a grounding, a certainness. There were times when Delia was doing better and taking care of everyone, keeping Terry and his hothead out of trouble, making sure Jennifer was doing her chores, teaching Jennifer to read. Their world was shifting that way now. Delia hadn't been holed up in her room for sixteen days. Jennifer knew that these moments, these glimpses never lasted as long as the other ones, the quiet ones, the sad ones. But for now, at least, a good moment.

They could talk again. Not about loneliness, but they could talk.

Dear Mama,

Noon siren and the smoke is not as much. Whatever fires caught in the city yesterday have died down, but the sky isn't changing back. The smoke has been replaced with black dirt, picked up north and sheared down by the winds. The black gets whipped into the air, outlines people, glimpses their movement. Then the dirt slows, and the crowd re-forms, shakes itself clean. Still so many people.

Mille-copters have been coming and going in a frenzy. All morning, their blades have cut the air, overwhelmed the explosions and church bells and talking. None of the Red Crosses have come through to take the dead off. The bodies have stiffened to the ground, skin burning black, what's left of their hands and bones, what the collectors didn't sever during the night. The dead used to get more attention from the Crosses and guards than the living. Now they're ignored.

Why won't you pick up the bodies? I asked a soldier at the food site.

It's no longer part of our mission, was all he told me.

I dreamed the dead had escaped the city, their spirits swirling above their bodies, the smoke, the sky. Then I dreamed that their spirits couldn't escape the plastic, that it was suffocating them. I have a piece of sharp glass I keep with me, and in the dream I took the sharpest edge, split open the plastic, let the dead spirits go, one body, then another, until one cocoon revealed Darl's face, his eyes staring ahead, fixed, burned so badly in the sun that they had glazed white, petrified, enlarged so the skin around them would never close. Here was someone I knew, among all the dead, all the bodies jumbled in the courtyard, someone I knew.

I cut the plastic away until his hands fell open. Even though it was night, heat rose off his skin, and I picked up a strip of the plastic, fanned his ankles and calves, his arms, those eyes, all I could do, until the heat had gone, risen out, the last of it, and the dream ended.

Mazy stays so close to me now, it's difficult to walk. This morning when we left the van, we saw a group rummaging through the church, a bishop gang, I'm pretty sure. The front of the church had already collapsed over the tall steps, opening the pews to broken wires and dust. The bishop gang didn't see us, too busy searching through the plaster and bricks. For what? I do have Lavina's knife, and the glass, but I don't know if we can stay in the van

*tonight. We have to be careful going there. It's Thursday.
Lavina hasn't returned.*

*The dead are starting to smell—those lying in the
waterless reflecting pools, under trees, those in the courtyard mummy-wrapped. No matter where we go in the
square, the wind picks up their decay and the syrupy plastic. Those in the medical tent, their decaying limbs get
bathed in antiseptic. More and more people are falling
dead. The ones from yesterday, their skin has dried out.*

*When Mazy draws them—all day she has drawn
faces of the dead and the ones alive, thinning cheeks,
eyes, and hair, whole sheets of faces—she marks the
dead with skin pulled tight. I'm afraid to touch her pictures, afraid her people will crumble. The sun is going
down, and it seems calmer—I saw specks of blue that
quickly dissolved in the smoke and grit. But it's only an illusion. I don't believe that Birmingham will ever heal.*

*The last siren is going, and all day, mille-copters
have been moving guardsmen and Crosses and supplies
in and out. Somewhere else in the city something is happening I think, something urgent. The black marketers
have stopped trading rations and money for ice, and despite all the people, and all the frantic movements, Linn
Park seems even more exhausted.*

North. Jennifer knew which direction was north—
Nineteenth Street and Mettans would take them. She

found Nineteenth by the library end of the square and
marked its direction with her finger, pressing the highway
straight across the map's wrinkles. Then Thirteenth to
Court to Weatherly Road. That put you out in Hooper City.
And from Hooper City, where could they go?

Whatley was east. Twentieth Street to Fifth Avenue —
Stay off 1st, the note warned. She kept pausing at the in-
scription — Fifth to Chesson to Whatley. Somewhere in
Whatley — 2607 — where the pencil lead had circled and circled, etching a small groove.

While Mazy sketched the surrounding refugees —
fragmented, shoving, disappearing — Jennifer looked at the
map. It was a torn-out square, a grid of the downtown area, a
few miles in circumference, and didn't extend to the desert
wall where she and Mazy and the others from the bus had
been dropped off five nights ago, where she had found stars
for navigating into Birmingham. Since then the stars had
darkened, smothered under dirt and smoke. She couldn't
find even one.

Like the afternoon before, and the afternoon before
that, they left the square as soon as the last siren ended, creating a routine that had worked against the camp's attrition — who would Jennifer recognize in the dead tomorrow?

But for now they were safe inside the van. She and Mazy
had finished supper, the blue flashlight cranked and set in
the middle, and Jennifer pulled out the map, checking the
streets and directions, again, careful to follow one route at a
time. If she jumbled too many streets, her internal compass
spun and spun her vision into a blur.

Focus on one thing, she told herself. *North*. But then she
remembered the church. She had spotted the bishop gang
there that morning. So when she and Mazy returned from
Linn Park, they circled Kelly Ingram through the bronzed
dogs and junked cars, by the apartment building called
Freedom Manor, by the statue of MLK posed, ready to address the empty street. They came to the front of the church

the full length of Sixteenth, coming up on it slowly, watching—Jennifer noticed no movement inside, but she had to make sure.

She put down the yellow can of water and took out Lavina's knife, holding it so it couldn't be pulled from her, and kept Mazy close as they walked, up the steps, past where the doors and the frame had fallen down the center aisle. But there was nothing inside, except in the first row of pews and bricks where a fire had been, black coals eating out a place in the carpet and loose bones—nothing smoldering, nothing warm. The bishop gang had eaten a dog, then left.

On the altar, burned into wood, the words *This do in remembrance of me*, and Mazy pointed to a stained-glass window in shards of blue, its center ripped out where a glass body had been—only glass arms left to hold the corners of the frame. The ceiling was so high, so cavernous, that Jennifer's breathing deepened and ached, and she saw Mazy inhale that same fullness.

There had been churches in Montgomery like this, so arched above her, full of the sense of sky, majestic, waiting for someone to sing. The church services in the mining camps had been held in squat buildings or trailers that swatted voices down, and Jennifer only had to attend a few times to know that God was a myth she didn't believe. But in the old stone churches, the empty ones with rounded ceilings, painted ceilings, majestic—there, in those places, that voice lived, that music she wanted to hear.

Then the blue glass darkened like the specks of blue sky earlier—the sun was being shut out by a new crop of sand, which the wind had carried heavily for miles, looking for the right place to shake free.

Jennifer and Mazy had scrambled out of the church and run back to their shelter. Since that moment, the wind had been striking at the side of the van in a fury as if that first storm in Talladega had finally caught up with Jennifer after meandering and searching.

"Tell me the letters in this word, Jen," Mazy said. They had finished supper and saved back one tin of rations to add with the other rations—three days' worth of food, five days if they ate very little, and two plastic bottles they picked off Sixth Street, filling them with water from the can. The yellow can was heavy, and she stretched out the numbness in her arm and shoulder from carrying it all day.

"Jennifer."

Mazy pushed her shoulder into Jennifer's back and the throbbing sharpened.

"Stop it," Jennifer said.

Mazy had the book of poems and was pointing to a word on the page. "This one," she insisted, and Jennifer folded the map.

"It's *soft*." Jennifer whispered *soft* like Lavina would, so strange to hear the echo of someone else's voice in your own.

"I know it."

"The first letter is an *s*." Jennifer drew the *s* on the back of the notebook with her finger. Mazy did the same. Then Jennifer wrote the letter down. "Lots of curves to an *s*," she said.

The pen wobbled and dipped when Mazy tried, but she abled through it without pausing.

"Almost." Jennifer drew a second *s*. "Slow through the curves."

Then Mazy did, repeating *slow*, repeating *curve*.

"That's it."

Mazy smiled. She drew another *s* and another until the curves became a natural movement in her hand. They finished the *o*, *f*, the *t*.

"What's the next word?"

But Mazy shook her head. "Not yet. I want to get this one right."

As she copied and recopied *soft*, whispering it, Jennifer thought of going north, of the street numbers, Nineteenth,

Thirteenth, how the streets kept shooting north eventually, always a turn to take them where Lavina had gone. Lavina was probably dead.

Jennifer looked down at the blanket and her stationery box, the black lacquer peeled where she had held it, belly sweat and hands, and grit, the blue light, anything not to look at Mazy. She shouldn't think about Lavina dead with Mazy beside her. Better to think that she was alive, that the money she had taken from Jennifer had helped secure a way out for all of them. But Jennifer still didn't understand why Lavina had gone north alone. And that kept eating at her: Lavina's decision to leave them.

There was a scratching at the back doors as if the wind had brought down a branch or unhinged a strip of iron. But it wasn't a scratching; it was a creaking noise, someone pulling on the door handle.

"Mama?" Mazy said.

Jennifer grabbed Mazy's hand and flattened the pencil to the notebook, turned off the small flashlight. The blue wilted into black, and Mazy inched closer to Jennifer, said nothing else, like they had talked about—"No one can know we're here," Lavina had said. But someone knew.

Jennifer grabbed hold of the knife from where she kept it under her heel, from where the metal burrs caught on the tough of her skin. During the day she kept it tucked in her waist, somewhere touching skin so she could feel it, be aware of it always.

They shouldn't have come back to the van. Jennifer had vacillated on what to do since they came across the bishop gang that morning. *If we go to the church and it's empty*, she told herself, *then we'll be okay*.

Black coals, bones—that's all they discovered. Lavina had said, "A hideout can only last so long," but staying in Linn Park at night had become too dangerous. And what if Lavina was outside simply trying to get in? Here, this spot, she would know to find them here. But if it were Lavina, they would've already heard her voice, heard her calling for her daughter.

The wind struck the side of the van, pushed underneath it, then receded. And in that lull Jennifer heard someone walking. Then something butted the doors. The loud whack made them both jump, the pencil and paper were lost, the flashlight rolled to one side—but she held on to the knife.

Something walloped the doors again. The pieces of cardboard slipped to the ground. And though the doors had been unsettled, they didn't break, the metal settled back. Nothing could be discerned through the small glass windows. Mazy dug her nails into Jennifer's wrist, and Jennifer didn't pull away.

The doors held again, were hit. And again. Then they buckled. The person walked closer and yanked until the doors flew open.

Pure black. The van had been opened up, a vastness into an even larger vastness, and the wind curled inside and something, though they could not see it, *something* lunged into the black air and filled the van.

It was that second or half second of uncertainty: that was all Jennifer had before Mazy was pulled from her. Jennifer let her body be pulled, or else she lifted her body up—she was never sure what happened exactly, but her body shifted up and over and down, and she brought the knife down and down again. Finally, the body she was stabbing turned before she could pull the knife out and knocked her against the wall. Something clattered, and whatever, whoever, was inside scrambled toward the broken doors and out.

Mazy had yelled and was crying, just like the person Jennifer had stabbed had yelled, but those sounds were just slowly starting to seep in, to make sense, and match up with what had happened. Just like the curls of wind and sand started to make sense again, covering her in a sheet, a blanket, a thin cooling.

"Did I hurt you?" Jennifer asked. She had stabbed into

the black air and anyone could've been under her—Mazy, herself—but she hadn't stabbed herself. There was no pain, no blood soaking her jeans and shirt.

"Did I hurt you, Mazy? Talk to me."

"No," the girl said, trying to stretch her breath out longer and longer. Jennifer moved over to Mazy, put her hands on the ground, felt the tire where the rations were, where her black box was. She fumbled with the lid, dug into the bottom for the sharp piece of glass, but no one was coming. They would've already come by now. Time still hadn't pulled itself back together completely, and there was no coherence of what should happen, what had happened, what would.

"We need the flashlight. Help me find it, Mazy." Both of them put their hands to the floor, the heat still rising from the metal until Jennifer knocked against the tube, grabbed the base, and clicked it on, and there was Mazy holding the knife, a flare of blood on the blade, but the girl didn't drop the knife, didn't jump away from it.

"Clean it off," Jennifer told her.

Slowly, Mazy wiped the blood on her dress, one side, then the other, and Jennifer kept shifting the flashlight to the broken doors. The light flickered on the chrome of the junked cars outside, the blowing sand.

"It was your mother's knife," Jennifer said. "You need to keep it. Can you do that?"

"Yes, ma'am." Mazy nodded. "What're we going to do?"

"You can't cry any longer. You understand?"

Mazy nodded again.

"And you have to hold that tight." Jennifer moved forward on her knees, grabbed Mazy's hand around the hilt of the knife and squeezed like Mazy had squeezed into her wrist earlier. "No one can take it from you."

Jennifer shoved the contents that had overturned back into the stationery box—letters, envelopes, pictures—and tied the box inside a blanket with the rations and two bottles of water. She gave Mazy the yellow can—a small amount of water was still sloshing inside, not much to worry with, but they would need it at the food drop.

Then she took the long ends of the blanket and tied them across her hips, shifting the knot in front, and they headed to Linn Park to the consulate. Jennifer decided she wouldn't leave until the government workers accepted their visas and let them go north.

Down Sixth Street the sand flew against them in clips and stung. They didn't come across any walkers, only fallen bodies. Occasionally, someone rose off the ground enough to cough out the strong wind before leaning back to the earth, but that was the only movement besides the sand. It sheered down, polishing buildings, metal poles, so hard to see. She made Mazy grab hold of her shirt and wrapped a rag over the girl's face. Mazy wrapped a cloth for Jennifer and she sucked a piece into her mouth, bit down, and held it. Then they came upon the reflecting pools that led up to the fountain, that led to the tents, everything so dry, but the crowd had dispersed, the storm had driven them into the buildings, and just the reflecting pools were left with dead bodies.

They walked alongside the pools to the fountain to where she thought the red line was, but the tents had vanished, the national guard, the Crosses. Those in the makeshift hospital were still on their wheeled beds, calling for nurses and doctors that had slipped out on mille-copters. The dust and wind swallowed up their voices. In the aisles she saw one figure, then another—collectors like locusts busy dismantling the sick.

Jennifer took the yellow can from Mazy—they wouldn't need it now—and led the girl to Nineteenth Street. North was Nineteenth where Lavina had gone and not returned. Fifth took them east, seven blocks to Chesson. The directions twisted through her mind like vines choking up a tree.

Jennifer made sure to keep walking, keep moving away from the collectors, but she paused when her light glimpsed the mound of cocooned bodies like dead wood, melted into one another, getting buried in the falling sand. By morning they would be completely buried, a sand dune in the landscape. And those bodies in the reflecting pools would be covered over—a field of upturned dirt—the homes and signs of the city blanketed.

"What're you doing?" Mazy said. When Jennifer didn't respond, the girl let go and walked a step back. "Jen?"

But how could Jennifer explain this familiar despera-tion, the sand thickening in her ears, dulling and persistent, the storm too big. Even if they escaped Birmingham, the desert would come looking. Jennifer had known this all her life, and the girl would come to know it.

"If we go north, we can get to my cousins and mama," Mazy said.

Take care of Mazy, Lavina had written, and already the woman's face was becoming something less real, grained as the weather, even those large eyes and rounded cheek-bones. But she had asked Jennifer to take care of her daugh-ter, and Jennifer had promised herself to do so, and her own baby. She had to get them out.

Jennifer and Mazy ran up Fifth. Still no walkers, no one. Here just long stretches of nothing, except, occasionally, the sky lighting up with an explosion or lightning from the dust storm. She wasn't sure what to attribute these moments to, but for every illumination, nothing moved toward them, no collectors or bombing gangs, bishop gangs roaming, noth-ing except mille-copters that used their own floodlights to cut into the sand wall.

Then they came upon a group of dead bodies, the blood still pooling. Some had clothes taken, and one woman, all her teeth had been dropped on the ground, waiting for someone to pick up and sew back into place. One man's leg had been sawed clean.

Jennifer had seen men and women sawed in half at the carnivals that came through the mining camps. Each summer a magician raised his hands or her hands and said, "Relax. Your friend is fine. Absolutely fine. I just need to put the pieces back together," neatly and always with no blood spilled.

At any moment someone would appear, attach the missing leg, reinstall the teeth, reverse the tiny holes in the foreheads and chests, tiny like deep wells in a sink, the blood pools gathering up pools of sand, mouths dusted in peach fuzz beards. Someone would emerge, *abracadabra*, and undo what had been done. The people would jump up and bow, surprised at their luck, happy to be alive and whole.

But not here, not these bodies scattered across the highway. Whoever emerged would come for the remaining legs and teeth and for them.

Jennifer turned off the flashlight. "Hold on to me," she said, gathering her shirt up and clamping Mazy's hand down. She stepped toward the wall, another wall in Gail's onion, high, rough, and felt along it, going as fast as she could with Mazy pulling her shirt. That pebbled feel—clay rocks. They were the rocks that Mat had dug out of the earth, everyone in the camp along the Alabama River smelling of iron when they came to bed, even the dishes holding on to the residue of the mines. Their work was here, cemented into these walls.

Keep moving, she told herself, and tried to keep track of how many blocks she had come, six or seven. Somewhere in the distance, a flash of light. Luck. A split second that allowed her to see the street name: Chesson. At the corner she turned along the wall, one block, another block. She tapped the flashlight on and off to read the numbers, but there was nothing except the cemented clay rocks and the horizontal sand. So they kept going until they found an opening, one of several places where the wall had been broken through, and inside there was a mirror Chesson Street in front of a row of houses. She read the numbers—2000, 2041, 2053, the sky lighting up—until they came to a gate for 2607 Whatley, opened.

The sand died and brought itself back. "Lazarus sand," Terry always called it. They moved carefully to the front door, everything dark, and she knocked, but nothing; so she turned the doorknob and pushed in; they both pushed in as a light flashed up from the ground into their eyes. There was a click.

"Don't shoot us," Jennifer said.

"Put down the knife," someone said out of the dark, and Jennifer stepped in front of Mazy. "What're you doing here?"

"I have a note from Teal Dennis," she explained, spitting the clump of rag out and pulling it to her neck, "for Mazy."

"Put down the knife," the man said. It was definitely a man's voice and growing stronger.

Jennifer turned, and Mazy squinted, moved into Jennifer's shadow. As she did, she dropped the knife. It scattered to the baseboard, into the darkness there, lost from them.

"Everything you're holding, too. Put it down."

Jennifer set the glass piece and the flashlight on the floor.

"The note," the man said.

She had it in her pocket with the map, and her hands shook so much, it was hard to get them out without tearing, but she managed and held the strips up in the light that kept hurting her eyes. They watered, tears coming down, trying to wash away the sandy grit.

Then the light and the man came forward.

We should run, Jennifer thought, *this one moment, we could back out into the yard into Birmingham.* But they stood there, and the light bobbed in his hand. He came up to them and around them slowly and shut the door.

"Don't touch me," Mazy said.

"I have to check you," he said.

"Let him, Mazy. It's okay." A few moments later, he took the strips of paper from Jennifer.

"What's all this?" He tugged at the knot around her waist, and Jennifer loosened it, laid the blanket down, slowly untying each end.

"Rations and water," she said, picking up the box.

"You need to leave that here." He tapped it with the gun barrel.

"They're letters and pictures, that's all." She opened the lid, and he shined the light down, fished through with the barrel and shut the lid.

"Come on," he said, pointing the light in front. Jennifer and Mazy eased forward until they were in a room where it was dark and the door was locked behind them.

They didn't speak, except Mazy breathing jagged and too fast. "Shh," Jennifer said, rubbing the girl's hair, the full length to the back of her dress, where it came down to her waist, combing through it. "Shh." The room was pitch and black and all she could smell was wood and coal and some of the grassy smell from Mazy's hair.

They had to come here, had to. The consulate no longer existed, and Lavina had never returned. That left trying to get through the storm on their own. Or Teal Dennis. But if Mazy had been her child would she have made the same choice?

You don't have a choice, Jennifer kept telling herself, yet she didn't quite believe it; there had to be something she hadn't figured, another way out of Birmingham like those who slipped into the sewers. The woman with the burnt scalp had claimed she knew how to get to the end of the city, certain that she could find a passage underground, and that kept gnawing at Jennifer. She was giving away three years of Mazy's life, and possibly her own if the *guia* would take her, too, and her baby.

She just hoped Lavina's instincts had been right, that Teal Dennis wasn't an organ dealer, that he was what he promised: a *guia* who had swept the desert for a long time and had plenty of contacts in the Saved World.

The door opened and shut as someone hurried past them, sat down. Jennifer let go of Mazy's hair.

He put the flashlight on the floor so they could see his face, the edges of the room, a small room with a table and chairs against one wall and paintings hung against the plaster. One painting was of a tree—silver-blue leaves and an orange sky, a path cutting through the sky in yellow-orange strokes, layered, swirling, the tree in silver-brown, green, the grass green and blue. The grass strokes pointed to the sun, the branch-shade, and the sky swirled and swirled until the silver leaves and their branches began to shift, began to rise.

"Who's Mazy?" the man asked. His face was bearded, and the only thing in his hand was the note and the map. He spread them on the floor, tapped them down.

Neither Jennifer nor Mazy budged.

"Come on. I'm Teal Dennis, and one of you is Mazy. Though it ain't Wednesday and it ain't five o'clock." He chuckled, pressing the tip of his finger onto the paper he had written on and handed to Lavina days ago. "But," he groaned, "I haven't been able to get out of here 'cause this damn storm." Then he rubbed the thick front of his neck and wobbled his large body into another position.

"Always the Birmingham weather that turns sour. I tell you, you live in a hell of a place." He howled again, scratchy-deep as his talking, and easy. It calmed Jennifer though she didn't want to be calmed by it. "Storm's going to end soon though, and we'll be getting out. So you're in luck, Mazy. If you'll tell me who you are."

Jennifer waited on Mazy, then took the girl's arm so they faced each other. "Mazy, we've got to do this."

"You're the girl," he said.

"No," Mazy said and stiffened. "What're you doing?" she whispered.

"Trust me," Jennifer said. "Where you taking her?" she said to Teal Dennis, and the man picked up the light and flashed it on them.

"Somewhere between here and St. Louis. That's my route on Snakeskin Road. But it could be anywhere in the Free Zones really where she winds up. Depends on the customer, where the customer lives."

"We need to get to the Saved World. Chicago."

"The Midwest *is* the Saved World, honey. But it ain't called the Saved World up there. It's still the United States, more like city-states now. That's what Birmingham was before all this mess, and that's what Chicago is—but I ain't going that far. I'm not a taxi service."

She wanted to demand that he take them, but he would just take the money like Lavina did.

"What does she have to do?"

"Farmwork—that's all the Free Zones are—mostly corporate farms. She might work in a factory or a house for someone. The customers choose, though I try to nudge them toward certain refugees."

"I want her to be in a house with a good family."

"A good family?" he howled. It turned quick into a cough and he had to rub his throat to soothe it. "Of course they're good families. Each and every one. But you're not Mazy's mother? Seems like I met her. Can't quite remember."

"No, she's not my mother."

"Her mother's gone. She left me in charge of Mazy."

"She's not gone." Mazy pulled herself loose and stared at the floor.

"Well, she's not here," Teal Dennis said. "You look healthy, both of you do, like I was told outside." He set the light over Jennifer's face, down her body. She had to work hard to keep her eyes from closing.

"Nothing's wrong with me," Jennifer said.

"How old?"

"Thirty."

"Thirty." He groaned like other people's age was something that ached him, and he stretched his back. The man couldn't get comfortable. "Your name?"

"Jennifer."

"I've got two contracts, Jennifer. If you want to join Mazy—you're bonded for three years until your debt's paid, then you're free. That's how it works." He unfolded two long sheets of paper, pushed them across the floor.

"Will you keep us together?"

Mazy looked up when Jennifer said this.

"I'll try, but I can't promise—"

"I need to know you'll keep us together."

He bent down and put the light between the contracts, so they could see his eyes, the deep shadows, how the light pulled the sharp corners of his large face toward the ceiling, broadening.

"I can make all the promises in the world, but it don't matter. You've got to get out of here. The government's pulled out—there's no more food, nothing, just a desert. You don't want to be here for the last of it. You don't want to be here when there's nothing left. Now, I need to know if you're going to sign these contracts. Storm's coming to a lull."

"She can't write," Jennifer said.

"Then you sign her name." He dropped a pen on the sheets and before Jennifer could take it, Mazy grabbed her.

"You're not signing for me." She said the words straight-out.

"I don't know where else we can go."

"My mama," she said.

"You have to trust me. I'm trying to get you out of here. It's what Lavina wanted. We'll die here."

"My mother is here."

"I don't know where she is and neither do you, Mazy."

"She's with my cousins."

"But she may not have made it."

Mazy sighed, and dipped her head, shifted her body closer.

"If we leave, will Mama be able to find us?"

Jennifer wanted to tell her yes, but, "No," she answered. "I don't think that's going to happen."

Mazy hooked her fingers tight into Jennifer's fingers. "Then I can't leave her. We should try to find her, Jen. Why won't you help me find her?"

"Because I'm not sure where to look. This is the only way out. Lavina talked to him. She trusted him." Jennifer looked over at Teal Dennis and Mazy did the same. "She doesn't want us to come looking for her."

"But I need to—"

"She's gone." Jennifer shook her head.

Mazy yanked her fingers loose. "You don't know that; you don't know where she is."

"But we'll be together."

"You can't promise that either. You heard him." Mazy turned, stared at the opposite wall, the painting with the tree, maybe her attention was there, the swirls and colors, what Jennifer had already found.

"Remember those bodies when we came here tonight," Jennifer said. "Laid out on the road, cut up and bleeding. I don't want that to be you. And all the ones you've drawn. Remember them. All those people lost."

Jennifer took the pen, signed under Teal Dennis' name, above the Delta Insurance representative, and still underneath there was a place open for *Buyer*. She signed both contracts, sent them back across the wooden floor, not even looking at what they said.

Teal Dennis took two small containers out of his pocket, opened one, and eased out a tiny object shaped like a *U*, like a horseshoe for a small pony.

"Open your mouth," he said to Jennifer, then gestured with it. When she kept still, he sighed. "I already explained how this damn storm's messed up my schedule, and you're lucky I'm still here. All this is—I need dental records for the insurance. My customers want their property insured."

"I'm not keeping that in my mouth."

"You don't keep it in. It just takes an impression. A few seconds and it pops out." He scratched at his beard, and she didn't say anything, so he strode over, and she opened her mouth.

"Bite down," he said. He held her chin in place, her teeth squishing into the wax frame. She could smell dirt and coal, but also chicken cooked fresh in his hands, not out of a tin. Then he told her to open up and wedged the small horseshoe out, the suction so tight, she thought it would pull down her entire row of teeth.

He set it back into the container and wrapped it inside the contract.

Then he handed the other horseshoe to Jennifer and leaned back on his legs. Something was hollow about his body, how it moved and jostled, like the dead wood trees that got washed up in the river, like his thick skin and clothes had been wrapped around a big whistling, nothing frame.

"She's got to do it, too," he said. "I ain't dealing with someone so angry."

"Mazy?" But Mazy hadn't stopped staring at the wall, the painting. "We've got to do this last thing."

Jennifer came around and hooked her finger into the

girl's mouth, opened it. She expected Mazy to bite at any minute. But the girl let Jennifer open it enough, let her place the horseshoe in, push it into her teeth, and take it out.

"There's just one more thing," Teal Dennis said. "That box of yours. I need to see it." He gestured.

"Someone's already looked at it once."

"I know. Just put it over here."

"They're my letters."

He tapped his finger on the ground, and she opened the lock like she had done in the foyer.

Teal Dennis shuffled his hands through the letters and down to the bottom and opened a few letters from her mother. He thumbed through Mazy's notebook and the book of poems.

"These sealed envelopes—what's inside?" He squinted at the address.

"Letters to my mother," she said.

"Mathew Harrison?"

"He's my husband."

Teal Dennis opened one of the letters to Mathew, started reading. *Those are my words,* Jennifer thought to herself and wanted to snatch it from him.

Slowly, he put it back, pushed the box to her.

Then he went to the door. "Come on." Mazy held on a little longer, but she got up, too, and they went down the hallway, still dark, but with other people with flashlights, and outside to where three vans sat, waiting. He put them in the last van, which was also dark, but when they got in, there were other bodies, so many, ten or fifteen or more, all of them, it seemed, women or girls Mazy's age, and one looked even younger, but it was only a flash—the doors shut.

For a second it was as if the breath in all of them had been sucked out, and then they all exhaled. Someone was crying, somewhere, more than one. Someone was praying, "Oh Jesus, Lord, please," always someone praying.

Mazy dug her nails into Jennifer's arm and Jennifer let her. The wind and dust hit the walls of the van, shifted it up a little, polished it, and fell back. Jennifer hoped to find windows, but there was nothing. All she could taste was the wax in her mouth.

Cairo, Illinois

Dear Mama,

So it's true. The Saved World, your flicker-photographs from Chicago, the sky there when it breaks free of clouds into patches of blue, no haze, just blue to breathe easy. The first time we stopped this morning, I looked south, the clouds gray and brown there, still full of dust. But those clouds lingered back, and above, white clouds stacked tall, stretching the sky's ceiling higher. Such depth to the sky, Mama, and between all that white collapsing on itself and rising? Blue, as if we had outrun the desert at last.

Mazy and I have made it out of Birmingham, smuggled out by a guia, Teal Dennis. We're in a convoy of three vans, and it's so dark in this cargo hull, lit only by splinters of light along the rear doors, when they shake open enough light for me to continue writing.

Each time we stop, I've counted—there are fifty-one women and girls. The only men are the drivers and the guards who travel shotgun. We stop to eat and "go piss," they tell us. Then they dig through the brush for propane gas tanks, full ones to replace the empties they leave in the same spot, under the same cover for the fuel runners. The men circle us with their hands over their rifles, talking about the next pickup at mile markers up the road.

Teal Dennis told them in Double Springs, the fuel runner put it at marker 57 near the Natchez Trace.

And that's where we stopped next—the drivers trying to get us to Pickwick Landing in Tennessee for tomorrow's auction.

In Double Springs, I heard a lonely hollowed-out sound that swelled, died. The woman squatting next to me noticed that I noticed.

She said she'd always liked the loon, but I didn't know what a loon was.

Just a bird, she said and stood up, pushing her skirt down into place. There's no time for modesty here.

You don't know it? She asked like she didn't quite believe me, and kept patting her skirt in the back, a spot that had buckled and wouldn't smooth.

I'm from the desert, I said.

She put her hand to her mouth, cocked her neck, and

made the call that the loon made. Then she blew at a long wavy strand of blond hair that kept landing on her nose, itching.

I learned to do that as a kid, she said. I taught it to my kids.

And the smile that had crept up, pulling at the corners of her lips—I don't even think she knew the smile was there—suddenly dimmed and she left. I stayed with Mazy and the other women until the loon answered back.

At marker 57 with evening coming on, that same woman said to me it was crickets just getting started around us, rubbing their wings, and cicadas working their wings—that's what we were listening to coming from the thick undergrowth.

Where you from? I asked.

She said Birmingham, and knobbed her hands around her hips, exhaling and stretching from the van's ungiving metal, the crooked shape it had forced on all our backs.

She told me that she had lost her house in Hill Valley, a protected zone until the storm, and asked if Mazy was my girl.

Mazy and I looked at each other.

Yes, I said, and Mazy didn't disagree, let me hold her hand. I wished I had told that to Teal Dennis.

It felt cool, a cool July evening and humid, the ground wet from rain that had come before us, and the plants and trees at the Trace—just like the blue stretching overhead, the white clouds all scattered into small bits turned pinkish blue-gray by the sun. At the Trace, the earth stretched out from us in green. Birds darted from the branches, sailed. This was what the dead birds in Birmingham had been before the storm, I could see that, before the children tossed them away.

Must have had her when you were young, the woman said. Hold on to her.

She uncrossed her arms to touch Mazy's shoulder, but Mazy pulled back, and the woman looked down like that was expected, her touch an offense. Of the two of us, she was the younger one with that crazy wave of hair flopping on her tiny nose, just floating there. Her children had to be young, too. Maybe they were dead or still in Birmingham. Maybe she left them behind.

Teal Dennis and the other men called out, raised their guns and whistled, rounded us up. That woman's in a different van than Mazy and me.

Riding in this hull is a lot of shimmying and jerks of what the road gives. The hard metal floor just hums through your bones, my baby's bones. I still can't get over that someone is inside me growing. It's a girl, Mama—I'm sure it's a girl. The van is always filled with a chorus of coughs—one person starts it and then everyone else joins, louder and louder, trying to outdo one another with their echoes, trying to get out that last dirt in their lungs. The guias have opened up vents in the back to keep us

*cool, and with it, a little more light, slatted like blinds over
windows. A few women whisper. I wish I could make out
what they're saying against the hum of the van, the vents'
whistle, the coughs and highway.*

July 3, 2044

Mama,

   *The auction has ended, and we're heading to
Pilot Oak, Kentucky, trying to get there by night for another auction tomorrow, a small showing for a group of
buyers.*

   *One of the buyers at Pickwick warned Teal Dennis
that a feud between two farmers had shut down Highway
22 at a section called Parker's Crossroads.*

   *Are the government agents going to mediate? Teal
asked.*

   *Not anymore. Not around here, the buyer said, swat-
ting at flies.*

   *Not even regional? No one out of Memphis? Or
Nashville?*

   *They don't come around here either, the man said. He
said everyone had their own property to protect. And the
city-states had to take care of themselves with the feds
pulled back east and all the problems there. Then he told
Teal Dennis, What's waiting for you on 22, if you keep
that way, two farmers claiming the same acres and neither budging.*

Teal Dennis asked if it was anyone he knew and the man answered that it was Floyd Stentson.

Teal Dennis nodded and rubbed at his beard. He said Stentson could be a little crazy, and asked if Stentson still drove an army tank around his farm.

The buyer nodded—*He still uses it to blow up trees*—and slapped a fly on his calf.

He said, *The other party in the feud is a corporate outfit—Tyler Foods. They're just as crazy.*

The buyer hadn't seen a government agent in months. He claimed they had all gone back east. Last one he saw was in a mille-copter crash. Someone took it down near Lutts.

Teal Dennis told him about Birmingham, that the national guard was swarming the city.

Or they were, he said. *They've pulled back, created a new border in Adamsville.*

The man shook his head—*It's their wreck and they'll never fix it. Never.*

Teal Dennis smiled—*Guess I'm going to have to shed a piece of skin off Snakeskin Road.*

That's what everyone calls this length of highways we're on, Mama, Snakeskin Road. When one piece of the road gets shut down, the guias shed it like the skin of a snake, and find a new path to travel.

Teal Dennis told the man thanks, handed him the papers and teeth casts for two women. Then he told his drivers to start on 22, cut off on 412, and work toward

Weakley County. They could get into Kentucky that way. He knew a fuel runner there.

And at the auction, Teal Dennis had lined up less than half of us; said he could get a better price in Kentucky. Mazy and I were some of the ones he saved back.

The other women were lined up and checked over by the buyers. Twelve were sold. Some as wives, some as field laborers. One was sold as a nanny. As the rest of us were corralled into the vans, other guias arrived at the landing, the wide lake behind them trapping the sun, and they trailed out their wares—men, women, I saw two babies.

The woman who had made the loon call, the woman from Hill Valley, I didn't know her name—she was one of the twelve, gone.

July 3—Night

It's night, Mama, and we made it just outside of Pilot Oak. Everywhere we stop is outside of town. The drivers rarely go through them because of roaming gangs. The farmers stay away from the towns, too, unless they know exactly where the roamers are and they can exterminate them without losing workers.

There are thousands of crickets rubbing, chirping. The sound overwhelms everything else. The campfires have died back to embers and the mosquitoes are biting us more without the smoke to confuse them.

I know soon we'll be put back in the vans, but for

now, there are stars, so many that Mazy has taken the notebook and is drawing them as negatives—her stars are black marks against the white page; she's trying to map the sky, the universe.

She said she didn't want to forget what they were like.

You'll see them again, I promised her.

I wish Mama could see this place, she said.

Earlier, when we were driving, the day was much hotter than these dying fires. They opened vents in the back of the van after the first stop. I could feel Mazy's sweaty arm next to me and her hair blowing in my face. She's calmer now.

I wish your mother could see this, too, I told her and I wished Mathew could see it.

I don't know what Chicago is like, if you have seen these same skies. Mat's father used to swear that these places existed.

About as close to heaven as any of us will get, he promised.

It was the one time I remember him smiling. I'm the one seeing what he wanted Mathew to see—everything is so vast. I've never thought of the world as endless, as beautiful, as possible. I wish my baby was born right now, here.

I've taken my shoes off, Mama, and guess what? I'm digging my feet into the soil, wet and cool, heat still coming off those embers.

July 4

Dear Mama,

Saw thistles this morning, a whole open field. The wind hit them, beat the stalks down, tried to, and then they stood, black and brown at the base, dried out above thick tufts of grass, some of the white fluff swirled, arced, and settled. Just for a moment. Each time the sun split the clouds out, there were mountains.

Hills. Not really mountains, some of the other women said.

We were in a valley surrounded by mountains, as far as I was concerned, swaths of green and something blooming red, yellow, the sun, its light at the tips of the cloud, like the fingers on a hand reaching around this gray-purple and tearing it down the center like so much bread. And warmth. Not blistering heat. Just warmth. Then the clouds closed up again and the hand of the sun was pulled away.

Teal Dennis' men gave us three buckets of water and sponges and said to rinse the dirt off. So I washed Mazy and she coughed on the water, said stop it, and so I put more water on her face like Terry would do, or I would do to him. She snatched that sponge and threw it at me and hit someone else, and well, Mama, we were all throwing water, scooping it out of those three buckets onto one another, laughing and hitting one another with sponges until the guards stepped in and said that we were clean enough.

That's when the trucks pulled in. The buyers. We all looked at one another, looked around at our soaking wet selves, our nervousness getting even more nervous.

So I just closed my eyes, then opened them to that circle of mountains, at that sun, a cloud rolling over the top, a swath of orange, something blooming red and yellow. The wind picked up and blew the thistles everywhere, and the guards said, "Line up," the barrels of their rifles pushing at our loose hands.

This is what I've seen since leaving Birmingham: a deerfly tried to bite me, tiny yellow wings, striped in black; a bird flew over, a hawk. It dove and swung in the wind, then kited higher. One of the men tried to shoot it.

Moths, fluttering from one grass blade to stalks to bushes, passing in the fire smoke. Oaks and pines with large vines crawling up. The wind here has a different sound than in the desert—there's more rush to the wind when it strikes leaves, abruptly dropping away. Black grass seeds collect on my leg, and sometimes the sky is as gray as dust cloud gray, but there's nothing dry about it.

My skin is filled with sweat, moisture. Mille-copters come overhead. When I hear them, the vans pull off onto smaller roads and stop and dust comes in through the vents. But like the buyer explained, there are no federal agents here now. The mille-copters vanish.

A tree with red berries that shiver, and the rain, so

much rain that doesn't evaporate by noon; loons and frogs; one frog cranks up, then another, and another as if they're calling on one another to see who's loudest.

The bark of huge oaks, gray and disjointed like rivers, not at all blackened and burnt as I've known them; brown branches, white berries, split from the trunk; and on one ground, flattened out pears, the limbs still bent full with pears with green lopsided sides. They taste cold and sweet here. Birds like to whistle here. The wind forces rain from the trees.

Sometimes we're let out in long-rowed crops.

That's cotton, one girl told me, and someone got stickers from pigweed. One woman saw me get sick in the morning. I had tried to walk behind a wide trunk, and she saw me bend over, said she wouldn't tell the guias. Sometimes the ground is covered in pine straw—swaths of earth.

One tree, its bark had peeled off, and between the branches sat the web of a huge spider, the ground below covered in a mat of brown pointed large leaves. And sometimes pine straws pierce the green leaves and dangle down or catch in the branches of other trees, then the wind brushes through.

Parched thistles lift and fall and lift, for how far? The quality of the light is different here. Always there is something living—bugs at my toes, around my mouth, looking for water, too.

A blue morning glory winding up a tree.

Huge white birds scuttering up from the ground.

The sound of trucks driving past on wet roads. None of them have turned back for us.

The wind curls around my entire body. Some branches knot up and curl into themselves. My stomach barely shows. Flattened pinecones; pears squished on the ground; and orange butterflies, black roots that shoot up from the sand and trip you; brown nests in trees, if you look up high enough and stay with your watching, the wind shifting it all, Mazy's hand swinging in mine. She lets me do that.

The barbed-wire fences are rusted, the wires tangled in streams and rivulets; and the sound of trucks on wet roads coring out the distance; leaves spread out like huge fans.

It is the fourth of July, Mama. Happy Fourth. At least I know you're in a safe place from what the guards and the buyers said today about Chicago, that it's well pro-tected, and one man said the city had as much influence as the whole federal government, that the US govern-ment no longer has control over the Midwestern city-states: St. Louis, Chicago, Minneapolis.

Mazy and I weren't sold in Kentucky. We're heading to Cairo, Illinois, now. Cairo, like all these small towns, has been abandoned for the large cities. But you must know this, must know what the world is becoming. There are only five women left, all of them in our van, so there's a lot more space for lying down. The vents are near the

truck bed, and when you lie down, the wind rushes over
your whole body.

   Jen

Those letters to her mother had been almost three
months ago, three months since Jennifer was bought in
Cairo and Mazy was taken from her, taken on to St. Louis,
or sold somewhere between.

She could barely remember that girl. No—the memory
was there. Jennifer had put Mazy out of her mind, that was
it, wouldn't think on her, except reading these letters now—
the two of them holding hands, their hands latticed, the
smoothness of Mazy's skin and the sweat between their fingers. Or sometimes Mazy leaned into her. That was the important thing—the touch, the closeness. If you touched
someone, you couldn't lose them.

But Mazy wasn't in Cairo. And Mazy's mother, Lavina—
her face marked up with dust and black holes, her voice
scratched out—Jennifer couldn't piece her back into someone recognizable. Lavina had abandoned them in Birmingham.

It was out of boredom that Jennifer opened the letters.
That's what she told herself, but she didn't really know why.
She dropped them into the black box, let them fall into it
with the ripped-open envelopes like making a fire of twigs
and leaves and brush. That would be a good thing, to burn
the box and everything inside it—a history she didn't want
to cross anymore. She would never get the momentum of
herself back, and by tomorrow Mazy's hands, the touch of
her skin, would toughen and wizen, become impossible to
hold on to. Jennifer would shoo the girl away, a straw broom
to the floor, and the letters would evaporate like smoke without burning any trace into her mind.

She put the box under her bed, gave it a shove to the
center, far enough that it dimmed smaller. Maybe one day

she could walk into her room and forget the box was there. If she pushed it far enough under.

Two floors below, Professor Jinx was flying over the piano, "Catching every key in sight and sending it straight to heaven," he would say when he wasn't in one of his blue tempers, the kind Mat had.

Professor Jinx had driven down from his club in St. Louis and been playing all afternoon—quiet, healing solos. But he was revving it up now—"Straighten Up and Fly Right"—that's what chords he struck, "hot, fast, and loose." She could hear his voice, that dry, sweet sound.

"I've had this parched scratching in the back of my throat all my life," he told her as if he was an old man, an old soul. He wasn't much over fifty.

That voice, it was rising up now, and she could almost hear the heels of the other girls stomping with the tricks from St. Louis, from Memphis, though it was too early in the evening for stomping, dancing. The mille-copters were just starting to buzz. She'd be expected to come downstairs and join the other girls soon.

Jennifer went back to the window and looked across the Ohio, the straight of it where it turned down and out of her reach. This is what she always did before going to the parlor, glance out over the river from her room five stories up in the St. Charles Hotel in Cairo, Illinois. The hotel had been built before the Civil War, and it was where, she'd been told, Ulysses S. Grant had kept his headquarters, and, before that, where runaway slaves had stopped on their journey north. Though she hadn't gone to the basement to see it, supposedly the underground holding cells still existed.

Jen's room sat in the southeast corner, and from there she could see the Mississippi River, too, just a catch of it from the south window, the rest of the Mississippi hidden under mimosa trees, the levee, the other buildings. But the east window displayed the full stretch of the Ohio, the hills of Kentucky banked on the other side. A little further south the two rivers conjoined and barges slipped slowly around one another with Cairo, this small leveed jewel, right between them.

Because it offered a better view of the Ohio, it was this window she stayed at most, watching the drifting water, and farther north along the Cairo bank, its houses there burned up and broken. In one house a skinny tree had coiled through a large hole in the saltbox roof. A maple that a john pointed out to her a week ago. He had flown in on a mille-copter from Memphis to St. Louis, said he needed a pick-me-up before seeing his wife, and Jennifer was just the girl for it. *Girl*—no one called them women here, except for Jinx. All of his songs were about women and mothers, and as he put it, "low down, wrong kind of loves."

"That kind of love," he promised, "puts everyone else's love to shame.

"And that kind of love is the kind I've endured. It's in my singing, my playing. Come closer if you want to know the depth of that lowliness." Jennifer always got as close as she could, as much as he'd allow.

It was still light out when the john from Memphis was done with her; he stood by the window swishing his tie in a knot, pointing at the maple. "Someone needs to fix that roof," he said. He smiled, sure of himself. Jennifer wondered what it was like to be so damn sure of yourself and wanted him to get away from her window, from her view of the world.

"Autumn's already started." He pointed again, and that's when she came over, saw the red edges at the top green crown of branches.

Every day since he left, she had come to look at the maple more than the river. The red had spread from the edges to the center vein, the green now in splotches. She looked and waited for the wind to catch the red, carry it; at times when that happened, something in her sparked. That's why she opened the letters. She remembered now:

she wanted to see if reading those words about Snakeskin Road could knife through the numbness even more. But it just made her hands ache for Mazy.

The rivers here didn't dry up, not like the Coosa. Barges came up and down, east and south to Cincinnati, to Memphis, and north to Minneapolis. She knew these names from her desert schools, from the tricks that flew in. The other girls talked about the barges and their destinations, too, that they might escape on one. The barges moved so slowly, and all day and night, surely they could swim out and sneak on board. Sometimes the barges did stop in Cairo. The St. Charles was here after all, the only thing left in town.

The hotel had been split into two halves, the upper half for clients coming in from city-states on mille-copters, clients with the most money, and where she was because she had never been a prostitute before.

"You're fresh," Ms. Gerald, the St. Charles Madame informed Jennifer on the first day when she was sold here, smiling deep and inviting, like this was a good thing to be.

Supposedly, after two years, Ms. Gerald moved you down to the bottom floors, which had been flooded several times despite the levee. If you didn't perform well, if you gave her too much trouble, she sold you downriver to the whorehouses there, the shanties where anything could happen to you.

Jennifer's debt would be paid in three years, but many of the girls had paid their debt and still didn't leave the St. Charles.

"Nothing to go to," one girl said. Lisa, from Atlanta. "When I pay off my debt, where am I going to go?" She never talked until she'd gotten halfway through a cigarette. It took the smoke and heat to warm up her vocal cords, Jennifer decided. She only smoked long, thin cigarettes that one of her regular tricks brought with him from Nashville. "There's no other place for us. Besides, this place is family."

She inhaled, her body clinging to the tight wrapper, the orange tip, lining her up with its line.

Cawood, who told Jennifer to say her name like a crow cawing for the woods—Cawood was also from Atlanta and big-boned and she said, "That's crazy talk. Period. Soon as I pay my debt, I'm done, done with it. I'm heading to St. Louis."

"Where in Atlanta you from?" Lisa always asked Cawood, always after Cawood made an assertion.

"I've done told you," she said, rolling her eyes, rolling them so far back that sometimes Jennifer thought Cawood would fall out of her chair with disgust.

When Lisa wasn't around, Cawood said to the other girls, "I've already told that skinny whore where I live in Atlanta. How many times? How damn many times is she going to ask me that? What drugs are she on today? Enwine Hills off Nance Road, house 123. It probably isn't there now, but I've answered her. You've seen me. How many times?"

"Too many," some of the other girls replied; they were the cheerleaders for any clash, and some laughed, Cawood lowering her head, swinging it low in disbelief.

The bottom two floors were for barge operators, truckers traveling off I-51, and smugglers, and the mille-copter pilots. The train on the levee never stopped, just kept pace with the river.

Jennifer had been downstairs, had seen *those* girls around the first-floor bar, General Grant's Bar it was called, *those* girls relaxing just like she and Cawood and the other girls on the third-floor parlor did, but only in the daytime when the house was quiet except for women resting, talking in their long T-shirts, in their gowns—that was the only laughter you heard then. Occasionally, someone came off the road and was quickly escorted to a room so everyone else could linger; or a mille-copter would stop, a business executive flying between the cities, between meetings, like her john at the window that afternoon last week.

So the hotel was, during the day, a hotel of women—except for the security guards roaming the fences, and up and back, floor to floor, and except for Professor Jinx, when he came in from St. Louis or one of the casinos, or woke up after an all-night playing. First thing he did was start his melodies, his riffs while the kitchen workers sprayed down dishes, cut peppers and avocados flown in or shipped in, preparing breakfast and lunches and tonight's meal. And Dr. Syeth would come in a few days a week to make sure no one was pregnant or ruined.

Ruined was Ms. Gerald's word for a prostitute who got HIV. "So-and-so has been ruined," was how Ms. Gerald put it, frowning, refusing to show her teeth. "Got ruined," the other girls echoed. Some cases were treatable, if still not curable, but some strains were too strong for the drugs. "Don't let that happen. Don't let a man do that to you," Ms. Gerald said.

The news of a ruined girl was always a good occasion for Ms. Gerald to reiterate the five house commandments: 1. Give nothing away for free; 2. Never steal another girl's john; 3. Never steal from Ms. Gerald; 4. Don't kiss with your mouth open; and 5. All the money you make goes to the house.

She would turn, as if in a hurry to get away, then "Oh, yes," she would turn back around. "Take care of your body. No bareback sex. Don't let a client ruin you." That was the sixth commandment, and Ms. Gerald was always threatening to add more.

But some tricks paid extra for sex without condoms. The extra went to the girls, and they'd hide it, hoping Ms. Gerald wouldn't find it in her raids—if a girl hung on to the extra, when a girl was at last free, she could go somewhere "in style," Cawood promised. And if Ms. Gerald found the extra, then there was the river, the baptism, the cleansing for such betrayals. The girls, all of them, were her investment, and she wanted return on her money.

Ruined was also Ms. Gerald's word when something happened to a girl that made her imperfect, imperfect enough that clients wouldn't use her again—like deep cuts on the face or a bottle "broken in the cunt," was how Ms. Gerald said it. That had happened twice downstairs and she'd had to hire more security.

"Don't worry, those johns got their own cutting," Ms. Gerald promised. But the rich clients, the ones on the top floors, whatever they did, nothing happened to them. Ruined women worked as cleaners to pay off their debt or were sold to farms or sent downriver or over to Instant Casino.

Instant Casino was in Paducah, Kentucky, less than an hour away by car, ten minutes by mille-copter. There were whores at the casino, too—"But not the good ones," Ms. Gerald said. "I own all the good ones."

Ms. Gerald refused to let the girls go until their debt had been paid, though many had tried to leave. After talking about last night's tricks and what they had requested, about the dancing and the Instant Casino musicians that had sat in with Jinx, and all the aches and headaches, and the food that had been served, stuffed pork—was that what the chef called it?—while they lazed around the parlor together on the sofas and cushioned chairs, the girls that had been at the St. Charles the longest told stories of those lost ones.

One girl hadn't been at the St. Charles a month before she slipped out on a barge—a good swimmer—and she waved and yelled out, "See you in St. Louis," to the girls on-shore. The next day her body came floating down the Mississippi, stiff like a plank of wood, her calico dress wrapped up around her throat.

Another girl snuck out with a client on a mille-copter. "I can't tell you the number of girls who've tried to steal out with some trick," Cawood said. "But this john wanted to marry, and Ms. Gerald wouldn't allow it, so he snuck her out. The Nashville police brought the girl back. That's the kind of reach Ms. Gerald has." Cawood went around the circle, nodding her head from one girl to the next, looking through each of their eyes and daring them to doubt the truth. "Ms. Gerald beat that girl and sold her to one of the shanties. Watch out for those men who want to marry."

There was the story of Roger.

"Oh, no, not this story. This one's not good," someone said.

"None of them are good," Cawood said.

"But Roger," Naomi continued, "he wanted to marry this girl so bad, he was ready to give away his fortune. He came from old St. Louis money. And she—all I remember of her—she was petite." Naomi was small, too, the oldest of all the girls. "Her name was Anne and she led him on. She thought he was her ticket, but Ms. Gerald wouldn't let her go."

"A tiny thing," Cawood agreed. Sometimes the girl's name was Margaret, and sometimes Stella, and Marla, or she had no name; she was just *that* girl who did *that* unfortunate, stupid thing.

"And then," Naomi pushed all the hair out of her face, knotted it and held it, revealing a washed, bare face, lips full with lipstick, "he came in on a Friday night, the parlor full of card gamblers out of Instant Casino. They had lost all this money, but still had some for us. And Roger went up to her room, cut through all that noise, and shot her, that petite girl, then cried over her body before shooting himself. That noise—we thought security had spotted a roaming gang and was running them off. Next morning, security found the two bodies. They had the bodies wrapped in sheets before I could see them."

Ms. Gerald refused, no matter the price, to sell her girls into marriage. "Once a man buys you, he'll do whatever he wants. Treat you like pure dirt. He'll throw you out when he's tired of your love. I've seen it." Ms. Gerald nodded her head strong on that one, stronger than Cawood nodded her head. The girls all speculated that something like that must've happened to Ms. Gerald, some man must've gotten tired of her love. It was the only time the veneer of her face peeled into a sadness, like that deepness in every river where you go down searching, but lose your way to the surface and lose the bottom and don't know where you are or what you were hoping to get—that's what her face became.

Ms. Gerald claimed she just wanted to protect her girls, but Jennifer thought it was about control, who got to own what body—and Ms. Gerald was determined to own as many as she could.

Those mornings when the girls talked about the lost ones, Ms. Gerald came out of her office, came right to the center, and perched on top of a table. She always sat on the tops of tables and never chairs.

"I had this one girl, she was pregnant. This one had somehow slipped past the doctor. Doctor . . ." Ms. Gerald snapped her fingers as if the doctor's name was right there to hold in her hand, but not quite, not quite could she take it. Then she scratched her scalp, her hands so pale, as dry-blue as vein—even when she pushed through her white hair, all wiry and brilliant, no red, no blood would rush into those hands. "Oh, whatever his name, I had to fire him because he let this girl slip by. He wasn't a very good doctor."

Later, after Ms. Gerald left, the girls said the doctor's name was Thurman and the father of the baby. The girl's name was Reseda. She was seventeen.

"So she had gotten herself four months pregnant when I noticed her belly." Ms. Gerald grabbed her small stomach through the pink jacket and lifted it. "She was dancing on the floor over there, and I grabbed her stomach just like this." She exhaled. "Beautiful brown skin on her."

"Not black like me?" Cawood asked.

"No, light brown." Ms. Gerald nodded.

"Then her skin wasn't as beautiful as mine." Cawood opened her arms wide as if there could be no doubt, and the others laughed.

"No one's as beautiful as you, Cawood, but she was still beautiful. I told her she had to get rid of that baby. I mean, whose was it? Next thing you know, with a baby she'd blackmail a client. And she said she wouldn't get rid of the baby. So I got the doctor and went up to her room and still she said, 'No, I'm keeping it.' Just like that, 'No, Ms. Gerald, I'm keeping it.' But she knew I wasn't going to allow a baby. I told her, 'You have to do what I ask' because, now listen up, I'm telling all of you this: babies are where *it* starts." Ms. Gerald went around the room, making sure every girl was paying attention. "Once a man gets you pregnant, he has you where he wants you. He has your pussy against the wall."

The girls hollered at that one. "Don't let him snatch that," someone said, and the laughing got stronger.

"So we left her, and I got security. I had the doctor, the one I had to let go and some guards—we were going to have to take that baby—and together we went back upstairs, the fifth floor. I knocked. Nothing. There was no sound when I called her out."

The girls said Reseda had screamed from inside her room. Some of them swore they heard her screaming, Ms. Gerald pounding the door, and the doctor, her boyfriend, he was begging Reseda to open the door, then nothing.

Ms. Gerald got up from the table and walked around to the glass doors, the ones that spread across the east wall, the entire east wall of the parlor, and looked over the sixty-foot levee that surrounded Cairo to protect it, and over that levee into the Ohio River and across the river into Kentucky, where the bank curled up and spread into fields.

"Black, black," she said. "When we finally got inside, the room was black. Her window had been lifted. Wind was blowing in and the doctor and I went over and looked down and there she was on the pavement below us, shaking. The fall hadn't quite killed her, hadn't quite done it to her." Ms. Gerald shook the cuffs of her pants, rubbed one shoe, polished it on the back of her left leg. "That's the thing about being on the fifth floor. It's far enough up to cause you pain, to hurt you if you fall, but not far enough to finish the job. So there she was, her baby lost, and lost herself. Poor girl." Then Ms. Gerald walked out onto the balcony, sliding the glass door behind her so no one could follow.

The closest hospital was in Memphis, the girls said. Reseda was still there, living on machines that the doctor paid for. And she did lose the baby. She did lose herself. Poor girl.

Then the girls walked out of the parlor to their rooms as if telling something this horrible was too much to deal with once you said it, once you spoke the truth. Even though the paths of the stories had been different, whether Ms. Gerald told it or the girls told it, the ending was always the same.

Jennifer often looked out her window for Reseda, her mind conjuring the body on the black pavement, the gooey tar that surrounded the hotel and spread to the chain-link fence—red hair some days, blond on others, black, brunette—the hair sprawled out and the shaking body and some dress with blood on it. Sometimes the body on the ground was her own. Jennifer stared and stared—she couldn't turn away from herself fallen; her baby was dead.

Jennifer looked at the pavement and touched her stomach like Ms. Gerald had touched her stomach when she told that story. Each time a new girl was bought, that story got told. Some morning, Ms. Gerald walked out and said, "I had this one beautiful girl," and recited it, set them all in the fold, again. It was a dare, of course. The St. Charles locked you up with bodyguards and fences, isolated you from the world. No freedoms, but safety. What was left was the dare—venture out if you think you can make it. You better make it. The world will kill you, snatch you up. Always that talk from Ms. Gerald and her girls.

Jennifer pressed on her stomach, but her skin through the fabric just felt numb. She had lost the ability to feel where her baby might've kicked. By now, Jennifer would've been showing.

Go back to sleep, she told herself and pressed up against the glass instead, thought how easy it would be to tumble, to fall and break apart. Yet the baby, the baby—she couldn't do that to her baby.

The baby's dead.

Someone rapped on the door. Ms. Gerald had sent one of the security to her room. The girls would've called her out, but the guards just knocked and left. They'd be back if she didn't come down, and this time instead of knocking, they'd simply come in and escort her to the parlor.

When she first got here, Ms. Gerald sat her in the office—the only time Jennifer had been allowed inside the office with its huge planters of lavender and artifacts from the Cairo Custom House and, most prominently, an engraved pistol and sword and Union soldier uniform pressed into a glass case—and said to Jennifer, "I own you now."

At the time, Jennifer was thinking of Mazy, the van back on the road, each second further and further away, a distance she'd never catch up to, and what would happen to Mazy now. Then she couldn't stop crying. She wanted to get up, wanted to run, but there was a guard at the door, so she sat there listening, tapping her feet, and digging at her eyes. *If I blind myself*, she thought, *blind myself to what's happening, then I'll erase it.*

Ms. Gerald walked to her desk, sat on top, and lifted the contract, the wax mold of Jennifer's teeth as proof of ownership. Carefully, she set them down. "You're in a brothel, and you need to get used to that. It takes some girls a while to get used to that. The good news is this: the St. Charles is an oasis, not a shanty. I found this place out of the wilderness."

Ms. Gerald told this to everyone: "I came to Cairo after the people left, came here with nothing and built a brothel out of the wilderness."

Cairo had been a city once. What happened to those

people, their lives here, where did they end up? But Ms. Gerald announced her *wilderness* line so often, so confidently, that the girls repeated it, and the regular johns said it to the new johns when they got drunk: "an oasis in the desolate Midwest, a brothel out of the wilderness." Then they laughed at the spectacular, improbable truth. How could this be? Yet here it was, the St. Charles thriving and nothing else.

Ms. Gerald had managed to supplant the other truths, all of the other histories of this place except for the Civil War, as if that were the only other time Cairo had existed. The other histories, no one cared to know. And where Cairo had ended, Ms. Gerald began. No one knew, not even Naomi, who Ms. Gerald was before the St. Charles, where she came from, why she came here.

"You're fresh, so I'm keeping you for the rich clients," Ms. Gerald said and explained the boundaries of the St. Charles Hotel, the squared fence and gun tower, the landing area for mille-copters, the generator and pump house, the security detail and guards, and the dangers beyond those boundaries. As she talked, she kept her arms stiff, her hands pressed to the desk edge as if it would fly away without her insistence. The white hair she kept pinned back, and she had on a gray suit that swallowed her up from ankle to throat. Ms. Gerald always wore suits—pink, blue, green, black. The stiffness in the fabric seemed to hamper her movements.

Finally, she repeated that any extra money a man offered, Jennifer had to give to the house.

"Number five of the commandments, all the money comes to me. I take care of my girls. Do what I ask, and a man won't be allowed to hurt your body."

"I'm not going to," Jennifer said.

Ms. Gerald sighed. "Don't think a client won't take a drugged up girl. They like that, some prefer it. I won't protect you unless you do what I say."

Jennifer was taken to her room, told to shower, dress,

come downstairs to the parlor at seven. But she didn't, and they knocked on the door. She didn't come down and they came back—Dr. Syeth, that straight black hair of his shagged over his forehead left to right, his face always sweating in that same pattern, left to right, as if his face naturally sloped that way, shiny. He always looked as if he'd rather be somewhere else, like he had to be careful—he knew the story about the other doctor, and he brought two guards to hold her down.

They drugged her and left the room, leaving Jennifer with a sense of the world splitting and moving at different speeds. She called out for Mathew, the baby, Mazy, Terry, Delia—like the flicker-photographs in her mother's letters, how the images started up, then got stuck halfway, these people slipped in and out, half real, unreal.

The second rhythm was of her room, the dimness of it, how the corners flashed and then fell into darkness, the piano playing downstairs, a client talking to her, splashes of laughter, talking, as he moved her body around. She couldn't move her body at all. And there she was split between the two worlds, simultaneously existing in both, slipping from one to the other like water, like the river draining in and back on itself, and she couldn't completely divorce what was being done to her from what her mind wanted to hold on to, but she couldn't hold on to anything. As if all of the world had become an impossible slippery air.

The next day, she had awful cramps, and then the blood, the fetus, all of it washed out of her. They all knew. The girls brought in towels and soaked up the blood and wrung the towels in the shower. Dr. Syeth told them to throw them in the river or burn them. "You should've told me you were pregnant," he said, wiping the sweat from his face. Her fault, all her fault—anything that happened to them, the responsibility was always with the girl. And they changed her sheets and left her alone for a while, left her with that emptiness.

"Pull yourself together," Cawood had whispered to her one day. The girls made visits to check on her, and Cawood sat on the bed and hummed whatever Jinx was playing downstairs. She kept picking at her nails, a stubborn yellow polish that wouldn't come off. "We've all got our losses just like you," she said. She smelled like lemons, like she had been cutting lemons. "I'm sorry, honey. But don't let this damn place and that damn woman pull you apart. That's what she wants."

It was Naomi who came the most. She had worked at the St. Charles for five years, and in the hierarchy, only Ms. Gerald was over her. Cawood was third in line.

She sat on the bed, smelling of lavender from Ms. Gerald's office, and looked through Jennifer's stationery box. She looked over Mazy's drawings, and read from the book of poems, the letters Jennifer's mother had written, looked at the flicker-photographs.

"I like this one of the Chicago River," she told Jennifer. "I'm from a town near Chicago. Braidwood. We used to drive there when the city was open. Our favorite thing to do was follow the river block by block." But she gave the readings in the wrong voice, the wrong pitch, not her mother's voice, not how Jennifer had imagined the poet with her name, the other Naomi, Naomi Shihab Nye.

Eventually she discovered Jennifer's money that Teal Dennis hadn't and took it. Jennifer had closed her eyes half in and out, but she saw what Naomi had done.

Ms. Gerald came in after a week. "Your baby is dead. You have to start working." She stood in the doorway, but Jennifer never answered, and when she woke up, Ms. Gerald had gone.

The baby was gone. Jennifer wondered, if she had given in, had done what Ms. Gerald had wanted that first day, would the baby still be alive? There was no baby. It was her fault. She had betrayed Mathew. That's how she saw it. And she had betrayed herself.

The thing that healed her the most was the music, not at night, the fast riffs, but during the day, Professor Jinx slowly building his chords, repeating them, getting his hands and keys in synch like he wanted. She could feel her body rebuilding and wanted to step out of bed to that music she had known in the desert—Billie Holiday, Ella, Peggy Lee—step toward that music, its sound rooted in her own breathing, and when Cawood hummed, the humming became flashes of—

Oh, sweet, sweet baby down on your knees,
Oh, sweet, sweet baby where you going to now?
Black like me, black like me, what will I do?
I'm so black, you're so blind to me.

"Don't stop singing," Jennifer said to her once.

"Oh, I don't sing," she promised. "My voice wasn't made for that. Just helps me pass the time, but thank you."

Sometimes Jennifer would get up and look out at the river, watching it drift and drift, holding her hands to her stomach, that hollow core of herself. She couldn't undo it.

Jennifer hadn't written a letter to her mother since arriving in Cairo and still couldn't write one. The baby was gone. She should jump, end herself, but somehow, she couldn't, not with that girl down there. Reseda. She kept seeing that girl down there. But what could she tell Mat or her mama now?

"You tell your mother, Here I am. Alive. And I'm okay. And I know you're going to say you're not okay, but you are. You're alive, you have to stay alive, honey. That's all you got. All anyone here has." That's what Naomi said. But Naomi had taken Jennifer's money, stolen a piece of her freedom for herself—her words couldn't be trusted.

Now, standing by the window, Jennifer could smell the wet wood and mildew of the room—it rained here so much. And she needed to go down.

Jennifer had hoped to get to Chicago, have her baby. She would've raised it with her mother until Mat came. She would've made him leave the desert. But she knew that was a lie—she couldn't make anyone do what she wanted.

A trick told her once that the St. Charles had slipped between worlds. "Kansas City, St. Louis are protected, civilized. All the city-states," he said, "most zones in Kansas City are protected. Everything between those two cities, everything around the St. Charles is a vast frontier. You must feel unsafe, don't you?" he asked her. "The frontier could easily swallow you up."

She had never answered him.

There was a scratch on the door—one of the girls. The girls scratched at the door like her mama's cat, Pearl.

"I'm going down," came Cawood's voice. "I know you're inside. Come down with me, Jen."

Jennifer looked out at the maple turning red, then at the river, the wash of trees just beyond, cypress and willow trees reaching over the river still green, the sway, the turn of green in the current, green turning black in the fading sun. The sway seemed to drink from that river water, seemed to cradle the river in that late sun. She wanted to hold and twist those branches with her hand and felt another spark. How to place it, she didn't know. How to use it for something that would keep her alive.

The first thing she noticed coming down the stairs was the sound, how it quickly magnified. She'd have a good foot on the stairs from the fifth floor, when there'd be that slight tremble at her toes, and the further down she walked, the tremble spread up her calf, around her hips, the full length of her shoulders, radiating down her arms.

"Feel that?" Cawood said. Cawood was already swaying in her dress, a raspberry silk wrapped close to her body, especially the small rolls on her stomach. "Hot love rolls," she called them, though she had gotten into a few arguments with Ms. Gerald about her shape, and its multi-faceted contours.

"I'm in fine shape. You see any man doesn't want to hold on to me? Dance with me? I bring the most money to this house." It was true, and always that talk about money quieted Ms. Gerald down.

"You just need to be careful," Ms. Gerald said, expanding her fingers outward, "with your figure."

"This figure?" Cawood straightened up tall and wide in her bones, locking her hips. "Nothing wrong with this figure." It was Cawood who could talk loud and get away with it. Only Cawood. In a month, she would be a free woman. "Not a girl," Cawood noted. "Woman." Like Jinx would say.

Jennifer was wearing a silver dress as tight as Cawood's, so that moving in it made her feel mummified. It was a dress that had been picked out for her, sequined, a size smaller than she needed. Some nights, most nights, the girls got to choose their clothes unless everyone came down wearing similar things.

"Black, too much black in this room," Ms. Gerald would announce and make them go upstairs, change. "We offer variety." The St. Charles offered every shade of girl from pearl to latte to ebony, short, tall, and big-boned, every pitch of voice, every shade of color in their clothes and their polish—that was Ms. Gerald's promise to her clients.

A couple of outfits got circulated depending on size. One was a cheerleading outfit with a bright yellow W branded across the blue front. A vendor out of Chicago brought in racks of dresses and tops and lingerie and pants for Ms. Gerald and the girls to pick through each month, and that's where the cheerleading outfit had been found. There had actually been five or six to choose from with different letters, mascots, and one with a megaphone over the heart, the fabric pressed inside a plastic casing.

"Couldn't she have picked the megaphone?" Cawood

asked a few weeks after the cheerleading outfit had been circulated through the house. "We all know what we are, whores, but damn, sometimes I just want to snatch that W off the front."

"That'll get you baptized," Jennifer said.

Cawood shook her head. "I've been through that. Burned my throat up. I've been beaten by that woman." When she said the last thing, she didn't smile, she looked angry. A lot of the girls looked skittish.

After Ms. Gerald had told them to go back upstairs and change out of all that drab black, one girl, Odette, returned in black pants, the same ones she had worn, with silver buttons down the sides. Ms. Gerald picked up a glass tumbler from the bar and came up behind Odette and hit her between the shoulders.

"Are you deaf? What're you doing?" Ms. Gerald struck her again, but the glass was too thick to break. Odette was tiny, tinier than Lisa, and Ms. Gerald knocked Odette to the ground. For a slight woman, Ms. Gerald generated a lot of power.

Odette had yelled, "Stop, God, stop," crying, and hurried out of the parlor with her body halfway upright like an ostrich. Ms. Gerald put the glass down, stared at the deep red ring the lip had formed in her palm. If the glass had broken, it would've done so into her. She shook her hand, walked off. No one looked surprised at what had happened. It was just an interruption, a pause before the clients flew in, and they went on doing what they were doing before.

"Shouldn't have worn black," someone admonished.

"I'm not wearing it for the rest of the week," someone else said, and a few girls giggled. Jinx started in slowly on a new song, and that's when the interruption, its last imprint disappeared completely, the world had circled back into its musical place again.

No one liked wearing the cheerleading outfit or the cowgirl outfit with its heavy leather chaps except for Lisa, though she had never been a cheerleader or a cowgirl. "It's just something different," she explained. Always at the St. Charles you had to explain yourself. An unclarified motive made you suspicious.

Tonight, however, was a dress night because a firm from Nashville had requested "ballroom girls," as Ms. Gerald put it.

As they walked down the stairs, Cawood was already lilting to Jinx's piano. Someone was playing a saxophone. Probably Dane Red. Everyone called him Dang Red when he got deep into a solo—"Dang Red, Dang," the tricks and girls would holler, "you've got something," and stomp. He'd go and go until his cheeks fired red and breathless, and he could go no more. He played the sax, and his younger brother, Benji Red, played drums. Benji always showed up after his floor shift at Instant Casino. Then he and his brother and Jinx would go until two, three in the morning.

"Come on, Jennifer, you got to feel it a little bit," Cawood said.

She did feel it, just not in the way Cawood did. The music tried to soothe, but something inside her ultimately wouldn't accept it, and though the music filled her, she had shut the music out. Whether it was Jinx's music, or some man she didn't want holding her holding her, or Ms. Gerald's commandments—all of these things filled her now and left her empty of herself.

At the bottom, with the trembling changed to shaking, the floor shaking strong, people dancing just on the other side, Cawood set her body in front of the exit.

"All the way down this stair and you haven't talked to me. Not once." Cawood asked questions this way— assertions to be denied or confirmed, then apologized for.

"Still that baby. Going to have to let go of that baby." Cawood nodded. She took Jennifer's chin and made her nod, too.

And that touch . . . how was it, Jennifer wondered, the

touch of someone's hand to your face could almost make you cry? This was something she couldn't shut out.

"Three months you've been carrying this burden, and I ain't saying you haven't done your work, but you're starting to depress me."

"It's not just the baby."

"I don't want to know—we've had this talk before. Whatever it is, I don't want to know about your family, who you loved before you got here, and neither does anyone else, none of these tricks. You've got to forget that world or you won't make it. Ms. Gerald's watching you. I've seen her. She'll put you down on those bottom floors. And those girls, you don't want to be one of those girls." She held Jennifer's chin straight with her own. "Now, you've got to do something that seems impossible, and I know, 'cause when I had to leave Atlanta, I felt the same way. You have to embrace this world, this small little speck, the St. Charles in Cairo, Illinois. If you're like me, whatever there was in Atlanta, whatever there was in Alabama for you, ain't there now. And this, too, the St. Charles, it'll be a speck to brush off your skin one day, just flick it off like it was never a part of you. As soon as you leave. I'm leaving in one month. But you've got to make it to the end. I'm not going to be around. I'm almost a free woman."

Jennifer took her hand and pressed it against Cawood's cheek, her hand so cool against Cawood's warm face. She took the back of her hand and pressed it as well, pressed out the coolness, front to back, and Cawood let go of Jennifer and let her arms fall by her sides.

"Now you got me thinking. My younger sister, two years younger, she did this to me at night when we had the same room. She could never keep her hands warm, even in the dead of summer, and she'd roll her hand, one then the other, on the side of my face, like my skin was biscuits for patting, and tell me, 'You so warm, Caw'—she called me Caw—'and I'm so cool. We even each other out.' She'd do that, and I'd let her until she fell asleep. All night I felt her hand on my face, even in my dreams. We were just girls." Cawood closed her eyes and nodded. Then she opened her eyes, those circles of white, the dark center, her black skin.

"I ain't going to keep having this talk with you, Jenny. I'm tired of having this talk with you."

"But you're so warm, Caw," Jennifer teased. Then "All right" when Cawood smiled.

"All right," Cawood said. She opened the door and Jinx's music poured into the stairway.

A trick walked up, took Cawood's hand like they had known each other forever, good friends, and Cawood said, "Where you been so long?" "Waiting on you," he answered so sweet.

Jennifer navigated into the noise before someone approached her. "Floating" was what the girls called it—she floated through the talking, switching bodies, long drinks in hand, the east doors open and screened, the first night of this, because it was cool, had cooled now, autumn as promised, autumn she never knew in the desert was definitely here. Some girls were already dancing in a huddle, the "St. Charles football huddle" they called it, with arms spread over shoulders, feet kicking to the center. The tricks broke in, peeled them out one by one onto the tiled floor, black and white squares that spread from the east end to the kitchen that shuttered the west end, the bar against the north, everyone talking, laughing. To her it was like being submerged in water, these conversations, the smoke, Professor Jinx, all of it just as heavy as water.

During the days, the girls went down to the river to swim—the Ohio because it wasn't as muddy as the Mississippi. If a barge came along, they waved and called to it until the barge operator honked back, Jennifer's stomach felt wet and cold, washed by the small tide of the boat's wake, the river for the moment like the ocean. And she'd dive in, swim hard to reach the bottom like she did at seven, twelve, and older—she used to race Mathew to the bottom to grab a handful of mud and bring it to the surface.

She went down and down until that river became as dark and muddy as the others she'd known—the Pearl, the Tensaw, the Coosa—before she rose to the surface, blowing the air out of her lungs like a whale. And waited, waited for Mathew to come up beside her.

But the Ohio just slipped past, barely rippling, moving quietly on to join the Mississippi. The barge had already gone by. Sometimes the other girls caught her looking for Mathew, and they stared at her like she was crazy—*What're you looking for? What crazy thing are you doing now?* They were all unnerved by how quiet she was, and no one would talk to her except Cawood and Jinx.

But the air in the parlor was thicker than the Ohio, harder to breathe. She stepped across the tiles, focusing on shoulders and belts and shoes, letting them blur together, and didn't look at the johns' faces. *Don't look above the neck or they'll approach.* Some girls did, tried to figure out the nicest or richest, the easiest johns to deal with, and tried to avoid the regulars who liked to bruise. Ms. Gerald said a little bruising was acceptable, but made those clients pay extra and sign an agreement for collection of property damage. "A binding agreement," Ms. Gerald explained to Jennifer that first day, "is still honored by city-state and federal law." The girls called it the "whore prenup."

"Which means," Lisa said, putting out a cigarette, "if you have the money, you can do whatever you want to your whore."

Jennifer slipped around the huddled girls still kicking their feet, to Professor Jinx playing quick, his cracking voice like Mat's father's records:

You got nerve, and you got gall,
Looking at my woman as she's scooting down the hall.
Yes, you got nerve, and you got gall.

But, mister, if you don't move your eye,
I'm going slit your throat, leave you to die,
And my woman, I promise, my woman won't even cry.

That voice of his was dry and sweet, like burning the driest wood and watching it turn and pop, blue and orange. Jinx was a small man, lanky, his brown fingers too big for him, shooting out the cuffs of his white shirt—always a white shirt—with fat knuckles and thick wrist joints, all those strong bones pegged into the back of his hands.

She didn't want to disturb him, but she stood by the piano anyway and waited for his solo to end. He had stopped singing, was counting off the notes *tet, tat*, that thing he did where he scatted with the keys up and up the scale, while Dang Red waited, plopped on a chair, one leg hooked back, ready to anchor him into a solo.

Dang Red was young, but so overweight he had to sit on a box or a chair every time he sat in, and the sweat on his arms and large face bathed his pale skin in a milky whiteness; he always wore what Jinx called a porkpie hat and his lips and nose were as squat as the hat, as if he had been squished in the front, smushed down from the top of his head and along those square cheeks, all of him into a square porcelain box. With one hit, he'd crack right open.

He clicked his fingers on the reed until Jinx eased up and swept his hands over the keyboard, graceful, slow, letting the piano catch its breath, and in the applause, Dang Red hooked his leg and sharpened out his first note. He was so crouched and pigeoned, his head under that straw hat so low, that Jennifer was afraid the sax would bump the floor and shatter. It was the way Dang Red held things and moved—everything about him fragile.

"Good to see you," Jinx said, his voice still dry, always in need of water. He nodded.

She nodded back. "You sound good tonight, Jinx."

"Every night."

"Of course, every night." And that's how it started, how he pulled her into his joking and teasing like she used to do with Terry, something familiar she needed.

"What do you want to hear? Anything?"

"I didn't know you were already taking requests."

"I just started. What you want?"

"How about 'Miss Otis' or 'Cotton Field'?"

He shook his head. "Not upbeat enough. You're just trying to bring us all down. The people won't have it, not this evening."

"I heard you playing Nat King Cole earlier."

"There you go." He smiled. " 'Straighten Up and Fly Right.' Want to hear it again? Now that Red's here, I can do it even better." But Jinx's hands slipped at the keys; he fell forward, tried to catch himself, and did, pulling himself up on the bench, rolling his shoulders and setting the tempo back.

Dang Red had kept his eyes closed this far, but when Jinx slipped he peered over to see what was happening.

Jinx waved Dang on with his big left hand. "I've got it," he called, and Dang closed his eyes, turned to the small crowd of dancers.

"I'm sorry," Jennifer said.

"Don't be. I shouldn't let you distract me. It's my own doing, not yours." Everything for Jinx was about perfection, no matter how easy he talked about playing hot, fast, and loose. There was nothing he hated worse than a loss of concentration. And when he got tired, his hands started to slip, couldn't feel the keys right. She'd seen him at those moments pick up a cup of tea and drink, grabbing the cup all along its sides. Those strong hands shook that tea like an old engine.

Jennifer had told him to rest more often, but Jinx wouldn't give up his all day rehearsing.

"This piano gets too lonely without my touch," he had

said, and this wasn't the only piano he kept company. He worked all the local casinos, had his own club in St. Louis— The Roll 'Em Pete—and he was married, though he seldom talked about his wife.

Jinx came to the St. Charles for a few days at a time, sometimes he stayed a whole week. Ms. Gerald kept a room open for him. Then he was gone, leaving everyone with a silence that made them less hungry for breakfast, less eager to get out of bed or wanting to do a single thing.

"As I see it," he told her often, "I don't have a choice in the matter. I've got to play." He kept wet, cool towels beside him on the bench to rest his hands on, and sometimes he'd ask Jennifer to get him a new towel wrung in water and crushed ice. The coldness kept his hands numb and going.

She was staring at his hands now, sweat dappled along the sleeves of his shirt. "What's your age again, Jinx?"

"You should never ask a young man his age. Why you doing that? You think 'cause I'm slipping on this piano I'm old? I'm fifty-six. My father didn't pass until he was ninety-one." He slipped a second time; just his left fingering.

"I'm causing you problems," she said.

Jinx waved to Dang Red. "I got it," he called out. "Keep going," another sweep of his hand cutting the light, those swollen knuckles crossed in hard skin.

"I wish you could stay." Jinx cleared his throat and looked up. She looked back, waiting, not ready to leave. She hoped he'd reconsider and tell her *I want you to stay*. But he wouldn't. Sometimes when she came over, he didn't say a word, just kept his focus on the piano. He had grumbled to her before that she was bothering him and to stop it. Once in a blue temper, he abruptly said, "I can't talk with you now."

The glass doors, on the east wall had been opened and the wind carried through the whole parlor, autumn as promised. There were two guards, one on either end of the wide sweep of doors, but not carrying rifles—rifles weren't allowed on the floor at night, so mostly the guards kept their arms crossed and stood like potted trees, watching, watching.

"Okay, I'm going," she said. "But when I come back tell me more about your father and play 'Miss Otis Regrets.'"

"We'll talk about him, I promise." Jinx liked talking about his father. "But 'Miss Otis' will have to wait until tomorrow. Just come down."

She would do that—come down and sit with him—and should've done it earlier instead of staying by that window, but she just didn't think of it. She forgot to do these things that were good for her. Like eating, she didn't do much of that either. Instead she thought about the girl who jumped from the fifth floor and didn't quite die; instead she thought about her baby, her missing baby. Talking with Jinx was like a thin piece of paper catching fire while they talked and joked, until he had had enough of talking. Later as she tried to remember it, grab it, the paper was ash, gone.

On the way to the balcony a client lifted her arm and the silver sequins pulled even tighter across her stomach. Jennifer almost shook free, but there'd be repercussions; she looked around for Ms. Gerald and couldn't find her, but it didn't matter. Jennifer readjusted herself in the dress, let him tow her onto the dance floor. He was smiling, beaming. "Hey, how you doing? How's it going? You married?" He popped his curly head back, laughing like of course she wasn't married, couldn't be. But Jennifer was. She jerked away from him without thinking, those words—she had been stabbed. There wasn't a wedding band any longer. Ms. Gerald had taken it. And she rubbed her thumb between her fingers.

"Yeah, that's my husband over there." She pointed to Jinx.

The man's smile soured. He looked over at Jinx, nervous, then back at her, this trick. He smiled again, disbelieving, "That old man?"

"He's not so old," she assured him. "And he's got strong hands."

His smile soured even more. "What's wrong, baby? Rather be with him than me? What you think you doing?" He was insulted and there'd be repercussions. So she stepped close, pretended to swoon into his arm so he could catch her, and when he did, she took his hand, righted herself, and whispered, "It's okay, baby," smiling. "Nothing's wrong." Waited, waited for him to smile back, and he did.

Underneath, she could feel that rumble-beat starting, everyone stomping on the floor. The trick looked past her, and she turned to look, too, everyone saying "Dang Red, Dang," yelling it and stomping. "You've got something." They raised their arms and clapped.

He had come off the chair, raising the bell of his sax, setting it out, his porcelain cheeks all fired red, and that porkpie hat tilted up all the way, about to fall off his square head. And she stood there lost to it.

"Dang Red, Dang." Everyone stomped around her, their noise rising, rising until she was in the river diving down, the thickness of the air, the music blurred, smoke like water. Jennifer closed her eyes, watched her hand stretch down, bend through the water to the mud, grab it and turn, race to the top. She held her breath and kept it, waited until she reached the surface to blow out that air like a whale surfacing, and looked to her other side for Mathew, waited for him to come up from below, to rise out of those dresses and suits and lights, the long wail coming from Dang Red.

Dust and sand cut at her skin. *Watch that sky*, Jennifer told herself, *watch it*, looking for stars as if by doing that, by focusing on the sky, she could push the sand away, the wind away, make it not exist anymore.

Then she heard the sputter and fizzle of the machine.

Jennifer turned from the sky as hands reached down and crossed to her shoulders, her head, hips, and feet, lifting her.

"Wait," she said. "Wait." But they had gathered all the corners of her body up like a flag, lifted her, and dropped her into the steel mouth of the machine.

At the bottom she started to roll, whooshing, tumbling in plastic against the oiled tines until the sound dulled. The plastic slipped over her skin, over her mouth, tightening, some huge spider cottoning her in a web. When she screamed, all of her breath pressed back into her, and her lungs tightened and burned. She tried to rise up, but her body was angled wrong, she couldn't get to her arms, her elbows, couldn't bend or scream.

Then the tines stopped and lifted her body, spit her out of the steel mouth. She lay there on the ground, looking through the plastic sheets crisscrossing her eyes, trying again to find the night stars. The heat in her was going cold, her body sinking in on itself until the plastic and the Birmingham sky tore away, and in that sudden violence, her breath returned, she woke up.

"Hey." Someone grabbed her arm. It was too black to see except the blue flow of light by the window.

"Go back to sleep," he said, a deeper voice than the way she remembered it, crackling, groggy. Or was it a second trick, a third. This one had wanted a sleepover. That's what the girls called a trick who paid to spend the night; they always were the neediest ones.

She kept rubbing the sweat off her arms and stomach, rubbing and crossing herself, but it didn't make her warm, sitting up in bed. She recognized her bed.

"Just go back to sleep."

It was colder, even at lunchtime now, and fewer girls wanted to go out to the river—only those stir-crazy insomniacs or those who wanted to swim, who liked standing in fish-green water or sitting at its edge. Crazy. Some girls slept until two. Jinx did.

But the St. Charles was just off the Ohio River bank. It was their only excursion off the hotel grounds, and the only exercise they got other than fence walking all six paved acres of the hotel, the generator house, and the parking lot.

"Just like prison," Lisa said, looking back at the security guard in tow, Douglas. If attacked by roaming gangs, Douglas, in theory, would have to stop them. Maybe not stop them, but at least hold the gang off and radio for help. The gun tower stood on the other end of the St. Charles, facing the city, useless. Some guards had pulled up chairs on the third-floor balcony to monitor and eat lunch. But the levee blocked the view of the river from the third floor except halfway to the Kentucky side. The guards never saw the girls on the Illinois bank, could only hear echoes of their splashing and what sounded like mumbling. If you wanted to see the entire river from the balcony, you had to wait for a flood. And if the river flooded, they wouldn't be going to it: eight girls, marching single file with one guard in tow, still rubbing sleep out of his eyes.

Jennifer wondered for a long time why Ms. Gerald didn't send a full security detail. Two guards trudged along on some outings, but they were never happy about going, and never more than two.

"It's because nothing ever happens," Cawood had told her. "In all my walks to the river, not one gang has attacked. Only one girl ever swam the distance to a barge, and she came floating back the next day dead. Lesson learned. For everybody." But that, Jennifer knew, had happened on the Mississippi. They never went to the Mississippi side of Cairo now.

Lisa pinched her thin cigarette and curled her other fingers around, inhaled. It was such an elaborate, awkward way to smoke and not much wind blowing, not much reason to hold it that way. But it was her habit, and she managed never to burn her hands. She flicked the cigarette. "I was in prison in Fulton County for three months. Guards watching everything I did. This is exactly what it's like."

"I bet the food's better here," Bethany, another girl, said. She had stringy red bangs she kept in a headband, her arms, legs, and face dotted with freckles. No matter how little or how long she stayed outside, no matter how well she covered herself, her pale skin always blistered, and she returned to the St. Charles with red patches like the sun had scrubbed her hard with soap. But Bethany had grown up on the Missouri River and liked to be in the water. As she walked, her silver bracelets clattered like dull bells.

"Yeah, what was that last night. Lamb?"

"Good, huh?"

"Yeah, it was. Never had that. Going to have to say something good to the new chef."

"He's cute."

"Cute," some of the other girls agreed. "What's his name?"

"Don't start in with that kind of talk," Cawood said and came to a stop. She stretched like she couldn't get her body to shift like she wanted, like she hadn't woken up right.

"Keep moving, mother duck." Someone clapped. Cawood was in front and no one could budge around her. She was always in front and had a key to the gate. Like Naomi, she had keys to everywhere in the St. Charles.

Lisa said, "You can get your body in order at the river."

"Please. It ain't like the river's going to disappear if we don't hurry and get there. And my point about the cute chef is this: if a man ain't paying, don't bother with him. I don't want any fighting in the house, especially over a man. We got enough tricks to deal with at night."

Some girls nodded and some asked Bethany to tell a little more about the chef, but she whispered to them, "See me later," and rolled her eyes at Cawood, who rolled her eyes right back.

They passed under the levee through a cutoff valve that was shut during floods, through the thick reeds, a pathway they had trampled, and then down the steep, sandy bank.

Some girls ran, flying past Cawood to the water like kites falling, shouting. Some girls got undressed; some had walked out in housedresses and took only their panties off; one girl had tried to sneak out in her red satin ballroom dress, but Cawood said, "No, too expensive"; and some had bathing suits on underneath, the bright fabrics gleaming at the sun. Everyone flattened towels to the bank, anchoring the corners with shoes and bracelets.

Jennifer kept her towel over her shoulder and sat on a strip of sand and mud and watched the other girls arc into the river, splashing one another like they were kids still, like that was something you would never lose about yourself if you could just find the right watering hole.

"Aren't you going in?" Douglas said. She could barely hear him. It was as if all the resonance had been pulled out of his voice a long time ago and left him with a hollow pitch.

"In a minute," she said. She didn't want to be reminded of his presence, the rifle and all the equipment on his hips and vest—he had a bullet-proof vest. Instead of feeling safe, she felt betrayed, remembering all those guards in Birmingham leaving on mille-copters, leaving them behind. And she didn't want him imposing on the openness of the beach and the river, where one surface overtook the other, the bodies vanishing in water.

She tried to focus on the bodies, but he kept swaying back and forth, his shadow drifting on the sand in front of her, so she stood up and walked to the edge.

"Take off your clothes and come in," Cawood yelled.

"Take it all off," the girls hooted, echoing the cries in the parlor.

Jennifer twisted her hair behind her ears and crossed her arms. She had on jeans and a shirt she had thrown on for breakfast, and she didn't plan on taking anything off.

"What you trying to hide?" Cawood splashed water at her, but Jennifer was too close to the shore. "Remember our talk? Remember what I said to you?"

"I'm leaving my clothes on," Lisa said from where she was standing waist-deep in the river.

"Well, of course you are. You're *Lisa*," Cawood emphasized the *Lisa*. "And Lisa doesn't take off her clothes."

"Unless she gets paid," Bethany said, and everyone laughed.

"A lot. You got to pay that girl a lot to get those clothes off," Cawood said.

"It's worth it," Lisa fired back, and sent a flare of water at Cawood. "Just leave me alone. I don't care if we're both from Atlanta."

"What difference does that make? Like we should be friends because we're from the same city. And I was never in prison in Atlanta."

"Leave her alone, Cawood," another girl said, and another one: "We have to take our clothes off enough as it is."

"But not like this." Cawood pulled her shirt up and tossed it, tossed her arms and hands up to the sky. "Just us and the sun and the river and no one else." She laughed, but her laughing died back quick, the wind sweeping across, picking up the coolness from the surface. She pushed out in the water to grab her shirt before it sank or slipped away, and kept out in the deeper channel.

A barge was coming from the bluffs at the highest point of the city, way up east, already honking to let them know he was coming. Some of the girls waved, but he was too far away to notice, not much more than a speck, and they had to be the tiniest specks to him.

Jennifer stepped into the water—it was too cold, and she

had to press into the mud to keep her feet from cramping. But as Cawood swam into the deeper channel, Jennifer stepped further away from the shore, letting the water soak up to her waist, the cold dissipating. She turned from the barge, looked at the river where it hooked toward the Mississippi.

One time she swam the Alabama River bank to bank, but the Ohio was much wider—and if she started out for the middle, Douglas would have what her mama called a "hissy-fit." He couldn't use the rifle because she was property. No way he could come after her, not with all the stuff he was lugging. She thought about that, swimming out there, no one but the sun and the river, like Cawood said, taking long backstrokes, and holding her breath, releasing it, and looking up at the guards on the third-floor balcony eating their lunch.

"She's calling you," Lisa said. "Ms. Gerald's girl Naomi. Hear me? She's calling for you. Wake up."

It was the *Wake up* that got Jennifer's attention. Then she heard the other—Naomi repeating Jennifer's name. She was trying to descend the bank gracefully, but there was no coming down that slope gracefully.

"She's calling you." Lisa drew her lips in tight, all the anxiousness in her voice and long cheeks ready to burst, and Jennifer wanted to say, *Relax. She's calling me, not you.* But instead she smiled, lay back, let her hair catch and pull into the water. She looked straight into the sun.

Since leaving the desert, she could see the sun, its blurred white mass like a nickel at times, like a melting quarter, though she had always been told not to look directly or it would burn holes in your eyes. So be it. In the desert they said the warning as a joke because the sun was never without its curtain of ozone. Look straight into the sun if you can find it hovering.

But here the sun warmed her face, and she could

breathe without coughing. She looked straight into the white center. "Burn," she whispered. It could burn straight through her for all she cared.

"Ms. Gerald needs to see you. Come on." It was Naomi. She had finally made it to the river and was trying to keep her shoes from slipping into the brackish water. Douglas moved up behind Naomi.

"Come on in," Jennifer said to her. "Take it all off." She liked parroting Cawood's lines. When Cawood pointed those words at Jennifer, she felt a tickle but didn't laugh. Cawood's scoldings and motherings and insistences caught her off guard, so she hesitated, not quite sure what to do with them. The words had to sit for a while. Then later, she repeated the lines as a way of saying, *That was a good one, Cawood; don't worry about me, I was listening, I'm still here.*

Jennifer heard Cawood chuckling in the back, her way of saying, *Glad you did, I hear you.* A lapse of time existed between what each of them said directly or not—they talked around each other all day and still there were these moments of connection like sisters, friends since forever, one listening out for the other.

Naomi stood there with hands on hips, balancing, afraid of the water, like it was some deadly pit of lava. She had on a linen suit that Jennifer liked, similar to the tan one Ms. Gerald wore. Maybe it had been Ms. Gerald's once, and she'd given it to Naomi. Naomi who had stolen Jennifer's money, who had read her mama's letters and the poems in a scratchy, thin voice, the wrong voice. Her lips full of red lipstick; her tiny body. Naomi with her hair in bobby pins and wiry strands of gray in her straight black hair, wiry wrinkles burned into her face. Naomi was afraid of those wrinkles just like Jennifer's mama had been and hoped everyone would notice her lips instead.

"You don't have to be so damn afraid," Jennifer told her. "You're like my mama. I feel sorry for you."

Naomi turned at Jennifer like Lisa had done, making the coat buckle at her waist, like Jennifer was crazy, that crazy desert girl. Why you asking me to come in that river? I'm not coming in there. Telling me not to be scared. You feel sorry for me?

"Ms. Gerald needs to see you," Naomi repeated.

"What about?" Cawood asked. "What you want with her?"

Naomi cupped her hand over her eyes and stared at Cawood's head above the brown water.

"It's nothing to do with you."

"I'm asking for her."

"Cawood, it has nothing to do with you," she snapped. Cawood sluiced a gusher of water at Naomi that didn't reach, and then Cawood turned the other way to face the Kentucky side.

Jennifer stepped out, but she didn't pick up the towel she had brought. Instead she just stood there, dripping onto the sand. Naomi had already started back to the St. Charles, her body angling up the bank in that linen suit.

"Now tell me, what does she want?" It took Jennifer a while to catch up with Naomi, but she did at the hotel entrance and grabbed her shoulder.

Naomi pulled away. "You were rude to me down there. Why?"

"You took my money," Jennifer said. "I know Ms. Gerald could've found it and taken it, but she does that to everyone. Why did you take the money?" For months, Jennifer had wanted to bring this up, but the two of them had kept their distance after that week when Naomi helped Jennifer recover. Naomi was Ms. Gerald's girl, like Lisa said, and Jennifer had felt there was no point in asking. But Naomi wanted something from her now, and Jennifer decided she wanted something, too.

"It's not your money," Naomi said. "Belongs to the house."

"You're not the house, Ms. Gerald is."

"How do you know I didn't give it to her?"

"Did you?"

Naomi wouldn't look at Jennifer straight on and shook her head, shook it to mean no or shook it to mean I'm not telling. Either way she was done talking and went into the hotel lobby, up to the parlor.

Jennifer looked at Jinx's piano all empty by the glass doors, saw the guards outside still eating their lunch, leaning back in their chairs, and she wondered how close it was until two when Jinx would appear, one of those rare moments you'd see him walking, long through the legs like a curved rail, and cranky, ready to play. They went up one more flight of stairs into the office, and Naomi shut the door behind them.

The room hadn't changed since that first meeting, the big planters of lavender, the navy Union uniform pressed in the glass case, except the glass was dustier, the sunlight striking it, the designs in the pistol handle. There was a guard by the door and Naomi went over to him. Ms. Gerald was sitting on top of her desk, a contract and a small case beside her holding a wax impression of someone's teeth. It was as if that first meeting, that first day, had reset itself into motion, only this time, Jennifer knew what would happen.

She heard a noise, someone breathing hard, sitting in the chair Jennifer had sat in, should be sitting in now. An elbow came into focus, the sleeve of a pale blue dress worn, a few tears, but not dirty, clean enough for visiting an aunt and cousins in Hooper City.

"Mazy," she said. It was Mazy, but her hair had been razored off, and there was a cut across her cheek, that knobbed cheek she carried swollen and red now where the scab had been pulled. But it was her, and Jennifer reached for her.

Mazy looked up, turned her eyes down.

"Where've you been? What happened to you?" She grabbed the girl, and for the second time since she had known Mazy, all of the girl's weight—there was so little of it—gave way easily in her hands. She didn't answer, didn't put her arms around Jennifer. Instead she brought them to the center of her body and shouted and pushed with all her strength, pushed Jennifer back.

She was shaking and crossed her arms.

"It's *me*, Mazy."

Mazy shook her head, kept shaking it.

"I was hoping you knew her," Ms. Gerald said. "She was sold to one of my regular clients in St. Louis by the same *guia* who sold you to me. Who is she? Mazy. Tell me about her. I just bought her."

"I knew Mazy in Birmingham," Jennifer said, and started to say her mother was Lavina, started to talk about the city, what had happened, how they had gotten out. But Ms. Gerald didn't want this kind of information. For three months, no one had asked about Birmingham. Everything around the St. Charles was empty, a forgotten land from here to the city-states. A few girls acknowledged, "Oh, it's a mess down there in Alabama," and sometimes a client would ask, Where you from? And Jennifer would say, Birmingham, and they'd echo the sentiment, What a mess, or go on to the next question, the next thing they wanted her to do. She finally stopped replying.

But one trick said—and he worked for the Nashville city-state—that the federal government couldn't maintain the border, the US government was bankrupt. They had already closed checkpoints in Louisiana and Mississippi.

"Pretty soon," he said, "the border will be a map line. That's all."

"What about the people in the Southeastern Desert?" she asked him.

"Still people in that desert?" he asked.

"My husband," she said, and he said, "Huh," just *huh*, like he didn't believe her. "I thought you were from Birmingham."

Then she forgot about that trick and what he'd told her until now.

But Ms. Gerald didn't want to hear about the desert, and Jennifer tried to think of the best way to answer. She looked down, pulled at her jeans, pulled the wet fabric from her skin. Ms. Gerald kept her office cold and the damp denim was making Jennifer shiver.

"How did you find Mazy?" she asked.

"I didn't. The client brought her to me. It was a favor for him since I depend on him for business," Ms. Gerald said. "He was tired of her. She was his servant." Jennifer looked back at the cut on Mazy's face.

"The girl did that to herself. The hair, too. Look at her wrists." But Mazy turned her wrists so Jennifer couldn't see them, no one could. "If she wasn't so beautiful, I would've turned him down."

Ms. Gerald leaned in. "Tell me about Mazy. Her temperament. What do you know? She has a different name than you—she's not your sister or cousin. But they can give you any name on these sheets." She tapped the contract, and picked up the small case, rattled the impression inside, stowed it in her pocket.

"She's a friend," Jennifer said. "I knew her mother. I was supposed to take care of her, but we got separated.

"Mazy," Jennifer whispered, pleaded. She wanted to hold the girl, but Mazy shook her head, inhaled and exhaled quicker and wildly.

"I can't calm her down." Ms. Gerald crossed one ankle behind the other and began to rock slowly. "She's no good to me. And no good to herself if she keeps working at those wrists. I can sell her to one of the shanties, but it'll be a loss. I don't want a loss." Ms. Gerald yawned. She always seemed bored when she talked, as if everything she said had been repeated and repeated, and she no longer had interest in her words, in anyone in the room, even herself. "Will you help me?"

"She's angry with me because we separated. I allowed it," Jennifer said.

"She's not just angry at you. The client told me she destroyed their kitchen in St. Louis. His wife had had enough, so here she is. What I need to know is, was she like this in Birmingham?"

"No," Jennifer said. "Not at all."

"I mean, can you reach her? Get her ready to work? Dr. Syeth's given her a shot, and she'll get drowsy. I'll have her taken up to your room."

"She's fifteen."

Ms. Gerald turned her hands over. "What can I do about her age? Nothing. I've had girls twelve work here. In the shanties, they start them out at ten." She gripped the edge of the desk, swung her legs stronger. "Fifteen is a good age to start. She's not ruined yet."

"Let her do something else. Mazy's been a servant."

"I'll never get my money out of her that way. And she's already used to being fucked. I know the client. You just need to get her ready like Naomi had to get you ready. She's in a brothel. It takes some girls a while to get used to that."

Jennifer stepped toward Mazy, but the cold denim pulled at her skin and Mazy bundled tighter into a ball.

"She'll calm down," Ms. Gerald insisted, and kept rocking her feet slower and slower like the gears of a clock dictating time, its fluctuations and pacing, when it should finally end.

That last day on Snakeskin Road, they lay back on the full stretch of the metal floor of the van, just Jennifer and Mazy and one other girl. The vents were turned wide open, turning hot air over them, that smell from the gas tank and tar; it rained once, and the air got damp, cooler, but they drove through it, and the air thinned out, again, took the sweat from their bodies. At least the air was moving, and it was dark, difficult to see Mazy, so they held one another's hands, taking turns rubbing the inside of their palms, touching, some game they invented, like scooping the fruit out of a melon.

Jennifer was thinking about the next stop, Cairo, Illinois. Chicago was in Illinois, and though she tried to recreate that state map in her mind, the crossing roads and bulleted cities, she couldn't locate Cairo. She knew it wasn't near Chicago, but it was in Illinois; she was moving, getting closer. And when they got there, she wondered how they might escape. The *guias* had kept everyone circled and had threatened to put them in chains after one woman ran off. They found her and beat her, kicked her, and because of her bruises, sold her cheap. No one else had run since.

There were almost as many *guias* as women now. It didn't seem possible to escape. But she kept thinking, they'd step out, and while the *guias* talked about the next marker where the fuel runners had left tanks, she'd grab Mazy and run. But the map just crumbled around her then into brush and groves that rubbed against her legs until they caught fire, the entire landscape she knew nothing of, lost.

When the van did stop, it wasn't a field. They were at the St. Charles, and the *guias* corralled them toward the entrance, told them to go inside to the bathrooms there. It was the first time all trip they had gone in a building, first time they had come to a town.

Though the town appeared broken, empty, the lobby of the hotel did not. A white wainscoting held up the bottom half of the walls, a relief of roses encircled in branches, and the upper half was painted in crimson with a gold gilding of leaves just above the chair railing. The stem of each leaf angled forward and directed you through the lobby further in.

The ceiling was tin, high up, the kind she had discovered ripped and curling onto the floor and countertops in Alabama homes with debris and rafters pressing down on them. But here the ceiling spread out in perfect squares, fans sticking down, slowly turning the cold firmament and the ovate medallions of the chandeliers.

As they walked through, Ms. Gerald watched them, said nothing. Then on their way to the van, Teal Dennis told Jennifer he needed to speak to her. "Hold up a second," he said, pulling her aside, and Mazy paused, but one of the other *guias* pushed on Mazy's back and said, "Let's go." She was trying to get a look at Jennifer, and fell forward, caught herself, looked back. The guard pushed on her, pushed until she moved, and it was at that moment—there was too much space between them. They had managed to stay close until now, and Jennifer started walking toward her, but Teal Dennis said, "Hold up, I need to talk to you, that's all. Just hold up." He wrenched her arm, wouldn't let go.

The sun glared through the open door and there was nothing but the black shapes of the women and *guias* and then just the white of the sun, the door swinging shut, the St. Charles security guards coming over.

Teal Dennis turned, walked out of the lobby where Mazy had gone, and Jennifer started after him, screaming, but the guards stopped her and took her to Ms. Gerald's office.

"I have to get back to the van," she said, catching her breath, her wrists sore, burning.

Ms. Gerald just looked at her and began to swing her legs.

Jennifer watched Mazy sleep where the guards had set her on the brown covers, and remembered the van, how the metal got on the back of your arms and clothes and the tar coming up in the vents, and Mazy getting pushed in the lobby, all that space between them impossible to gather.

She looked out her window, but the girls had come in already, the Ohio River slowly working its way south, the sun pulled off its axis somewhere going west. So Jennifer went over to Mazy, rubbed her hair, where the long strands used to unfurl, where she used to comb out strips for braiding, the scalp over the hard bone. Then Jennifer lifted the hand to her face, took her other hand and pressed both into her chin and mouth and breathed dirt, salt, citrus—orange or lemons, a bitterness to Mazy's skin, so familiar, but she couldn't find comfort. The tears plashed on the worn dress, on Mazy's face, and Jennifer rubbed them off, rubbed them back into the line of hair.

"Tears will do no good," she whispered, something her mama often said, adding, "The desert won't hold them."

That's when she noticed the girl's wrist, the left one, turned, marked in cuts back and across, the blood sticky, and she went to the dresser, pulled out a shirt, bit it, an old shirt tasting of cedar, and tore it, gingerly wrapping the raw skin—she didn't want to wake the girl—and wrapped the other arm the same.

"I'm sorry," she whispered. "I should've kept you with me. I should've come looking for you," as if these words could heal Mazy, could change her body back. She dried her tears as they came and told herself, *No good; nothing's good.*

There were small bruises, purple splotches above the elbow, along the calves where the dress lay, covering everything else. At least Mazy's body had let go of its shaking; she was resting, still wearing her shoes, and Jennifer unbuckled one, peeled it from her foot.

Below them, the piano—it was two, Jinx playing. He had barely started when he came to a halt.

She could see his hands trying to bend out of the night's

sleep. It was too early for them to shake. He was staring at
the piano like he did, his jaw hinged loose, staring at the
piano like it was some new, amazing thing he had to figure
out. He'd spend all day figuring it out.

Then he struck the keys, the same notes. He'd do this
over and over, build the song "From the center-root," Jinx
liked to call it. "I start right in the middle, work both directions—build a little toward the start, then come back to the
center-root, build toward the finale." Eventually that
melody, that root circled through the whole piece until it
was done, and he'd work on the next song. All night he in-
serted those roots into his solos, and she'd stop wherever she
was in the St. Charles, expecting them, fragments of music
that had purled through her head all afternoon, unfolding
in the space around her.

"Are you all bad luck when it comes to women? Is that
really how you got your name?" Jennifer had asked the first
time she met Jinx. She'd heard him through the floor in her
room for weeks and knew of him from the other girls, and
walked by and said nothing. But on this night, she sat at the
bar listening until she got restless, then got up halfway
through a song about a woman named Lucille—

> *Lucille, Lucille,*
> *You done stole my car, my coat, my shoes,*
> *Ditched me on this dirt road*
> *And left me with the muddy bottom blues—*

and walked over to him. It was the third song in a row about
women treating him bad.

He didn't answer, just kept on playing. When she didn't
move away from the piano, he said, "I guess I'm not all bad
luck; you're here. I'm married—my second wife. She's stuck

to me so far—that's two women, so I'm not totally jinxed, though I've had my share of low-down love, the wrong kinds of love." He shook his head.

"The truth is, some people look at me suspiciously. They think my name sounds like I'm getting into trouble or causing it, like I'm a bad omen. But the truth is—since you asked—it was my father's nickname when he played in New Orleans, played the piano morning and night: the Swanson Club, Tipawa. He had the fastest hands. You couldn't catch those fingers with your eyes, no way; he'd be on to the next key. So the others in the trio started calling him Jink with a *k*. For a long time that was his name. Everywhere he took me with him, people called him Jink.

"But my father had a second side—jokester, trickster. One time when I was in high school, I picked my hair out as far as I could. When I walked, it floated." Jinx laughed. "I had my own private cloud of hair, that's how I saw it. My father kept his hair all slicked back, straightened, and cut short, so it was my rebellion—hair. That's all I possessed." He put his hands out like there was nothing to his body to own, not now, not when he was in high school, not ever. Then he dusted one hand down the front pearl buttons of his shirt. He was thin like Terry but had muscular fingers, arms. Terry carried his muscles in his shoulders.

"My father, he was a big man. He told me to cut my 'fro or birds were going to nest in it." Jinx crooked his neck so Jennifer could get a better look at the whole slab of his head. "See what time has done to my beautiful hair?" He rubbed his fingers through the tiny, flat curls. "Scruff is all I grow now," and he shook his head, disgusted.

"My father did that to me constantly. Came by and picked at my 'fro with his hands, yelled, 'Watch out. A bird's getting in that hair, nesting down.' And I jumped. Always, I jumped. He got me so many times." Jinx laughed and this time his voice departed. He had to clear the gravel out of his throat before he could go on. "See, he got it in my mind—

birds in my hair—got me thinking about birds, red, blue, hawks, wrens, worried me with it constantly. I woke up in the middle of the night shooing birds away from the bedposts. Wasn't a bird there. Man was a trickster.

"His friends got the same treatment. As my father put it—'I'm just helping people let go of their blues.' Then he'd dig at my side, smile, and I'd tell him to stop. And he'd tell me I was being too serious. Always told me I was too serious. His job, he said, was to try to ease me up some.

"So he did enough of this fooling at church, and at Jack's Grocery where we shopped, and just walking, my father loved to go walking in the French Quarter, and strolling to his clubs until after a while people started saying, 'Look out. Here comes Jink. He's going to play some trick on you. Those fast hands, watch out. He's going to jinx you,' and they all moved out of his way. Smart thing they did.

"Wasn't long before his name got changed. Everyone started calling him Jinx. His real name was Edward Smith, but Jinx, well, that's a hell of a lot more interesting. My mother called him 'Edward'—she was the only one, insisted on proper names at her table. When he passed, I took up *Jinx* out of respect."

"What's your real name?"

"It's Jinx," he said. "That's my real name. Fits with all the troubles come on top of me. Especially from women." He squared himself with the piano, straightened his neck—

Lucille, Lucille,
Come on back down this road.
You'll find me waiting till sunrise,
Then I ain't going wait no more

Jinx always wore white long-sleeved shirts, tuxedo shirts with silver buttons, pearled buttons, like his father; always had a story to tell about the things his father did. His voice was frail and dry and sweet. There was a sweetness to his sound that flowed through the words and yet was so fragile like it might crumble and contradicted the way Jennifer had always heard the songs, especially Billie Holiday and her sad tones that wouldn't let up. Jinx's voice always let up, always wanting a drink of water.

"Why you like this old music?" he said one afternoon after she had dragged a chair over to listen. Jennifer had slouched forward, elbows on her knees, her chin cupped in her hands, making requests for "Miss Otis," "Strange Fruit," and "Traveling Light," reeling off the names without thinking. "Now, someone you know had to love this music or you had to love it. Which is it?"

"Don't ask me that, Jinx," she said.

He stopped playing, looked straight at her. "What happened to you?"

Jennifer sat up. Without the music the earth slipped, just enough that she had to make sure her bare feet were on the cold floor, and her body was indeed her body sitting up in a chair.

He was always demanding in that way, wanting to know the history of things, how people were connected. But it was too much to reveal her parents, Mathew, her baby. Everyone at the St. Charles knew about the baby and that was enough. Just the thought of telling more weakened the threads of those people inside her, and she wondered how much longer she'd be able to hold on to them. She couldn't lose them.

Jinx sighed, started back on the lower keys. "I ain't trying to scare you," he said. "It's just, I'm always telling you stories. I'd like to hear some."

He said nothing else and after a while, she refound those center-roots and submerged, wedging her chin back into her hands.

Through the evening Jinx played what the clients wanted and when no one wanted anything, he played piano solos. Later when everyone was upstairs finishing business or, if lucky, an early night and resting, well, you heard Jinx working through his center-roots again, but faster—what he had started slow at 2:00 in the afternoon and wouldn't finish until 3:00 or 4:00 a.m. He struck the keys, paused, then let the keys tumble, quick tempo like his father, one rhythm into another—like tumblers inside a lock—then the lock clicked and he paused to call the sun back from the other half of the world. The pauses grew and grew as the hours slipped, as if the distance between river currents had grown too great, all the magnetic pulls of the world stretched to their end, and leaving just a pool of black water, unmoving, silent.

Mathew loved that kind of music—big band, swing, blues. It was the music of his father, Mr. Chris, who loved it and danced to it. That year before his death, Jennifer got Mr. Chris to dance with her in the boxed kitchens of the houses they lived in. A few times, she got Mat to dance. But he was in too much awe of the steps his father made and never tried to emulate them.

When they first started dating, no matter what they did—make love, eat, kiss, sleep, drive—they listened to Billie Holiday, Nat King Cole, Dinah Washington. It was so much a part of Mat, how he moved through the world, and she wanted to get close to anything, everything that was a part of him. They planned to get married, but a few months before the wedding, Terry passed. He came up from a mining hole coughing; his lungs shut and air gave way to blood.

That's when the desert and all its vastness swirled against her and knocked her down. There was nothing to grab on to but wind and blowing sand, nothing to steady her falling. Every day, Mathew held her in bed and told her, "I'm sorry, Jen. What can I do? Just tell me. Anything."

She wouldn't answer; she couldn't. Those words were like a wool she couldn't tear or reach around to throw away.

All she heard was the wind sweeping the sand; his voice, the touch of his fingers were just another sweep of that same grit. Mathew smelled like clay, like the deepest core of the earth—he'd never get that out of his skin, just like Terry. All day, he held her and she suffocated under the smell of red iron. When she had the strength, she picked up his arm, moved it off without explaining.

When she went to her mother's house, Delia leaned up from the table and without any acknowledgment said, "Terry," just kept repeating his name for Jennifer to answer to and "Why did he?" Then long silences. Jennifer sat at the table across from her or on the sofa, cooked supper in the kitchen, and wouldn't answer, wouldn't dare give anything except for those plates of food and tea. She waited for her mama.

One night, a couple of weeks after Terry's death, Jennifer drove over and found her mother at the table with an envelope.

"How are you?" she asked. Delia had looked especially worn the last few evenings, wearing that old ghost again. Jennifer worried that Terry's death might send Delia so far down, she'd never climb out.

As much as Terry had meant to Jennifer, he meant even more to her mama. She had depended on him to get through her days, to survive the desert. They had only been in Alabama for seven months. Jennifer had latched onto Mathew, but Delia still had no friends. And Jennifer didn't have the strength to replace Terry, nor the desire. She was old enough now not to hate herself for that selfishness.

Delia was at the table, head crooked in her hands, where they gripped the thick black-gray hair that would be Jennifer's one day; those hands held her up, suspended. She was looking at the far wall, and Jennifer thought the two of them might sit awkwardly in that small room as usual. But then her mother said, "I want to get out." She let her hands drop, they knocked the table, and she turned to Jennifer.

The skin around her eyes was burned and swollen, so her eyes looked even smaller than usual, painful to look at. But it was the first time since Terry's death she had acknowledged her daughter.

"Mama, you should do something about your eyes."

"Let's go for a jaunt," Delia said, saying *jaunt* like Terry would, and she showed enough of her teeth that it could be mistaken for a smile.

Jennifer quickly said, "I've got my truck," surprised her mother wanted to go anywhere. Delia never made suggestions, never wanted to do anything, as if by sitting alone, she could wait out her depression, wait out her life until one or the other ended.

"Just let me get something on." Her mama put the envelope in her pocket, tied her robe, and went to the back.

Jennifer looked around the room—so spare, the desert trawling a gust of wind across the north side of the house. Then it fell back to catch its breath. They were in Richmond, not far out of Montgomery, and she thought they might drive up the river to the capitol ruins there.

September 29, 2044

Dear Mama,

I'm closer. Yet there is no way I can reach you, no way to get to where you are. I'm in Cairo, Illinois, and I wish I could be in Chicago. It shouldn't take that long. I think of that distance, how little of it there is between us, and yet I cannot get to you.

I can't leave Mazy. She was separated from me two months ago when we left Birmingham. She's hurt, Mama, but she's in my care now. I can't tell you what has happened here, what has happened to me, because I don't

want to remember this day and yesterday, and all the
days that lead back to July. If I think of them, allow these
days to define me, they build on top of me like so many
stones until they have pressed me out of existence.

It's the same as when I think of the miles from Cairo
to Chicago, each mile magnifying, accumulating until it is
impossible to cross, infinite. I have felt this way since
coming to Cairo, and I can't help Mazy like that. Her
mother asked me to take care of her, which I will, and
then find a way to get both of us to you.

I need you,
Jen

Jennifer sat on the edge of the bed going through Mazy's notebook. It was lunchtime and Naomi had brought up plates of food and a wardrobe of clothes. "I'm guessing she's a two, but I also have some size fours. I don't have any junior sizes." Naomi laid the plates on the table, then transferred the clothes from the crook of her arm to the dresser. "One of the bras should fit," she said and asked if there had been any progress.

"She's exhausted," Jennifer explained. "I don't know when she'll wake up. Those cuts are going to need time to heal."

"One guard's in the hallway in case she gets violent again." Naomi walked to the bed, looked the girl over. "She's sleeping so hard."

"Did you hear what I said about time?"

Naomi nodded. "I'll talk with Ms. Gerald."

That had been an hour ago, and none of their murmurings, none of that noise or the smell of cooked chicken had gotten Mazy to wake up.

Jennifer sat on the edge of the bed and flipped through the drawings, kept going back to the people she recognized: a woman with puffy cheeks, her hair trailing off into the light and her hands clenched onto the can of water, bony fingers clutching that can like it was her last possession in the world. Light sluiced down her throat, one of those rare times when the sun had made it through the haze.

A man with fattened jowls and a mustache pulled over his lips, sores on his arms, and a thick wrinkle across the top of his nose where someone had pounded at the center of him and brought his eyes down like a bull, serious and tired.

One woman had on a plain shirt—Jennifer remembered its color, blue. The woman's hair had been pulled up and over her forehead to wave back at her ears, blond, and it hung loosely to her shoulders. Jennifer had watched the woman skim her hand down the middle, put in a barrette, clamp the left side out of the way. She tried to do the same to the right, but the barrette she was holding split apart. She placed a hand to her cheek; Mazy had drawn out the point of her nose in gray pencil, and her eyebrows pinched to the center. In her other hand she kept rubbing the barrette.

And one woman with a shawl—it was actually green like the skin of a lime and cleaner or at least brighter than the other shawls Jennifer had noticed in Linn Park, so striking. It was as if the color wrapped around the woman protected her somehow.

Clothes blew around, shirts without bodies the children tried to catch. When they hit the back of someone's calf like leeches, they had to be scraped off.

And dead birds everywhere, their beaks half-open, and cats and dogs stretched out with their mouths open wide as if they were just tired and panting, trying to catch their breath. Only they wouldn't move, would never move.

Another drawing, of a boy, a scar over his eyes and a wide blunt nose like the blunt end of a hammer, half his bottom teeth missing, that collarbone raised on the left side more than the right. Jennifer remembered that the boy never wore a shirt.

The other children—boys with fat faces, lips too tiny to hold much, making sure they stayed close to an adult. Just the arms of the adults had been drawn onto the page like broken-off tree limbs.

A bicycle tire.

A woman with a lazy eye that drifted far to the left corner as if trying to catch something behind her and a wild tuft of hair like a gray crow's nest; her shirt, collared, a man's collar, wide on her, leaving a wide ring on her neck, sunburnt. Mazy had penciled the neck in black.

A cross with fake flowers that someone had staked into one plot of the square. It said *Go Now, Papa*—for days no one touched it.

A different man, his nose curved where it had broken, and the long curve of a scar that stretched across his face and nose, and another scar that pulled up one corner of his lip— so many wrinkles, like rivers and creeks for tears to cut the paths deeper, drop from his jaw, catch in his hand.

A plank of wood with *Steep* written on the side.

Mazy had sketched pages of buckets and bucket lids and tin cans, a door that had been pounded, the latch pounded back sideways, the tin piece in the frame coming unnailed, falling out.

There was an entire page devoted to a woman Jennifer had not seen, a deep hollow in her neck where the Adam's apple should've been, that's where her chin sunk into black, where the wrinkles first started, where she might collapse into the pages, disappear. Her hair was thick, long, straight, full for a woman in her fifties, sixties; but maybe she was younger like all of them, the desert having scored her face hard, maybe it was the thick-wire eyebrows that kept her eyes dark and focused out to somewhere in the smoke and wrinkled elbows that kept her in place.

Mazy drew arms and legs straight as witch brooms and hands that curled back like the feet of birds. Even the dogs, mottled white with coal faces and ears and noses, carried a solemn, hungry look. The haze stirred their shadows into one thick circle, one long knot unknotting on the ground, stripped from each dog, each person, a corner indiscernible.

Always in the center, the reverend stood on his box, hands toward heaven, wrinkled elbows, dark-circled eyes, coil on top of coil-vein, a belt of broken leather, his mouth open. The scar above his lip set his mouth separate from the rest of his face, deep lines to a wide sandbar chin. In Mazy's drawing, it looked as if he was waiting for rain to drink.

She remembered pieces of stone, beard, chipped paint, wood, faces stretched wide, dark overalls, thumbs missing on hands, bald heads, worn-through jeans.

Not just people but pieces of wire rolled up, the wind blowing across, one tree where birds had made a nest out of wire. And paper that would whip up, hit you in the face, a smokestack rolling around having fallen from somewhere, and pieces of rock from a building that people kicked, plain dresses that stretched all the way down to the women's ankles, dirt-white and some cornflower pattern, cracked bowls, and piecemeal plywood, electric wire lines that dipped into the streets, abandoned chairs upside down—all of this, Mazy had drawn, had spent each hour watching, sketching.

Jennifer was sweating, breathing hard like she did after the nightmares of the harvesting machines, but she couldn't shut the notebook, couldn't stop remembering. On the last page, Mazy had drawn a picture of Jennifer.

She had marked the thick black hair, and a fierceness in her eyes; those eyes stared hard into things, wild into things, searching. The planes of her face were cut by toughened long cheekbones, scattered with freckles, her lips drawn up in a silent pull as if she had taken the words from someone for herself and would not let them go. Mazy had discovered the wrinkle at her chin, where it frayed into two paths, and the wrinkles at the corners of the eyes trailing down like her hair. But that fierceness, it was something Jennifer wanted to recognize in herself, but couldn't. She put the notebook down and walked to the window. The faint reflection in the glass was too bland, her wrinkles smoothed away, ghostlike. She looked back for the picture Mazy had drawn, for herself.

It was when Jinx started playing that Mazy rolled and stretched in bed and sat up.

"It's okay," Jennifer told her. "It's me. No one else." She picked up the notebook, brought it closer, but the girl shifted to the other side.

So Jennifer left the notebook on the covers and went back to the chair and table, flipped on the lamp. The only other light came from the window, the sun coming through in streaks of gray; all morning the clouds had been gray and that waiting for rain set a heaviness into each movement, the lifting of things, even sitting down.

"There's no one else here, I promise. You're in my room. One of the girls brought chicken up to eat, but that was a while ago. I don't think you'll want it now."

Mazy looked at Jennifer, watched her, and Jennifer kept searching for the missing long hair, the way Mazy's face used to be—thinner, her eyes smaller. Then Mazy reached for the notebook.

"I can get you something else from the kitchen. Are you thirsty?"

Mazy didn't answer, just flipped through the pages until she got to the final drawing.

She looked up, then back at the portrait, and Jennifer straightened her shoulders. She felt as if Mazy was looking to see how *she* had changed, what *she* had lost in her face, judging, measuring, calculating something as well.

"You do this?" Mazy asked, lifting one of her wrapped arms.

Jennifer nodded and pointed to the bathroom. "The sink's in there. You should take them off and wash the cuts."

Mazy went back to the picture, traced a finger over the page.

"I can get you something to eat." The lines on the page had been etched like braille, its own language for decoding. At least the girl was calmer.

"You left me," Mazy said. "They took me to St. Louis. Chained me inside the van because I refused to leave without you."

"I tried to get outside."

"You promised we would stay together."

Jennifer marked her feet against the wooden floor. "I had to get you out of Birmingham. I didn't know what would happen after that."

"Then you should've left me to find my mama."

"She wanted you out, too."

"She was looking for my cousins and my aunt. She asked you to take care of me until she found them." Mazy set the book down, then picked it up and slung it at the bathroom door. "I don't even know what happened to her."

"I'm sorry," Jennifer said.

"Not good enough." Slowly the girl stepped out of bed. "I don't trust you."

Jennifer watched Mazy's toes dig at the wood, the bedposts holding the frame; the book was somewhere in the corner, she couldn't see it. "I'm not asking for that."

"What are you asking?"

Jennifer wanted Mazy to be okay, and here she was alive like Naomi had said—this is the miracle, this is what you hold on to. But there was also what Ms. Gerald wanted.

Mazy peered around the room. The green walls had faded in the gray light; they needed painting. Nothing had been hung, not even a full-length mirror like Jennifer had found in some of the other girls' rooms. She set her eyes on the rosewood dresser and the long green, black rug going from the bed to the center. To the right—the table, chairs, and lamp, their legs and cords entangled. The bathroom, the south and east windows.

There wasn't a television—the only one in the St. Charles belonged to Ms. Gerald, though Jennifer had never seen it, never heard it. No phones or radios were allowed either. It was always strange to be with a trick in the middle of a conversation or in the middle of sex, and have him blurt something out as if suddenly talking to himself. But it was the phone embedded just under the ear; he was in conversation with his father, a wife, a lover, his boss, his children, someone else. And Jennifer covered her mouth, laughing, though she didn't mean it, was afraid to, but it happened.

Sometimes the client laughed, made a joke about coitus interruptus. "I know this is ridiculous," he'd say, or "I'm ridiculous," roll his eyes, and continue talking. Sometimes he just walked out or turned over in bed, and she was left to stare out the windows of her room or the parlor—a reprieve until the trick wanted her again.

It was never what was said, the lies or truth of the words that sent her spiraling the other direction into that blue low-downness that Jinx always sang about, or the intense, angry conversations. It was the artless talkers, the soft-spoken easy ones, how they gave their words away, how those words, she could tell, were being received.

Sometimes, while a client slept, Jennifer touched the knot underneath his ear, felt the plastic and metal underneath the skin, and remembered the collectors, how they cut and pried open the phones like digging oysters out of shells, then chiseled and pulled the wire-roots to keep them intact. She always wondered how far into the neck and ear the wires had been sewn. In the desert camps nothing like this existed.

"Where am I now? Who do I belong to now?" Mazy asked.

"Ms. Gerald, the woman you met, owns us. You're in the St. Charles. It's an old hotel."

"But where am I? This isn't a city-state."

Jennifer shook her head. "You're in Cairo, Illinois. We're squeezed between the Ohio and Mississippi Rivers. You can see them from the windows."

"I flew along the Mississippi yesterday," Mazy said and walked over to a window, the Mississippi side, that slip of river curling under the trees. "First time I'd been in a mille-copter. The pilot kept dipping close to the water, zigzagging because of the winds."

"The St. Charles is the only thing left in Cairo. All those houses out there are abandoned."

"Like Birmingham," Mazy said.

"What was St. Louis like?"

"I lived in a protected zone called Blue Ridge," and as she stretched, Jennifer saw small lines of blood, where they had dried in the fabric. The cut on her face had scabbed all the way across and it pulled her cheek taut. She kept looking out the window and back at Jennifer, the gray changing her face light, then dark as if the full length of the day, from its first beginning to dusk was happening all at once in Mazy's expression.

"Those broken walls in Birmingham. It was just like that in St. Louis, only they weren't broken. So high, you couldn't see over them. Used to walk along those walls. All the time running errands for my family. Kept waiting for someone to break through. I'd hear explosions and jump and people wondering what was wrong with me."

"You had a family?"

Mazy shook her head. "They didn't have any children. They wanted me to call them mother and father, but I refused. She beat me for that, Ms. Hammond. That was her name. With a mop handle, anything with a handle—I remember when she lifted a chair to me.

"When she beat me, she got all upset, and my body turned numb. I thought, This is what it's like to be dead, this numbness. Do they beat you here?"

"Sometimes."

"Do you ever wish you were dead when they beat you?"

"No," Jennifer said. She didn't tell Mazy it was because she felt she had already died. Since her baby's death, she lingered. That was the mystery to her, the lingering, how she was able—she had only been whipped twice for not fucking enough clients, not bringing in enough money. Ms. Gerald used a horse whip across the shoulders that she kept in the glass case. "I haven't seen anyone beat that bad."

"I won't take it anymore," Mazy said. "That's why Ms. Hammond got rid of me. That numbness started to burn." Mazy drew a line down her breastbone and clenched her fist at her stomach. "I'd wake up at night on fire, sweating." She moved to the window.

"Every day, Ms. Hammond sent me to the store for groceries. 'Need some bread, child,' like I was her child. Told me to walk. It was good exercise for me. So I was always going along the walls. Everything was clean in Blue Ridge, not dusty or dirty. All the people so clean. When I got back with the bread, she'd say, 'Where's the eggs? The chicken? I need a fresh chicken, child.' And she'd walk through the kitchen and ask the cook if there was anything else he needed. Then I would be off, again, along that wall. Every day like that.

"Of course, I knew what was on the other side—Birmingham, that world, those people wanting to get through the concrete. Their hands were on the other side pushing. And I didn't want to run away and get caught by them. I knew what they would do. I did run away once. She beat me for it. Got me on the floor and started kicking. Whatever you do, don't let them get you on the floor. I had to see a doctor. For a while, I wasn't allowed to walk by myself. Hell, for a while I *couldn't* walk." She drew a line down her breastbone again, sat down on the broad windowsill, put her back against the glass.

"One day, there was a man stealing bread—happened when I was in the store. I had a whole list of things for Ms. Hammond, and I was just getting to them, and somehow the man had gotten into Blue Ridge—he hid under a car. That's how he got through the checkpoint, the police think. He was obviously not from Blue Ridge. He was dirty. He wasn't dressed properly." Mazy glanced at the shoulder of her dress, picked it up to look at the bruise, and looked down her arm at the bandages, then crossed her arms, shivering. "He wasn't proper. Ms. Hammond was all about proper. And the police came in and shot him. That's the law. You get caught stealing, you get shot. Eye for an eye.

"Everyone there said he deserved it, and everyone who talked about it later said he deserved it, and the police hauled him off quick and the store was mopped blood-clean. But before they shot him, I remember the man saying, 'I'm hungry' like all the people in Birmingham used to say in Linn Park. Those people." She pointed to where the notebook was. "And he said, 'There's no food in the rest of the city.' He was angry. They shot him.

"Everyone said *thank you*. The officers couldn't finish their work for all the congratulations. I just stared at his body. Some people started laughing because the bread he had stolen had gone poof, up in the air. That's how the checkout woman put it, 'They shot him and the bread went poof.' She raised her arms, 'Poof, up in the air.'

"The bread slices fell all over the ground, all over his body. He was covered in slices of white bread and some people were laughing, how ridiculous he looked. But when you're hungry like we were in Birmingham, saving those rations, when you're hungry like that, you're always hungry like that. I started picking up the bread.

" 'No,' the checkout woman told me. 'Don't do that.' She came out from behind the counter and took my arms, held them. 'You get some fresh bread for your mother.' But I had already stuffed a good bit in my pockets and I kept picking it up. Then one of the officers came over and looked at me and asked if I was all right, and where did I live. I didn't want to get shot, so I got up. As soon as I got out the front door, I ran home and put all of that bread under my bed just in case," Mazy said. "Just in case.

"But Ms. Hammond found the food, made me clean it out. I'd hide food, and they'd find it. Finally, I got so hungry, I went into the kitchen and took everything, all that food hiding in the cabinets and fridge, set it on the counters and tile." Mazy twisted her hand, emptied it into the whole space of the room, then held her arms tight again, shivered. She kept looking past Jennifer as if nothing was recognizable, not even the shapes of walls, the line joining the ceiling and the floor, as if the corners didn't exist, as if Mazy and Jennifer weren't here or anywhere.

Jennifer and Mazy stayed quiet with each other just like Jennifer and her mama had stayed quiet that night driving out of Richmond to Montgomery. She hadn't traveled along the railroad tracks that followed the Alabama like Terry used to do, the gaps in the ties smoothed over with sand, getting as close to the edge of the bank as possible until her mama would say, "This isn't some daredevil show." And Terry, embarrassed, would relent.

Instead, Jennifer stayed on Highways 40 and 54, which mostly stayed off the river, dipped close enough a few times to glimpse the wide snakish water, then veered into the wheeling dust that started on the ground before stirring toward the sky. Throughout the day, you could see the dust devils rise until they exploded back into air having lost the force of the hot-cold helix inside them. In the darkness, the headlights only captured that beginning spiral, the dust slipping over the cab, then away.

Her mama had slouched against the passenger door from the beginning, content on not talking, just like all their drives together. The truck shook Delia's face and neck until she was lulled into sleep, shook the wrinkles loose, and Jennifer tried to follow the lines, where they betrayed her mother's age—just like her mama's hair, this face would be hers when she was older. At least with her mama resting, there was a softness, a flexibility opposed to the rigid frame her body woke with, setting against the spare houses, her time alone, the grit, and chores.

In Montgomery the buildings were half-covered and imploding, the weight of the sand too much. Jennifer drove up Dexter to the stone steps of the capitol, its domed roof missing—it had been lifted and carried to Birmingham by skycranes in 2014, the year Jennifer was born, leaving a huge, cratered ceiling for gathering up whorls of sand.

"You stopping?" her mama asked, and peeked, yawned.

"Just for a minute," Jennifer explained. It wouldn't be a good idea to leave the truck idle. The engine had been doing weird things, sputtering when it sat too long, getting cold or clogged, especially with dust blowing. The dust always worried Jennifer.

"I keep expecting people to come out of those buildings," Delia said. "All these years, and still every time we come to a town, I look for people." She had brought a shawl—even now in the hottest part of summer Delia wore shawls or something long-sleeved as if she could never get warm—and she sat up more, hooked the shawl around her, its spiral of red, yellow, brown, the wind whipping against the hood of the truck. "When Everett passed, it was like someone slapped me hard in the face. For a long time I looked for him walking back in the house. But it was just you, Jenny, in the house. And now Terry."

Jennifer's cheek stung, and she wanted to say *I'm sorry, Mama, it was just me in the house.* She had failed—a daughter instead of a husband, a girl instead of a man, and a woman now, still not the right companion. Her confidence, her existence washed out of her, exhausted with the burden of what she was not.

"I know how much he meant to you," she said. "Both of them." Jennifer put her elbow into the crook of the door frame and leaned that way. "I wish Terry was here."

"Some people, they should never pass. They're too good for death. He was. But Jenny, I have some news. We don't have to stay in the desert." Her mother pulled out the envelope, the one from the table. "Your Aunt Bobbie, she's been able to get visas and money for us to come and live with her in Chicago." Delia placed the envelope on the seat beside Jennifer. "Mathew has a visa, is that right?"

She nodded. "He's had it since he was born. He's had it all this time and just hasn't used it."

"Then we can all leave, Jenny. You and Mat can marry in Chicago. I know you got your plans set here. If you want the ceremony—"

"Hold on, Mama. You're talking too much," Jennifer said, and pulled up the sheets of folded paper. She glanced at the letter, the words *Dear Sister,* and *persuaded,* and *visa,* and *I can't wait to see you and Jen, Love, Bobbie.* Aunt Bobbie. Jennifer had only seen flicker-photographs. Much taller than Delia, but she had that same lope and roundness in her shoulders, carried herself like Mama—slow, purposeful. She wore glasses, the kind that came to a point at the top end, making her eyes into cat eyes. And she had curly red hair—Where all that red comes from is a mystery, Delia had said—neither she nor Jennifer had a trace—and Bobbie's hair was the curliest of the three. She left Louisiana before it turned into a dust bowl, and now she wanted them to come live with her. They had no other living relatives. Paper-clipped to the letter were two permissions to transfer, one for Jennifer, one for her mama.

Jennifer smiled, the visas heavy like mining scrip, the kind of paper that wouldn't easily tear or dissolve. "Why is she helping us?" The answer seemed obvious, but every bit of good news in the desert had a catch.

"Because of Terry's passing. My sister works for the government. Did you read what she said?"

"No," Jennifer said. "No." She reached across, grabbed her mama, digging into the holes of the shawl.

"Now, don't worry," Delia whispered. "We're going to be close. We'll have our chance in Chicago."

If anything Jennifer squeezed tighter, but all the strength washed out of her; she didn't believe they would ever be close. For her mother to actually say it, say it was possible, just made it worse. But Mat—they could leave the desert together and have a life in the Saved World—this was possible; this is what Jennifer held on to.

"I'm glad we'll be out and finally have that chance. I've just been no good here to you, to myself."

"It's all right, Mama," Jennifer said, and tried to take hold of that word *chance*. If she just pulled tight enough, maybe she could wring out all their disappointments, their reservations, and the distance between them would dry up, collapse. Her mama wanted it to be so. She said she did. Jennifer pulled and pulled and waited to experience something beyond hollowness.

"Let's get on back," Delia said. "You talk to Mathew. I just wanted to drive out one more time like Terry loved."

It was true. Terry did love the jaunts, and they loved the long monotonous drives because of him. Yet he never kept track of the miles they traveled. Jennifer knew it had taken seventy-four miles from Richmond to Montgomery, yet with him, it didn't matter. The trips went like this: she asked Terry the miles on the odometer, and he rattled off some number, yawning, uninterested. A little while later, she asked him again. Sometimes he just said two or six million, something so wrong she knew he was lying, and she craned her neck at the odometer.

"Stop bothering me with that," he finally said. "It

doesn't matter how far we've gone. Just look outside. Look." He waved his hand through the cab like his arm was broken, flopping it goofily around like a broken-winged bird. So she sighed and leaned on the passenger door, and looked, anything not to look at that recalcitrant man and his stupid, stupid arm.

It was always outside so dark and black, you could barely make out the bank, where it dipped down to the blacker river. The headlights just glared into the pitch, blinding, revealing the edges of some other world, immense. They were going into it fast.

"Look," he was still whispering to her.

When Delia had left for the Saved World, she sent Chicago to Jennifer piece by piece, in letters and in flicker-photographs. There was one of Pearl, her mama's tabby, splayed on the bed, pawing at her mother's hand until she rubbed its white belly. The paws froze, the picture came to a stop. And the streets of the city, her mother walking the sidewalks to share it with her.

On the nights Mat worked, Jennifer had mulled over the people in those ten-second clips. What did they do? Where were they going? The number of bodies always shocked her, how quickly they walked by, their faces blank and focused, then gone out of the frame.

But Jennifer's favorite was of Mama kicking her feet in the Chicago River. It became Mazy's favorite, too. Whenever the legs stopped kicking, Mazy set the letter under the bed lamp, and the light started the silent movie over, Delia's legs paddling, her shoulders lifting, then curling over her arms straight as pegs, and the whole time her lips were opened wide, happy. Aunt Bobbie must've taken it, or perhaps someone her mama met, someone plucked out of that large, engrossed Chicago crowd. The note at the top had been short—

June 19, 2041

Jenny,

    The sky has finally_____, so I've gone

to the river. We don't get_____. I

love you. Wish you could be here.

    Love,

    Mama

All of her mother's letters had been censored by the government office in Birmingham, when the office was there and Birmingham was the entry city into the Saved World. They controlled the desert mining, food shipments, the schools, even television. But just like the flicker-photographs, the incomplete lines, the absences drew Jennifer to Chicago even more.

It had been nine years since her mother left the Southeastern Desert, nine years since Jennifer tried to convince Mat to use their visas. But he wouldn't leave his father and so she stayed while her mother sent photos and letters, the absences building and building.

"I think your mama's pretty," Mazy said.

"She wouldn't think so."

"Why?"

"I don't know. She just can't see any beauty in herself; she never has." Mazy had just taken another bath—she had had five over the last two days, and this was the longest one so far. She smelled of soap, vanilla covering up the orange-metallic of her skin, sweating out the water, her head wrapped in a blue and gold bandana.

"Did you ever tell her?"

"What?" Jennifer asked.

"That she didn't see herself the right way. That she was beautiful."

"No. I never tried to talk her out of it."

Mazy put the letter back up to the light and the legs kicked again. "She seems happiest in this one."

"It's Chicago. When we leave here, we'll go there."

"I'm too tired to go anywhere," Mazy said and leaned against the pillows she had propped against the headboard. "It's just too much trying. I don't believe in it."

"You have to keep trying. Promise me, Mazy." It was the same argument they had after Naomi brought them supper a few hours ago.

Naomi set the dinner plates on the table, the glasses of sweet tea, and told Jennifer, "The girl's progressing fast" as she took up the dirty plates and forks and knives from lunch.

Jennifer said Mazy needed more time and could one of the servants bring the food tomorrow?

"You need to show her the kitchen," Naomi answered. "She needs to start getting her own meals. Her room is almost finished." Before leaving, she went over and talked with Mazy about makeup for the cut on her face.

"You're doing so well, she's going to tell Ms. Gerald you're ready for work," Jennifer said.

"You act like you don't want me to get better."

"I want you to stay with me as long as they'll let you."

Then Jennifer explained Ms. Gerald's five commandments, the story about the St. Charles being found *out of the wilderness*. She didn't tell Mazy about the girls who died.

Mazy said she had already figured out what the St. Charles was, but didn't want to be touched anymore. "I told Mr. Hammond that. Gave him a black eye once. It didn't stop him. And Ms. Hammond knew and never stopped him—" and how could Jennifer do this, wasn't she married?

"There are worse options here," Jennifer said. She looked at Mazy's wrists, the purple marks on her arms, and felt that emptiness where her baby had been, where the unborn child bled out of her. How could emptiness form such a thick knot?

"But you'll get through it. We'll get out. You have to believe that, Mazy. You have to keep trying." She repeated everything that Cawood had said and everything that Naomi had said, a string of words that disintegrated as soon as they were spoken. "Listen to me, Mazy."

"Stop it," Mazy said. "You don't even believe what you're saying." She went to the bathroom, turned on the water.

For the last few days Mazy had walked back and forth to the windows, Jennifer pointing out the girls at the river swimming, their names, and do you want to swim? The girls from the first two floors swam in the late afternoon, the sun blurring them into shadows on the water.

Mazy stepped up to the glass and watched, then traced back through the room until she had covered every inch of it, and washed the cuts and found a yellow sundress that worked and a white pullover sweater that she took off and put back on, complained that it was scratchy, complained that she was cold, and wrapped her sheared head in the bandana.

Jennifer had picked up the notebook. Its spine was now broken, but the pages were still intact, and Mazy drew on the empty sheets that remained. Each time Jennifer came near, Mazy closed the book. Jennifer heard her crying in the bathroom, in her sleep—and that was the only time, in her sleep, that Jennifer could touch her, try to soothe her.

But the girl had been in a good mood since their argument and her long bath, humming along with Jinx's voice like Cawood would do and was probably doing right now somewhere in the St. Charles, only Mazy's voice was smaller, quieter. Both Dang Red and Benji Red were playing with Professor Jinx tonight. Mazy stomped the floor to the stomping going on downstairs, her feet swinging from the bed. Jennifer wanted to take her and dance.

"Does he ever stop playing?" she asked, smiling. Jennifer hadn't seen the girl show such a full row of teeth since they were on the bus in the Talladega Forest.

"Thank goodness, no," Jennifer said, and told the story of how Jinx got his name.

Then she had taken out the flicker-photographs—Mazy had never seen any before.

They sat on the edge of the bed, watched them under the lamp and talked about Jennifer's mother until Mazy said she was tired of trying. Jennifer promised they'd get to Chicago.

"Then you'll have your mama. My mama's dead." Mazy dug her shoulder at the pillows.

"You don't know that."

"She's dead and she ain't coming for me. And if she isn't dead, she still ain't coming for me. She left us in Birmingham, Jen." Jennifer couldn't see Mazy's face. "I don't trust you." She let go of the letter, just let it fall to the covers. "You'll let me go again."

"I won't."

"You will. I know it. You won't take me to Chicago. It's better for me to believe you won't take care of me. And how can you? Ms. Gerald's the one owns me."

Jennifer picked up Mazy's hand and rubbed the inside like scooping flesh out of a melon.

"I don't know what to do," she said. "I want you to be okay."

"I told you, I'm numb, I'm dead. I don't want to live."

"Mazy, please."

"I don't trust it." Mazy pulled, but Jennifer wouldn't give her hand away. "You let me go once. And my mama's gone."

"But you're alive."

"I want to believe it," she said. "And I want to trust it."

"Then do," Jennifer said.

Below them the stomping had picked up and Jinx was flying through a solo. Jennifer caught the center-root, what Jinx had been playing all day and breathed it in, held it, and held on to the girl's hand, and tried to steady Mazy's shaking but couldn't. She felt her own blood twist and shift through her body, so hot, and all she could think of, holding her mama that night in Montgomery, the hollowness. How her mama had asked for a chance and how Jennifer decided against it.

October 6, 2044

Dear Mama,

I try to sleep, but I can't sleep. It's a partial sleeping I do, and I've gotten good at it. Always, I find myself drawn to the windows in this hotel—looking past the lights, the shadowed roofs that turn across the night water. I remember how desperate the river made you when Terry died, how I missed you when you took the bus to Chicago, even if the way we left each other wasn't good. For nights, I drove over to your house and waited for you so we could go driving, jaunting. I've never told that. I should've come to Chicago then. The world has gone all backwards on top of me.

Remember how the desert sand just washed over us, Mama, over everything we were. Here in Cairo I'm no longer in that harsh weather, though we do have land clouds that roll in, carbon clouds out of Missouri. They sit on top of us for days in grayness, then roll on, break apart. Some fish die, and the trees are sick for a while, but they recover and we can go outside. I've only seen this twice, and the truth is, Mama, the Saved World is more beautiful than I thought it would be.

The river turns outside my window and the trees, especially the ones on the Kentucky bank, dip their branches into the water. The water pulls them down, lets go, and the branches rise up, up, then get pulled down again as if fish are nibbling the ends bare. Whenever we go down to the water, I sink my body under, and the fish bite my legs and hips, those lazy branches shifting, turning like my arms turning. I wish Mathew was here.

And Mama, I don't know how to help Mazy. She's calmed now, asleep. She's better. But the truth is, I can't protect her, except these few days she's in my care. It's wrong of me to think otherwise, to tell her otherwise. But I keep thinking of those stories, the girls who died here because they couldn't wrap their minds around what was expected of them as slaves, as whores. Three years, Mama. I don't know if she'll make it, not after what happened in St. Louis.

Don't hold judgment on me. Please don't hold judgment. Mazy cut her wrists in St. Louis. You could help me if you were here and Mathew—I can't write him now. I don't know what he would think of me, and I lost our baby.

I can't write any more now, Mama. I shouldn't have written that. But I have lost my baby, and I've got to somehow help this girl. And for what? To linger like I linger? I don't know what to do.

"This water will never go dry," Mat said. He nodded and kicked at the bank, pushing sand and mud into the rivers. They had gone to where the Ohio and Mississippi converged at a shoal. The sky, it was full of stars like that night on Snakeskin Road, so full that it seemed the universe would break apart, and those black paths in the sky would be the black paths of the rivers twisting and going, washing the stars away.

"We get so much rain here," Jennifer said. "Every few days."

"Nothing gets washed out?" he asked. Always when she dreamed of Mat now, he showed up curious, full of questions about the Saved World, his boots still on. He wasn't taking them off, rolling his pants up, cajoling her, *Let's go, Jen. Come on in with me, Jen.*

"It floods a lot. That's what I hear. But when the water shrinks back to the rivers, everything returns—all this green." Jennifer was on the edge of the water, too, a few steps away from him, but she didn't come any closer. "Mathew, I have to tell you something." The darkness kept cutting out, black, blacker, so at times she could glimpse the bones in his head and hands like familiar outcroppings, and then the shape of him would fall into the black, impossible to find. She couldn't find him now.

"The baby's dead. I know," he said.

"Mat—"

"What could you do?" he said. "What could you do, Jen?"

She wanted him to put his hand on her stomach, at least turn and look at her. She could see him now, had found him, again, a fixed point like the river, the sky, nodding, looking out at the water.

"No use having a baby in the desert anyway."

"We're not in the desert. We're in the Saved World. You've come this far to me, and I need you."

"I can't stay, Jen. I've got to go back," he said.

"To what? There's nothing in that desert, and I need you."

"There was nothing you could do," he said. "I don't blame you, Jen." And he started along the bank.

"You shouldn't leave me," she said. "Can't you see that? You shouldn't keep leaving me."

But he kept going. Above them that field of stars was so much more than she could hold, and at any moment, she knew they would fall and the earth would fall away, and the only thing left would be her echo still circling, calling for him to come back.

"They're swimming again," Mazy said.

There was still a piece of a dream, Mathew at the river, and Jennifer yawned, swatted her hand at the flattened sheets and coverlet.

"Do you want to swim?" she asked, stretching, looking, and found Mazy at the window. Jennifer kicked the covers down with her feet.

"Well, it's a little chilly," Mazy said. She had the pull-over sweater on, and pants, and who knew how many layers of shirts underneath the sweater—yet still her body was like a twig.

"We don't have to swim. We can just watch from the bank or dip our feet in."

"Is the water cold?"

"Not bad," Jennifer promised. "You'll warm up to it."

"All right, I want to go."

They found Douglas on the balcony and he agreed to walk them down. A few minutes before, they had come through the parlor and Mazy sat on the piano bench, flattened her hands over the closed lid, slowly opened it back.

"He doesn't want anyone touching the keys," Jennifer said, and checked behind her for Jinx, but he didn't appear. She wondered if he had left for the casinos or gone back to St. Louis. Mazy touched the piano lightly, soundlessly as she worked her fingers from the middle out to the ends and back over each white and black note, her fingers levering up and down. She had to perch on the edge of the bench to get to the floor pedals.

"You think he'd teach me?" she asked.

Jennifer had never seen him teach anyone or offer to do so. But maybe he would, and she told the girl just that, *maybe*, and they went to the kitchen, grabbed leftovers from the fridge, piled them into sandwiches while the cooks cleaned squash and onions and crowder peas in the deep sinks. The knife handles and spoons smelled of garlic, and the back kitchen door swung open, someone on the stoop wringing the neck of a chicken, those white feathers flying against the cook's fist. He roped the bird down on top of the other dead ones.

It was chilly like Mazy had said, a little foggy after the storms last night, and they both ran down the bank in front of Douglas, didn't stop until they got knee-deep in the water.

"I'm mad at you," Cawood yelled at Jennifer.

"What for?"

"You wait until now—a whole week—before you let the rest of us see her, like she's *your* private property. I'm Cawood," she said to Mazy and smiled.

That graciousness irked Jennifer so. "I'd like some of that kindness, too," she said, and Cawood frowned at her while the others introduced themselves.

Shivering, Mazy brushed at the water her jeans kept soaking up. She walked backward to the shore.

"Where you going?" Cawood asked. "Don't be afraid of us."

"You see the girl shaking. She's cold, that's all," Lisa said. Her blond hair was wet to the scalp and neck, no longer blond, and the rest of her was hidden under the black water. "Cawood can be a little bit of trouble," she warned Mazy.

"I'm not trouble." Cawood splashed Lisa and Lisa splashed her back and that set everyone splashing. The ritual.

Now Mazy was really shivering, but laughing about it.

She pulled down the edges of her bandana tighter and balled up her soaked towel and sweater, threw them on the shore.

Jennifer took Mazy's hand and pulled her out to the other girls. "You'll get warmer the deeper in you get."

On the Kentucky bank the hardwood leaves had started to turn yellow, some orange, almost a peach color, all of them tinged like the red maple. The girls came in, formed a loose circle around Mazy and Jennifer.

"Welcome, Mazy," Cawood said—she was the closest— her voice low, whispery. "This river is the best thing about the St. Charles." She opened her arms at the foggy sky and shouted, which all at once made Jennifer nervous and elated, as if something of her had slipped out in that shouting, ricocheted off the water and up to the sky along with everyone else. Then Cawood said, "We do this every day until winter gets us."

"Not the yelling. That's all Cawood," Bethany told her, and the other girls chuckled and some hissed "trouble" under their breath. "Have you turned tricks before?"

Mazy didn't answer.

"Have you had sex? You're young," Lisa said.

Mazy looked behind her at the bank; it had gotten further away from them; and she glanced around at the different faces, not sure where to pin her gaze.

"Were you raped?" Cawood asked.

"Cawood," Jennifer said.

"Don't start on me. You've had your time, Jen. You've been holding on to her for too long. Now we get to talk."

"Raped," Mazy managed, and with that she started to leave, but the girls closed in. "Hold on," they said, "wait up."

"Don't be ashamed just because someone raped you. Most of us been through that," Cawood said, and many of the girls nodded, said, "uh-huh," and Mazy stopped.

"Let her be, Cawood. She isn't ready," Jennifer said.

"Oh, you're ready. Kind of work we do, you're always

ready for. Trust me." Cawood went past Jennifer and came up to the girl. "Someone rape you?" She nodded until Mazy nodded.

"Hurt you?" She picked up Mazy's wrists and rubbed over the cuts. "No trick's worth cutting."

"That's not why I did it," Mazy said.

"Then why?"

"I was angry—" Mazy stopped, looked down at her wrists, the hands holding her, and started to say something else, gasped.

"Cawood," Jennifer said; she was behind them still, and Cawood shifted her back so Jennifer wasn't able to see Mazy and Mazy wasn't able to see her.

"Doesn't matter, whatever happened," Cawood said. "Let it go. No more cutting." She lifted the blue and gold bandana. "What you hiding under here?" and Mazy reached up to her skull as Cawood tossed the bandana between two girls, Mazy spreading her palms over that nakedness.

"Pretty. Your face is much prettier without that hair. You need to stop hiding." Cawood took Mazy's hands down.

"You just throw him away, right here in this river, toss him. That man, it was one man?" Mazy nodded. "It's happened to all of us, a trick doing something we didn't want. But you throw him away, and all that cutting, you throw it away, too, until it's nothing, until it doesn't exist, and only you, that's what's left.

"Next time a trick tries something you don't want, you scream at him like you heard me scream—it'll scare the hell out of him, I promise. He'll think you're some devil. Tricks don't want to mess with the devil." Cawood broadened her shoulders and everyone laughed. "It's all a performance— what you have to do to survive," she whispered. "You've got to learn how to perform." Then she raised her voice. "Johns don't want to be shamed either. Up and down this river are shanties where tricks can do what they want to a girl. But you're protected here." She looked past Mazy at Douglas and the other guard, Oliver. Mazy turned to look. "Some trick starts to hurt you, just scream, and the guards will take him out. Won't let him back in the St. Charles.

"And remember this, when you're in bed turning a trick, it's your bed, take control of it. Most times, that'll be enough. You can come down here, wash tricks away easy. But if you don't work, Ms. Gerald will sell you to one of the shanties, and you'll still have to fuck. Or you'll be in a field working your back against the sun instead of a bed. It takes all of us to keep this place going."

"That's right," the other girls said, "all of us."

"You need to start working," Bethany said, her freckles patched into red blisters.

"Get it over with tonight," Lisa said. "I've got a wig, a brown one you can borrow—wavy, long. I bet your hair was dark brown."

"She's not ready for working," Jennifer told them and stepped around Cawood.

"She just needs to get it over with," Lisa snapped back. "Before I got sold here, I worked at Instant Casino and the casino in Natchez. Saw girls cut and beaten by tricks, saw them die. No one did a thing."

"You're scaring her." Jennifer moved closer, but Mazy pushed her hands out.

"I don't want you around me."

"Mazy—"

The girl shook her head and Cawood grabbed Jennifer's shoulder.

"Don't." Jennifer shook loose, wheeled. "You're bullying her." She was right up on Cawood, and Cawood breathed in, exhaled long and slow.

"Why you picking a fight with me?"

" 'Cause you don't know what's happened. I'm worried about her."

"She's got to take care of herself," Cawood said. Mazy

was walking back to shore, and Jennifer wanted to follow, but hesitated.

Some of the girls swam out to the drop-off, where the channel turned deep, and dove under, laughing; others leaned out over the water, let the surface hold them, cool them, the wind picking them along like driftwood. They faced the sun, where it was burning away the fog.

"She won't make it on her own," Jennifer said. "She's not all right; she's told me."

"I'll look after her like I've looked after you."

"All your caring hasn't made me any better."

"Yet here you are, still alive as far as I can tell."

"But you're leaving in a month. We've got three years."

"You'll get through it like I did, Jen, and she will."

"I'm not happy, Cawood."

Cawood busted a laugh so loud Jennifer thought the river would crack open. "Is that what you're after, happiness? Who ever said living had a thing to do with being happy?"

"Then what's the point, Cawood? What can I hold on to?"

"Nothing. There's no point to it, just like there's no point to death. You think you'll be happy then?"

"I bet your sister had a hard time with you," Jennifer said and stomped off through the water as much as the water and the bottom mud would give.

"It was the other way around," Cawood called out. "She gave me all the fits in the world, but I did love her."

"Did? You *did* love her? You still don't?"

"No, I *still* do, but she passed. She didn't get out of Atlanta."

Jennifer stopped and the river sloshed up against her legs; she turned. "Cawood—"

Cawood just shook her head. "Bringing up my sister. That's none of your damn business. None of your right. Don't do that again. I don't want to think on it, and I've told you that." She swam for the deeper pool of water with the other girls and wouldn't turn around, wouldn't look at Jennifer.

"Cawood," she called after, and from the other direction, Douglas yelled, "Hey."

He and the other guard, Oliver, were yelling for Mazy to come back—she was walking along the shore—and Oliver said he would shoot. But Mazy was property. Ms. Gerald didn't want her property damaged or gunned down. Still, in Birmingham, guns went off by mistake all the time, people shot when no one should be. He pulled his gun. Mazy kept walking, moving a little faster.

Jennifer hurried onto the beach and told them, "I've got her. Don't shoot. Hold on, Mazy." She looked up. You couldn't see the St. Charles, not the third-floor balcony where the other guards had stretched out in chairs, resting after eating, and she felt dizzy like the current and mud were still pulling her feet and ankles in, her shoulders pulling the other way.

Then Mazy ran and Oliver fired. But that was all, one blast into the air, the three of them running after her now. He radioed the other guards, and the ducks along the bank jumped into the river or sliced the water a small distance, then raised up and flew across.

It was at the point where the beach curved, where Mazy could've gone out of sight if she turned up the bank into the empty houses and buildings of Cairo; it was at that point she stopped, and they caught up to her quick. The men grabbed her, bound her, Jennifer asking if she was okay, and pleading, "Don't harm her."

Two huge black birds clapped from the shore and sailed heavily toward the sky. Where the birds had been, where Mazy kept staring, was a body tied to a tree. It was an old white oak, bent and heavy-trunked leaning out at the water. And where the trunk leaned, the body had been tied, a rope

across the forehead, one across the neck, stomach, and
calves like a ship's figurehead, a sign hanging from its neck,
the wind picking at it, knocking.

Douglas walked up, swiped at the sign, missed, and
reached for it again more slowly. He kept looking over the
face—eyeless, noseless, earless, the mouth eaten back into a
wide gullet. He kept looking as if it was someone he knew.
And Mat, for a second Jennifer thought it was Mat—she had
dreamed of him. He had walked up the river; but she had
dreamed him, it wasn't him now, and yet she said his name.

"No hunters," Douglas shouted, turning the sign so they
could see the spray-painted words. "Another poacher from
Qillen's farm. Should we leave him?"

"Why does Qillen tie those bodies up so close to us?"
Oliver spit at the ground, scraped his foot over the spit and
buckled a collar over Mazy's neck, pulled, wrapped the
leash around his hand. Mazy kept staring at the body; she
hadn't moved.

"He's always tying poachers up by the roads. Have you
seen the one on 50 between here and Instant?"

Oliver shook his head.

"Should I cut him down?"

"We're not dealing with that." Oliver radioed the other
guards, many of them already on the beach.

He waved. "You can stop your running." They slowed,
and one guard put his hands to his knees.

"Ronnie, are you that out of shape?" Oliver snapped.
The other guards chuckled.

"He used to be a sprinter," someone said, and the heck-
ling grew louder. Ronnie managed to raise one hand and
swat at the closest body.

Behind them, the girls were still in the water. If any had
been panicked when the gun fired, Jennifer couldn't tell.
Their voices boomed upriver, joking, singing, the huge
black birds circling.

●   ●   ●

There was a scratch at the door. It was Naomi, and Jennifer told her to come inside, but she stood against the frame, her hair drawn severely at the corners with bobby pins before it fell straight to her jacket like three sides of a square so her face could be fully seen. Nothing was hidden in those eyes; her distrust was never hidden. Jennifer always felt she was facing her mama, a piece that kept shifting before Jennifer could catch up to it and name it, know it exactly.

She said, "Mazy's already in the parlor. You need to come to work like everyone else."

"What did Ms. Gerald do to her?"

"Nothing," and she shifted into the hallway, into its weaker light with the odor of stale cigarettes and plates of barely-eaten food. "Worse things have happened than a girl running away and failing. Like when you got here and lost your baby." She looked at Jennifer's stomach, then back to the stairwell. "It takes a while." And there it was—that knot where her baby had tried to take root and was now gone.

"Besides, Mazy said she was ready to work."

"I need to get dressed," Jennifer said, and Naomi tapped her watch as Jennifer shut the door.

"Just know you're expected."

After they came back from the river, Mazy had been taken to her new room, and Jennifer was left with the girl's clothes and the notebook. A servant came for the clothes, but the notebook stayed; and Jennifer looked at the drawings Mazy had recently done and kept hidden. They were all of the room, different angles of the furniture and windows, how the curtains pulled against the walls, and the Kentucky shore and the river, that long bank on the other side.

Jennifer wanted to go to the windows, but couldn't now; she didn't want to see those birds circling, didn't want to think about that tied body stretched above the water. Qillen was a name she had heard of. He owned the land north of the St. Charles, a tobacco and corn farmer. And what Douglas said, that other bodies were tied to trees along highways—Jennifer kept pacing the room, looking at her walls, imagining bodies just beyond them, every direction, all those bodies had her boxed in. So she retreated to the bed, opened the notebook back up.

Mazy had drawn a picture of Delia's legs, just the legs kicking, and Jennifer took out the flicker-photograph to set it beside Mazy's drawing. She stared one to the other, the one in motion, the other still, and at first the motion of the photograph kept her attention, but then it was what Mazy had done, how the one leg dipped down, the lines around the anklebones out to the toes.

She put a hand over her mama's face in the photograph and gazed at the legs, tried to imagine what Mazy saw. Then she put a finger on Mazy's lines, felt along them, ingrained so deeply. She traced it and traced it. Her mama was in these lines, and herself, and Mazy, crossing, twining, breathing, while the other legs fluttered on the periphery.

Jennifer took her mother on one more drive, a short one from Delia's house on Ted Lane in Richmond to the bus waiting in the town square of Sardis. At 3:00 a.m. the bus departed for Birmingham, and from there another bus to Chicago. It was only thirteen miles from Richmond to Sardis and her mother was already on the front porch with her one piece of luggage when Jennifer arrived.

She tossed it on the truck bed, and they started out.

"Where's your luggage?" her mama said. It should've sounded like a joke. Jennifer had said for weeks she wasn't going. But Delia said it straight, a mother's order, and Jennifer felt the pull to oblige. The truth was, Jennifer had thought of going, even now with so little time, with Mathew refusing and at the clay mine, a part of her, no, every bit of her wanted to leave for the Saved World.

"I'll get there," Jennifer promised. "Mat just needs a little more convincing. His father's here." Jennifer had been telling herself this for days.

"Chris wants his son to go as much as you and me."

"He won't go, Mama. We've already talked about this. I don't want to talk about it."

Delia sighed, and for a few miles they stayed quiet, but she kept looking out the window, fidgeting. She had on perfume, but Delia never wore perfume, and where did she get it? Maybe that's why she couldn't be still.

"Why don't you come anyway. He'll come after, he loves you so much."

"You wouldn't have left Terry here."

"But I want you to go." Her mama slapped her hands on the dashboard. Like a child, Jennifer thought. It was something Jennifer would've done once.

"Why won't you come with me?"

Because I don't love you. She could've said that to hurt her mama, and even thinking it made Jennifer scold herself—by allowing those words to go through her mind, the sentiment might become real. And what if it was real? It wasn't. She did love Delia, but she was also scared of her, of what might happen with the two of them alone and no Mat to talk with and console her.

"I'm getting married, Mama," Jennifer said.

"He'll follow. He loves you so much," she insisted.

"Stop, it, Mama." Jennifer put her hand over Delia's and squeezed.

They continued on the highway and Jennifer kept her hand on her mother's so Delia wouldn't talk, then a sign for Sardis brightened in their headlights, and just ahead of the sign the bus headlights cut slivers into the black sand, heading north.

Jennifer left the truck idling and opened the tailgate, slid the luggage across the bed, and handed it to her mama.

"Jenny, I promise things will be different."

"I'm getting married. Then we'll come. I'll talk him into it." Her mother was tall. Jennifer always forgot that. Maybe Jennifer was a little taller, but she usually found Delia sitting in a chair, and when she stood it was like being next to someone Jennifer didn't know as well as she thought she did.

She walked her mother to the bus and the driver came out. He had on a gray suit and blue cap and checked her ticket and visa and put her bag in the compartment underneath the seats efficiently and without grunting like Jennifer had earlier.

"You have no idea how hard it is to leave your girl here, your only girl," Delia said. She put the tickets back in her purse, closed her eyes.

"I know, Mama."

"You know nothing of it," Delia said. "I know what you think of me. I know you don't like me."

"Mama," Jennifer said. "I love you. Doesn't that count for something?"

Delia stood there, as if she was judging those words, trying to decide if she could believe them. She looked at the ground, then out at that desert, taking the whole desert in. "I carried you in my body for nine months, doesn't that count for something? Maybe I shouldn't go. Not like this—"

Terry had told Jennifer the same thing about nine months. It was something the two adults must've spoken of between themselves and agreed on—nine months, that should count against all the other.

"I'll get there, Mama," Jennifer told her.

"I just want you in Chicago," she said. "Safe. With me."

"I know," Jennifer said. "I love you."

"I love you, too." They hugged, and her mother's body felt bulky and awkward. Delia got on the bus and the driver stood out by the door trying to light a cigarette, but couldn't in the dirt-wind blustering stronger. Finally he put the cigarette back into his pocket and checked his watch and went inside.

Jennifer waved to her mama though all she could make out were darkened windows and the long silver body of the bus, brighter than the driver's suit. She headed back to the truck. The wind kept whistling the sand by her in huge ribbons, her headlights sputtering down, then flashing brighter.

That damn engine's not going to hold, Jennifer thought to herself, and hurried to the cab, but then she slowed down. She was going to be in the desert until Mat decided to go with her. There was no rush to leave. If the truck broke, it broke. She stood there watching the engine rear and putter.

"Go ahead and break," she said, but it wouldn't.

Jennifer came down in her green dress, the material thinned from use, a favorite dress that had been in her closet when she arrived and belonged to a girl before her. Sometimes she'd take the collar, bundle it up in her hand, and smell the sweat that was not hers, as if by smell alone she could know that girl. She was a brunette, her hair lighter than Jennifer's thick black, but just as thick and straight. The dress was tight on Jennifer's stomach, so it had to fit the brown-haired girl better; she was smaller, a few inches shorter. There was something about her sway, the way Jennifer moved in the hips of the dress; she could pick up the hips of the other girl—no, not the hips exactly, but that sway, she could pick up the girl's motion. Sometimes, the material threw her off balance as if the dress was expecting the other girl and how she walked and danced. Jennifer had only worn it a few times. Never washed it. She didn't want to lose that girl who she liked to imagine had gotten free of the St. Charles, one of the lucky ones.

The stairwell door vibrated when Jennifer put a hand

against it—people already stomping. And Jinx, he was singing, playing loud, just him tonight, no one else, not Dang Red or Benji. She held there. Last time she had been in the stairwell at night, this very spot, she had touched Cawood's face, and they had talked about Cawood's sister. She was dead. Something cold went through Jennifer. She wouldn't bring it up again—not her place, not her right. Another person she had no right to know of or feel for, like Mazy. She wanted to go back to her room, lie down, sleep. But there'd be repercussions. Naomi would come looking for her. If Delia was here, she'd say, "Stop feeling sorry for yourself." As if that's all it took to stop, as if her mother ever stopped.

She opened the door, and the sound came full in the lights, the room whirling, Jinx singing:

My baby's the best thing I got
Hot light burning white off the sun,
Lords knows, I do all she asks
My apple, my peach, my spicy honey pot.
My baby, she's the one that's hot,
Burns out the moon with her fingers where they run,
Keeps me on my knees, my queen bee,
Sipping from her sweet-sweet honey pot.

She made sure not to make a grand entrance, kept to the wall like those infamous wallflowers she couldn't be much longer, and looked down at the shoes and bare feet turning, kicking. Already there was the St. Charles football huddle; eight, ten girls laced together, kicking their toes to the middle and heels back out as tricks peeled them out until only five remained, then four, Jinx doing what he called the upper key boogie-woogie special. In that back and forth and fast rhythm, those garish bodies and suits, Jennifer found Mazy. She was dancing with two clients and Cawood nearby. They laughed, and Mazy had on a wig, but you couldn't tell it, a blond one Jennifer had seen on Lisa. Mazy was dancing like dancing was her second skin. The girl looked over, then looked away quick, took the hands of one of the clients and pressed them against her sides. He moved his hands up and down and the other one put his hands on her, too.

Jennifer cut across the floor. Someone grabbed at her. "Hold up, baby," he said, but she kept past him to the lounge—where three girls were taking a break between johns, smoking—and past them into the bathroom. She tried to avoid the full-length mirrors Ms. Gerald had hung for examining your body's growing contours, and locked herself in a stall, vomited.

There was for a moment euphoria, her strength growing like she could push through the stall door, every door in the St. Charles, but they just led to empty hallways and stairs and more doors, and then a window, then the sky. She shook that sky out of her head and calmed enough to lean back, breathe. *This*—she had forced Mazy to leave Birmingham for *this*.

Someone came into the next stall and retched; all night there'd be retching. Like washing tricks away in the Ohio River, retching was another St. Charles ritual, though this one was unspoken. Ms. Gerald was serious about keeping your figure thin. On Friday mornings, they had to be weighed, and for each pound gained over the week, the girls lost kitchen privileges. One pound equaled no breakfast until the next weighing, two pounds equaled no breakfast or lunch, and anything over five pounds led to mandatory fasting. So the toilets in the bathroom smelled more like soured milk than piss no matter how much they flushed and the servants scrubbed.

Jennifer waited as the girl stepped out, then up to the mirror, cleared her throat, gargled, and washed her hands. She had already seen the red heels and tried to erase them, not wanting to attach those heels to a pair of legs and face.

When Jennifer returned to the lounge, the three girls were gone and Naomi was standing there. It was one of Naomi's duties to clear out the lounge and stalls, herd the girls back onto the main floor with the clients. She slipped past Jennifer without speaking, like she was tired of talking to people, tired of giving orders.

The music, the mood in the parlor had changed. Jinx had begun a slow song, and except for a few couples, everyone had retreated to the bar or the balcony, the glass doors there open, replaced with screens for the cooler nights, the guards stationed to the sides like potted trees, like every night—still immovable. Jennifer caught the red and white flashes of a mille-copter, then another. They were coming from the east, from Instant Casino.

Then Jinx slipped, snagged right in the center of a center-root, and in that pause, the dancers continued to turn in place, a slow box move, and she heard the shuffle of people below, that other world from the bottom half of the St. Charles, girls turning mille-copter pilots and truckers and barge operators. She always forgot they existed until they made noise. The shuffling sounded like fish hitting their heads inside a bucket. Then Jinx sat on a chord, and the music washed back over that parallel world.

"Why don't you take a break," she said when she got to the piano. "Talk with me a while."

"Got to finish up this song. Stand a minute." He repeated the chorus, *My sweet baby, I'll take you dancing tonight*, then swept his hands across the lower notes to the upper ones, a move he called the "escalator," and stopped— all these things she knew about him—his hands, their habits that had become more recognizable to her than her own.

As he rubbed them together, people clapped, and conversations filled the empty space. His hands looked sore, shaking, and Jennifer sat on the bench, took them.

"No low-down love songs tonight?"

"I'm just getting warmed up. I'm starting them off with

some nice, pretty songs, then I get to the truth, all that sweet love's going to go bad. Just wait. I got a whole evening to make love go bad. Ow, don't press so hard," he said, and Jennifer let his palms sit in hers. She picked up the towel, a few slivers of ice still in it, and laid it over those wooden knuckles, swollen. Above them, the ceiling fans were turning too slowly to do any good.

"If my fingers ever fail me, that'll be the worse day." Jinx kept twisting his shoulders and arms through his long white sleeves, trying to ease the pressure on his wrists.

"You've still got your lungs."

"I know, but take my hands, I might as well die," he said. "They're attached to my heart, my lungs, my brain. It's all wired down to the fingers." He twitched them, but it didn't help them steady. "I'm worthless if they go. My father had to stop playing the piano in his eighties—I couldn't practice around him after that, he got too upset. I had to go to my club, The Roll 'Em Pete, and my wife took care of him."

"How long you been married?" Jennifer had always wanted to know about this woman in St. Louis.

"Thirty years."

"Thirty years and you're singing songs about bad love?"

"Before I knew her," he raised his voice, "I knew bad love. Don't doubt me. I had my share. She's my second wife." He flashed two fingers. "First one I was married to, loved this woman so much I didn't know who I was. I didn't care if I played the piano. That's right," he nodded, "that serious. My father told me I'd lost my mind, and I had. We lived in Kansas City. I was working at Ophelia's enough to pay rent and supper, and it wasn't long before she started telling me she needed more time to herself. Well, I didn't understand it because I couldn't stand to be without her. Why would she want to be away from me? Then I found her with someone I knew, we both knew. Never will forget that. Strolling up Wyandotte and there they were on the other side of the street, walking, holding each other, right out in daylight like they were doing nothing wrong. Never will forget how vulnerable that made me." Jinx stared off, frowned, and Jennifer could see it—if she wasn't careful, her questions would make him quiet, cranky, send him into a blue temper.

"I'm sorry, Jinx," she said, but didn't know what else to do, how to keep him from sliding. And still she knew nothing about his wife in St. Louis.

"Enough of all that," he said. "Where you been?"

"Taking care of a girl."

"The new one?" He nodded toward the bar, and Jennifer looked through the hot, bright, all the colors and bodies, the smoke heavier until she found Mazy with the same two tricks and Cawood.

"Thought Cawood might be taking care of this one."

"Looks like she is now," Jennifer said.

"What, you jealous? You're attached to her, I can tell."

"I'm not jealous." Jennifer bit at the inside of her cheek.

"Uh-huh." Jinx cleared his throat. "What's her name?"

"Mazy. We met in Birmingham, and I promised her mama I'd take care of her. It's my fault she's here."

"Birmingham's no place for anybody now."

"But she's here, and she's so angry with me about it. And I don't blame her. She misses her mama."

"She's young," Jinx said. "You have to give kids time to forgive. She can't hold that grudge always."

"You don't know Mazy. And like I said, I don't blame her."

"So let Cawood take care of this one. Move on."

Sometimes Jinx could say the most hurtful things without even trying, and she wondered why they stayed friends. Maybe they weren't friends, and it was his blunt way of reminding her. He had said move on. But where could she go? There was no place for her and he knew that. She looked around the parlor, over at the balcony at the tricks standing, looking for someone to approach.

He sighed. "I don't know what to do for you, Jen."

"I'm not asking for anything," she said. "You know I'm married just like you are."

"I thought you told all the guys you're married to me?"

"I tell them that, but I have a husband in Alabama, nine years. And what's he going to think when I'm done at the St. Charles? Like your first wife—what she did. You think he's going to want me when I'm done?"

"It's different. She was two-timing."

"I'm doing worse than that."

"Stop," he said but wouldn't look at Jennifer now—it was the same look she expected from Mathew. He'd turn from her, allow the numbness to seep back in over the emptiness in her bones, her skin. His gaze, his hands—he'd keep those from her. "I'm going to play a song. One that's going to lift your spirits, get you out of this mess. You'll see."

"No, Jinx," she said and held his palms tight, tried to stop them from moving—she was the one sliding now and needed his hands, but they twitched, shifted.

"I've got to start playing," he said. "Now let go."

"Linger a little more, Jinx. Rest your hands with me, Jinx."

"I've rested enough. I've got to do my work. You can stay here."

"You never let me stay," she said. "Besides, Ms. Gerald won't allow that." Jennifer released him, set the towel down.

He put his fingers right at the center and banged out a chord. "What am I going to do with you?"

Jennifer stood up. "You're letting me go."

"If a man loves you, he loves you no matter what," Jinx said.

"Maybe. Maybe he loves you until he thinks you've betrayed him. Like all your songs tell it, like you yourself tell it." And she walked off.

"Don't listen too closely to my songs," he called after

her, and clicked fast over the keys. Then, "Wait," he said and got up from the piano.

Slowly, he came over. "Why's it got to be like this?" he said. "You walking away?"

He reached out and grabbed hold of her arm. Rubbed it, his hands wet and cold from the ice. "Come downstairs tomorrow, and I'll play some songs. Just get through this night and come down tomorrow. See me."

"What makes you think I can't get through the night?" As soon as she said it, she wished she hadn't. There were so many other things to say. Better things.

"I don't know." He looked down. "I'm just worried about you, Jen."

She took his hand, held it carefully. "It's good of you. And I'll be here tomorrow, all right?"

"I'll be expecting," he said and nodded and walked back to the piano.

For a moment, she felt better. Then Mazy came out on the floor with the two clients, and Jennifer sat at an empty table to watch them.

The whole evening went this way—Jennifer and Mazy swirling around each other, avoiding each other. Cawood wouldn't talk. Every time a trick came by, Jennifer got up with him and found at least one other girl to chat with until the trick started talking to the other girl more. Then Jennifer went to the bathroom or the bar, somewhere, anywhere else. The maneuver had been nicknamed "the bump and run." Bump into someone else, leave your trick there, and run the other way as fast as possible.

Even though Mazy made sure not to look over, Jennifer watched her—so much like her mama, Lavina. She had those same knobbed cheekbones and wide, moon eyes, and that smile, that full row of teeth. *Take care of Mazy until I can get back to you*—that's what the note from Lavina had said.

As she watched Mazy, she wondered about Lavina, and her own mama, Terry, her baby, Mat and what Jinx had said about a man's love, and Cawood's sister, and sometimes there were glimpses of Birmingham, the dead being lifted into harvesting machines, Mazy's drawings of their arms and legs and faces. For months, Jennifer had lost these parts of herself, misplaced these people—how does one misplace people?—but with Mazy here, suddenly they bloomed. At times like this, they overwhelmed her, consumed her, each image pressing down, becoming the other, and there was nothing to be done about it until she lost them again.

She sat listening to Jinx play "What Did I Do to Be So Black and Blue"—his voice cracking high but gruff. That music, Jinx's music, and the river, the only two things in this place that ever healed her. And it never lasted. She looked at Mazy, wanted to ask if she was okay after what happened earlier. But Mazy seemed like that body tied to the tree, like she had already forgotten what Jennifer could not, like she had never seen it to begin with.

Naomi passed through the room, and Ms. Gerald came down from her office twice and circled. Neither said a word to her, but like Jennifer they came to watch Mazy. Another girl doing what was expected.

And when Mazy finally left with a trick, even then, Jennifer held on to see if she would come back down. It was all Jennifer's doing and no way to undo it. She hated herself. But this time, all the self-righteousness she had pointed at her mother was gone. She hated herself for what she had done to Mazy. There was nothing else, just like Cawood had promised, nothing to hold.

There was a scratch at the door. Jennifer thought it was Mazy, hoped it was, but it was Lisa.

"Come on," she said.

"What?" Jennifer said.

"Just come on." Lisa was still whispering, but with such urgency, Jennifer didn't say a thing to the trick lying asleep in her bed, just left him, slipped on the green dress, closed the door, and followed Lisa down the hallway. And she didn't ask Lisa *What?* a second time because she couldn't. Lisa moved too fast, staying ahead of her, the hallway empty, cold, always colder than her room.

The wall lamps flashed up in their steps; between the lamps, shadowed curbs of wallpaper and carpet, and in the distended blackness of the ceiling, the space between her and Lisa grew longer. Jennifer couldn't catch up.

Lisa opened the last door to Cawood standing over a bed, and Mazy in a chair at the far end with her knees up, arms folded, and sheared head burrowed down. On the bed was a trick lying on his stomach, his back wrapped in sheets and blood.

"She cut him into a mess," Cawood explained. "Broke a water glass in the bathroom. The pieces are everywhere."

Jennifer kept hoping the body would move, but it didn't. And in the dried blood coming through the white sheets she saw what Mazy cut into his back, the lines of a trunk, the round whorls of bark on the spine, and branches stretching over the shoulders—a tree bleeding through his skin that Jennifer could not reverse, could not sew up. "He's dead."

"Just dead drunk. He'll come out of it eventually," Cawood told her. "She didn't cut him deep. More like she engraved him than anything else. We wrapped his back and the bleeding's stopped. I mean, he's lucky we got here when we did. Who knows what else she would've done—she's lucky." Cawood tilted her head sideways at Mazy. When the girl didn't look over, Cawood crossed her arms, sighed. "He needs a doctor. And I don't know what he's going to do to her when he wakes up. He's going to be hurting. You know what Ms. Gerald will do."

It was a tree, straight, then curved where the roots sank down into the hips, and around the trunk, spots of blood like stars, like leaves falling, at the shoulders the thin beginning of branches, his arms just dangling, his whole body.

Jennifer started for the chair, but Mazy tightened.

"I heard her through that wall crying. She was whimpering." Lisa pointed. "She wouldn't open the door, so I got Cawood to let us in."

Jennifer kept walking, moving from the lamp to the window, tucking her bangs behind her ears.

"We found her like that," Lisa said, "with him on the covers."

"She was doing so well tonight. I thought she was ready."

Jennifer stopped. "Mazy," she whispered. The girl remained bundled, no shoes, blood on the dress around her legs. Jennifer turned to ask Cawood about the blood.

"Don't leave me," Mazy said.

Jennifer turned back. "I'm not going to," she said and reached in.

"That man's mille-copter is out there but the pilot isn't going to wait. He needs a doctor."

"We're coming," Jennifer told Cawood, and "We have to go now," she said to Mazy. "You have to come with me. You understand what you've done?"

"I know," Mazy said.

"You have to get up." Jennifer helped her and lifted her—the girl's hand was sticky with blood from where she held the glass but she hadn't cut her wrists or any other part of herself. Her hands were shaking like Jinx's, her whole body, and her bones felt pared and hollowed like Jennifer could lift her, the easiest, most breakable thing.

"Take her down to your room and wait. I'm going to open this door and yell, yell so loud, the guards'll come running. When the guards come up the stairs, you get the hell out of here, the gate to the river." Cawood handed her the key. "Try to catch a truck on the highway. Over at the bridge into Kentucky. I wish I knew a path, knew some people."

"But Cawood," Jennifer held up the key, "Ms. Gerald will—"

"She won't. She might not even figure it out. I've been baptized by that woman, like I told you. Not doing that again. I'm out of here in a month, I promise." Cawood shoved an envelope into Jennifer's hand. "It's what Lisa and I've been hiding—almost eight hundred. There are smugglers will take you to Chicago, or at least get you near for that. Now go."

"Caw—"

"You going to make it, you need to go." And they slipped into the hallway, the elongated shadows and lamplight, slipped into Jennifer's room.

"There's a trick here," she whispered, setting a finger to Mazy's lips.

He kept snoring. "Snores louder than you," Jennifer said, and reached under the bed, pulled out the black box, placed the envelope inside, made sure the lock was secure.

When Cawood yelled, the doors in the hall were flung open, and even the trick on her bed turned. She waited until the heavy feet, the boots of the guards came through the stairwell before she and Mazy slipped out, all the way down and out the gate that Jennifer had walked through so many times. But Jennifer didn't go to the Ohio, the bridge. She took Mazy through Cairo to the Mississippi side, and kept looking back, kept thinking someone would come, Douglas and the other guards, or the roaming gangs out of the houses, but if they just kept moving, running, maybe nothing could get them.

They made it under the levee to the Mississippi, and kept going along the bank until Mazy slipped, and Jennifer lifted her up, a stream of barges coming upriver like there were always barges. For a moment they raced the ships, then Mazy, swiftly, silently, dove in and began to swim.

Jennifer called to her, watched her slip from the bank,

then clutched the box and dove in, too. The stacked barges sat halfway out in the water, chugging slow-footed with what looked like coal, the moon catching flashes off the pyramided freight. They were heading north to St. Louis or Minneapolis. She could barely see the girl, but could hear her thrashing and followed after the sound, breathing, diving into the water, and back up, Mazy ahead of her, and the barge lights cutting off the Missouri bank on the other side.

Her lungs and muscles started to burn. She hadn't swum like this in years, and her lungs filled with heat and too much cold water, but she couldn't stop now and reached out, the thrashing ended. She grabbed the iron siding and tried to call for Mazy, then found the girl holding on to the edge, breathing hard, lifting herself as Jennifer drifted to a ladder, pulled herself up, too. She tossed the box onto the coal, and sat next to the girl in the front. Behind them, the black pile sparkled. They both looked back at Cairo and the St. Charles, watched it for a long time, the land slipping away, the dark trees, this separate island they were on. Overhead the stars from Mazy's notebook glittered; it was as if the book had opened, and the stars had been tossed to the sky, those stars back into a universe, wide, so wide, impossible to navigate.

She thought of that story about the girl who waved to everyone from her barge and the next day came floating down the river, dead. She looked over at Mazy shivering and grabbed hold of her, gathering the girl into her arms; the warmth of their skin worked against the cold. Then she looked at the stars slipping past, and breathed.

October 13, 2044

Dear Mama,

    I'm close to you, closer than I've been. I'm on the Illinois River just past Beardstown. A smuggler, his name is Patrick Carson, is taking us to Starved Rock by boat and from there, his connection, LT, will take us to Chicago.

Patrick Carson tells us over and over that LT owns five Cadillacs, and he'll be up to meet us in one of those.

It's a simple plan, he says. We'll get you to Chicago. Don't worry.

Every day we get closer he tells us this, and I'm starting to believe him; believe that Chicago will be my home. He's been smuggling people and shipments up the Mississippi and Illinois forever and a day. Everything to him has taken place in forever and a day.

These small towns along the river aren't dead, he promises us. He tells us, I could stop anywhere along the river and see people. People coming down to fish off the banks, in motorboats and pontoons, not just barges and tugs. This river had a life to it of people. And who knows what's coming next.

When he starts rambling like this, Mama, he stares at the trees and the sky like it's the last time he might see them and says that the river is a vacuum now, but someone will fill it.

It won't be those isolated farmers or the corporate ones. They're too tied to the land. This river.

Then he throws his hands up in the air as if the expanse of his arms can reach out, touch every part of the water.

Someone's going to take her. And it won't be me.

They'll run me off—after Patrick Carson told us that, he shook his head and returned to the helm.

When we go through the locks, Mazy and I hide in the V-berth, even though Patrick says he's been paying the valve operators for years and knows their first names. He always asks about their kids.

Extra money comes in handy with kids, and he winks, believing Mazy is my younger sister. Most of the time we stay hidden in the quarters, but occasionally we get out on deck, especially night. I'd like to tell you that Mazy and I talk like we did in Birmingham, that she asks me to read to her and teach her to read, that we are close like sisters after all we've seen and known together, at least friends. But she maintains her distance, draws in her notebook, doesn't want to acknowledge what happened, doesn't want to acknowledge me.

It took a while before the notebook and the stationery dried because we had to swim to a barge in Cairo— everything got waterlogged. The operator let us stay on until St. Louis and introduced us to Patrick Carson. For so long, our luck ran the other way. I still worry we'll come out from hiding in the V-berth and Patrick Carson will have sold us like the guias on Snakeskin Road. But it's just him, and he's carrying other supplies more valuable than us.

He said he's mainly taking us because he wants company.

He said—*It gets lonely out here, and I'm tired of making this trip without anyone. Besides, it's a simple plan.*

Sometimes when I look out at the shore, I expect someone to be there, waiting, because for months our luck ran the other way. But now I'm close to you, can feel the distance reeling, vanishing. I want you to understand when Mazy and I arrive, what happened to Mazy is with her like it is me, like those years in the desert remain with you.

She asked me if I thought she was crazy.

No, I told her. The world's what's crazy.

She told me, but I can't get all of it out of my head, Jen, the way those people were killed in Birmingham.

She never talks about what happened to her in St. Louis. I haven't brought it up because I'm afraid she'll turn violent, afraid of what she'll do to herself. When she found out we were going to St. Louis that night we left Cairo, she almost jumped off the barge and back to shore. I told her we weren't going to the house she lived in, but I still had to hold her to keep her from jumping.

I used to think that if you survived something long enough, no matter how horrible, then you'd truly escape the thing you were trying to get away from. It would disappear and so would its hold over you. I thought I'd forget the desert like you seemed to be able to in your letters and photos. But I've looked back over your words, faded from the river, and the pictures, some of them no longer transform in the light, and now I see all the ways you've never forgotten the desert; its mark is on you. It's on us, that dust and wind, what it's carved into us and taken.

I have nightmares of Birmingham. For a while I dreamed of Mat, but he's gone from my dreams; I can't bring him here, and maybe I shouldn't any longer. Since losing my baby, I wake up at night reaching between my legs for the blood and the fetus, try to catch it before it's gone like a fish slipping from my hands in the river. I can't stop having that dream. I don't know what Mazy dreams, but losing her mother, and what she saw in Birmingham, what happened in St. Louis—all of this stays with her.

She'll need the two of us to keep her together, to keep her from hurting herself, to heal her. What has happened will always conspire against her living.

I love you,

Jen

October 14

Dear Mama,

We're nearing Starved Rock. Patrick Carson has told us the story several times because it's one of his favorites, of how members of the Illiniwek Indian tribe fled from another tribe, the Potawatomi, to the rock. The Illiniwek held there instead of coming down to face the Potawatomi and died of starvation. I keep thinking of that choice—and there were no good choices, death was certain either way, but they chose to last on that rock as long as possible. For a long time that's what was being done to us in the desert—we were being starved out of existence, and we remained. Then I think, Mama, I did that to myself when my baby died—I can't say that I've finished grieving, but I can say I no longer want to linger and starve. I want to reach you in Chicago. I want to give you that chance you asked for years ago. I want to give myself that chance, and Mazy.

October 15

Dear Mama,

Tomorrow we will be at Starved Rock and then soon, very soon, we'll be with you. I'll hold you for a long time and not let go, and I'll hand you these letters, let you read them all so you'll know what's happened to me and Mazy. Please, please welcome her. She is part of me now.

Today, Mazy showed me her notebook—all the pages are used up. When we get to Chicago we'll need to get her more. I can't wait to see what she makes of Chicago, what she sees in that world through her eyes, her hands. Mazy showed me her sketches of the Illinois River, its slow water and flat banks, the trees turning, their leaves drifting on the currents away from us. She has a picture of you—well, of your legs kicking that she made at the St. Charles—and a picture of her mother, Lavina.

She said she couldn't draw it for so long.

I had it in my mind, Mazy told me, what my mama would look like, the expression on her face—anticipating what might happen next; my mama was always anticipating things. That's why she put me with you, because she *didn't think she could get me out of Birmingham. I think she knew how bad it might be and hoped against it, hoped more than anything in the world I'd be alive.*

Did I get that? Mazy asked.

What do you mean? I asked her.

Did I get that anticipation, her wanting me to be all right? Did I do that in the picture for her?

I told her yes, and placed my fingers like I always do now to the page. Because to really know what Mazy has drawn you have to touch the page, follow how the lines turn. I've often thought those indentions and lines are their own language, and I've come to realize that in her markings is an essence of these people, some part of them she has set down, maybe the only thing of them left, and when you touch that page, Mama, you touch those people, wherever they might be, they're suddenly with you, alive.

So I touched her mother's face, and Lavina was with me, just as I touched your legs kicking in the water and you were with me, that distance between us gone, and the river, this one, all of them, I have followed their currents on these pages to get to you.

Tomorrow. Good night, Mama. We will see you tomorrow.

I love you,

Jen

Rosser

Adamsville, Alabama, was the new post. Had been for two weeks, but I doubted it'd last long. Used to, I went straight to Birmingham with the deserters—they had a nice setup. Dropped off my bounty and got paid in less than an hour. But the desert had closed in, and the government pulled the border back. They squeezed Birmingham underneath it and left all those people there, dying.

It took me half the night to get paid for two men and a woman. Had to sit with them in a cement cube, and one man, he was the shorter one, I had already kicked him before we came in and cautioned him about it, but he wouldn't stop crying. I told him to shut up, he was crying like my mam, like his mam, like every fucking mam in the entire fucking world. That did no good. I would've hit him but you couldn't do that on the premises without getting paid less.

Some of the patrollers looked over at me with my head all bottled up in my hands and they chuckled. I knew one of them, had dealt with him all summer—he had a square head that rolled on his chin-neck every time he looked down to sign papers.

"It ain't funny," I yelled. "Hurry up."

They kept chuckling, and that short man kept crying. Geez.

Turned out they were from Suttons Corner, Georgia, on the Alabama line—got fifteen thousand dollars when I was finished and they were to be shipped to a limestone work camp in Telfair. When I left, I left the crying for the wind crying and blowing sand all through Adamsville like a dust fire. That's all I could hear, wind and sand making its promise—in Birmingham they were doing a killing—soon enough, the desert would come here, too.

High Street had three bars, and from what I could tell, it was the only street with anything happening in this town. It had a lighted church, but I wasn't going near that church, and one bar had been set up in a supply store. The sign hadn't been changed—*Stel's Fertilizer*. One bar looked as if it had been in Adamsville forever—called The Halladay. And the other was a converted elementary school. It didn't have a name, just lights in the glass windows.

That was the one with classrooms full of drunk patrollers and guards and Red Cross volunteers and whores. You didn't like who you saw in Ms. Krenshaw's seventh grade English, you could step over to Mr. Flumb's eighth grade math. Those were teachers I had once, and I kept imagining them stepping into the rooms. Neither one could keep us quiet.

At the end of the hallway stood a pair of double doors and a string of clear lights that opened to the school gym; the bar was all the way across. If I had to name this joint, I'd call it School's Out, or something catchy, like The End of the World.

"Tomorrow, everyone will get up with headaches and

start the world over." I told the bartender that, and he just gave me my drink. So I drank and talked with other hunters, patrollers, and guardsmen. I drank and listened the rest of the night as much as I could through the conversations wheeling and circling to the steel rafters and falling back on top of me.

One officer said the government had abandoned Linn Park. He kept trying to rub the sweat off his hands. Never seen someone sweat so much. "That was the last consulate we had. All the other food drops were shut down last week. We've left those people to the bombing gangs and roamers."

"And the storm," I reminded him.

"Doesn't sit well with me, but it's just too many people to deal with." The whole time he kept looking side to side, yet wouldn't look across the table, too ashamed of himself, his bald head like a dull pendulum, unhitched and wilting. But he didn't know me enough to have to bare his shame. "And there's no money."

"What do you mean no money?" I was used to the feds not doing something 'cause they didn't want to. A lack of money, however, had never stopped them in the past. The government had lived in bankruptcy forever.

"They've moved all the guardsmen from Louisiana and Mississippi here, but"—he shook his head—"they're not returning. No money. The government's just keeping this section from Birmingham to Atlanta patrolled. They're worried the desert will take Atlanta next. Most of the mining is south to Florida anyway."

"They still turning the mines into work camps?"

He nodded. "Accelerating it, building those camps as fast as they can. Someone's making money. They've talked about transporting prisoners from the Carolinas. It shouldn't affect you any, if you're worried." He looked up then, smiled. "You'll always have a job."

"I'm not worried," I said and finished off my rum. But I knew why he said it—if prisoners started coming down, the government wouldn't need Alabama deserters. And for years the government had paid good money for those people.

At one time the Southeastern Desert had too many inhabitants, and the government wanted them bottlenecked, didn't want them fleeing north, just like they didn't want anyone leaving Birmingham now, so they made it a criminal offense and marked runaways as deserters as if they had belonged to the US Army, as if they had abandoned their country.

If you brought in a deserter, you got paid enough to keep doing it. I've done it for nine years. When the government opened the work camps, they started paying real money. None of those people in the camps ever get out—they work until their death. Then someone in the government said, Hell, why not make all mining operations in the Southeastern Desert an extension of the penal system.

Since 2014, residents had worked government-run mines, but there was hardly anyone left in Mississippi and Louisiana, just on the Gulf Coast, and the same attrition was happening in Alabama, in Georgia. Now the government was building work camps to replace the old mining jobs.

"Justice." I had this argument so many times with other hunters and patrollers. Most everyone claimed it was all about justice. Those residents tried to leave the desert; they should be punished.

"But the desert's part of the US," was what I always reminded them. "Those people are citizens."

"They're getting justice."

"They're getting rooked." Not that it mattered.

"And you're getting paid," I've been reminded.

"That's why I do it," I always tell them, but that's not quite right. The money helps—money always helps—but when it gets down to it, once you start a line of work, it's just easier to stay in that line.

Several black marketers shifted from table to table selling jewelry that collectors in Birmingham had taken from the dead. They kept repeating the same thing about having more stuff than they could get rid of—lots of necklaces and wedding rings, photographs of families that had become a fetish and traded throughout the post like baseball cards. They had gold and silver fillings, and size elevens and twelves in men's shoes.

I wear an eleven and a half, but they didn't have any half sizes. So I bought a pair of twelve loafers that looked like real leather and had scarcely worn through the sole. There was this one jeweled cross I almost bought, with turquoise and diamonds—fake ones, I was sure of it, but I almost took it anyway. Mam used to have one.

"It's clean," the seller promised, like all the death had been washed off, like you could wash it all off; and those jewels did shine; he kept rubbing the cross with a towel.

Finally I had to get up and go to another table 'cause he wouldn't. The bar smelled like beer and vomit and smoke and floor wax. Any second the school basketball team would emerge, and we'd have to clear out, let the ghosts play. That floor wax was getting to me, the whole place was, so I left.

Outside, the storm was still going. It had come from Mississippi, piling a ton of dirt on Birmingham, and we were getting some of it, too, but the ozone was secure here. Tomorrow the dust would end and the sun would click up and up its ladder, no problem. But the truth was, the ozone was more wobbly than secure, that tear over Alabama wasn't finished tearing, and when I had asked the officer where the border was now, definitively, he chuckled, said, "Definitively, they're waiting until everything settles. They've changed it four times in the last week. So far it's holding about ten miles south." I got stuck on that.

Usually when I came in, I took out a room and stayed on post until I spent my money down, but I was anxious—the ozone disintegrating, the winds pushing storm after storm, throwing the earth at us, and everyone in the bar just annoyed with the weather like always. They had grown static and debauchery gets tiresome after a while. I was getting closer to fifty years of age—that was part of it, too.

I used to tell everyone that change was routine on the Southeastern Desert border, yet I couldn't stay that night and walked past the church with its lights still on, hoping to catch repentant sinners from the schoolhouse. They were playing a hymn on the organ—"At Calvary." My mam's favorite. And I started humming it, 'cause I know it like my mam made me know it, and the dust was blowing around me, but it couldn't hurt me, not here.

The sky was all black, a fake black, and in the light, the dust made yellow whorls. Fire. So I got in my van and headed up to West Sayre, across Jett Mountain. That was the latest route for *guias* out of Birmingham; they squeezed through on Highway 5, and so many passed, it was like a salmon run. They were heading up to Tennessee and Kentucky on Snakeskin Road. All you had to do was follow.

Three things I remember about Old New Orleans where I was born and raised until I was six.

Water. All this water around me and dead dogs floating in it, though when I told Mam about it when I was older, she said it wasn't just dogs, but cats and people's clothes, debris, water all the way to the roofs, and people, those pale shoulders hunched, and their clothed backs swollen up, and black skins.

"Lots of colored people there," my granddaddy said. He was Cherokee and black and all mixes of white, but always denied any color in himself.

"Memory is a funny thing, isn't it, Rosser?" my mother said.

I remembered seeing my yellow dog in the water, floating. Mam never said if that was true or not; she didn't answer; she looked somewhere else.

The Superdome. We were in this huge warehouse—the Superdome, Mam said it was. I just remember sitting down on this bottom field and these bright lights at the top, so high up, it felt like the whole world had been crammed on top of us, what remained of the world. There was a woman in front of me in a wheelchair, and I watched her and the back of her blue leather chair.

"I'm going to get us some food." Mam patted my head, pressed me to the ground, but I squirmed out. "Stay put," she warned.

"Mam," I said, like, of course, I'd stay put, why would she think otherwise, but really I wanted to go. She said the same thing to my older brother, Theo, but without any head-pressing, then she left.

Then he left. I remember grabbing hold of his shirt and Theo jerking away and giving me that look—"Don't." So I didn't. It was just me watching this woman in the blue wheelchair. I existed behind her what seemed like forever in this new world, and she was constant, she didn't vanish. I wanted to touch her arm and say something.

"She was sleeping, just sleeping." That's what Mam told me for years afterward.

I snapped back, "She was dead. I know it. I keep having the dream and she was dead."

Then Mam would shut up as usual, not wanting to fight with my memories any longer.

My father was from Orleans. Never saw him, not one time. He probably died in that hurricane. Mam said he wasn't even in the city then probably. Already gone. "He was always getting out of things before something bad could happen."

But I'm fairly certain he died in that hurricane, was one of those dog bodies. I'm just not sure which one.

They never did put the city back together. And there was another hurricane, then the dust storms. But we weren't there for any of it. We left to Newport, Kentucky, where

Mam's father was, where her people was. That's about all I remember.

I'd been holed up in West Sayre, fallen asleep I don't know how long, when some vans came by, whizzing. There may have been more to come by earlier, but it was just that small convoy that got me stirred. Everyone drives the same white vans so you can't tell what's in back. There were three in a row, and I figured *guias*—they liked sweeping out fifty or more deserters at once and that took about three vans. I waited a bit, then headed out.

For cargo, I had food and water and all the propane tanks I needed to get to California or Canada, not that I was going that far. You just never know how long you'll be on a run. The tanks knocked against one another, especially when I hit potholes on the highway. I kept trying to find a steady rhythm in them, but couldn't. It didn't take long to realize the *guias* were heading up to the Natchez Trace. I knew a fuel runner there. And nothing, nothing had happened.

But you don't get trouble as long as you drive on federal or state roads. Get off on these narrow county blacktops and dirt strips—and eventually you'll have no choice—then you might run into farmers. They'll want to know who the hell you are and where you come from. Once they figure out you're a bounty hunter, they'll take everything of value out of your pockets—money, knives, pictures—so it doesn't get bloody before they kill you. Roaming gangs kill you like they do cattle and dogs for supper, but there's not many left. They're the people from these ghost towns that didn't make it to Louisville or Memphis, didn't get enslaved. Roaming gangs have to constantly move. The farmers have almost eradicated them.

Just last summer, patrollers were on the federal and state

roads and mille-copters, helping out truck-carriers between the city-states. Hell, ten years ago, Union Chapel and Jasper, all these towns still had people. All of it gone. Supposedly, the city-states are protected, but I want nothing to do with them. That's what Birmingham was. Now it's under the border, suffocating.

Newport has one part of itself that faces Cincinnati from across the Ohio River, one part with a shopping mall, high-rise condos, and an aquarium. You go back from there to Fifth Street—some banks and businesses—still pretty nice. Keep coming down Monmouth to Sixth to where the Brass Ass Lounge is, and *Girls, Girls, Girls* flashing in pink neon on the marquee. Keep coming back, and the roads haven't had much work done. Dixie Chili and Beach's Sewing Center are still boarded up, until you get to Twelfth and Anne.

That's where Mam's daddy lived, and where we lived after we left New Orleans. Theo was always going to the shopping mall on the river, strolling up there. That's before they built the wall on Fifth and closed it off from us.

"At least," my brother said, "we can still get into the Brass Ass."

They let him in though he was only sixteen, 'cause they were starving for customers. Plus, he looked older and thicker than boys his age. We had the same brown hair, but his lay down flat and serious on his head and mine was always cut too short by my mother and spiking.

"Have at it," I told him. There was no *we*—I couldn't get in. "Looking is all you're going to get." Then I shifted a few steps out of his way in case he wanted to give me a slug. His favorite target was my left upper arm, and once he slugged me so many times in a row, the whole side of it turned black. Still I said things, daring him to. Crazy.

But before the wall, Theo was able to go to the shops,

and he lived all day trying on clothes, watching movies, and the river—he said he especially liked watching the cars shoot across the bridges, as if he were part of that world. Our mam, she was somewhere else. She'd come home for a few days, then be gone. I was left with my granddaddy.

Granddaddy wore an orange cap and a jacket, a light brown one, dirty, all of it, and faded around the shoulders. Even in the humidity of Newport, in hot July, he had on those heavy clothes. Most days, he never talked, just came outside and sat in his chair—a peeling blue aluminum thing, not very comfortable—allowing the steel back to straighten up his back as he smoked cigarettes, one leg crossed long and dangling over the other.

"He's cooling off," Theo would say and shrug. But Granddaddy was always out in the sun.

Sometimes he pointed at things. A bird maybe. Mosquitoes. I couldn't tell. I was on the porch, on the far side looking down.

"Hey, old man," I'd say when the mosquitoes started to get me too many times, "let me have a drag on that cigarette." And I'd come off that porch, jumping on the boards so they quaked and scared him. I did this in the summers when I was eleven and twelve, finally big enough to think myself a bully. "Hey, old man, I got a lighter right here."

He had one, too, though sometimes he turned and let me light his cigarette. I'd be up on him. If I wanted, I could push his body down with my body. I always waited until he pulled out a new cigarette and wanted it lit before I stepped off the shaded overhang and approached.

He gave it to me to light, and I did, took the first puff or two, gave it back. Sometimes I ran off with it.

"You're stupid," I'd tell him. "Stupid."

Every time I stole a cigarette, I'd wait a few days, try it again. He still turned to me to light it. His memory was so rattled.

One day after watching him from the other side of the

porch, I came over and took his pack of cigarettes straight out of his pocket.

"What you going to do about that, old man? What you going to do?"

"Boy," he said, and he curled his fingers at me, gesturing, "boy." I went and put my head next to his. "Those are my cigarettes," he said. That's all.

I stood up.

"I know whose they are," I said. "Take them from me." I dangled the pack out in front of his nose.

He just breathed, like he could breathe those cigarettes in if he did it hard enough.

"Boy," he said. "I'm going to whip your father's color out of you."

"He's whiter than you are," I said. But by that time, I was already across that yard, and as soon as I got out of sight, I slung those cigarettes out and tore them up—good cigarettes—just tore them and stomped on them. I started to head out on Monmouth to find Theo. But to stand there with my brother and have him pretend that he couldn't hear, no matter what I said, no matter how much I talked, to have Theo look at everyone and everywhere but not look at me—the thought of it was too deflating.

I exhaled and looked down one end of Twelfth Street to the other, this house, that house. Someone had a fake eagle in the yard with all the brown paint coming off the wings, and a girl who was younger than me stood up on her toes from behind a fence; her nose was on the wooden top, her small dog barking. I didn't like dogs, was scared of their sudden movements and noise, kept dreaming of dogs in that New Orleans floodwater.

Underneath my shoe that cigarette pack with that stupid camel was looking happy with itself, like the painted sand dunes behind it was a better place than where I was. It didn't seem fair, so I snatched the camel up, marched back into the yard.

I was going to give it to Granddaddy, I swear, give it back to him, empty as it was, but I got halfway and I spotted him crying. Crying over stupid cigarettes. So, I hurled the pack on the ground and pointed. "Come here if you want one," I said and went inside the house, making sure to slam the door.

Next day, he walked out into the yard, facing the sun in his jacket and orange cap, even though it was hot, crossed one leg over the other and pulled out a cigarette. After he finished smoking, he put his hands on the armrests and kept them still. Then I came outside and sat on the porch. The mosquitoes found me quick.

I guess those sand dunes and that camel was a sign of the kind of work I'm doing now. I never think about that unless I come across those kind of cigarettes. I was twelve then and left him alone after that.

Above Natchez Trace, I drove through a dead zone, a swath cutting over Highway 20; I couldn't see no end to it. It had peeled the land away east and west, trying to touch the sun coming and going, gashing through a field of millet and pines. There were some dead Herefords with bleached faces and tongues, their stomachs bloated and splitting, their necks and legs stiff. All of it probably from a carbon cloud.

Some carbon clouds drifted from the cities and dissipated—everything grew back fine. But some, the mercury was too strong and killed the land off, especially if it settled in a valley until the wind got deep enough to blow it back out.

There were fissures in the ozone, too, ruptures that could last for months, burning stretches of land until they healed, but everything not rooted to the earth could avoid them. The carbon clouds were so thick, you couldn't see where you were going, where it stopped; everything got trapped inside. The whole state of Kansas was a dead zone for years after carbon clouds settled there. This one on 20 carried three miles by the road.

The *guias* had been at the Trace. I found their empty propane tanks and hung on for the fuel runner. It was the one I knew, Bo Wasson. He said they were taking women to an auction at Pickwick Landing. All from Birmingham. And not just this group.

"They're keeping you busy today."

"Yeah." He nodded and took a swipe at his forehead, the sweat and loose hair. "I've got to refill these tanks and get them to another mile marker."

I'd been paying Bo for years, and there were several fuel runners in Kentucky and Tennessee that I also knew, but that was it.

After the dead zone, I passed a few truck-carriers and more white vans returning south and one guy in an Impala. A 1960s Impala; 1960s. Baby blue with fins and rounded taillights and the frameless glass. Now that was it. I thought about circling, asking him to trade that Impala for my van, but I wouldn't trade if I owned that car. No one in his right mind would trade. I wondered what he was doing up here.

Next I hid the van several miles out of Pickwick and cut through the woods to the landing.

It was cool there under the oaks and a scattering of cottonwoods, pines, wind off the lake, and I lay flat on the pine straw and leaves the rest of the night, staring up at those branches sweeping back and forth against the moon, a full moon. Sometimes I looked down at all the shadows over me, cutting, crossing, but they never sewed my body up fully into a shadow. They did the same to the moon, revealing faces—there were always faces in the branches, but none I recognized or could make into someone I wanted. I couldn't sleep.

In the early morning the *guias* and the farmers showed up.

Pearson Whaike was with them. I had stolen two deserters from him some years back. His farm was up on Hohenwald, about four hundred acres of tobacco, and he didn't have many guards, not much of an operation. I thought he'd be forced out by now.

Someone had built a fire and was turning meat on wooden spits. The fat sizzled, burned, and the smoke drifted up for the trees to absorb. My stomach wanted me to go down there and reach into that fire, take it. And the women and girls and men stood one at a time on the block while the auctioneer reeled off numbers. The farmers raised their hands until "Sold," the auctioneer said, and that deserter was removed, a slave now, the next one hauled up.

I took photos of those blanked faces, washed out, some of them streaked red from crying. I took pictures of the *guias*. Teal Dennis was the main one. He'd been doing this longer than me. More vans and trailers showed up and they brought more meat and wood to the fire—the smoke had spread all through the branches. I stayed a while, but it was too much to take in, too many people I'd never be able to find. Always best to leave the hunting simple—Teal Dennis was the one I started with. I cut back across the woods to those vans heading into Kentucky, wanted to see how far west he was going.

On Twelfth and Anne, the days spun lazily like time had stopped in Newport. Theo and I went to school or didn't, came home or didn't, then one time when I was fourteen, I came home and it wasn't just Granddaddy in the yard— Mam was on the porch, dressed up. I mean dressed up in a black skirt and white blouse. She was always pretty, with those small eyes, and curls she stuck in place with hairspray. But Mam never bought white 'cause she said the minute you put it on, it got dirty. Someone must've given it to her. She was going to revival.

"What's getting revived?" I asked her like I always did, being smart-alecky, and she dusted her hand on the railing, exhaled deep like she was cleaning out the air in her lungs and the air around her; she didn't say a thing.

At other times, she would look down or tighten her lip, and that's when I knew I had gotten to her. Don't know why Mam was nice to me, I didn't deserve it.

I said to her I wanted to go.

"You don't even know what it is," she said.

"I don't care. I want to get revived."

"It's a church service," she said. "You'll think it's boring."

We had never gone to church unless someone was married or dead, but I had seen enough of the white walls and colored glass to know the church didn't want me—not the way I was dressed, not in my worn shoes, and my hair that Mam butchered on the porch, always cutting out bald patches.

I looked over at Granddaddy. He had fallen asleep. I crossed my arms.

"All right," she said. Mam was such a pushover. "Go wash your face."

"My face isn't dirty," I told her but I did it, and did it fast, 'cause sometimes she'd say wash your face, and by the time I come out, she'd be gone. But this time she was waiting, leaning on the porch railing with her back to me.

My mam had a nice figure, her hair up in a swirling bobby-pin bun I could never figure out how she put together. And the length of her body tapered from her shoulders to a red ribbon she had tied loose around her waist so it caught her hips. The afternoon shadows crossed over her back, and when she breathed, the shadows carved out different pieces of her shoulders and neck, and some of her was left in the sun, a late sun, making those other places brighter than normal. I stood watching and would've stayed that way content, but somehow she noticed me and turned and looked at me so strange.

"What?" she said. Then, "Come on now, Rosser." I had said nothing.

We walked down Twelfth, up Grandview. It was a long curvy hike up into the hills behind our house, and for a while I thought my mother didn't know where she was going. She wasn't the best with directions, and I asked her several times, and she said, "I've got it, Rosser. You can go home if you're tired." But I wasn't even sure I'd figure out how to get back home.

At the top, down a side street, Biehl, there was a square tent. I remember it was all staked out with new rope and wooden stakes, but the green canvas was old and blackish-green. It smelled wet from rain.

As soon as we got in, Mam sat down on one of the back folding chairs and I sat beside her. There were people still coming in, taking up seats, and the preacher, he was this thin man with gray eyes. Those eyes had an energy to them, a brightness like my mam's hair earlier, and his hair was slicked back and parted down the center over his nose and the buttons of his shirt. He came up the aisle and gestured, "Y'all come on up to the front, if you want, you can come closer." Mam said we were good where we were.

"If you change your mind," he said, gesturing his hand toward a wooden box with a wire-mesh front—a cage—sitting on the grass. It had a Bible on top. "You're always welcome. My name's Preacher Spoon." He smiled.

My mother thanked him by batting her hand, and he took it, just for a second, then let go and trotted back down the aisle.

Wasn't long before another man came and sat next to her. He said something low. I couldn't quite make it out, but Mam laughed like she knew him, and leaned that way, leaving the side of my arm tingling, chilly despite the heat. They were laughing, laughing too easy, and in front was Preacher

Spoon, just him and his Bible, those gray eyes all serious. Next to his legs, the small cage. Something kept slipping around in that cage. It was a snake. Two snakes.

He cleared his throat, everyone quieted and settled, and he started.

I was watching Preacher Spoon when Mam got up all of a sudden, dusted the bottom of her skirt, and began to walk out. I grabbed hold of her arm. Hadn't done that in years, hadn't done that since the last time we had gone somewhere together.

"I'll be back," she said.

"No, Mam. I don't know how to get home."

"I'm not leaving for good," she whispered. We were both whispering because the preacher's voice, it was already in a steady cadence.

"No," I said, and she shrugged me off, made sure not to look at me.

I watched them cross onto Biehl—he had his arm low around her waist. The preacher raised his voice. I turned back around, the emptiness in those chairs growing, and I kept thinking at any minute a snake would leap up from under one of the seats and bite me, that those serpents were already slithering behind my legs where I couldn't see them, choosing the best, most juiciest part of my ankles.

They weren't under there. It was crazy talk to think that way, and then Preacher Spoon said, "Jesus," drew out the name Jesus like the wind had forced it into his mouth and Jesus had come for his name here and now, the savior's spirit was with us.

The talking got stronger and louder. He was going into it. That voice, the way he talked and breathed—I couldn't move.

I followed the three vans to Cairo, saw them park across the river at the St. Charles brothel, and I turned around.

Teal Dennis was going farther, I was certain of it, but he only had a few women left. Most were sold in Kentucky to Bixon Farms—that was the logo on the truck, a beat-up Ford with a shit-soaked trailer, and I had come across the logo on several fences rusting. Bixon would be the second stop, St. Charles the last, and Whaike's farm in Hohenwald first. If I was lucky, I'd finish the whole run by August, taking just a few deserters from each place, only my share.

Pearson Whaike's farm was in a hollow looped inside a grove of evergreens, and the compound was as I'd remembered it. He kept the field slaves in quarters outside the main house, and parked his tractors and harvesters and trucks next to the barn. Half the outside lights needed bulbs, and there were broken holes in the chain-link fence where small deer could wind through. His overseers walked two together across the grounds at night. I watched them fall asleep, and on the next night with new guards, the same thing happened.

In the mornings, the slaves came out to be fed, and then to the fields, but whenever the slaves were allowed a break, only one guard took them to the woods. Pearson was never out in his fields, and they were harvesting cantaloupes now instead of tobacco. A long rectangular box had been hooked to the rear of the tractors—only three were in the field, sixty acres, each tractor culling different rows, and I could hear other voices and equipment in the adjacent clearings divided by this narrow strip of woods and could smell the dirt being spun out of the wheels and diesel.

All the new slaves, the women from Teal Dennis, had been placed in one gang with two overseers and a driver. They took turns walking the women to the edge of the field to piss.

It was the third morning, and the driver and one overseer stayed up at the tractor, guzzling water as usual. Their laughing and talking echoed like the ghosts of circling birds as the other guard walked down to the woods behind the slaves.

He said, "Don't go far in. I'm watching," and stood on the periphery with his rifle on them. They must've kept the workers in chains at night 'cause they rubbed their wrists and ankles continually, painfully.

Slowly he came out of the sun, it was hot, and moved under the shade of the trees where a draft had started leavening; he moved under the shadow until his whole body was swathed in the cool dark. I slipped behind him, gagged his mouth, and cut across his neck. Then I lifted my shotgun on the women.

"Keep quiet," I said and tossed out pieces of rope. I had them tie each other's hands.

They kept looking at me and at the overseer's body.

"Don't look at him," I said. "He's gone," and I snagged the loops onto a leash and hurried the slaves down the center of the wooded strip where an old cow path still winded.

The other guards yelled for their dead man, not knowing he was dead. They were yelling loud, something about *Stop messing* and *Come on—Pearson wants this field done today*, and I knew they were coming for him, their echoes getting louder and more urgent. I shut the women in, locked the back doors, drove off humming. Humming has always relaxed me some, takes my mind just enough out that I can drive straight. It's never a particular song, just the sound, the noise of it rattling in my throat. Once I hit Highway 43, I knew the guards wouldn't catch up.

That first night of the revival, Preacher Spoon closed with the hymn "Serpent Handler":

Signs of God lie upon his believers,
To stamp out Satan the Great Deceiver.

Drink poison, behold the serpent's head;
Lay hands on the sick and raise the Dead,
Ye shall not be harmed,
Ye shall not be harmed.

While everyone sang and clapped, he brought up the wooden cage. He carried it down to the first row and everyone passed it, the rattlers backing up heavy in one corner and striking against the screen-mesh front. Some people refused to hold the cage. One person bobbled it and dropped it, which caused four women to faint. Preacher Spoon promptly revived them.

When the box came to me, the snakes were coiled and rattling, growing heat. My heart was ready to burst, holding on to the wooden ground underneath those snakes, and I could feel them coiling tighter and tighter around my veins, a tightness my blood couldn't escape or catch up to.

Preacher Spoon had to pull the box from my grip and he carried it back down. That ended the sermon, except to tell your friends, your kin, your neighbors. I felt all woozy in the chair, like all the wooziness was going out of my pores, and I couldn't put myself back together. But finally my sweat hardened into salt and I ran home.

Next evening I asked Mam if she was going. The revival was happening every night through Friday, but she said she had a date and started humming "At Calvary." Though we had hardly ever gone to church, Mam had gone as a child, and when she was in a good mood she hummed and sang those hymns, and when Mam cut my hair she did, and taught them to me for the hour it took, and that made me hope cutting my hair was something she liked to do.

So I walked to revival by myself, moving up two rows closer, and someone had brought in a set of wooden pews from an abandoned Tabernacle Church on Ninth, slid them over the grass earth in front.

Preacher Spoon appeared from the back this time, not

showing up until after seven and the people talking louder than normal, which I've found they always do when something hasn't started they believe should, and there was a slightly larger crowd. He tapped my shoulder.

"Where's Mama, little lamb?" he asked and looked at the empty chair beside me.

"I'm here," I told him.

"Yes," Preacher Spoon confirmed and patted my head, and moved up, speaking to the women in the next row. He talked with everyone down the aisle like he knew them, like they had all been friends since birth and had at last found one another again. It was so relaxed under that green, musty canvas, like what afternoons are like before thunderstorms, and everyone glad it wasn't nothing worse once it's over.

Preacher Spoon started preaching, his box of snakes right beside him and a table on the other side and only one lamp on the floor which reversed the shadows up the buttons of his shirt and face toward the top pole of the tent.

It became hard for him to breathe he had so much to say, his eyes shut. But at the closing of a thought as he gasped for air, he opened those eyes, and that gray and that energy behind them shined out on you. It had to be God or the Devil or Jesus, someone with more power than Preacher Spoon. The congregation said amen. He inhaled a breath and they amened back, like there was an exchange of breath from those of us in the chairs, and Preacher Spoon, back and forth the word of God, and his voice rising, falling, rising, until he said, "In Mark, chapter 16, verse 17, follow along with me, the words, 'These signs shall follow them that believe: In my name shall they cast out devils; they shall speak with new tongues. They shall take up serpents.' " He reached down with his eyes still closed and hauled up that cage and set it on the small table and felt around the wooden sides of the box, then the steel front like he had no eyes at all, never had them, didn't need them.

"In Luke, chapter 10, verse 19, the Lord says, 'Behold, I give unto you power to tread on serpents and scorpions, and over all the power of the enemy: and nothing shall by any means hurt you.' So says the word of God; it is truth. The word will abide forever."

He opened his eyes and opened the latch, pulled out the bottom shelf, and took one snake in his hand, up his arm, sliding, like a long vein of his own, the flat head pointing into the congregation, and Preacher Spoon closed the other one in.

"Ye shall not be harmed, ye shall not be harmed," he said, holding the snake in the reverse light, its white belly blinding. "Now I call you down here to the front, to the Lord. Ye shall not be harmed."

A man the size of two men walked down. He quivered but managed to open his fingers all the way and Preacher Spoon gave the snake over, a diamondback that glimmered, then was eclipsed by the man's body. He turned to face us, fell to the ground with the snake trying to coil and jut. It wanted nothing more than to be let go of. The man, it was like he'd been chopped at the knees, sent down to pray, but he hadn't been bitten. Not yet. I was waiting to find out what that rattler would do.

Preacher Spoon took up the other snake and called everyone to rise, to come down and join, to give over to the Holy Ghost. He started singing "Serpent Handler."

And while he sang, the congregation prayed for the word, for forgiveness, and truth, rising, but each prayer was its own, with its own cadence and offerings—the words clashed against one another, yet wanting the same disparate, holy thing.

One snake was a copperhead, the other a diamondback, venomous snakes you couldn't hold, and yet they were being held. Their bodies crooked and jutted—no easy place for their motion along the hands and arms that would never replace the flat of the earth. Everyone was trying to latch onto the rapture and some people rising up, singing it, "*Lay hands on the sick and raise the Dead, Ye shall not be harmed,*" going down. All of the women going down, but none were my mam.

It was easy, one of the easiest hauls I had made. My luck was running good.

The whole trip to Adamsville, nothing happened on the roads, and in back the deserters never yelled or tried to break out the doors like one guy did back in April. He jumped onto the highway like it was a river that would catch him soft and it killed him.

They didn't even cry once we got inside the cement block at the post; they were too jolted, too much had happened in a short time and they had grown unsure of everything, of themselves. Only one of the deserters begged, "Don't make me go back into that," when she realized we were in Alabama. "I can't go back into that." The words soured in her mouth. But we were already in the cement block, and she was getting processed. I sold them for fifty thousand. Right there, the whole crew, fifty thousand.

"That's the most money we've given out," the cash officer said, smiling big like I had made her day, but she hadn't been here long. I'd seen hunters pull in more.

The only glitch was that the patrollers couldn't verify one of the women. She kept looking around, scared just like the others, trying to figure out the sudden walls and steel cages. She had a small face and barely any chin and hair cut straight across the back as if my mam had done it—rough, uneven. She told the officers a name, it wasn't real, and fingerprinting, DNA, signatures, nothing came back. Still they took her. She was probably someone Pearson bought from the old Mexican *guias*. Who knew how she got to Mexico, where she came from before she was smuggled north.

I was cautioned not to bring any more unidentifieds

because what if it was a citizen; patrollers don't like you turning over US citizens, even if they had been enslaved. I knew several bounty hunters turned back for offering too many unidentifieds at once and forced to sell their cargo cheap to organ dealers. If you kept doing it, you got black-listed. And if you want to know it, right there, that's just how screwed up and illogical the rules were, the whole process outlined in a manual issued back in 2014.

The first haul was always the largest because the desert-ers hadn't adjusted—all the shifting from Alabama to the farm, and then rescued—some deserters actually believed that's what I was doing—it kept them from finding their cen-ter. By the time they realized what was going on, I'd resold them to the government. But it was early; maybe my luck would hold. There was that chance, so I didn't stay in Adamsville, didn't even head over to The End of the World Bar. The weather had calmed; the sun slipped down red and the crickets reemerged from their hiding places during the storm. What was left on High Street, a layering of sand like snow flurries.

Teal Dennis sold nine women to Bixon in Kentucky—I had recognized the name from fence posts but that's all I knew of them. They just didn't look to be a huge operation with the secondhand truck and trailer. I wouldn't get all nine runaways—more than my share, too many to coordi-nate. And to be honest, I was still in disbelief at Pearson Whaike's seven, how easy it was. Still don't know how I got seven.

"One more haul," I said, whispered it to myself and stretched. Fifty thousand. I doubted I'd get that much money in one trade again. Suddenly all that money was a burden. I had to do something with it, had to spend it, and the thought of it exhausted me.

I'll spend it later, I decided, and restocked the propane tanks and water tank and drove right back up through the

Natchez Trace on 43, 195, 16, came right up through the dead zone; the Herefords split open to vultures gathering the last bit of dusk. I wondered how long it'd take before any green returned to that track of land, and when I'd rest. I hadn't slept for days.

Night came on as I crossed 33. Then I took County 291 winding into the Sanctified Mountains, then 86 that struck out through Jals Valley; the sun was long out of it, and that's when I heard the train.

It was coming right next to me on 86, the tracks just to the left under a string of old telephone poles and wires stretched out in loops that touched the earth where some had rusted through and broken. It was catching up—power trains moved quick and reached two hundred in straight-aways, but Jals Valley was too curvy for that. Still it was going. I said, "Hell with it," gunned the accelerator, and there we were side by side racing, the road going and going, but there was no end except all that remained undefined and unknown. We would cross there and keep crossing to the next and the next.

I was right alongside the engine blowing hard smoke. That was the important thing, I told myself—I was right there. But all I noticed was its one light in front, a miniature sun, and the smaller backlights streaming down the long body. My feet and ankles started burning—if the road turned too fast, I wouldn't be able to angle out of it. I opened my window to hear better, the train and my van going, when suddenly there was an explosion, and I thought I'd been shot, but I hadn't, it was the train.

Maybe it was the light, the small sun had burst out, or the engine had gone out in a steel flare, but then I saw truck lights come on and zag, a whole swarm zagging over to the train, some people running with long sticks, rifles firing—roamers. I kept going, lucky as hell to get out.

•　•　•

I had a snake in the yard, small, black. I was watching it not move, and I wasn't moving either, the two of us waiting on whoever moved first, when Theo came out the door.

"What's going on?" he asked and did it in such a way like whatever my answer was it wouldn't satisfy him.

"Quiet," I said. "I'm aiming to pick up that snake." I pointed.

"Where?" he asked. He looked over at Granddaddy, then back across the sweep of the yard. The grass had died brown it was so dry, windless, and his big head was full of snot. He kept rubbing his fingers under his nose — summer colds were the hardest to get rid of, Mam said. And he stood there with all that snot and heft I could never undo.

I pointed harder. "There," I said and felt him pass on my left. I started into a lunge for the snake, but he clubbed me in the arm and I fell over. From the grass I saw the heel of his boot strike at the head. He did it again and again, the snake's body vaulting up, then falling, twitching at the grass blades.

"It's just a garden snake. What you want to pick it up for?" he said and looked across the yard at Granddaddy like his question was a joke and the two of them were in on it. Granddaddy put a cigarette to his mouth, puffed out some smoke, set his arm back on the rest. Theo walked out onto Twelfth.

I watched the heels and cuffs of his jeans, the snake turning the dead grass because there was no wind to do it. I pulled up on my knees like that man praying in the tabernacle, and the sun eyeing the back of my head. My arm was sore. I put my hand up close to the smear of blood in the raw skin, but still I couldn't grab hold of that snake.

It was Friday night, the last of the Holiness Signs Revival and Mam promised she'd go with me. She got dressed up in the same white blouse and black skirt — it was more a brown-black color than I remembered—and it pulled out the brown in her tight curls and the flat moles on her skin. I had those same moles, red and brown patches.

We were on the porch and I said, "Let's go." She looked me over.

"I've already washed up," I promised, and she smiled. Then she nodded out beyond the yard, a man walking up, that man from the first night.

I was about to ask her who it was but didn't bother—she'd been seeing him all week. He was stooped like Granddaddy, but a little wider, still spindly, elongated like a pancake, and his face was all bearded, gentle, too gentle, so all you could notice was him smiling back, a ridge of teeth, and Mam said, "Harold, let's go, it's starting soon."

We walked up Grandview. Mam and Harold, they laughed and joked and I just kept looking up the blacktop, looking up to the curves peeling off like apple skins, round and round leading to more blacktop and more curves, switchbacks that kept going until, if you weren't careful, you'd lose your balance and fall.

Preacher Spoon came over as soon as we arrived and took our place. He was happy to see Mam, I could tell, but not as much to see Harold—his smile waned. It was good to have someone on my side, and he made his offer to sit in front. Mam batted her hand, started to say we were good here, but I stood up.

"Let's go down there."

"Rosser, I don't want to. This is good," she said and contorted like she was aching at a joint in her body that shouldn't be provoked.

"Well, I'm going," I said and marched up to the front left pew. It was empty, just me, and that long slab of wood. You could pile that bench up with snakes like I had dreamed it and lose the boundaries of your own skin inside their squirming. I had to close my eyes and tell myself *Stop, don't let the world get away from you.*

Wasn't long before Mam sat next to me; Harold next to her.

She sighed. "You've embarrassed me, Rosser. When we get home . . ." She pinched my arm, the same place Theo had slugged me, and I said, "Ow," but she never finished the threat; she didn't have to. When I got home, Granddaddy would be at the table eating soup or one of those bread sandwiches he made without peanut butter or jelly or anything, and later Theo would open the door at 2:00 a.m. as loud as he could, and Mam, she wouldn't be home. Empty. All her threats were empty.

We didn't talk after that, and she didn't talk much to Harold either except in curt replies. Meanwhile the tent got so full, it couldn't hold all the congregants. They had showed up every night, more and more people, and tonight was the largest—standing by the ropes and stakes, their bodies swollen out into the clearing. Biehl Street dead-ended on a hill that overlooked Newport. You could see rooftops and the tops of condominiums over the Fifth Street wall and the ones in Cincinnati with blue and yellow warning lights, but you couldn't see the river, that's all there was. That canopy had been staked right up to that precipice where the road ended.

Right in the heart, right up front was Preacher Spoon with his hair slicked into wings and those closed gray eyes, and that Bible he kept pressing with his hand, opening and pressing down on the pages, like he could stamp those words into his skin, into his blood, into his soul and ours.

He had already taken a bottle of fire and held it under his chin. I glanced over at Harold's fat beard and wanted to put the fire under it until I smelled burning hair. There were three lamps of light on the floor throwing the shadows up at sharp angles against one another, so you were never sure which path to follow, which shadow was the most real, the most true to the contours of Preacher Spoon's face and the words coming out. Tonight, he had four boxes—some of the congregants had brought in snakes. As the sermon closed down, people were getting in fits, praying to the Holy Ghost as loud as they could, praying into the arcs of those shadows. And it hadn't cooled any, the night was betrayed; all the bodies and the sweat and mustiness of the green canvas.

Mam had grabbed my hand during the fire under the chin part—Mam was a big old scaredy-cat.

Then Preacher Spoon felt around the mesh gate. "Have you ever looked inside someone's soul? Found it hollowed out?" Preacher Spoon stopped and looked through us all. "My soul has been that kind of soul. Until I let the Lord in, allowed the Lord to fill me, and wash me with His blood."

He took up a snake. "I ask you to come down with your shames and disgraces and your empty souls. Let the spirit fill you tonight."

I didn't know where my soul was, what it held or lacked, just like I don't now—nothing, inside me is nothing. And that must've been why all those people came to the front, 'cause inside them was nothing, too. When the women started walking to the front, I said to Mam, "Why don't you go up there?"

"What do you mean?" She was already clutching on to Harold and had turned her body to the side, away from the commotion.

I nudged her. "Take up a snake, Mam."

"Rosser," she said my name with as much gravel as she could and rolled her eyes. "I think we should go, that's what I think." She looked for Harold to say something in agreement or nod, but he just looked straight ahead, mesmerized like I had been that first night, like he had lost where he was, stuck to the wooden back.

"You the one who brought me on Sunday," I said and crossed my arms. I wasn't budging.

But then it was like the spirit took over, or at least what I thought that would be like, what the spirit had done to all the other people. I got out of my chair aiming to walk right toward Preacher Spoon and take up one of those snakes. Mam's hand reached for me, but I wiggled out before she could—the spirit did that, helped me wiggle out.

I walked forward, stepped around the dancing ones, the ones with fire, the ones with snakes, ready to fill my soul with whatever it took, and Preacher Spoon said, "Come on, little lamb; are you ready, little lamb?"

I nodded and opened my hands out and he placed that snake down, a bright diamondback on my wrists, and after he did, I knew that thing was not of me. I had hoped the spirit would fuse us, me and the snake, and I'd be washed through with the blood of Jesus, a blood other than my own, but we remained separated by our skins, our cold blood. I was cut off, having betrayed myself for wanting.

I heard Mam. She was right there yanking my hands away, saying, "Put it down, Rosser, let go." I opened my eyes and she was still shouting and other people were, too, but they were lost inside their own shouts and didn't hear my mother. Preacher Spoon pushed them back, made a circle around her, and Harold came forth, and Mam, you could see the puncture on her arm. That snake, it was somewhere, everywhere.

Harold said call a doctor, yelled it to the congregation, and Preacher Spoon said, "No, the Lord will heal her."

Mam looked at me, aching, clutching her arm above that purple lump, the two small holes.

"What you bring me here for?" she asked.

What was left of the spirit that had filled me, left me.

"Mam," I said, and she shook her head, and kept her eyes pinched closed and wouldn't look up.

I ran from there.

There's one thing about running and what I know the Lord must've known when he put this world in motion—it never ends. You think it will, you'll want it to, but it never ends. Don't believe me, just place your hands against the earth, try to stop it.

They had a lot of overseers at Bixon Farms and echolocation gates around the compound and dogs. The nine deserters were split up, and I could only find six of them that matched up with the photos I had taken at Pickwick Landing. They may have already sold the others or were using them in the house. And the land, it was sprawling, well over a thousand acres of corn, peas, tobacco, pine groves, hardwoods, and pasture.

A creek ran beside one of the butterbean fields, and a fence line for another farm, Galtson, across the creek. The stream ran through a pine grove and that grove spread out and touched on several other fields of corn, and one pasture that was used for hay. They had already done at least two cuttings, the hay bales stacked on the far side like tall swirling comets, and the pasture had grown enough to be cut again into windrows for drying.

For days, the six had worked the butterbean field; but there were just too many overseers and other field slaves and the dogs were there. I counted four, all bull-mixes, and watched the workers bend against the sun, load bushels, turn along the rows. It was work I did when I was younger, when farmers used field hands instead of slaves. You had to get on your knees to pick the butterbeans at the ground, and the stems hard to pull. I watched them pick and pull for days and couldn't figure out how to steal them away.

Sometimes you have to give up; you follow the night and morning routines but an opening just isn't there. And I had stayed at Bixon too long, that uneasiness of land and trees around me too familiar.

Then on the fifth day, a culling gang went through the butterbeans to finish them off—nine slaves, one overseer,

his dog, and the tractor driver. Three of the slaves were deserters Teal Dennis had auctioned. I didn't like that only
three were out there, not after I handed seven into post just
last week. But I kept telling myself, "Only your share—that's
what you take."

The van was at the far side of the pasture by the hay
bales, and I had walked to the pines, and through them to
the edge of the butterbean field, the creek ran along it. At
the other end was a logging road through hardwoods, deep-
rutted, that opened into a long field of corn, and on the
other side, another stand of pines, and a field of crowders
and purple hulls where the other gangs had begun the harvest.

I scoped the driver—the edges of his round face, then to
the center ear, his nose, and his large neck up to his hairline—short hair, curled white. The overseer was younger
and his face long, narrow. They kept moving, I wouldn't be
able to get both cleanly. There was the dog, too, shifting in
and out of the rows. I walked around the edge of the pines to
the thicker hardwoods and waited.

It was a long day, around five when they were done, and
the tractor came out first with the butterbean bushels on the
rear trailer, followed by the truck with the field-workers
locked in the back cage. It was the same type of cage used
for hunting dogs. The overseer had the keys and his dog was
up front.

I could no longer hear the other gangs working several
fields over. The tractor's engine quavered, chopped loud at
the branches, and I placed the rifle against the swell of a
maple, scoped the black center of the driver's ear, and
pulled the trigger. I checked the bolt, counted, shot into the
truck, and the glass shattered.

The tractor driver fell under the rear wheel, but the ruts
had been carved so deep from the logging that the tractor
kept straight until it slipped into the cornfield and vanished.
The truck, however, jolted to a stop, and the slaves fell into

one another moaning. They had been soundless killings, clean, but the dog was yelping, and I couldn't get it sighted until it pushed around the overseer and through the shattered glass.

Forty yards. I fired, missed, but in its jump, the leash caught and jerked the dog's speckled head up, left it hanging at the running board choking, scrambling. Took two more shots, and that last cry the dog made sailed through the branches, up into the air—the highest thing, I couldn't keep from ascending. They would hear it in the other field.

So I took the keys from the ignition, opened the cage, tossed three ropes in, and told the others to tie the runaways' hands. I had to point at "this one" and "this one," threatening. They kept huddled to the back, "Don't shoot," they said, and "Mercy," praying, wailing. Then I told the three to come out and they wouldn't and I aimed the rifle in, said for the others to push them out.

There was a gap where no one moved, and that's when I heard the dogs. The tractor had vanished into the corn and I couldn't see through it, but that sound of dogs and trucks was just beyond us now, approaching.

I shot one of the slaves, one I didn't want, and he fell over.

"Push them out," I said, and this time the others did. I hooked the knotted ropes to the leash and headed the deserters across the bean field. Behind us, one slave jumped off the truck and started through the hardwoods, but the rest closed the steel door back, rolled the dead one to the front as a barricade. I could still hear them whimpering, hear their prayers.

By the time we got to the field edge, someone was shooting at us, coming on in a gray truck. I fired back, and we slipped through the pine grove. Between the canopy and the fallen straw, the air tightens into a stillness in a pine grove; you become aware of each breath, each step by the trees sewn perfect into the earth, that stillness working against your motion, wanting you to stop. But you don't. You accelerate from bole to bole, the sun cutting paths of light across you, then darkness, then the same light like breath as if you can breathe in light and dark, keep them and make them into you and you into them.

There was no road through here; the gray truck would have to stop at the field's edge, so we got to the pasture easy, and the women kept running despite the shirts, men's shirts that hung to their knees sweaty and catching. Still, the deserters had been running faster since the gunfire, and my van was just beyond the hay bales on a field road. It met up with the creek and turned onto a dirt road that became County 46, and only a few miles to State 13.

But halfway into the field, a dog crossed from the pines, brown and coaled, and I knew we were not faster than any dog, so I wrapped the leash tighter around my hand, pulled, and did not look behind me in the grass whirring.

I tried to think of the distance, how little of it remained, hoping that was enough to will us to the end.

Suddenly the leash jerked my arm and shoulder back, pulled all of us into the seeding grass like we had caught a large fish. But it was the other way—the dog had caught us and taken down the last one.

It's said in Matthew, "If your hand or your foot causes you to sin, cut it off and throw it away. It is better for you to enter life maimed or crippled than to have two hands or two feet and be thrown into eternal fire." So I cut the leash where it held her and pulled the other two up, untangled them, and we left that woman on the ground to fight the brown dog with her hands still tied.

As we neared the end of the field, a second dog jumped the last woman and this time I felt my shoulder pop. She yelled like the other one had. I cut her rope to us, and this dog turned, locking its bite, a yellow dog like the ones in my dreams. I fired, killed it—but I knew it would come again and again for me, would never be dead.

The overseers were in the pasture now taking aim, scoping us, as the other dogs swam through the grass.

Only one slave was left. She was running slower even without having to carry the others, breathless; there were shots; we kept past the hay bales and they were coming and the dogs were coming, and my shoulder I didn't know if it would hold.

We ran along pines that cut the sunlight in and out as if the Lord was cutting the length of the light upon us himself, what He would allow us to have, to give, enough. I shoved her up front in the cab and drove off in the shots firing.

It was when we got on County 46 that she slumped against her door, and I thought fainted, but I found the blood pooling in her seat, and pushed her arm, "Hey," I said, "we made it out." Pushed again, but she didn't move. I grabbed her black hair, pulled it to the side, and watched those closed eyelids, didn't dare open them, didn't want to see them.

Just like that my luck had run the other way. I kept that dead body until the next morning when I crossed the dead zone above the Natchez Trace and cut the engine and looked down that line where nothing grew, the vultures working on the carcasses still and flies grinding in angry black spots, and across that border, the wet grass verdant, the branches and leaves catching the wind turning. I rolled the window down to hear that shushing rise, cease, rise. It cleared the air of the smell of blood. And I knew I had to dump that body in one of those places, but I sat there as if she were still dreaming and would wake up. Then I'd drive to the post, collect my bounty.

That night my mother got snakebit, I didn't go home to Granddaddy and Theo. I was afraid Mam would show up, or never show up. The more I thought about it, the more I decided I didn't want to find out what happened. So I hitched to Lexington and worked on horse farms there and farther south in tobacco and cotton fields; I've worked my share of purple hulls and peach orchards, too. I had an eye for surveying, knowing the full measure of a farmer's land, could tell the bale yield of his cotton just by looking over the acres in July. I started riding shotgun on drug runs with other field-workers, and read the Bible until I was done with it, and wouldn't step into a church.

Once I started driving, I ran drugs and guns along the Cumberland Parkway and north and south through the Gap. When I got older, I was a carrier along the Southeastern Desert border, and a *guia*, then a hunter. But in my twenties, when I made those runs to the city-states, when the city-states were just forming, I avoided Newport every time I came near Cincinnati.

But one afternoon after finishing a run to the Licking River, I took Highway 9 to Monmouth and followed the streets down to Twelfth and Anne. Granddaddy wasn't in the yard in his rusted chair, his faded coat, the chair was gone, and a chain-link fence had been put in. I opened the latch, walked up to the door, nervous as hell about it, but I did it. A woman answered.

She had thin black hair, not at all like my mother's curls, though they could've been the same age, and a cross around her neck and an old work shirt that must've been her husband's because it fit her too big. It had dirty stripes that begged for washing, and her nose jutted out like a rudder, pulling up the center of her lip; her lip had a gash on one side, a scar from when something gouged it or she hit something. She told me that she'd bought the house from the bank and had never known any Lewis families, and her mouth stayed open like there was more to say, but for a long time, she just looked at me, studying, and said nothing.

"You could check at the courthouse," she finally said and messed her hair, ruffled the back feathers of it as if that cooled her off. It was a hot day and heat was drifting out from behind her where the fans were blowing, doing no good.

I looked out across the porch where I used to sit. It was empty, no chair, but my legs already had that pull in them and my shoulders leaned, but that was all, just that leaning toward. It was afternoon and the light was doing like it did those years ago, strips of it coming under the overhang, only Mam wasn't on the rail, humming.

"Are you all right?" the woman said; she had stepped back into the house and latched one hand to the doorknob.

"No, ma'am," I said, "I'm not all right. Not one bit of me." I was shaking—too many ghosts here I knew of and couldn't find, and I backed away from her. I had worried her enough. I thanked her and she was already shutting the door and locking it; she said nothing else.

I drove up Grandview to Biehl, got out, walked over the clearing. People had thrown trash, even old refrigerators and ovens, rusting, junk thrown down the side of the cliff, and that's where I sat, where the tabernacle had been staked years ago, and closed my eyes, imagining the angles of the lamps, the shadows they cast onto the green ceiling. I could hear Preacher Spoon's cadence, his breathlessness, and feel the snake roll in my hands that was not of me, and Mam, where was Mam?

The mustiness of the canvas was in the firmament still, and the voices striking against one another struck into me. When I opened my eyes, the tears had stopped and left the rooftops blurring into a rivulet tucked and sloping toward the dingy wall on Fifth, graffitied now with charred inscriptions and bright splashed letters. I could make out the word SO in orange and the number 29, and beyond that the terraces and balconies of Cincinnati in a gray smog dissipating.

I always delivered my cargo to the edge-towns of city-states. I never been inside one, will always keep on the outside of that world.

• • •

I still don't know if Mam is dead or not, but the Lord never did me any favors. The more I read of Him, the more I lost the threads of myself. And I decided, after my time in Newport, not to look for those people, my people. I decided they did not exist.

It was October when I left Adamsville. After the mess at Bixon, I didn't want to go out, but every day I looked at those pictures, the ones I had taken at Pickwick Landing and Pilot Oak, Kentucky, and I knew there were five runaways that had gone on to Cairo and beyond it. One had curls like Mam. The whole time at Pickwick she wouldn't look at the farmers bidding, kept staring at those on the auction block; she saw herself there, just like them, afraid.

One of the women had blond hair that was long in back, short bangs, and her slitted eyes kept working against her rawboned cheeks whenever she closed them; she tried to keep her eyes closed, maintain her focus on the ground.

The next one had black hair, thick, and the lines, you couldn't tell it in the picture, but they were strong for such a young face, and a girl beside her—they held hands at both auctions; the woman with the lines, she refused to let go of that girl.

The last woman was shorter than the others, even the girl; she kept her hair pulled off her face so you could see all of it like a bald mountain scored by the wind, brown skin, baked, her eyes set deep, the lines of her mouth turned inward, unopened. I knew what Granddaddy would say about her.

The photos were two-inch squares that fit in the center of my palm. I took them out one at a time, sometimes I pasted all the photos against the sweat in my hand, and kept them in my pockets, and I burned the others, their faces to ash.

Maybe those five women weren't in Cairo. The *guia* had sold one, maybe two at the St. Charles before he headed out. And maybe none were there now, but it was the *maybe* I got stuck on. I knew I should forget them, burn their pictures like the others. They were too many weeks removed, too far gone.

But for over a month I centered the photos in my hand. For over a month I took a room in Adamsville and went to the bars and stayed outside of the church and slept and slept on the bed to make up for all those weeks of not sleeping. I woke every day and there it was in the desk drawer, the Bible. I didn't want to pick it up, but I knew where the passages were, the ones always calling me. You can avoid the Lord all your life, yet that won't do any good. So I took the Bible and tried to will myself out of existence like the Lord had done, like my father did, like I did to my mam and brother and grandfather.

I drank strychnine like I had seen Preacher Spoon do because "If they drink any deadly thing, it shall not hurt them." The word abided in me, and I was unharmed.

I burned my wrists, my fingernails black, peeled them off, set fire in a bottle to my feet, under my chin, and I said into that room and beyond its walls, "Who of us can dwell with the consuming fire? Who of us can dwell with everlasting burning?"

I answered, "It is me, it is me. Damned and protected, both sides of the Lord's curse. It is me." But I did not vanish in that smoke or the dreams that followed, the second death where dogs came rising out of the flood, one of the dogs my father.

The next morning in the thin light, I looked out over High Street from the balcony, cleaned the .260 and the shotgun barrels, polished them in bluing. The cars and trucks stayed dusted in sand, unchanged. Later I heard the church choir—

Happy in Jesus,
All my sins forgiven;
Happy in Jesus,
Now I'm bound for heaven;
Happy in Jesus,
A life restored to living.
Redeemed and sanctified,
Because my Lord was crucified.

But the Lord had done me no favors. I took the hotel Bible, set it on fire in the sink—the pages held together, too thick to do more than smolder. So I tore the pages out and burned them, and still I knew I'd never be done with the Lord until He was done with me.

I should've gone up to West Sayre and followed out a new gang of deserters. That was a smart plan, but I kept bringing out the photos until they took hold—if I couldn't will myself out of existence, I'd will them into existence. It was decided: they wouldn't vanish. I wouldn't let that happen. So I restocked the propane tanks, and the water cistern, and rations, and bought cartridges and new rope and a Tawl knife with a pearled hilt off a marketer. Then I left for the Ohio.

First, I stopped at Instant Casino in Paducah. The casino was back a ways from the river on Jefferson, a row of wired-off buildings and parking lots built out of the rubble of old houses. You could shift from the hotel to the casino without ever knowing the river was there. All through the Midwestern Free Zones casinos and brothels and churches had popped up, all of it heavily guarded. You weren't allowed in Instant until you checked your weapons. But down that river was the St. Charles—only an hour's drive by car or boat—and gamblers were all the time shuttling between the two places. It didn't take long to find someone going over.

His name was Ed Cochran, and I saw him staggering into the bar, which was a cove. The bar had the fewest lights, and you had to talk over the loud country-swing and bluegrass. I made sure not to sit next to the speakers. It hurt my ears.

They had brought the ceiling down with tiles and air-conditioning vents. The rest of Instant was well lit to catch cheaters at the tables, but they left the bar dark and cold; and it wasn't summer, it was autumn for Christ sake. Then Ed walked up after playing blackjack, complaining that he'd lost too much money, said he was going to the St. Charles with the rest of what he had.

Two prostitutes tried to talk him out of it, draped their silk sleeves across his back. He shook his head, brushed them off. "I always go to the St. Charles. That place was built out of the wilderness. You know the story?"

"I know it," I said and came over and bought him a whiskey and told him about Ms. Gerald, what she had done, told him what he already knew, that General Grant had made it his headquarters in the Civil War, that the underground railroad had run through it, that Ms. Gerald had restored it out of a dead town. I talked fast, said I wanted to come along, and if he'd drive, I'd pay for us both.

"All right," he said, overwhelmed. His eyes kept drifting toward the ceiling, and I followed them, but the ceiling was too black to find a place to fix on and hold. Only then, after we had agreed to go together, did he ask me for my name. That's how drunk he was.

Ed Cochran was a corn distributor for farms in Indiana and the Illinois valley, and his chin jutted out like the squared head of a diamondback. His nose had widened with age; my nose was doing it, too, though mine had gotten broken once and was more crooked. My face had widened out as much as my brother's, what I remember of him always, so much bigger than me.

Ed Cochran's bones kept pushing out through his shirt.

He hardly had any shape to his body except for thin, and his Adam's apple was a knotted bone stuck in his throat. Every time he talked, that knot forced his words out in a whisper. He only had four fingers on his left hand, and was strangely proud of the way he lost his thumb, pressing it against an irrigation gun. He had four hundred dollars left from the blackjack table and smelled, Lord he smelled—his body, his clothes, all of him soaked through with whiskey, a cloying sugar. I told Ed I was a truck-carrier taking a full load of kaolin from the Southeastern Desert to St. Louis, and it wasn't long before we were on Highway 50.

He kept swerving through the dark, and I had to grab the wheel.

"Why don't you let me drive?" I asked.

He said, "It's my damn car," and slapped at my hands.

"At least keep your eyes down here on the road and not the treetops," I said. I made sure he was looking down before I let go. Each time he swerved, we went through the same routine.

He had an old Ford Power, the 2020 model, red with white stripes, and red seats, leather ones, and cat-eye headlights, squared front and rear, a convertible. Any minute, I thought the wind gusts would blow him out into the stars, or at least the branches that hugged the road. But he turned his knobbed shoulders down, clutched the steering wheel, and barreled ahead.

When we got close to the St. Charles, I made him stop. "Just for a second."

"What for?" he shouted after me as I jogged up the shoulder. "I want to get there. We're almost there." His voice wasn't slurring as bad, even some of the whisper of it had roughened deeper with gravel and anxiousness. He was sobering up, and I told him to wait a second; it wouldn't be long.

"I'm carsick," I lied and kept jogging until I came to the tree we had passed where a body—that's what it looked like—had been roped to it. I wanted to read the sign hang-ing off the neck: *No Hunters*.

"That's longer than any second I've ever known," Ed squeaked out and coughed.

The face and stomach were all eaten up with flies, and when you stepped in close, you could smell it rotting. I felt around his pockets for a wallet or a card, but the overseers had taken everything, even his shoes. It may have been someone from Adamsville. It may have been someone I knew. Several hunters talked of coming this way, but they were as faceless to me now as this one.

"All right. Come on, I'm going to leave your ass," Ed Cochran shouted.

"I'm paying," I reminded him and got back in, catching my breath, wiping my hands on my jeans, but I couldn't get the wet smell of the dead off of me.

"Don't make any more noise. I ain't stopping."

We drove on to the St. Charles, flashing by two more bodies on that road.

I kept grabbing on to her hair, the separate lengths of it, holding it tight, until finally she pulled away, flicked her neck like a horse, and sat up on the bed. We had been fin-ished for a while, so I knew the touching was over. I just didn't want it to be. What I felt—the warmth suddenly cold, and the way I thought of it, like the warmth had come from the two of us and lingered between us—that wasn't the case. It had nothing to do with me, had belonged to her. When she pulled away, she took the warmth, and it was over.

Still I wanted to touch one more time down her body, the full length of it, and measure myself to her skin. She asked if I smoked, and I told her I didn't but, Lord, I wished I had a cigarette, 'cause if I had one, that would've brought her warmth back.

I had already paid, and she started getting dressed, and

so I did, and that's when I said, "I got one more favor," and took the photos out, set them in her palm. "Do you know any of these women?"

"I know two," she told me and nothing else, handed them back until I gave her more money, then she pointed to the youngest girl, she pointed to the one with black hair.

"They worked on the top floors—the rich johns." She rolled her eyes to the ceiling where the piano music had played all night faintly over us, and she retied the loose strands of her blond ponytail.

"Are they here?"

She was still looking down, tightening. "Probably dead. That one," she touched the girl, "cut a trick all up."

"Killed him."

"Just cut him. He's alive. And that one," she touched the one with black hair, pressed a little harder, "she left with the crazy girl. They slipped out and that man has a bounty on them—the one got cut—is that what you're here about? You his bounty hunter?"

I smiled and rubbed the back of my neck. I still had a headache from Ed Cochran's driving. "I don't know him. That's not what I'm here about," and I looked across the room at the window. "Which way they go?"

"St. Louis. Chicago—everyone thinks they're up to Chicago—the one with black hair has someone in the city. Hell, they've probably already made it or something happened to them. It happened last week. But what I heard, they got on a barge to St. Louis—swam right out to it on the Mississippi." She walked over to her window, looked out like she wished she had done it, too.

"That's what a barge operator told one of the girls. Said he dropped them off in St. Louis. But the rivers take you everywhere from here. I like to think they got away," she said. "There were two girls helped them escape. Got baptized by Ms. Gerald. That's what Ms. Gerald does, puts you under water till you almost drown, baptizes you. I've had it done to me.

"And one of them, a black girl, she wouldn't do it, refused to let the guards put her under. I saw the whole thing, all of us did. She got beat, got hurt. Does no good to help someone." She turned from the window. "Why you want them?"

"They're deserters."

"So you're a bounty hunter for the government?"

"I just need to take them home."

She smirked and lowered her head at me. "You ain't just taking them home." She was daring me to say otherwise, and I didn't. "You know you can get kicked out of this place? Ms. Gerald doesn't allow bounty hunters."

"Only if you say something."

I stared back at her until she wouldn't look at me at all.

Her hands, she couldn't be still with her hands, kept fitting her blouse over her breasts and at her waist, kept tugging on the buttons, up, down. She sighed. "I know a little more."

So I got up, paid her, sat back on the bed. I watched her put it with the other money and roll it inside a sock.

"They got on a boat in St. Louis. That's what I heard, going to Chicago. But they probably already there. You too late."

"Probably," I said.

"You got all that money, why you want *them*?" I had already answered her once, but I had given the wrong answer, not one to her liking, and I had another chance to give the right one.

Really I didn't know why—how you got obsessed with people, how they consumed you, and you never even know them.

She was sitting close now, and I placed my finger at the corner of her eye and down her cheek and neck, down the crook of her elbow, her hand until I started to feel warm again, and she touched my hair, kept brushing through it like my mam had done when she cut it, fluffing it out before scissoring off the ends.

Couldn't sleep like she could, but I didn't wake her, and I snuck outside where it was chilly, the only sound coming from the third-floor balcony—someone on the piano. Whoever was playing was still at it. I'd heard the same man at Instant. He wouldn't stop playing that night either. Hell, it had to be near six in the morning.

I looked up at the balcony, the few lights there and someone hurried up a side stairwell. It must be the servants' entrance, and I started that way, got to the bottom of the long ascension of steel rungs, and stopped. I was waiting for something. Maybe permission to go into that world—the rich johns like the blond whore had said, but the guards would throw me out. But that piano player—he must've known the two deserters.

Then the door opened and five, six guards came rushing down. I stepped out of their way and did so casually, but I knew I might have to run if they started coming for me. *They don't know you*, I told myself, and sure enough, they swept on by.

"Where you going?" I shouted. They just kept on until they reached a gate and opened it, kept running and never answered.

Wasn't long before more guards appeared at the main entrance of the St. Charles and took after the first group. I followed behind them, a path by abandoned houses and brush, all the way down to the long bank of the Ohio River.

They had flashlights pointed, rolling over the water, and rifles drawn on one woman and one man knee-deep in water, walking slow-footed to the shore. The woman was in front, the man a few steps behind. They didn't have on any clothes.

"We were just swimming," she said, cursing the guards all huddled up.

"You can't come out here and you know it," someone from the huddle said.

"Just having fun. We ain't going nowhere. Now get the light out of my eyes," and she stood, crossed her arms, not budging.

"Don't shoot us," the man pleaded.

"They ain't going to shoot you," the woman turned and snickered. "They ain't shooting me either. They're cowards."

"Come on out or we'll get Ms. Gerald in on this."

"Not until you get that damn light out of my eyes." The water had to be freezing, but the woman's face turned an angry red.

Then someone uttered okay and they lowered the flashlights, the rifles. The two skinny-dippers waded through the shallow water and onto the shore, where they grabbed their clothes, wrapped themselves in towels. The whole time, the flashlights flickered in and out, tunneling up at the sky, unraveling, dissolving into black tangents.

The woman kept telling the guards to move, to give her space. The man, he quivered and lowered himself to the ground, begging the guards not to shoot. They just chuckled and ignored him.

I was at the top of the bank, right before it sharply descended, and had sat down to watch, the water dusky, turning, drifting away from those people. Somewhere on the water were those two runaways.

Calmed me to be here. All this water and nothing on it. Then slowly a light crept up the bank and hit me straight-on so I couldn't see.

"What's that?" someone said, whispered it like I might get spooked and run.

"I'm not a *what*," I said.

"What're you doing?" This time someone yelled and the rifles came up, aiming.

"Just watching," I said and put my hands out to show I didn't have a weapon. "That's all."

"Don't move," someone else called, and I said, "All right."

I wished then I were back in bed sleeping, holding on to that woman's hair, the warmth of her back and shoulders.

The only good thing out here was the music from the piano still working its way down from the balcony, the river soaking the music in deep and carrying.

Ed and I returned in the morning, and his driving had improved—he no longer skidded toward any ditches as he slowed down to point at the dead hunters on the side of the road. He asked if that's why I made him stop last night.

"I've never seen that done to a body," I explained.

"Those damn bounty hunters mess up my business," he said. "They get what they deserve." He honked at the last one we passed and yelled at it.

I slouched against the passenger door, and the rest of the trip, he talked into the embedded phone in his ear, lining up the farms he was planning to visit. "After lunch." He winked at me. "I've still got four hundred dollars to blow at Instant."

I nodded and slouched back over. The vibrations lulled me into half dreaming, but kept me awake, too, and that wind, it was flying around us. I don't know how he could talk on the phone in the wind. I tried to sleep. Before too long we hit a bump, and I stared out at the hood, that beautiful red, kept seeing myself riding down to the post, swinging open the door. I looked over at Ed talking away, holding on to the wheel.

"Why don't you let me drive?"

At first he didn't answer, then I asked a second time, and he looked over at me, studied me. He was a little annoyed and told the person on the phone he'd call them back.

"It's my car," he said like he said last night. "We done settled this, and we're close anyway."

"Just another ten, twenty miles," I told him and yawned. "Not much. Just let me give it a spin."

He glanced down at the speedometer, moved that square chin of his into the steering wheel to get a better look. Then he started speeding up, was trying to do it carefully so I wouldn't notice.

"Where you driving your truck to?" he asked.

"St. Louis," I said. "Just want to see how it drives, Ed."

The branches here were turning. It was autumn, and they were just starting to fill out with yellow and orange, and the red maples. They stood out the most along the fence lines.

"Pretty through here," I said, but Ed wouldn't look at the trees.

I pointed to the side. "Stop right there," tapping my finger at the top of the windshield.

"I ain't stopping," he announced and sped up more.

"You're going to get us killed if you don't slow down. Pull over right there." I pointed up ahead to the curve, a wide shoulder spreading out in dirt and gravel.

"You have to make me."

"Make you?" I leaned over halfway. "You think I can't make you?"

He looked at me and looked at the shoulder.

"Just slow down."

And he did, stopped the car on the side of the road. There was sweat on that chin, on that Adam's apple, coming off in small drops. He wiped it away, and the smell of whiskey was getting stronger.

"Now just get out," I said and grabbed his hand. "Turn it off. Leave the keys."

That hand was shaking, the skin dry and papery, shaking like that man last night coming out of the river, trying not to. Ed cut the engine, opened the door, and stood up so fast I thought he might fall. He didn't. He just walked around to the other side, and I got into the driver seat.

He stood next to the car like he wasn't sure what to do, like he'd forgotten who he was and where he was, like he wanted to forget this moment, like he wanted to reverse some things. And he kept looking over the car like it was the last time he was going to see it.

"I had this Ford Power—it was rusting in a farmer's garage. I got it from him and fixed it up. He just gave it to me, and I did all the work myself." His Adam's apple kept working up and down, and the sweat on his face had thickened into a white grease.

"You did a good job," I told him and cranked it, pressed the accelerator all the way in. Next I rubbed over the top of the dash, the smell of antifreeze coming up in the vents.

"I can call a patrol."

"You should've done it already. But there's none out here."

"I'll call the casino."

I sighed, looked out at the highway. It was curving, but there was no way to tell what was going on beyond that curve, if someone was coming, and what would they do?

"You could call them. You go ahead. You want to do that, go right ahead. And if I show up at Instant, they'll take your car back, kick me out. Then I'll be waiting for you." I shifted the gear.

"But that's if I show back up. I don't know where I'm going really," and I looked at the trees, the fields beyond them that kept going and going. You could tell it, they wouldn't stop until they had wrapped around the earth; and somewhere there were crows, I could hear them starting out over those fields, that journey, and something picking at the leaves in the underbrush. I looked back up the road we had just come. "Hate for you to waste a call like that."

The whole time Ed had his hands on the passenger door.

"I fixed up this car. Put a new 426 engine in. You know how hard those are to find? Got it painted, billboard stripes, the seats . . ." He was shaking his head, and the sweat beaded off.

"You did a good job," I told him and looked at his hands, counted the nine fingers, and looked up at him, waited. "The day's coming on," I said.

He took his hands off.

I went back to Instant, got the supplies, enough to last a while, and put them in the trunk, headed north.

When I was a carrier, I stopped at the edge-towns around Chicago, but smugglers coming up the Illinois River from St. Louis met their connections at two places: Morris and Starved Rock.

That was some time ago. It had gotten overused, and the government raided the drop-offs, closed them down, but the government was barely here anymore, so maybe the runaways had gone up the Illinois River, were on it right now. Maybe they had already gone through, or traveled some other route, or somewhere else, or maybe they were dead like the girl last night claimed.

I decided to go to Starved Rock because it was south of Ottawa, the confluence of the Illinois and Fox Rivers. They might take Fox up to Sheridan instead of going on to Morris. Had to think that way. The one with black hair, the girl with wide cheekbones, they had managed to stay together and were on the river still.

Highway 51 was a long drive through the flattest land, an endless ribbon of harvested cornfields, and the sun just sat there at the end of the day touching the earth and nothing else. At dusk, fireflies zagged into the cornstalks and out, streaks of light I passed by, unable to catch up to.

I sped by several fires next to the road, roamers huddled
around. Back when the government was still patrolling, you
didn't see gangs this close. The smoke from their fires would
appear at the edges of fields, and at night, you could make
out beads of red-yellow flame. Now the road was as much
theirs as anyone else's.

After passing a sign for Heyworth my car began to sputter. I had to pull over, rotate the empty propane tank with a
new one. It didn't take long, but up ahead was another fire,
and bodies around it, just specks that didn't move. I kept my
eye on them, kept looking behind me, but nothing was coming except those fireflies and the broken cornstalks rattling
toward the west when the wind struck. I got back in and
drove a little piece more, stopped.

There were only four men, all in long blankets, so I took
out my shotgun, stepped to the fire to warm my hands.

"Too cold tonight," I said, nodded but no one acknowledged me. I kept my grip tight on the shotgun. They might
be carrying rifles under those blankets. And what if someone
was hiding out across the road? But I doubted it. They just
looked worn down, too tired to fight, all mudded up and
cold except for the heat on their faces. Still I knew what I
was doing was crazy and, still, I couldn't stop myself.

I sat down, let the fire's warmth burn into my skin, my
whole body, trying to work off the cold and numbness of
driving.

"What's it like in Normal?" I asked. Normal was just five
miles away.

"We left there," one man said. "Had no choice." He was
straight across from me. "Town's been on fire. Wouldn't go
through it if I was heading north."

That's when I noticed the spots on his face. Should've
noticed it already, and the same on the others, paper scars,
pockmarks. Diseased.

I stood up. They were all dying men. Out in the field a
little farther two bodies were laid out in wide shadows. I

couldn't see the full shape of the bodies, what the Martz disease had eaten through. And how many bodies lay between here and Normal? How many had been left in that town to burn?

The dead and the houses, the streets, the air, everything was getting burned to keep the plague from spreading. The same thing had happened in Lawrenceburg over the summer.

"Is there a road I can use to get around it?" I asked. They had closed all the roads off in Lawrenceburg, and I didn't like the prospect of cutting through fields.

"Highway 43 should get you far enough out of Normal," the man said. "It was still open when we got out. My family's from Lincoln. My father worked at Inland Tools before everything closed. We've been living between there and Normal." He coughed and grabbed at his chest inside the blanket—it was a yellow blanket, with old threads roughed up like tangled horsehair.

I knew what was under those blankets, what Martz disease did to the stomach and the ribs, how eventually the ribs cracked and splintered from coughing. I had seen that, seen ditches full of people dead from the disease, seen bodies strewn across fields, left for the birds to pick away. Outside of Lawrenceburg, you could smell that death burning. I could smell it now.

These men had wandered here and stayed close to the road. Someone would be by to shoot them. Or they would starve or the disease would bore into their liver and finish them off.

I held the shotgun out and they didn't move. It could be me to do it. Maybe they wanted that, expected that.

"Be doing us a favor," the man said. He was watching me now.

"I'm not here for killing."

"Why you here?" he asked.

"I'm not doing that."

Their eyes stared deep into those flames as if the heat and light were all that was keeping them alive. I watched the fire soak up the air and lick at it. With enough branches and enough time it could go up and up, reach beyond the moon and beyond, the whole soul of the earth in one flame, then black and gone. Did they see that, too?

Slowly I stepped back, got in my car, and drove on.

I circled Normal by 43 like he said, the smoke so dense I was barely able to keep the car from the drainage ditches—but the smoke lifted and for miles the sky and fields were cleared. The clearness, however, didn't last—someone had set tires blazing across 51—and then shots, they were probably just a warning, the farmers trying to hold the roamers back, but I turned around, gunned the engine, and cut off onto Route 17 to Goose Lake on the Illinois River.

The lake was empty all night, but in the morning two boats crisscrossed each other and weaved around the sloughs heading north. I watched—one boat had six people on board—yet I didn't see the two deserters. They might be in one of the cabins, and it wasn't unusual for smugglers to travel in pairs.

The sun was out and the boats kept crossing, going up the lake. I got back in the car, drove ahead until I reached the Route 18 bridge and again set my binoculars on the boats. As they moved under me, I could hear the hum of the engines, but couldn't feel the hum through the concrete. They headed to a buoy not far up, and one boat, the one in the lead with the six people, honked at the other. The boats made a circle and returned to the bridge and then south of the lake, puttering.

They had been racing, that was all. Not who I was looking for.

I got in and followed 26 past Sawmill Lake and Senachwine. At Senachwine I came across a marooned houseboat in the marsh and cord grass. I watched it for hours shift in the wind, the water before climbing inside. Empty. There was no food in the cabinets and only the sound of water sloshing against the hull. There was one pot on the stove and something had dried black from the center up the edges. I lifted it, smelled the iron but that was all. I couldn't get my luck to turn, and I slung that pot against the cabinets and lowered my head, rubbed it. So much time I had wasted.

I kept along the Illinois River but there were no other boats, no one else, just the water hiding all that was under-neath and the sun gathering at the surface. On the far bank—trees, their branches leaning out, scooping up water and letting go, brushing small pulses into the current.

Finally, I reached Starved Rock, rolled the Ford deep under a stand of birches, and walked down to the line of the river there.

The water shimmied, and out in the middle of the Illi-nois was the dark and long trees of Plum Island, and to the north Starved Rock, the lock and dam with its caution lights, the sandstone bluffs and canyons. The sky was too thick with a black-grayness to see beyond it. A storm was coming, bullfrogs already calling to one another, anticipat-ing, and the lightning getting close like all the fires the day before around Normal joining into one crooked passage. I ran back to the car, put the top up, and slept with the rain beating down, beating down, washing me in and out of dreams.

All day I watched the boat ramp, the stone dock there, then back up to Starved Rock, Eagle Rock along the edge of the river, hiking the pathways through the woods.

Route 178 that crossed the Illinois below the ramp had

collapsed years ago, leaving half arches and columns of cement and steel rods that jutted out, sluiced the water down-
stream. The columns stood like a gateway into a forgotten
world. The trail paths had grown over with brush, and scrub
oaks, and ferns, and the wooden platforms and signs for the
state park overlooks had worn through, broken and empty of
people. Only the sound of the woodpeckers marked the
emptiness.

In late afternoon, the water shimmied in the flat aim of
the sun; it was icy when I put my feet in, burned all the way
up my calves, and yellow and red leaves fell in around me,
eddying downriver, latching onto my wet cuffs and wrists.
Only one barge had come and gone through the lock where
the river tumbled out, and I kept my feet in the water until
they grew so numb I couldn't feel them.

After supper, I burned three pictures in the shrinking
fire, their faces absorbed into purple and black tailings, let
them go, and kept the other two. The woman with black
hair, one corner had bled from where I held it, the sweat in
my hand smearing her arm and the gap around her into
dust, and the one of the girl had crackled along the edges
and a crease along her face split her in half as if the mouth
and shoulders belonged to another ghost altogether. They
were ghost people I kept coming for, like myself, my family.
I'd wait for them a few more days, then head back to
Adamsville; I'd burn their pictures, too.

The branches formed a jagged opening overhead to the
stars, a new moon. Always the stars like the Book of Jude,
"The wicked are wild waves of the sea, foaming up their
shame; wandering stars, for whom blackest darkness has
been reserved forever."

Forever. Was it true, our wicked bodies stretched across
the ether? Those same stars had fallen into my stomach,
grinded against themselves into me. I could not fill my soul
like Preacher Spoon had wanted, like I wanted, not even
when I held the snake's belly. I had placed the universe in

my belly, and still I could not escape the nothingness of my own existence.

As I sat there, the sky shifted against me as if heaven was as solid and immovable as the earth and scuttling against the branches. That's what the wind was doing, its hollow whirring, spilling ghost people back and forth across the ether I could take but never hold.

I dreamed all night of those men by the fire.

I drove up, got out, and shot them all in the face, cutting away their disease, dropping them to the earth.

But it wasn't over—the dream looped back—I was in the car again, driving up to the fire, the bodies waiting. I told myself, *Don't kill them this time. Wait until you're done at Starved Rock. Once you're done, you can go to Normal, find these roamers, put them out of their misery.*

I stopped the car, got out, pulled the shotgun waist high, and shot the back of their heads. I couldn't look at their faces again.

As soon as I killed the roamers a second time, I was back in the convertible driving up to the fire and the black earth around me slowly receding. I got out and came up to those flames to warm my hands.

"It's getting cold tonight," I said, and they looked straight into the embers, waited.

Never once did they turn on me. Never once did they do a thing to me. They knew why I was there. And the fire— it never went out. No matter where I was in the dream, I could see the flames on the periphery, shooting off flares, rising.

One time in Newport, Mam had pneumonia and before it was done with her, she also got pleurisy. Every time she shifted in bed, it hurt. Breathing hurt.

"I don't want to breathe no more," she kept saying over and over, half dreaming from the drugs.

Theo said she'd die for sure, and we'd be motherless as well as fatherless, but the nurse who visited our home from the outreach center said it was nothing like that. "Your mother will be okay," she promised. "If she gets worse, just call me," and she handed Theo a strip of paper with a number. "I'll get her back to the hospital."

Theo waited until the nurse left, then balled up the paper, and threw it in the trash. "That woman can't save her," he said.

"How do you know?" I asked.

"I know," he said, yelling, daring me not to believe him.

As soon as he slipped upstairs, I dug that strip of paper out of the trash, kept it with me. Memorized the number, which ended in 8934—I still know that part.

At night, I had dream after dream of walking in and finding my mother dead. But all night she kept me awake because the pain made her call out. "Breathe," she'd say. "I don't want to breathe."

Though it was hurting her, at least I knew she was alive, at least she woke me from the nightmares of finding her still body.

Sometimes, I got so worried about it, I felt my way along the dark hall until I was at her bedside making sure her covers were rising, sinking. I listened to that raspy voice and frail cough. Lord, that cough cut into me, into my lungs.

I fell asleep on the floor sometimes, and Theo, if he discovered me there in the morning, would kick me awake.

"Told you to stay in your bed," he'd say. "Don't bother her. Is he bothering you, Mam?"

She was trying to move her arm at him, though it hurt her, and kept telling him to stop. Just that one word, *Stop.* *Stop.* Even after he told her he had stopped, she kept repeating it like the word had gotten stuck on her tongue.

During those nights when she was sick, her voice held a different kind of singing—it was the last of her, what she'd whisper before she died—this voice, slipping out from her room, down the hall to me. She was telling me, *This is what death sounds like, Rosser.*

And the truth was, when Theo kicked me, it didn't hurt, 'cause I knew Mam's lungs and sides were in worse pain. I was feeling nothing compared to what she was. It actually made me feel an allegiance to Mam, like I understood a little bit of the pain, what she was going through, and just like death was kicking at her, Theo was kicking me. I understood.

Months later she was better and gone again. "Shacking up," was how Theo put it, "with a married man on Eighth and Commerce. She'd been better off to die."

"No," I told him and raised my hands, but he saw them coming and took them.

"You need to give up on her," he said and threw my hands back at me and spit on the ground.

All I knew, she was gone, and that coughing that kept waking me was gone, and that silence at night, it would get to be too much in my dreams like someone was pressing a thick heavy glass against me, trying to press my body down into the bed until I was no more.

The only way to break the glass was to jump up, so I'd jump up and suddenly be awake, sweating, sweating so much, and realize there was no glass. And I'd start crying and not know what to do, or where to go.

I was still sleeping when I heard a laugh like a crow; it hung there circling, pricking me awake. Then I heard voices circling from the dock and I took the rifle, checked the breech—it was loaded—and worked my way along the path.

One car. A boat at the dock with a raised helm, its wooden hull scratched up, needing paint. The Cadillac trunk was open. One man stood with his hand propped on the roof behind it. A black roof, polished, gathering up specks of sunlight, and his clothes were the same black, and his skin the lightest brown. He was a good bit taller than his car and he kept his other hand on his belt where the gun was holstered; next to him were the two women, the deserters, holding each other like months ago at Pickwick Landing, like they had remained inseparable. The dresses, blue and green—even from this distance they hung worn from the shoulders, draggled, faded.

There was another man loading boxes into the trunk. He was younger than the big man at the car, kept his lips shut tight, long-waisted but short; every step was about keeping his body aligned. The smuggler from St. Louis was unloading his boat. They met halfway, made the transfer, and split back up, the sun blurring the edges of their arms with the same beads of white pressing on the water current and the roof.

The smuggler wore a dark blue cap, wide in the front and as salt-dried as the orange one Granddaddy'd had. He kept his head tucked under it, making his face too dark to know. But he was the loudest. Everyone laughed at what he said, what he did. Even the young man sometimes grinned until he revealed his teeth, and shook his head.

I walked along the tree line until I faced the hood, the driver's corner—that was as straight with the front as I could get—eighty, ninety yards—and I stayed back of a wide sycamore, its bark peeled onto the ground. I was careful not to step on the peelings.

Then the trunk shut.

The smuggler said, "Hell, that's it," clear and ringing. He hugged the two women, slapped the big man on the back and called him partner, and said, "Next time, LT." They stood there, all five bunched together, and LT handed the smuggler money. He turned to leave, and LT's helper, the young man, opened the door for the women. His gun was holstered, too, and his shirt was untucked from carrying the boxes, the wind catching the edges of the white tails and twisting them. I fired, bolted the cartridge out, and everyone scattered to the ground. The young man fell as the women slipped behind the trunk with the other men.

For a long time, forever, they stayed behind that trunk, and the blood of that man pooled on the ground, soaked through his shirt; the rear door was still open.

Then the smuggler ran toward the dock as LT came to the front of his car, shooting at the woods, just firing into the trees hoping to catch something, to scare me long enough. My shot hit the windshield glass, and the two runaways edged along the wheel to the back door. I slipped the bolt into place, shattered the glass there.

The girl fell, but the other woman lifted her, pushed her into the car as it jerked, and I fired, struck LT in the arm, I saw him grab it, and fired again, missed, and the Cadillac sped past me. I couldn't hear. My ears had popped and were swirling now with a thickness. They ached from the reports, and I knew then, I should've stayed on LT.

The boat headed out.

The black-haired woman, the older one, had fallen lifting the girl and couldn't reach the moving car herself. Now she was running to the opposite woods, away from the dead body that had tripped her up. I fired into the air. She kept running. And as I pushed a shell in, locked it, I knew that was the wrong decision, too. She was gone.

The boat had already passed the fragile columns of Route 178, splitting the river, and I found her trying to work up the sandstone ledges toward the bridge. Her olive dress, it was that shade of green, kept snagging on the thin boles knuckled into the earth.

I yelled out, "I'm coming. There's no need to go any higher." That's when she saw me. She took a good look and dove into the water, so I jumped in after her.

The boat had already slipped away, and only faintly the motor chopped at the air because of my plugged ears; the water didn't help. Why she chose the water—why deserters panicked the way they did—I could never figure, but I swam until my lungs burned, until I grabbed her foot, pulled her leg under, and bound her waist. The two of us held in the river, struggling; she kept hitting, yelling in the brackish water.

"You're going to drown us," I said, but she wouldn't let up, no matter how much I threatened, no matter how much I squeezed and hit back. But eventually she tired, and I hauled her to shore and kicked her in the stomach. "Could've drowned us." Kicked her again and again until she coiled up, lay there unmoving in the grass, leaves, and dirt.

When the breath returned to the runaway, she inhaled it in a long sustained draw. It tightened and coiled inside her and came back out a dark, sad moan. Quavering, lost, the moan cut into me like those women crying under Preacher Spoon's tent. For a long while, I was afraid to touch her, afraid of so much grief.

Jennifer

Jennifer heard a door close, it was a car door, but it could've been that door from when she was twelve, trapped on one side, her mama on the other. She was just as blood-ied now, and in her mind she pounded that door. She could do it, break it open. "Mama," she said, "open up. It's okay. It's me." She pounded though she wasn't striking anything at all. Her hands had been tied. She couldn't move, and she could feel her hands, how they dangled there, numb.

She stopped.

She looked up at the sky—the car was moving, reeling—and she knew even though she was here, Mazy had gotten away and would get to Chicago—she had to. Jennifer's mama was waiting in Chicago, lingering, writing letters Jennifer couldn't respond to, and that distance sprawled and poured over her.

The wind blew her hair, crossed the blue of the sky into strips of glass, and that hair stuck to the blood on her forehead and mouth; she chewed on her tongue but there was no dust to roll and keep. It took a moment to calm her breathing.

She had lost her baby, Mathew's baby, and was glad it had already passed because surely the child would be dead now. The engine and the road buzzed in her stomach. At least Mazy had gone on—Jennifer had been able to do that much—the girl would make it.

Clouds drifted overhead and her lungs still burned from the river. And she knew, all these rivers had held her body up, the mud-water had shifted around her. "The earth's blood"—that's what Terry called rivers, driving along the edges, and when she went down, at each place, to clean off the dust and dirt, she found her history carried along the currents, shifting, returning, waiting for her to know it again.

Where was she going now?

Patrick Carson had asked if they wanted to make a run to his boat when they were stuck behind the trunk. But Jennifer had to keep going to Chicago. It was all she had left. She gave Mazy her box; something told Jennifer they might not go together.

Up front, the man was humming, his right arm dangling over the middle, relaxed, and his hair, the wind kept pushing, flying it around. He was humming, splitting the wind, and she smelled the warm leather of the seats, her own blood.

The wooden knuckles of Jinx's hands spread over the keyboard—she could see it clearly. He was at his piano at the St. Charles working through his center-roots, creating them, lengthening them, shortening them until they touched the different ends of the water and that black space between the currents and into her, the sound came into her, the water lapped and lapped over her, refusing to leave.

Rosser

I tied the ropes strong around her wrists and ankles, tied her arms to her waist and legs, dumped her body in the back, secured her with the belts, and I took out the shotgun, angling the barrel into the floorboard on the passenger side. I left the Remington in the trunk with the propane tanks and food. Then I cranked the engine, reached back, and said, "Don't worry. I'm just taking you home."

Halfway down 51 I let the top down and started humming. It was "At Calvary," Mam's favorite. I didn't realize that was what I was doing and I didn't dare sing it—my voice was nothing good. But Mam always sang it with a cheerfulness, setting her shoulders into it, swinging them, her whole body arched at the world, ready—it was the one time when she was sure of herself and I became sure of myself. She had what she called a "mid-range voice," and the notes never reached too high, but it had a smoothness that carried me and carries me still.

I thought of the light that afternoon before we went to the revival, how it swung under the porch overhang and lighted across Mam's back and how happy she seemed, and even when she giggled with Harold, the three of us walking up Grandview. As much as I didn't like Harold, hated him, it was nice to hear Mam giggle. Her voice shot through me, and I smiled, even though it also pained me.

Later that night when she got bit, her face was all contorted and flushed, and the moment right after, while Harold and Preacher Spoon argued over what to do with her, I wanted to reach down with my failed hands, *lay hands* on her like Preacher Spoon talked about and redeem us both. I'd put my hands on her red sash and lift her to the Lord. Then the red sash unraveled in my mind, just a skein of satin with no body to hold; and she was gone.

The sun was burning strong across the acres of cut corn, and the fields left with only a few remaining husks rattled as if I were driving the wind that rattled them, and the Lord, there was no way He'd catch up. Before me the flat side of the earth stretched out, unending.

Dear Mama,

I'm hurting. And the sky, it has tilted slightly, has moved toward me. A selfish thing to think, that the sky would tilt toward me. But what it is, I'm having a difficult time stopping myself from unraveling like a small dust devil when it loses its center and breaks apart. Scatters. I keep pulling into myself so I don't scatter. I find you here waiting. Your presence is comforting. Once I'm healed enough, I'll get to you and Mazy. She'll be with you soon, I promise. Even this hurt turning through my body, the pain will slow, and I'll find my way north.

If I could reach my hand out, I'd touch your shoulder. Remember how you slept on Terry's shoulder and I slept against the passenger window on our jaunts? I could put my hand out and rub your arm, pull you awake. That smell of diesel, and outside the door, the wind blowing the dust against us and a little farther the river. Right now I'm riding in a car, but the driver can't go this way forever, just like Terry couldn't. He'll have to turn.

The wind keeps knocking at the door and glass, so much that the sky has been pulled and is tilting toward me. Almost Mama, I can feel your cotton shirt catching in my dry hands.

I'm putting my hand on you now, Mama. Pull me to you. I'm ready.

Acknowledgments

This book came together with the help of many people. I want to thank Jana for her love, caring, patience, insight, and editing. Dylan for his paintings. Maddie for our conversations. And Jessi for her laughter. I want to thank my father for his stories about his parents and about my hometown. I want to thank him for answering all my questions and for his thoughtfulness. My mother, for her kindness and attentiveness and for the stories about her parents. Ron and Judy Evans for their caring. Noah Eaker for his guidance, his insights, and for taking this project on. Juliet Ulman for her editing and sincerity. And Joshua Pasternak for his encouragement. Amy Stout-Moran for her advocacy. Stan Corkin for a place to write. Russel Durst for time to write. Jay Twomey, Michael Griffith, and Brock Clarke for being sounding boards. Tony Grooms for his graciousness. And Molly Gaudry and her dog Reinita, who visited during the hot Cincinnati summers to keep me company.

About the Author

JAMES BRAZIEL has published short stories in *Berkeley Fiction Review*, *Chattahoochee Review*, and *Clackamas Literary Review*, among other journals. *Weathervane*, a chapbook of his poetry, was published in 2003 and nominated for a Pushcart Prize. He has also been the recipient of an Individual Artist Grant from the Georgia Council for the Arts. He currently teaches creative writing at the University of Cincinnati. *Snakeskin Road* is his second novel.